STRAYED

C.T. DANIELS

For my wonderful family who has encouraged me and blessed me more than I could have ever asked for.

If you're new to the Ebon Sky Series, thanks so much for coming aboard. Feel free to stop by my website and read the first book in the series, Branded for free. Http://www.ct-daniels.com. Happy reading!

ACKNOWLEDGMENTS

This work would not have been possible, first and foremost, without Jesus Christ. Every time I thought I wouldn't be able to finish this novel or handle the setbacks and disappointments associated with writing and publication, he kept me going, time and time again.

I also want to thank my amazing wife, Laurilee Anne Tracy, for standing by me through the course of writing this novel and always supporting me through the crazy decisions I've made to be able to follow this crazy, writing dream. Her support has meant the world to me, and this novel would not exist otherwise.

To my parents, you have always been there to love and support me and, from an early age, encourage me to follow my dreams. I love you both, and I am so blessed to have had you in my life.

As always, I want to give a special thank you to everyone who was involved in the development and production of the play this was all based on, Falkland Road. To Harley Erdman, your tutelage in writing and development was invaluable. To

Savannah Van-Leuvan Smith, you have always been so supportive of my work and put in so much work to make the play a success. To Camee Manderfield, you have been such a blessing, from your amazing dedication to the play to your unwavering support to your invaluable assistance with the audiobook and book trailers. Of course, none of this would have been possible, as well, without Julie Digiusto, Samantha Creed, Tiahna Harris, Leah Bugden, Daveth Cheth, Dillon Crocket, Stephen Lajoie, Rachael Hobson, and Jordyn Albert. You all were brilliant in every way, and considering this novel follows the opening moments of our play, your performances are now immortalized between these pages because of the continued inspiration you all give me.

To my audiobook crew, Camee Manderfield, Michael Normand, Eddie King, Christina Chenier and Laurilee Tracy, thank you so much for all the work you put in. Even though I haven't had the time to put the audiobook all together yet, I am so grateful, and I can't wait to finally get all of it edited.

And to everyone else who ever helped me out along the way: Shane Adams, Dan Johnson, Donna Saloio, Jasmine Marino, Demi Bernice Eslit, Will Power for teaching me play-writing, Hannah Cushman, Ashley Cummino, Julie Norval, and everyone else who has ever encouraged me or supported my work. I could not have done this without any of you.

PREFACE

There's nothing more surreal than the end of an era. For the past few months, I've thought long and hard about how I was going to feel when I released this book. And truthfully, I never managed to nail down anything of worth. The truth is, I don't think I ever thought the day would come. After eight years of getting to know these characters and their stories, watching them develop before my very eyes, I don't think I ever thought the time would come when I would say goodbye, when their stories would be complete, when I would move on to new characters and new stories.

I suppose, in a way, I will never truly say goodbye. These characters are now a special part of me, after all. Each of them carry an aspect of myself within the pages of these three books, whether it's their personality, their backstory or simply a detail about their lives. But I think that only makes the farewell even more difficult. It is bittersweet to say the least, to on one hand know that I finished the story I never thought I would finish but on the other hand wish there was more story to tell. But alas, this is no Harry Potter universe. This was the ending I've been planning for almost a decade, and no amount of sentimentality can change that fact.

However, it does allow me to focus on the road ahead.

What comes next in my author career?

That's a funny question to ask myself because, for a time, I didn't think there was a next. This was a series that I felt compelled to complete, but it has been my purpose for so long that I have a hard time seeing the path past this novel. At one point, I even half-expected to drop dead the second I published it because my purpose would be complete. However, since that time, my mind has been buzzing with stories, with fantasy stories, romance and satires that make me excited to pick up my pen and start on something new.

And I can't wait for you to see what my next project is going to be.

This is a work of fiction. Names, characters, organizations, places, events, and incidents are either products if the author's mind or are used fictitiously.

TRIGGER WARNING: Due to the graphic reality of the subject matter, this story deals with graphic descriptions of physical and sexual abuse. Reader discretion is advised!

1

RECAPTURED

TOLEDO, OHIO

*S*everal, feeble streams of fluorescent light flooded through the one-inch, open slat on top of the dumpster, converging and combining to create a single, grey stripe in the center of the half-filled receptacle. As quietly as she could, Blair scooted into the back corner, afraid of accidentally illuminating even a single strand of her naturally reflective hair, lest she give away her position. With each, slow step she took, the crunching sound of what she could only assume were plastic bags, week-old food and styrofoam cups echoed across her metallic surroundings.

Thankfully, at least for the time being, she was alone, which meant the sound of her movements would fall on no one's ears but her own.

While Kayde continued to lead their pursuers on what Blair hoped would be a wild goose chase, she hunkered down against the dumpster's frigid, oily walls and waited. Her skin crawled as she slid down the wall, landing on top of what she tried to imagine was a plush, lavender-scented mattress. However, not even her imagination could disguise the nostril assaulting odor that emanated from the jug of rotten milk she had just forced open with her backside. In that moment, every inch of her body felt rotten, but even if she was to spend the rest of her days stuck in the mire, feeding upon the week-old remains of half-eaten meals, it was still preferable to working at the salon for so much as a day longer.

For what felt like an eternity, but in reality was closer to seven minutes, she waited, unmoving, and stared at the grey stripe before her, trying to think of anything but what she feared most; Kayde had been caught, and it was only a matter of time before she rejoined him in chains. Closing her eyes, she envisioned him rushing to her side, taking her by the hand and leading her unto their freedom, but most of all, she dreamed of finding Natasha and running away. Only this time, they would be somewhere happy, somewhere safe.

Where they could live a good life, together.

Suddenly, the sound of rushed footsteps cascaded down the alleyway toward her. Instinctively, she held her breath, unwilling to move or even make a sound. As the steps came to a screeching halt beside the dumpster, a shadow fell across its slat, eclipsing the tiny strand of grey that had been her only light in the darkness. Hopeful, Blair perked up, preparing to make her escape. However, just as quickly as they had come, the footsteps continued past her, rushing in the opposite direction.

Shit, they must be right behind him.

Squeezing herself tighter into the corner, she locked her breath within her lungs and stared up at the space between the dumpster lids. There, a few seconds later, a flash of dark hair bounced calmly past the opening. Under the alley lights, it shimmered ominously, like blacklight in the middle of an already pitch black room. It was a dark gleam that Blair would have recognized anywhere.

It was Lena.

Shuffling toward the center of the dumpster, Blair raised her ear to the opening and listened.

"And I know about your sister, Kayde," Paul laughed.

Damnit! This isn't good.

As Paul, Lena and Kayde continued to argue, Blair raised the dumpster lid slowly and, planting one hand on the metal and keeping the other latched to the edge of the lid, hoisted herself out of the dumpster and onto the concrete below. As her feet hit the ground, she closed the lid slowly and without a sound. Then, she rounded the corner and hid herself amongst the shadows.

At the end of the day, Kayde was the most dedicated and loving brother she could have ever asked for, but his poker face was about as convincing as a five-year-old who had just been caught with his hand in the cookie jar. It was only a matter of time before he gave up her position, even if only by accident.

Peering cautiously around the corner, she saw Kayde backed up against the brick wall with Paul and Lena closing in on him. Instinctively, his eyes shot straight to Blair and grew wide.

And there it was; she was made.

Quickly, she retreated into the corner and forced her body against the side of the dumpster, preparing to hear yet another set of footsteps rush toward her and then to be yanked back by the collar and dragged unto her doom. However, hardly even a second later, she heard a smack, followed by the rapid shuffling of feet and, just a few seconds later, a thud. Curious, she checked back around the corner. There, she saw Lena with her hands around Kayde's throat. Beside them, Paul hoisted himself up from the ground, clutching his cheek with madness billowing from his eye sockets.

Then, Lena's dropped Kayde to the ground, and without a

second's hesitation, Paul seized him by the shoulders and hurled him to the ground.

"You stole her from me!" he screamed as he pounced, slamming Kayde's head mercilessly into the concrete. "How could you?!"

As much as Blair didn't want to leave in that moment, as much as she wanted to be there for her brother, to dash over to him and rescue him from the onslaught, this was her only chance to escape.

And she knew Kayde would want her to take it.

So, staying on the balls of her feet, she scurried toward the back end of the alleyway, sliding her hand along the brick wall to maintain her balance. As she rounded the corner, she hoped that the night wouldn't end the way she feared. She prayed that Paul would relent, that Kayde would end the night beaten but alive.

That the next day, between her and Violet, they could get him out.

However, as she rounded the back corner of the alleyway, a monstrous sound rang across the treetops, dropping her to her knees.

Bang!

"KAYDE!" Violet screamed.

Stuck behind the wheel of Kayde's car, she was helpless to do anything but watch the bullet embed itself in his chest, listen to the gun's blast echo through the otherwise empty parking lot and feel her every dream of love crumble as he fell lifeless to the ground. Immediately, she froze, her hands locked around the steering wheel. Her knuckles dug into the leather until chunks of its surface became lodged beneath her fingernails.

She watched as a man and a woman stood over his body, staring pitilessly at the life that was slowly draining out of him. Violet's heart skipped a beat as the smoking gun, which was still in the dark-haired woman's left hand, came into view. Her hands began to shake, and the blood inside her veins boiled instantaneously. In that moment, she wanted nothing more than to rip the pistol from that bitch's clenched fist and wedge a bullet in her brain. However, before she could act upon her fantasy, the man and woman both spun around to look down the alleyway and took off in a dead sprint toward something that had caught their attention on the other side, leaving Kayde alone, bleeding out, on the pavement.

Immediately, Violet leapt out of the car and darted across the parking lot toward him. As she neared him, she could see the pavement around him fill with crimson from the bullet-hole in his chest. Throwing herself to her knees beside him, she brought her fingers to his neck, checking for a heartbeat.

Thump... thump.

It was faint, quiet, as though his body was barely hanging onto a thread of life.

But it was there, meaning there was still hope.

In that instant, all thoughts left Violet's mind except for one; she had to save him. Tossing his arm over her shoulders, she pushed against the ground with all her might and lifted him to his feet. Then, she took off toward the car faster then she had ever thought possible. Within seconds, she was opening the rear, driver's side door of the car and laying Kayde across the backseat. Then, she jumped into the front seat and, sticking the keys in the ignition, threw the car into drive.

As she sped out of the parking lot, searching furiously for the quickest route to the hospital, Kayde whispered with what sounded like the last strength left in his bones, "Blair..."

"I'm sorry, my love," Violet choked, trying to hold back the flood that was welling up behind her eyes. "But I don't care if it's Mother-freaking-Theresa we're trying to save; I'm not letting you leave me, not for anyone."

Reaching into the backseat, she took his hand in hers and held on for dear life. Weakly, he did the same, and for the next fifteen minutes, all was quiet. The only sound, other than the roar of the engine, that she heard was her own, bated breath and fervent whispers that begged for Kayde to hold on, to keep going, to survive.

Because if he didn't, she wasn't certain that she wouldn't just drop dead alongside him.

As the lights of the hospital grew in the distance, Kayde's hand fell, limp, from her grasp. And instantly, she could no longer control the monsoon that raged behind her eyelids. Throwing the car into park outside the emergency room and not even waiting long enough to take the keys from the ignition, she bounded out of the driver's seat and toward the front desk, her knees buckling beneath her with each step she took.

Darting through the front doors, her legs didn't stop moving until she nearly collapsed headlong over the top the desk of the receptionist, who, instead of rushing to her side as she had hoped, simply looked at her and calmly asked, "How can I help you?"

"My... my boyfriend," Violet stammered. "He — he's been — there's no time to explain. Just send someone now!"

As the receptionist grabbed her phone to call for help, Violet rushed back out the doors and flung open the back door to Kayde's car. Then, she waited. Over the course of the next, thirty seconds, which felt more like hours, she stood, frozen, outside the door, gazing down at the motionless heap that, only a few hours ago, had been the love of her life. However, at this point, he was unrecognizable. The color had faded from his skin, and the life had left his eyes. From where she stood, she couldn't even see his chest rise and fall, which would have at least given her hope.

In a moment, hope had died, and in its place stood emptiness, despair and rage.

After that, everything was a blur. The emergency room's doors slid open, and a horde of nurses rushed toward them with a gurney in tow. Violet took a step back as to not get in their way. Grabbing Kayde by the shoulders, two of the nurses hoisted his body, which slumped in their arms as they hauled him up, onto the gurney while the other nurses strapped him down. Then, they wheeled him off, through the doors and down the hall, with Violet close behind.

As they smashed through the double doors that led to the operating rooms, one of the nurses turned and grabbed her gently by the shoulders, stopping her just outside the doorway.

"You'll have to wait here," the nurse informed her.

However, she wasn't having any of it. "No!" she screamed. "I have to see him."

Pushing past him, she leapt toward the door, her arms outstretched to stop it from closing. However, before her fingers could so much as graze its surface, the nurse wrapped his arms around her, stopping her in her tracks. With all her might, she pushed against him, trying to muscle him out of the way, but it was no use. By the time she managed to push him back even an inch, the doors had already closed and locked in front of her, leaving her with no choice but to wait.

"Only doctors and nurses beyond this point," the nurse said as he finally released her, brushed past her and headed back to work. "I'm sorry, ma'am."

Inconsolable, she threw herself against the wall and slunk to the floor. In the moments that followed, she lost all track of time, all trace of existence. A heaviness, like a million drops of rain, weighed on her heart. For an amount of time she couldn't even begin to count, she sat with her head in her hands, motionless, deaf and blind to the outside world and determined to die in the lobby before she so much as took a breath.

Suddenly, a hand landed on her shoulder, breaking her trance. With a sigh, she looked over at the grey-haired man who was now sitting on the ground beside her, dressed in a mono-chromatic suit and tie and looking like a man out of time, stolen straight from an old, black and white crime drama, complete with a chiseled jaw, receding hairline and handlebar mustache. In his eyes, he held what was supposed to come across as concern but to Violet was little more than the practiced pity of a tired cop who was hoping that he stumbled upon an easy case.

His hand still resting on her shoulder, the detective asked, "You the girlfriend of the kid they just wheeled in there?"

"I would have liked to be," she answered, turning away, pulling her knees to her chest and resting her chin atop them.

With a tired smile plastered onto his face, he offered her a weak handshake. "Jeffrey Demoor. Toledo PD," he said. "Were you the one who found him?"

"Yeah," she sighed.

"I'm sorry to hear that. No one should have to go through what you did. And I hate to bring it up, but I need to know. How good a look did you get at what happened?"

Just then, the hallway doors opened, and a doctor walked out, dressed in a pair of bloody scrubs. Immediately, Violet leapt to her feet. Quickly, the detective followed suit. As she rushed over to the doctor, her eyes begged for him to give her good news, to say that Kayde was stable, but all she was met with was an expression that shook her to her core. Upon seeing her, the doctor's eyes became downcast and shifted to the floor.

Then, he sighed, "We did everything we could, but he lost too much blood. I'm so sorry."

With that, the strength left her legs, and she collapsed to the floor beneath the weight of a river of tears. Burying her head in her hands, she screamed out every last ounce of breath in her lungs. Then, once every, last tear had fallen to the earth, forming a small puddle beneath her, she felt something strange rise up in her bones. It was no longer despair. It wasn't grief, nor was it sorrow. Instead, a fire ignited inside her chest, raging like an inferno and coursing like lava through her veins. Furious, her hands quivered, and, when she opened her eyes, it was as though flames shot out of them, scorching everything in sight.

Standing up, she turned to the detective and said, "Regretfully, I didn't see a thing. All I know is that he called me up and said he wanted to meet at the mall, that he couldn't stand this damn city anymore and needed to find a way out. But when I got there, the lot was empty. Well, except for… him. I'm sorry, Detective. I wish I had more to give you."

"Did he have any enemies that you know of?" the detective probed. "Anyone you can think of that would want to hurt him?"

But she shook her head. "No, I can't imagine what kind of monster could have done this. Kayde was the nicest, most beautiful soul I've ever known."

"Would it be too much for you to show me where you found him?"

"Listen Detective, I know you have a job to do, and I don't want to get in the way of that. But right now, I think I need to be as far away from this as possible."

With a sigh, the detective reached into his suit pocket and pulled out a business card. Handing it to Violet, he said, "Trust me, I understand. I can't even imagine having to process all this in months, much less right away. If you think of anything that might help, you have my card. Give me a call."

As she left the hospital that night, she knew; it would be a summer's day in the arctic before she ever dialed his number. In fact, she hoped that detective wouldn't come within fifty yards of Dragon's Wing.

Jail wasn't a good enough punishment to pay for their sins, to make up for the hole that now resided in her heart. The only thought that filled her mind was revenge.

She was going to find that dark-haired bitch and make her pay.

But first, there was something she needed to take care of, a promise she had yet to keep; she had to rescue Theresa.

IT TOOK EVERY OUNCE OF STRENGTH LEFT IN BLAIR'S BONES JUST TO stand. Even as she did, placing her hands against the building's wall, her knees felt like jelly beneath her. However, she didn't have time to process, think or grieve. If they knew who Kayde was, they must have known who she was, meaning that even if they hadn't seen her, they would know he would die before leaving without her.

Which meant she needed to run.

Immediately, she took off, running as quickly as her gelatin legs would take her, and kept herself pinned to the wall, both for support and guidance. Within seconds, she heard the echoing shuffle of footsteps down the alley and the clanging of the dumpster as the lid opened and slammed shut again. Then, the footsteps started toward her. She tried to run faster, but her pursuers gained with every step she took. Soon, they were at the entrance to the alleyway, and any head start she had been afforded had disappeared.

At this point, it was clear that speed would not be her savior this night. If she was going to end the night unbruised, she would have to get creative.

So, instead of running, she stopped dead in her tracks, and, choosing to use the darkness to her advantage, she tiptoed into the woods and dropped to the ground. Her skin scraped against leaves and branches as she crawled deeper into the woods. After a few seconds, she stopped. Then, without a sound, she covered her body in sticks and leaves until the world around her disappeared.

As did she.

The eight minutes that followed were excruciating. While Blair hoped her cover would camouflage her from her enemy, she also knew that, without the tread of her feet to follow, Lena and Paul would be forced to search the woods for her, which could inevitably lead to their feet landing directly on top of her. As she heard their feet brush against a pile of leaves nearby, every muscle in her body grew tense, as though she was Atlas, holding the weight of the entire world on her shoulders.

With every second that passed, the crunching sound of leaves underfoot grew closer and closer until even her cover shifted with each step her pursuers took. She felt the heat of their flashlights scorch her back, and she held her breath, praying that she had managed to construct her cloak without any rips or tears. Seconds later, her prayers were answered as Paul and Lena moved quickly past her, their feet landing only inches away from her.

And finally, she breathed a sigh of relief.

Even as their footsteps faded into the distance, Blair refused to move out of fear that they were simply hiding nearby, waiting for her to make a move. However, she also knew that her time in the shadows was limited. Eventually, daybreak would come, and she would be found out, which meant she had to make her escape while the darkness was still her ally. So, carefully shifting her weight so the leaves slid silently off her back, she stood up and slunk around the side of the mall toward the parking lot, where she hoped Violet would still be waiting.

As she rounded the front corner of the mall, however, she found an empty parking lot. It was completely devoid of life. Paul and Lena were gone. Violet's car had vanished into the night. Even Kayde's body had disappeared, replaced by a puddle of his blood. Immediately, her heart sunk. Without Kayde, she wouldn't have the chance to say goodbye, but even worse, without Violet, she had nowhere to go, no way to get there and no one to help her. Even if she got away, she would be on the streets, hungry and homeless.

But even still, it would be better than the life that was behind her.

As she turned toward the open road, she locked eyes with Izzy, who was sitting beneath a nearby lamppost with his arms crossed and a devilish smile across his face.

"Bet you weren't expecting to see me," he laughed.

Once again, Blair's knees buckled, and she staggered backward, crashing into yet someone else, who immediately latched onto her shoulders and spun her around.

It was Paul.

"Looks like your train's already left the station, Grace," he chuckled.

"Not that it would've mattered," Lena said, stepping out from behind a tree across the street. "There's not a hole on Earth we wouldn't have dug you out of."

With only one option left for survival, Blair sold her soul for just a mite of good will. "And that's exactly what I told him," she pleaded. "I swear, I didn't want to go. I told him that I wouldn't, that I couldn't betray you like that, but he wouldn't listen. He forced me to come with him."

An amused smile crept across Paul's face. "And how exactly was that?" he asked.

"He — he wasn't the brother I thought he was, not at all like the person I knew back home," she stammered. "He said that I — that he would find a way — if I didn't go with him — he would make it so you would punish me like you just did to him, that otherwise my life would become a worse hell than it already was."

Suddenly, the smile left Paul's face, and he glowered at her, saying, "And yet here we are. I guess it must have been fate."

"Wait, please, don't-"

Before she could finish her plea, Izzy's oily hands wrapped around her mouth, silencing her. "What do you want me to do with her, boss man?" he asked.

"Dark-room her," Paul ordered.

"Aw," Izzy whined. "I was hoping to complete the sibling circuit."

"All in due time," Paul replied.

As Izzy dragged Blair back toward the salon, she tried to scream. She tried to fight against him, but he was too strong. And she was helpless against him. From the mall, he hauled her down the street, through the doors of the salon, up the stairs and into a room that, in the months she had been there, she had never actually seen, though she had heard countless, horrifying tales of its darkness. Inside, there were no windows, only a single, black door, and the walls were covered in black. Otherwise, it was empty, apart from a thin, twin mattress along the right-hand wall, a small toilet on the opposite side and a sink. Other than that, there was nothing.

With a villainous cackle, Izzy slammed the door shut, immediately banishing every trace of light from the room and plunging Blair, literally, into the same darkness she had worked so hard to escape. With shaking hands, she looked around her but saw nothing but a thousand, ebon hands reaching toward her on every side, their fingers outstretched to take her with them into the black. Closing her eyes, she took a deep breath and tried to quell the anxiety within her, but the vice grip it held on her heart remained, as did the legion of black hands around her. Dropping to the floor and placing her hands on the ground in front of her, she crawled toward the bed. Her only hope was that a night's sleep would find her waking from this nightmare.

However, it was not meant to be.

As she laid her head onto her empty mattress, a chaotic rumble resonated from every direction, causing her to jolt up in bed. Starting as a low hum but quickly escalating to a furious blare, it was undeniably music, though to Blair, it sounded more like chaos. Between the manic beat of the drums, the low, growling crunch of the guitar and the ear-piercing screams, it sounded like hell itself, like the torturing of a thousand demons, of which she was undeniably one. She tried to shield her ears from the sound, but its waves penetrated her defenses, sending her reeling onto the bed.

And though she would try to drown out the screams, they wouldn't allow her sleep, not even for a second that night.

2

NEW

TOLEDO, OHIO

"How long are you going to keep her in there?" Lena asked as Izzy and Grace faded into the night.

"That's entirely up to her," Paul answered as he looked over her shoulder at the puddle of blood that sat, alone, at the entrance to the alleyway and sighed. "But right now, we've got bigger problems. Looks like Kayde's bitch nabbed his body."

"Shit," she muttered. "How much time do we have?"

Linking his arm with hers, he led her across the street toward the houses. "Depends," he replied. "How good a shot did you get on him?"

"Right between the ribs."

"Then we've got plenty. The hospital's, what, fifteen minutes from here? I doubt she'll even get him through the doors before it's curtains, which means we're looking at ten minutes before the hospital calls it in and another twenty-five before any detectives show. After that, I'm guessing a ten minute interview and another fifteen back here."

"So, an hour?"

"Like I said, plenty of time."

After scurrying up the steps and into Lena's apartment, they strolled into the kitchen, where they grabbed two pairs of gloves, a couple masks and safety glasses, as well as a handful of cloths, vinegar, two, coarse brushes, a vial of sodium peroxide and two, five-gallon buckets, one of which they filled with cold water and detergent and the other they left empty. Then, with their supplies in tow, they hurried back to the mall, where they immediately got to work.

Kneeling beside the pool of blood, they used the cloths to soak up as much as they could before tossing the soiled rags into the empty bucket. Then, while Lena poured half of the water across the stain, creating several, crimson rivers that flowed like tree branches across the grooved pavement and into the sewer drain that sat beneath the sidewalk's lip, Paul donned his protective gear and dumped a thin layer of sodium peroxide into his gloved hand. Soon after, Lena set down her bucket and followed suit, and together, they sprinkled the sulfuric powder over the damp ground, covering every inch.

After that, there was nothing left to do but wait for the solution to do its job.

As Lena scooted back against the wall to rest, Paul doused his gloves with water and shook them out over top of the mess before joining her.

"Well, that was quite the fix," she sighed.

"Yeah," he agreed, leaning his head against the wall and staring up at the night sky.

Turning to him, she laid her hand on his shoulder and asked, "How are you feeling? This has been… quite the last, few months."

He opened his mouth to speak but closed it again just as quickly.

The truth was, even though he tried to hide it, even though he tried to convince himself that Lena's shot hadn't been the final nail in his coffin, he didn't know how he felt anymore. He was reeling, lost at sea without a compass to guide him home. After everything that happened with Redd, Paul thought he had left the animal behind in Detroit. But, it had followed him, across a hundred miles, and was now taking over everything. Every thought, every move, every word came with its moistened breath falling across the back of his neck. If he didn't do something quick, his kingdom would topple, leaving the beast as king and his humanity in the dungeon. In that moment, storm clouds raged all around him, striking the ground to either side of him, and he felt trapped, like no matter what he did, his life was doomed to be like living in solitary confinement, separated and estranged from everyone and everything.

Even from himself.

As he stared into the distance, Lena's gloved fingers laced with his own. He looked over at her, and, though he may not have been able to see the smile beneath her mask, he saw it in her eyes, which glimmered under the alley lights, lighting the night sky with every color of the spectrum.

"I know it's dark now," she assured him. "But the sun's on the horizon. The night can't last forever."

"That… actually almost made me feel better," he said, unable to keep the faintest of smiles from pursing his own lips.

"Well, it's not all blood stains and dying bunnies up in here," she chuckled, tapping her forefinger playfully against her temple. "At least not all the time. Just… don't tell the others."

He looked back over at the fading, crimson stain to his left. "What if we've been going about this all wrong?" he asked.

"What do you mean?"

"We can't keep this up for much longer, pounding our heads into the same brick wall we've been fighting since Detroit. I mean, think about it. At Illuminate, not only did Erica turn on us, but we were dealing with at least one runaway per month. So, we did the only thing that made sense. We cut out the brute, replaced our whole roster and gave them everything they could ever want. But even with all the changes, Monica still stepped out and got arrested. Then… this. It's like nothing's changed. So, the problem couldn't have been the location, the girls or even Redd. It has to be-"

"The control."

"No matter how we try to swing it, make it sound like an oasis, those apartments are still a prison. But what if they weren't? In the end, more than anything, our workers only want one thing: a life outside our walls. So, what if we give one to them?"

Letting go of his hand, Lena leaned forward and clasped her hands in front of her mouth, and for a moment, she didn't move. In fact, she hardly breathed. She simply stared at the wall across from her. Then, without a word, she grabbed the bucket of water, poured half of its remaining contents over the stain and, taking the brush in her hands, began to scrub vigorously at the bands of scarlet that still lingered on the concrete. Quickly, Paul followed suit, and soon, the ground was covered in enough elbow grease to effectively camouflage it, as though nothing had happened at all.

As Paul grabbed the vinegar and poured it in wide, looping swaths across the nearly empty space in front of him, Lena sat back on her knees. "How do we know they'll stay?" she asked.

"Because they'll have nowhere else to go," he answered as, taking the brush once again in his hand, he scrubbed the area down once more. "Most of them have no education, no job prospects and, in this economy, nowhere to go but from shelter to shelter. Besides, after tonight, they'll be far too afraid of what will happen if they don't."

"Sounds like Russian roulette to me."

"I always was a gambling man myself."

"I'm just not sure how many chips we have left to bet."

"All I need is one. Loan me Grace. Think of her as a one month, free trial. If she runs, we'll keep things as they are, no muss, no fuss. But, if I break her..."

"Hell, after tonight, if you can put *that* bitch on a leash, I'll let you have the whole, damn kennel."

{}~{}~{}~{}~{}~{}~{}~{}~{}

Over the next week, Paul and Izzy refused to allow Grace so much as a moment's rest. During the daytime, she was kept undressed, blindfolded and relegated to her corner mattress, where, at fifteen minute intervals, she was met by client after client who had been given specific instructions to inflict upon her whatever punishment or pleasure their twisted hearts desired. On the slow days, Paul would even offer two-for-one deals to his customers as to keep the stream constant and torturous, like the slow dripping of a broken faucet. Then, once night fell, all Paul had to do was press a button on his computer, and a pair of concert-grade speakers he had built into the walls of the dark room did the work for him, subjecting Grace to deafening, intermittent blasts of death metal music.

During those seven days, they deprived her of everything, save for one bowl of unsweetened oatmeal per day, which Paul personally served her at the end of every shift. It was a regrettable situation, one Paul would have rather been able to avoid by simply selling her off to the highest bidder, just as the Russian had done. However, after what Grace had done in New York and now in Toledo, she was essentially worthless. With another owner, she was bound to cause even more trouble, which would soil what little reputation Paul had managed to maintain after Redd.

The only choice he had was to break her before throwing her a bone.

At the end of the seventh day, he ventured up to the dark room with a lantern instead of a meal in his hand. As he opened the door, he held his beacon in front of him so he could see what sort of shape she was in. For all the benefits the dark room provided, the one downside was that with sensory deprivation also came a monitoring problem. Even with night-vision cameras installed in every corner of the room, he could only make out the obvious; she was unclothed, her hair was mangled, and her movements were erratic, frenzied and generally frustrated.

Outside of that, he was as blind as she was.

What he saw when he entered the dark room was nothing short of chaos, as though an angry mob, armed with pitchforks, had decided to gut the room like a school of fish. Used condoms were strewn about the room beside piles of blood-soaked foam. The walls were covered in dents, holes and scratches, and a rancid odor inhabited the room, emanating from the clogged toilet that was filled to the brim with what looked like three days worth of bathroom trips.

As Paul's gaze shifted to the back corner, he caught sight of the mattress, which had been shredded and torn, with what looked like claws marks running in jagged lines across its surface, all of which led toward Grace, who was huddled in the corner with her knees held tightly to her chest. Dark lines encircled her bloodshot eyes, and her arms were covered in cuts, bruises and dried blood from what Paul could only assume was self-harm.

Immediately, her eyes shot up at him, widening. She looked down at his hands and, after seeing they were empty, began to shake uncontrollably as sweat dripped from her brow. Terrified, she forced herself against the wall, as though she was literally trying to push herself through the wall to escape.

"It's okay," Paul said, holding his free hand toward her. "I came to see how you were doing."

Although Grace didn't speak, there was a perceptible change in her expression, shifting from terror to despair. Her eyes sunk to the floor, and her shoulders tensed. Approaching her, Paul bent down to her level and lifted up her chin, bringing her eyes to his. Inside them, he saw nothing: no color, no movement, no life. They were filled with only darkness and brokenness, like a raging, black storm that would soon envelope everything.

Perfect.

"Have we learned our lesson?" he asked.

She nodded.

"I'd prefer to hear you say it," he said.

With a nervous gulp, she replied, her voice breaking, "Y-yes — yes, sir."

"And what did we learn?"

"That it — that I should — I mean, shouldn't run away... ever."

"Good girl. And if you try again, what's going to happen?"

"Y-you'll find m-me, and it — it'll only get worse."

Paul smiled. "Now, that's the answer I wanted to hear. So, what would you say to getting back to your room? I promise, we'll let you sleep this time."

"Really?!" she exclaimed "I mean, yes sir — if you think — well, if it's okay..."

Placing his hand on the underside of her forearm, Paul stood Grace to her feet and led her toward the door, explaining. "There is one condition, though. I need you to do something for me, an experiment of sorts. We're going to try something a little different. For now, this change will only apply to you, and it'll be temporary. But, if you do well, if you don't take advantage of our kindness, Lena might give me the green light to make it permanent and for everyone."

Upon entering the hallway, Grace shuddered and, breaking free from Paul's grip, held her hand in front of her eyes to shield them from the hallway lights. "Sorry. Just... not so used to using my eyes. What do you need me to do?"

"It's okay," he said, standing off to the side to allow her to adjust to the light. "Basically, everything stays the same. You'll work your usual days at the salon. But, once we hit quitting time, you can do whatever you want, go wherever you want, as long as your back at the house by midnight."

At that, her eyes shot up, and, squinting at the light, she stared at him, confused.

Chuckling, he continued, "No catch, no glass slippers. Dead honest. I want you to go out and make friends. If anybody asks, you work at the salon and love it. And if any of those people just so happen to be desperate for work or don't have a place to stay, I expect you'll do what you can to convince them that this is the right place for them. How does that sound?"

"Well, I mean," she stammered. "Y-yes — yes, I can do that. That sounds fair. What's my quota?"

"For now, zero. All Lena wants to see is whether or not we can trust you to do this."

"And if you can't?"

"You'd better make sure we can, because I am not in the mood to clean up any more blood stains."

AS THE FIRST RAYS OF SUNLIGHT FLOODED THROUGH THE OPEN blinds of the top-floor bedroom of his new home, Florian lay atop a half-sunken, blow-up mattress on the floor of the otherwise empty room, staring up at the ceiling with Janelle by his side as he had done for every minute of the seven hours since they had laid down the night before. For the third night in a row, he had been unable to rest, consumed with thought and worry instead of sleep. In just one week since leaving Dragon's Wing, everything had fallen apart. Without a job, he applied for unemployment, which should have been enough to keep the two of them afloat. Regretfully for him, however, Paul had taken the separation personally and, instead of reporting that Florian had been laid off, as Florian had hoped, wrote the government a scathing letter which detailed a fictitious, yet convincing, narrative about how Florian walked out of work during a lunch break with the promise of bringing back donuts, only to never return again.

Because of that, he was deemed ineligible for unemployment benefits, meaning he and Janelle had no income, no food and little hope of paying even the first month's mortgage.

All it took was one step inside their house for their poverty to become immediately obvious. Since every, last penny of Florian's savings was needed to pay for the essentials, such as the mortgage, electricity and insurance, little was left over for furniture, food or appliances. And, since he had sold everything they owned before moving to Toledo in an attempt to save money on moving costs, every room of their house was now empty, save for their mattress, the kitchen appliances that had come with the house, a couple lawn chairs in the living room, an old, tube television they had found on the side of the road and a beat-up DVD player that sat on the living room floor. Two months earlier, if someone had told Florian that this would be his fate, he would have been devastated.

But as hard as it was to swallow his pride, as much as he still worried about where he would find their next meal, he was happier than ever because, for the first time in his life, he was free to be himself.

And there was nothing left to hide.

Crawling silently out of bed as to not wake Janelle, Florian tiptoed down the stairs and into the kitchen, flung the fridge doors open and searched for something he could prepare for a surprise breakfast in bed. However, all it took was a single glance in the fridge to remind him; they didn't have enough money for food either. Apart from a stick of butter, a half-empty bottle of ketchup and a block of cheese for those late-night cravings, it was empty. They did have one thing, though, one cheap and safe bet for a delicious meal: ramen.

And lots of it.

Pulling two packages from the over-stuffed cabinet beside the fridge, Florian turned on the hot water while he moved to the other side of the kitchen to grab a pair of spoons. Then, once the water had heated enough to scorch the skin off a raccoon, he held each, half-opened cup of ramen under the water until they were full and closed the lids again to allow the noodles to cook. It was a far cry from the meals he wished he could provide Janelle, the culinary delights he dreamed of serving, but it was only temporary. At least, that was what he told himself.

After the noodles were sufficiently cooked, he poured their meals into a pair of ceramic bowls he had inherited from his grandmother, garnished them with a generous dash of cilantro, placed them on a plastic tray he had borrowed from the local food court and slunk back up the stairs to their room.

Sitting on the bed next to Janelle, he placed the tray on the mattress in front of him and leaned over to whisper in his wife's ear, "Good morning, sweetheart. Time to get up."

But she didn't budge, not that he had expected her to. If he had learned anything since they started living together, it was that Janelle never woke up without a struggle. The world could have been ending around them with sirens blaring from just outside their room, and the only waking sound she would make would be to ask for five more minutes of sleep. On school days, he often found that the only way to get her out the door on time was to set her alarm with enough time for five hits of the snooze button before she actually had to leave. Even then, she would only ever manage to make it out the door with thirty seconds to spare. On Saturday mornings, however, as it was that morning, hope of waking her up was settled comfortably between slim and none.

Which left him with only one option.

So, he whispered again, "I have food."

In an instant, as though the tickle of his breath contained a thousand volts of electricity, she shot up in bed. Like a bloodhound on the hunt, sticking her nose out and sniffing around voraciously, she searched for her meal. Finding the bowl of ramen to her right, she snatched it up and stuffed half the noodles into her mouth before he could even muster another breath. Then, she paused, another forkful dangling haphazardly over the bowl and halfway to her mouth, looked back at Florian and shot him a sheepish grin.

"Listen, don't judge me, okay?" she chuckled, her mouth still full of food. "Sleeping builds up a hell of an appetite."

Smiling, he teased, "I know, right? All that lying there doing nothing. It's a wonder no one's ever thought of it for weight loss before."

"That's brilliant!" she exclaimed, shuffling over to face him. "It'll be the new weight loss fad. 'The Sleep Gym.' We should totally do it!"

"'It's the weight loss system of your dreams.'"

"'You won't even know you're exercising.'"

"Who cares if it won't work? I mean, it's not like anyone

actually uses a gym membership anyway. As long as people are throwing away their money, it might as well end up in our trash can, right?"

"Have I ever told you how much I love you?"

Florian sighed, "Even atop a blow-up mattress with nothing but ramen for miles?"

"Even in a back alley with dumpster-picked leftovers for weeks," she answered, locking her arm with his and leaning her head on his shoulder.

"If you were smart, you'd have run a long time ago."

"Well, my parents always told me I was a dumbass kid. Might as well lean into it."

"But you and Iris deserve so much more than I can give you right now."

Sitting up, she placed her hand on his cheek, turned his face to face hers and asked, "You quit for a good reason, right? Because they were exploiting their workers?"

"I couldn't live with it anymore," he sighed.

"Then you are giving us exactly what we deserve. A caring, loving husband and father, who will teach our daughter to stand up for what's right, just like her daddy," she insisted.

"But what if that's not enough?" he asked.

"That will always be enough."

Once their breakfast had settled nicely inside their stomachs, Florian got to work. With job prospects looking increasingly bleak, considering the fact that, technically, he wasn't even qualified to do the job he had been doing for Paul, it was becoming clear that he would have to rely on the government to provide for his family. It was certainly a shot to his pride, but, short of going back to Paul with his tail between his legs or turning to petty theft, it was his only option.

That afternoon, he called up every government agency he could think of: Food Assistance, Medicaid and Energy

Assistance. Then, after collecting every, last piece of documentation or proof he needed, he took his favorite suit from his closet, ironed it until it bled steam and dashed to the library to fax over what he needed and print off at least three dozen copies of his resume, which, of course, had been thoroughly redacted to only show what he wanted potential employers to see. After all, the work he actually did for Lena and Paul wasn't exactly kosher in the world of legitimate work.

And as much as Florian would have liked to simply erase his time at Illuminate and Dragon's Wing, it would have taken far to much effort to fabricate a business degree, considering he never went to college. However, it didn't take long for him to mold that experience to his likening. Instead of painting himself as a bartender or receptionist, as had been his official titles, he labeled himself a talent scout. He highlighted his ability to perceive a person's capacity for a job and convince his mark that they couldn't afford not to accept the position.

He may not have been proud of what he had done, but there was no way in hell that pride was going to win out over the well-being of his family.

So, dressed in his best suit with a stack of resumes in his hand and an intricately designed "Looking For Work, Take A Resume" sign taped above his head to the side of the building, he stood along the side of the street in the heart of Toledo's business district ten minutes before lunch hour. As the clock struck twelve, he straightened his tie and fixed his hair. Then, the madness began.

From every side, business men and women flooded onto the street, their stomachs leading them in search of the nearest cheeseburger and fries. As they passed by, Florian took a resume in his hand and held it toward the horde, hoping that someone would take it. However, no one did. In fact, barely a soul so much as acknowledged his existence. They simply strode past him as though he was a ghost, crying out for salvation into empty space.

Not about to be denied, he cleared his throat and took a step into the mob, announcing, "Talent scout, looking for work! Ready to interview on the spot!"

"Out of my way, dumbass!" someone yelled as they barreled past him, spinning him almost completely around.

As he regained his footing, he slammed headfirst into another businessman, sending them both plummeting to the ground. Florian held his hands out in front of him to keep from ruining his suit, but it was no use. The force of his fall sent him skidding across the pavement, which tore at his suit like a lion's claws. He grimaced as he heard the unmistakable rip of cotton and felt his skin scrape against the cement.

Before he could stand up to pick up his resumes, which were now strewn about the ground, the businessman stomped over to his side and loomed over top of him. "What the hell do you think you're doing, standing in the middle of the sidewalk during lunch hour?" he asked as Florian saw what he could have sworn were flames billow out of the man's nostrils.

"I didn't mean to run into you, I swear," Florian pleaded, holding his arms defensively in front of him. "I'm just looking for a job."

"Then maybe you should find one like a normal person," the man said.

"But you see, my wife's pregnant, and-"

"Well, you should've thought about getting a job before you knocked her up."

"But I-"

"Just get out of here with your begging, you lazy bastard," the businessman growled as he bent over, picked up the resumes that hadn't already been trampled by the hungry, stampeding herd and stormed off, stuffing the stack in the trash.

"And why don't you stop being such a bitch-ass, pompous... And I'm talking to myself," Florian sighed, taking off his ripped coat and leaning against the side of the building.

Once the crowd died down, he made his way across the sidewalk to the trashcan, where his resumes sat underneath piles of discarded food, wrappers and other, unwanted items. Pulling what papers of his he could still find, he sorted through them in an attempt to uncover at least one that remained undamaged. But regretfully, after sifting through every, last paper, that was all he found, one, crumpled resume that wasn't covered in grease, ketchup or mustard stains.

So, with his last resume in his hand, he sat against the building, underneath his sign with his coat over his head as rain started to fall.

After another twenty minutes of waiting, all seemed hopeless. At this point, he was alone, drenched to the bone, and the only hope he had of finding a job was sitting, waterlogged, in his hands, its ink bleeding from its pages. No employer in their right mind would take his application now, much less offer him an interview. With a defeated sigh, he stood from the sidewalk, ripped the sign from the wall behind him and walked, head down, toward the nearest bus stop.

Yet another day was going to end with another bowl of pork-flavored ramen instead of the celebratory dinner he had hoped for.

He didn't make it more than ten feet toward the bus stop, however, before someone called out after him, "Hey kid, wait up."

Surprised and admittedly curious, Florian stopped and turned around. When he did, he was met by a white-haired, bearded man who was dressed in an immaculate, cashmere suit with a large, black umbrella held over his head, and was rushing over to him.

"I passed by you at lunch," the man said. "Heard everything that asshole from Terman's said to you. Honestly, I still don't know why Frank hired that kid. He's got an ego the size of Nebraska, acts like he's the Pope's adopted son, and he's not nearly good enough of a lawyer to get away with treating people like that."

"I don't mean to be rude," Florian sighed, looking behind him to see his bus pull up to his stop. "But if you've come to mock me, could we wait until I'm back with a new stack of resumes for you to toss in the trash tomorrow? My wife's expecting me back in thirty."

The man smiled. "Then we'll talk tomorrow," he said. "When you come in to work. I like your moxie, kid. Life kicked you in the teeth, but you kept on fighting. I may not have a big, fancy job for you, but I do have a janitor's uniform with your name on it, assuming you're willing to work for it."

"Full-time?"

"You got it."

"Benefits?"

"I wouldn't dare offer the job without them."

"A corner office that overlooks the city?" Florian asked with a wink.

"Don't push it, kid," the man laughed.

"Figured I'd give it a shot." Florian shrugged as he took the man's hand and gave it a firm shake. "I guess I'll be seeing you tomorrow."

3

HORIZON

DETROIT. MICHIGAN

"You have to believe my husband's a good man and that he can still be saved."

Sitting in the back of Shepard's cruiser across from a very alive Rebecca, Bradie couldn't bring himself to speak. The words just wouldn't come. He felt like he was in the middle of the hundred-yard dash. But, the gun had already fired, and he was still standing at the starting line, watching the other runners fade into the distance. Confused, he looked over at Shepard, who gave him nothing to work with but an unhelpful wink. Then, he checked in with Anna, who he hoped would somehow be, as usual, several steps ahead of him, but she looked just as lost as he was.

"Sorry to drag you straight into the deep end like this," Rebecca said. "But this was the only way."

"The only way to what?" he asked.

"To get one step ahead of this mess."

"What do you know?"

"That you catching Redd was little more than a knight's sacrifice."

"So that's how Paul sees this," he sighed. "A game of chess."

"And those girls were nothing but pawns to him," Anna growled, her voice shaking with anger.

Nodding sadly, Rebecca reached across the car and taking Anna's hand in hers. "We're going to change that," she said.

Pulling away, Anna scoffed, "Good men don't see women as tools they can just throw away when they cease being useful."

"Sometimes good people lose their way," Rebecca replied.

"You can't be listening to this," Anna pleaded, looking to Bradie. "Paul Cross needs to be put behind bars. We should be throwing away the key, not handing it to him on a silver platter. Those girls we rescued, those *real* people he hurt, deserve justice. There's no redemption for men like him."

"Redemption is for everyone," Rebecca insisted.

"Something tells me she's not planning on giving us a choice other than to listen to her," Bradie said.

"Then she's no better than her bastard husband," Anna accused as she flung open her door and turned back to look at Rebecca, hatred pouring from her sockets. "I don't know if you understand this, Rebecca, but your husband is hurting innocent girls, taking their lives away from them. And you still think he's a good man? You still want to save him? I hope you enjoy hell."

With that, her door slammed, and Anna stormed out of the car, stomping across the lawn and planting herself against the back of a fire engine on the far end of the blockade. Then, she held her head up high, flared her nostrils and stared daggers at Rebecca, who looked back at her with tears in her eyes.

"I'm sorry about that," Bradie said. "This is all a bit... personal for Anna."

But Rebecca shook her head. "Don't apologize," she insisted. "She took it a lot better than I did when I first found out."

"And how exactly was that?" he probed.

"Good luck getting that out of her," Shepard laughed. "When it comes to details, Rebbie's mouth is locked tighter than Fort Knox."

"If I tell you where he is, there's nothing stopping you from hauling him off in chains," she explained.

"Then what's the plan?" Bradie asked. "I can't imagine you would have gone so far as to effectively fake your own death without one."

She smiled. "We'll get to that; I promise. But first, you need to know that we're not playing just a single game of chess with Paul. He always has two boards in front of him, and both matches are intertwined. I thought I could force him to concede by taking myself off the board, but I was wrong, just like you were when you tried to take the legs off of Illuminate. I didn't understand it at first, but Redd was on the right track, except he fell for the false king."

"So, why don't we just go for the quick checkmate and take him off the board?"

"Now you've asked for it," Shepard chuckled.

With a smile, Rebecca explained, "Because then you're falling for the same play. You keep looking at Paul as the king, thinking that beating him will end the game when, in reality, he's nothing but a knight. Even Lena only functions as the bishop."

"Then who's the king?" Bradie wondered.

"That's the thing; there isn't one," she replied. "And I think that's the whole point. A kingdom without a king can't be toppled from the outside because, for every knight or bishop you capture, another is standing right behind it, ready to take its place. But, if you can turn a knight against its own, you stand a chance of reaching checkmate."

"And how do we do that?"

"By playing both boards. If Elle and I are taken off the playing field, it'll force him to concede one of his matches. And, assuming I'm right about him, if we play it right, losing one board will force him to see the error of both."

"Which I assume is where we come in."

"Precisely. I only need two things. First, Shepard, I need your police report to say that you found my body in the wreckage."

"What about Ellie?" Shepard asked.

Rebecca shook her head. "She was with her aunt when it happened, and that's where she'll stay. That's where you come in, Bradie. I need you to talk with your friend from The Pulse, the journalist. Have her write up an obituary for me. Specifically, it should mention that I left behind a daughter, who, after being abandoned by her father, has to now live with her aunt."

Scratching his head, Bradie said, "But The Pulse is a local paper. How is he even going to read it?"

"Let me worry about that," she answered. "Once those pieces are taken care of, the rest should fall into place."

Then, she looked at Bradie and said, "I know your girl isn't my biggest fan right now, but believe me, this is the only way. Can I count on you?"

Looking into Rebecca's deep, blue eyes, Bradie sighed. At this point, he liked her plan even less than Anna did. Everything about it flew in direct opposition to everything he had learned at the Academy, everything his father always told him about truth, law and justice. If someone committed a crime, they needed to pay. Even without a badge, it was still his duty to make Paul face the system and pay for his crimes.

However, if the last, few months had shown him anything, it was that the system was broken. When guilty men go free and innocents are imprisoned in their place, the only justice left is the kind that good men make for themselves.

So, with a hesitant sigh, Bradie nodded, to which Rebecca responded, "Thank you, Bradie."

If only I knew how to explain it to Anna…

As his hand gripped the door handle, through the reflection in the side-view mirror, he saw Anna glaring at him with an inferno behind her irises, her entire body tense with rage. Her shoulders stood as stiff as chromium, and both her hands were balled into fists at her sides. As he approached, she shook her head disdainfully at him.

She opened her mouth to speak. However, before she could say anything, he grabbed her by the arm, pulling her around the front of the blockade, and whispered, "We'll talk about this on the way home."

"No!" she exclaimed, ripping her arm from her grasp and facing him head on. "How could you even think about anything but throwing him in a cell to rot?!"

"She knows him better than anyone," he insisted.

Throwing her head back, she laughed, "Obviously. She knows him so well, which is why a detective from over a thousand miles away, who had never even met the man, was able to figure out he was a monster months before she had a clue."

"You're not being fair to her."

"Why are you on her side?! She's not protecting a man; she's harboring a monster. Every second he's out there, more girls are having their lives stolen from them. More girls like Erica, like Monica, like-"

"More girls like you."

With tears in her eyes, she pressed her palms weakly into his chest and yelled, "And you're letting him do it!"

Without saying a word, Bradie threw his arms around her shoulders and pulled her into his embrace. As he held her, she pushed against him with all her might, trying to force him to let go. However, he refused, instead holding her even tighter than before and allowing all her rage to funnel through his body and flow into the ground beneath them. Soon, her body began to shake, and he could feel his shoulder soak with her tears. Then, she collapsed like a falling star into his arms. Her knees buckled under the weight of the atmosphere, dragging her toward the earth, but he held her in place, like he was holding the weight of the world on his shoulders, refusing to let her fall.

"If she's right," he whispered in her ear. "We'll have more than justice. We'll have the tide on our side."

"I know," she choked, her voice muffled by his shoulder. "I just don't understand. How can she know what he's done and still think him to be anything other than a monster? How could anyone?"

"The same way I see my shadow and know it's only an outline. You said it yourself after his daughter's birthday party; the person he was around us, around his wife, was too real, too genuine, to be completely removed from who he is. Maybe all he needs is a shove in the right direction," he explained.

Taking a deep breath, Anna allowed all of the anger and rage she had kept bottled inside to bleed from her body and pushed herself away from Bradie. Then, she looked him dead in the eyes and asked, "So, what do we do?"

"First, we find Nina."

For the entirety of the forty minute drive from the accident to Nina's office at The Pulse, neither Bradie nor Anna said a word. Instead, they sat in silence, Bradie watching the road while she stared out the side window. With every second that passed, he could feel the tension envelop the air around them and constrict his lungs, making it nearly impossible to breathe. In that moment, it didn't take words for him to know that she was feeling it too. Up to this point, they had been in the driver's seat, uncovering every clue and turning over every rock on their own. All of the dominoes had fallen at their will. Now, the field was being set with pieces they didn't think should be there, and they had no other choice but to play along.

As they pulled up to Nina's building, Anna tapped nervously at the door handle, as though she was trying to find any reason at all not to open it. However, once the ignition turned off, she relented, forcing the door open and stepping out onto the asphalt. A second later, Bradie did the same, and soon, they were standing outside Nina's office, staring up at the wooden giant that stood between them and the point of no return.

Gulping, Bradie asked, "Are you sure you want to do this?"

"No," she sighed, raising her hand to the door. "But it's the only play we have. We have to at least see where it leads."

Knock.

Knock.

Ten seconds later, the door opened, and Nina stood behind it with an amused smile on her face. "And for my next act," she laughed. "I will make you both disappear."

Then, as quickly as it had opened, the door closed again, followed by fits of laughter from the other side. Meanwhile, Bradie and Anna looked at each with eyebrows raised, unsure of exactly what had just happened. Obviously, they had missed the joke.

"Perhaps I should stick with my day job," Nina chuckled as she opened the door again. "Now, don't just stand there like a couple doofuses. Come on in! I was just about to call the two of you, but now, here you are! So tell me, what brings you to my humble establishment?"

Taking them by the hands, Nina pulled them inside her office, which was small, consisting of only enough room to fit her desk and three chairs. As Bradie tripped over the threshold, he was surprised to find her office in complete disorder. Literally nothing in her office seemed to have a place of its own, which stood in stark contrast to the way Nina had carried herself up to this point, organized to a fault. Her desk was cluttered and messy, littered with news clippings, stacks of paper and what looked like at least a decade's worth of colored pens. Then, in staggered, unmeasured groupings, framed pictures of Nina with notable, local celebrities were strewn about her walls beside what appeared to be every article she had ever written, including her most recent piece, titled, "Dirty Judge Caught with Pants Down."

Plopping down in the chair across from the desk, Bradie answered, "I need a favor."

"Just say the word," she replied.

"It might be a little… unethical," he explained.

"After the gem you gave me, you could ask me to kick a kitten, and I'd knock her right through the uprights. Well, as long as she's not, like, too adorable or anything."

"I need you to write a fake obituary."

"For who?"

"Rebecca Cross."

"The trafficker-wife?"

"Yeah," he said, nodding. "All I need you to do is say that she died in a single car crash after her van burst into flames along Interstate Seventy-Five. Also, make sure you note that her daughter, Eleanor, is being left in the care of Rebecca's aunt after being abandoned by her father."

"She thinks it will make Paul second-guess his life choices," Anna sighed.

"Either that or don a cape and cowl and dangle us off the edge of a building until we talk," Nina said, fluttering her lips behind a forced exhale. "Is that all you need?"

Reluctantly, Bradie nodded.

"Then it's done!" she exclaimed with a dramatic rap of an invisible gavel. "And now, I have something to ask you."

"Shoot," he said.

"Let's hope it doesn't come to that," she laughed. "But, it may involve a bit of flying. See, I've got a friend down in Vegas, the talking head type. So, I was talking to her about what happened with the trial and all that jazz. Well, get this, apparently her audience eats those kinds of stories up like they're frickin' ice cream. So, she said she wants to have the three of us on her show to tell the whole story. We've got to move quick, though, before her schedule fills up. What should I tell her?"

Feeling a plague of frogs suddenly clog up his throat, Bradie stammered, "Well, I mean — I don't know. That's quite a-"

"We'll do it," Anna answered for him.

"Good." Nina smiled. "Considering I already told her we'd go on for the Christmas special."

"But that's in a month," Bradie said.

"And your plane takes off next week," she said, taking a trio of tickets from her pocket and handing them to Bradie. "Figured you and the family could use a vacation so I persuaded my friend's network to set you up, all expenses paid."

"What's your angle?"

"I am offended by the accusation! But, if you must know, let's just say there's a little something in Vegas I think you'll want to see."

"And I take it we're not the only ones going on this little, family vacation."

Pulling another ticket from her jacket pocket, Nina flashed it in front of him with a wry smile. "I won't be shacking up with you and Stacy if that's what you're asking," she replied. "Though, I can't said I'd say no if the opportunity presented itself."

"I think we'll take a pass. No offense," Bradie laughed.

"Maybe another time, then," she replied with a wink. "Either way, trust me; you're going to want me along for this."

Pittsburgh, Pennsylvania

POP!

"Shit!"

Suddenly, Violet's car jerked up and forward as she sped down the left lane of the highway, week-old tears still streaming down her face. Within seconds, her ears were ringing with the squeal of metal on concrete, and the nauseating odor of burnt rubber and smoke invaded her nostrils. Before she had a chance to react, the tail of the car swerved to the left, threatening to steer her into oncoming traffic. Instinctively, she followed with a hard snap of the wheel, and the car returned to neutral. Then, as she slowed to a crawl, she frantically checked her side view mirrors, trying to find her way to the shoulder.

This, however, turned out to be no easy task. On either side of her, cars sped by, veering around her bumper with trumpets so loud that it sounded like a furious army had surrounded her on every side. Then, to make matters worse, the car behind her lit its high beams, which reflected off her rearview mirror, nearly blinding her. At this point, she had no other choice. She would either have to take her chances in oncoming traffic or come to a stop in the middle of the highway and hope nobody mowed her over.

Or, she would have to take matters in her own hands.

So, taking a deep breath, she pressed the gas pedal to the floor and broke hard to the right. Seconds later, she was flying across the right lane and straight onto the shoulder. As her vision returned, she found herself dangerously close to the edge of the highway, which, as she only now realized, overlooked a steady, downward incline into a dense forest. Immediately, she hit the brakes and spun the wheel back to the left. As she did, the back end of the car bounced haphazardly along the pavement.

Then, the driver's side of the car went airborne, rising up into the air like a bird in flight. Terrified, she closed her eyes, gripped the steering wheel and prepared for her descent.

But it never came.

By what was either tremendous fortune or the guidance of the fates, the car slammed back to the ground in the upright position, and Violet immediately threw it into park, turned on her hazard lights and shut off the engine. Then, after climbing across the seats as to not be saved by the heavens only to get run over by a drowsy driver, she stumbled into the night air and checked the trunk for a spare. Regretfully for her, Kayde was never the most detailed person, which meant that he had neglected to keep a spare in the trunk, and without a phone, Violet was left with no way to call for help other than to beg.

With her winter jacket tightened around her shoulders, she stood behind the car, facing the stampede, and tried to get their attention. She waved her hands above her head, yelled at the top of her lungs and jumped up and down, but no one paid her any attention. For thirty minutes, she jumped until her legs felt like they were about to fall off.

Desperate, she collected a hefty handful of rocks from the side of the road and hurled them across the highway, hoping to call attention to her plight, but all that earned her was an earful from the brass section. She even unzipped her jacket and lifted her shirt over her head, flashing the entire east side of I-80 in the hopes that a pervert with a heart of gold would find it in his heart to help her, even if his only aim was only to get laid. But, no matter how hard she tried, nothing worked. It seemed like her only hope was for a police car to drive by and arrest her for indecent exposure. At this point, however, even that seemed like a pipe dream.

After another fifteen minutes of begging, she leaned against the trunk of her car, exhausted, as despair overtook her, flooding into her heart and pressing against her ribcage. The headlights on every side faded to grey, and in that moment, she began to wonder whether or not she should walk into the center of the road, close her eyes and hope Kayde was waiting for her on the other side. If she was being honest, she no longer knew why she was holding on so hard to what little breath she had left in her lungs. The truth was, she didn't have much left to live for. Kayde was dead. Her parents were long gone, and all she had to her name was a couple hundred dollars stuffed in her backpack. The only thing she had was a hastily-made promise to rescue a girl she didn't even know.

And once that was taken care of, there was nothing keeping her from a date with a noose.

What difference does it really make if I end it now or in a week's time? Is one life really worth all this?

As she was about to take her first step toward the highway, she heard the sudden squeal of brakes followed by tires skidding across the rumble strip. Seconds later, a pair of headlights encased her body in light. Turning toward the light, she narrowed her eyes and held both arms out in front of her face to block the light. When her sight finally returned, she saw in front of her a pick-up truck, which was being driven by what looked to her like the mascot for the local, sports team. He was dressed a football jersey under a matching hat and jacket with a scraggly, unkempt beard that ran well past his steering wheel. As his truck rolled to a stop in front of her, he rolled down his passenger's side window. Then, she approached.

"What seems to be the problem, little lady?" he asked in a thick, southern drawl.

"Seems my tire didn't have the will to live anymore," she

answered, climbing up on the foothold and leaning through the open window. "And apparently, neither did my phone."

"What happened to your spare?" he probed further.

"Don't have one," she sighed. "It's my boyfriend's car, and he isn't — wasn't — exactly good with, you know, cars and stuff."

"He with you?"

"No. Regretfully, he's not… around anymore."

"I'm sorry to hear that."

"What's done is done, I guess. Any chance I could use your phone to call for a tow?"

"Sure thing," he replied, taking his phone from the cupholder and handing it to her.

After calling the tow company, she handed the phone back to him and said, "They'll be here in twenty. I'll be fine by myself for that long. I don't want to keep you from wherever it is you have to be."

"Nonsense," the mascot insisted, waving her off and unlocking the passenger's side door for her. "You'll catch your death if you wait out here that long in the middle of November. Come on in. Get a little fire in them bones."

"I don't want to impose."

"It's only an imposition if you put your death on my conscience. Get on in here," he said as she wheeled around the front of the car and sat across from him. "Now, would you look at my manners? My momma woulda slapped a whoopin' on my ass if she knew I'd known you this long but hadn't gotten your name."

"Violet."

"Billy Ray."

"Like the country singer?" she asked, suppressing a chuckle.

"When my momma heard me cry, she said it broke her achy breaky heart," he laughed.

"She sounds like a good woman," Violet sighed.

"She was," he agreed. "What about you? You look like the type of girl who comes from good people."

"I wouldn't know."

"How come?"

"They didn't stick around long enough for me to find out. Seems fitting though, since, one way or another, everyone leaves."

"I'm sorry to hear that too."

"Me too," she sighed, turning away to stare out the window.

After that, neither Violet nor Billy Ray said another word until the tow truck came. Then, they said their goodbyes, and she rode with the tow truck to the nearest repair station, where she dropped the car for the night. After assuring the tow truck driver that she could find herself a place to stay, she pretended to cross the street to look for a hotel, only to double back the second the tow truck disappeared down a side street so she could huddle into the back seat of her car and grab a little shut eye.

After all, between the cost of the tow and the inevitable price tag attached to repairing a blown tire, she was running out of money and fast. If she stood any chance of making it to New York so she could keep her promise to Kayde, she was going to need every cent she had.

Opening the back door, she shuffled into the back seat, laid her head atop her crossed arms and, curling her legs into the fetal position, covered herself with her coat in an attempt to at least keep somewhat warm. However, it was no use. The fall air was far too frigid for her to find even a moment's rest. For the entirety of the six hours between laying her head down and the opening of the shop the next morning, she stared at the back of the driver's seat in front of her, wishing she had Kayde's arms around her to keep her warm.

The next morning, she met the shop owner at the front doors as he opened up and secured herself that day's first appointment. An hour and a half later, the job was done, and she dug through her backpack for every, loose spec of change she could find. After suddenly becoming two-hundred dollars lighter, all she had left to her name was twenty-five dollars, which was just enough to fill her car with a tank of gas for her return to the Big Apple.

It looked like this was going to be a one-way trip after all.

She was still fifty miles from the city when her gas light flipped on, meaning she had exactly that far to go before she was running on fumes. As she crossed over the bridge into the Bronx, the dial fell to empty. She could feel the engine sputter as she sped through the toll booth, tossing her last quarter into the machine in a feeble attempt to at least pay them something.

From there, it was a slow, monotonous crawl into the city. Taking the third exit into downtown, Violet searched frantically for a parking lot or a back alley, somewhere she could stash her car without risking a tow. But most of all, she needed a place she could sleep without causing too many problems and a spot under the street lamps so she wouldn't invite trouble.

Thankfully for her, it wasn't long before she found her refuge: St. Mark's Cathedral. Regretfully for her, however, just as she was about to pull into the parking lot, the engine gave way, causing the car to roll to a full stop in the middle of the street. With a sigh, she stepped out onto the cold, city street and shuffled behind the car to give it a push. Pressing her shoulders against the bumper, she dug her feet into the concrete and threw her entire weight against the trunk. However, no matter how hard she pushed, the car refused to move so much as an inch.

Suddenly, just as she felt she was finally about to make some progress, her knees buckled, sending her crashing to the ground. As she hit the concrete, she leaned up against the back of the car and tilted her head back, screaming into the cloud-filled sky, "You've got to be mother-freaking kidding me!"

"Is there a problem, miss?" a voice on the other side of the car asked.

Standing up and craning her head around the rear of her car, she was met by a gathering of about a dozen kind-faced, old men in priest robes led by a young man with slick, plat-inum hair, who looked quite out of place in this particular crowd.

"I ran out of gas," she lamented. "I was hoping to make it into your parking lot, but apparently it must not be God's will for me to park myself here."

"Or maybe He just wanted to give us the opportunity to offer you a spot first," the young priest offered, extending his hand to her. "Father Christopher, at your service."

Shaking his hand, she replied, "Violet. Just Violet. Thank you so much."

"It's our pleasure," he said as he waved for his following to join him.

With the might of the church behind her, it didn't take long for Violet to steer the car into a spot on the far end of the parking lot under the street lamp. As the car rolled to a stop, she took out her pack and rifled through it, trying to find even a bit of spare change she could donate as thanks for all their help. All she could scrounge up, however, was three cents, which she offered to Father Christopher.

However, he refused, saying, "Knowing that we helped a friend in need is payment enough."

"Are you sure there's nothing I can do to help?" she asked.

"Well, you can tell me one thing," he answered. "Do you have a place to stay tonight?"

With a sigh, she shook her head.

Seeing her despair, the faces of the priests fell. Father Christopher turned to the oldest of his clergy and leaned in to whisper in his ear.

Then, he turned back to Violet and said, "Well, in that case, welcome to the Chateau Saint Mark. We don't have much, but we do have warm air, a few blankets and a room in the basement you can sleep in. All we ask is that you help keep the place clean for Saturday Mass, at least until you get back on your feet. How does that sound?"

"I couldn't..."

"Nonsense! We insist!" he declared to a chorus of nods and approving murmurs from the other priests.

Before she had another chance to refuse, he wrapped his arm around her shoulder and led her through the front doors of the church, followed by his elderly entourage. From the main lobby, they traversed the right-hand hallway, descended the stairs and stopped outside the first door on the left.

"Welcome to your new home!" Father Christopher exclaimed as he opened the door with a flourish, holding his back to the door so Violet could step inside. "For as long as you need it."

Taking a cautious step inside, she peered around the room, which was modest in size and only big enough for a twin-sized mattress, an end table and an oak dresser. The walls were made of solid, grey cement and were covered in dirt and dust, sparsely decorated apart from an exquisite, oil painting that hung above the bed. Mesmerized, she took a step forward and knelt atop the bed. Then, she leaned forward as though under a spell until she was only inches away from the canvas.

It was the most extraordinary thing she had ever seen. In the center, there was a man in a white and red robe, walking along a dirt path. On every side, he was surrounded by throngs of people and was covered by a light that seemed to emanate from his very being. Behind him, a woman lay, sprawled out on the dirt with her hand stretched toward him. Her fingertips grazed against the hem of the man's cloak, as though she was trying to steal even a spec of his light for herself. Beyond all of this though, what struck her the most were the woman's eyes. There was such beautiful desperation contained within them. It was as though she had no hope left in the world but to touch his garment and hope it would make her whole again.

"Do you like it?" Father Christopher asked.

"It's beautiful," she replied.

"Father Williams will be happy to hear it," he chuckled. "Occasionally, considering we're in the middle of the Bronx, we'll run into others like yourself, people who need a shoulder to lean on for a time. Over the years, it became such a regular occurrence that, a couple years ago, we decided to turn the old, storage closets in the basement into shelters of sorts. But that wasn't enough for Father Williams. He told me it wasn't home without art. Personally, I think he does fabulous work, some of the most beautiful pieces I've ever seen. I used to ask him why he never tried to make something of his art but for him, doing it for the Lord is more than enough."

"What happened to the woman?" she asked. "The one in the painting."

"Well, she was healed. With just one touch of his cloak."

"That doesn't seem fair."

"It was a miracle. I think, by definition, those transcend the meaning of fair."

"But what about everyone else? Don't we deserve to have our afflictions taken away too? Some people give up every-thing, sacrifice everything, only to find sickness and death, and all this woman had to do was touch a man's cloak. It's not fair."

As she spoke, the corners of Father Christopher's mouth turned downward. He stood from the door, walked over to

Violet's side, placed his hand on her shoulder and said, "Something happened to you, didn't it? Before you came here. Something you're running from. If you're looking to talk, I'd love to listen."

With a cringe, she brushed his hand off her shoulder and deflected, "It's nothing. I'm just a little tired. You know, long drive from Ohio and all. I think I could just use a rest."

"I understand," he replied, standing from the bed and walking out the door, closing it behind him. "If you ever change your mind, we're here for you."

What good does talking do me if I still end up alone?

4

RUN

EAU CLAIRE, WISCONSIN

*F*or three days after leaving Duluth in her metaphorical rearview mirror, Natasha walked both day and night with nothing but a jacket on her back and a few scraps of leftovers and thirty-seven dollars and eighty-four cents in her back pocket until her legs felt as though they might just fall off. Under normal circumstances, the week-long walk to the edge of the Illinois border, where she hoped she would be able to scrounge up enough loose change to cover the bus fare to New York, should have been a literal walk in the park. After all, she had survived far worse in her lifetime than a never-ending stroll. In fact, when she first ran away from home, she had scoured the streets of Detroit for the better part of four days in search of food and shelter with little more to show for it than a tickle in her ankle.

However, what she had never accounted for was the toll pregnancy had taken on her body. After only five hours, every step became labored. Immense, shooting pain ran all the way from her ankles to her stomach, and it wasn't long before she found herself under a tree along the side of the road, trying feverishly to catch her breath. Then, the next day, after a night on a shelter-grade mattress and another seven hours of struggling along dirt roads, her legs gave out, forcing her to institute an hourly break in order to merely survive. She knew her best option was to pick up a cardboard sign and negotiate her way across the States. However, the last time she tried to hitchhike her way across the country, she was taken away in chains.

And she would rather take her chances on the open road than risk returning to her cage.

By the end of the third day, she was miserable and exhausted. Her legs and feet felt like melted butter, and the pressure on her chest from the thirty mile-per-hour blasts of icy, November wind was unbearable. So, unwilling to spend another hour wandering the streets of Wisconsin in search of yet another homeless shelter, she stumbled into a truck stop along the highway and prayed for relief.

Opening the doors to the attached convenience store, she was greeted by the biting, hollow voice of the cheese-topped, larger-than-life register attendant, who bit his lip as soon as she entered and said, "Hey there, pretty lady. Welcome to Clear Waters Convenience, where our prices are as satisfying as a dip in Dells Pond. How can I be of service?"

"I was hoping," she gulped as she approached the front counter. "I mean, wondering, if there might be an open cot I could crash on for the night?"

Looking her up and down, he sighed, "Sorry, beautiful. We've got to keep the beds reserved for truckers. Company policy."

"Just one night. Please, that's all I'm asking," she begged. "It's like negative twenty out there, and I've been walking all day. Couldn't you — maybe — look the other way, just this once?"

"Well, I get off in two hours. If you can wait that long, there's always room in my bed."

Involuntarily, Natasha's eyes closed, and she shuddered, a thick column of ice cascading up her spine. Her body shook, albeit not noticeably, as her shoulders tensed as tight as a millionaire's fists around his fortune. Breathing in deep, she took a shovel in her hands and buried her apprehension six-feet-deep.

Then, she looked up at the attendant, batting her eyes, and said in an all-too-familiar, breathy tone, "I don't know if I can wait that long. Maybe we could skip the foreplay and get straight to business."

"Would you look at that?" he chuckled, his cheeks manifesting a flamingo-like shade of pink. "Looks like a cot just opened up."

"Lucky me," she sighed as she took him by the hand and led him into the back office.

As the door to the manager's office closed, Natasha backed him up against the cabinets and sunk her lips into his with a desperate ferocity that caused his knees to buckle and hers to turn to gelatin. Quickly regaining his composure, he ran his hands across the small of her back, then down her pants. As he did, a deep ache settled in every spot he touched her, begging her to run, but even still, she persisted.

As he tugged at her jeans, trying to drop them to her knees, Natasha broke from his kiss and raised her finger to his lips. "You've been working all day," she whispered. "Why don't you let me do the heavy lifting for a change?"

Shaking, she brought her hands to her front and fumbled at the buckles of his khakis. A moment later, they fell to the floor. Quickly, she followed suit. Then, closing her eyes, she tried to drown out the disgrace that ran across her taste buds and down her esophagus like venom, but the shame soaked through her skin and bones, infecting her very marrow. It may have only lasted three minutes, but for the rest of the night, his aftertaste lingered on the tip of her tongue no matter how many times she tried to scrub it clean.

But nevertheless, it was over.

Leaving the last shred of her pride, as well as the attendant, who was still writing with pleasure, on the office floor, she made her way toward her new room at the back of the truck stop, stuffing her pockets full of yogurt-covered pretzels and gummy bears on the way and booking it around the corner before anyone spotted her.

After all, she had just traded away her dignity. She might as well get her money's worth.

Found but lost.
Person, still product.
Freedom has cost,
But others make the profit.
Open fields, nowhere to go.
Unchained, yet fettered.
Target locked, but I don't know
If this storm can be weathered.

That night, despite the exhaustion that shadowed her soul, Natasha couldn't sleep. Every time she closed her eyes, a nearly infinite void as black as coal lay behind her eyelids. There, deep in the recesses of her consciousness, stood a cage, made of pure white. Inside the cage sat the darkness, festering like a disease and seething with rage. On every side, small, black hands pressed against her prison bars, threatening to break free. And even though she knew the darkness could no longer harm her, that, thanks to the love gifted her by her newfound family that was waiting for her back in Minnesota, her soul was stronger than it could ever hope to be, she still feared that, despite it all, she would eventually prove too weak to hold it back forever.

So, instead of sleeping, she lay on her side, staring at the bare wall before her, refusing to allow her eyes to close. "What am I going to do?" she whispered to herself.

In response, the doubt in her heart said, "Fold."

The shame in her skin replied, "Run, just like you always do."

Then, finally, the darkness in her soul growled, "No matter how hard you try, you'll always be a worthless, weak coward."

But just as she was about to give in to the voices and sink into the depths of her despair, another voice rung out over the others. It was soft and warm, and its sound reached inside her heart and drowned the darkness beneath its light.

It was Blair's. "You're the strongest person I know," she assured her.

"Then why does it hurt so bad?" Natasha asked.

"Because this isn't the life you're meant for," Blair replied, her voice smooth and clear, as though she was right there, hovering over top of Natasha like a guardian angel, as though her breath was ticking Natasha's ear.

As she closed her eyes, she could even feel Blair's arm wrap around her waist and hold on tight. "I wish you were here," Natasha sighed. "I should have never left."

"You did the right thing."

"But you're alone."

"And you're safe."

"Why didn't you come with me?"

"This was the only way," Blair insisted.

"It was terrible," Natasha admitted.

"I know," Blair whispered.

"The way he looked at me. Like I was-"

"A play thing."

"He thought he knew me."

"But he didn't."

"He tricked me," Natasha said, her hands shaking with anger.

"Who are we talking about now?" Blair asked.

"The bastard who took everything from me," Natasha answered.

"He doesn't matter. Not anymore."

"These days, he's all I can think about."

"It'll all be over soon."

"Will it?"

"I promise," Blair answered.

"I wish I had your confidence," Natasha sighed.

As the words rolled off her tongue, Blair's arm slipped from Natasha's side. Immediately, she opened her eyes and found herself alone, once again staring at nothing but the clear canvas in front of her with only the dull ring of Blair's voice echoing in the back of her ears.

"What are you going to do?"

And for the first time since she left the Pierson's, since she woke up in the hospital, since long before the warehouse, Natasha had an answer.

Whatever it takes.

Leaping out of bed, she marched out of her room and dashed through the seemingly endless maze of back hallways toward the doors. As she burst out into the night air, her eyes immediately locked on to a running truck at the far end of the parking lot. In the driver's seat, an older man, as evidenced by the long, grey hair that was tucked messily underneath his camouflage hat, was leaning back with his head on the head rest and a copy of the newspaper open to what she assumed was the sports' section. Despite his grandfatherly appearance, he wore his perversion, literally, on his sleeve in the form of a naked woman sewn onto the shoulder of his black and white hunting jacket. As Natasha approached his door, leaving herself fifteen feet away, she became even more convinced that he was the perfect mark.

Behind his newspaper, perfectly hidden by its pages, he held a copy of Jerk-Off Magazine, open to a grainy picture of a naked Latina, who, from where she was standing, looked suspiciously like Jasmine. Stepping onto the foothold by the driver's side door, Natasha pulled the cut of her blouse down to expose her breasts, put on her best smile and knocked softly on the window. Startled, the hunting jacket almost jumped out of his own skin, instinctively closing his newspaper and magazine and throwing them to the other side of the cab.

Rolling down the window, he exclaimed in a thick, southern drawl, "Holy shit on a stick, little missy! If you'd have knocked any louder, I'd be needing a change of my knickers. But, for a pretty little thing like you, I can certainly find it in my heart to forgive. What can I do you for?"

Biting her bottom lip, she answered, "I thought you looked like the kind of guy who knows how to have some fun."

"Oh, do I now?" he asked, peering down her shirt and sighing excitedly. "What's the asking price?"

"Well, I'm headed east," she answered as she walked her fingers up his sleeve and ran them through his knotted hair. "But poor, little me, I don't have a car to take me there. So, I was thinking I could give you a ride for a ride. Extra rounds if you take me all the way to New York."

"You've got yourself a deal, sweetheart."

As she stepped back onto the asphalt, the hunting jacket opened his door and joined her in the back lot. Then, taking him by the hand, she led him back through the truck stop and into her room, where she got straight down to business.

It was a dance she knew well, but this time, she was the one leading. He put his hands on her waist, and she swayed her hips to a salsa rhythm. As he followed her lead, pain flooded through her entire body, like sandpaper against her flesh.

She almost collapsed from the dry, stinging pain, but she clenched her teeth and bore it all, knowing she was dancing the dance of freedom, for both her and Blair. There was no agony on earth that could have compared with the joy she was chasing. So, Natasha closed her eyes, and the rest of the world faded away except for the faint melody that kept her stepping in time.

Then, after another four minutes spent going through the motions, it was finally over.

Collapsing onto the bed next to her, the hunting jacket sighed, "And the Good Lord said she was good."

"So, how far are you going to take me?" she asked.

"As far as your sweet, little heart desires, kitten," he said as he stood up, offering her his hand.

And as the truck's engine roared to life that night, Natasha leaned her head back against the polyester and finally drifted off to sleep.

5

ANGELS

TOLEDO, OHIO

*P*aul stared down the barrel of his gun and into Kayde's eyes, his finger resting on the trigger, ready to fire. All around them, the alley lights glimmered and flashed with violent bursts of electricity that glistened off the gun's barrel, lighting the night air with a brilliance that rivaled the stars themselves. Desperate, Kayde pleaded for him to relent, but Paul simply smiled.

For there would be no grace this night. He was judge, jury and executioner, and the blade was about to fall.

As he pulled the trigger, time slowed to a standstill. Slowly, the muzzle exploded with brilliant flame, firing off in all directions. In turn, Kayde's eyes widened to the size of saucers, and his pupils narrowed, fixated on the bullet, which broke through the walls of flame, barreling toward him in perfect, clear revolutions, like an Olympic skater, fluid and pristine. As the projectile neared its target, the alley lights reflected off its brass casing, shining directly into Paul's eyes.

Instantly, the space around Paul filled with a blinding, deafening white that burned against his skin like thermite. He held his hand out in front of him to protect himself from the deluge, but it vanished beneath the haze that pulsated along with every breath he took. Meanwhile, a faint hum resonated in the distance, followed by a hissing wind.

Then, everything flashed again, but this time, not with light. Instead, the world blazed pitch black.

In the blink of an eye, the darkness overpowered the light and enveloped everything within his sight, except for his hand, which was still stretched out in front of him. As he stood there, surrounded by an infinite expanse of black that stretched out in every direction as far as he could see, a frigid, icy breeze blew past him, making his hair stand on end.

And he felt cold, lonely, as though he was standing inside a black hole, a void in which nothing existed except for him.

As he gazed upon the darkness before him, grey lightning arced across the darkness. All at once, thousands of bolts flew like many, thin vines, separating the void into both ground and sky, where the only plain on which lightning didn't flash was the one on which his feet rested. Then, as though lifted up by a celestial force, the pulsating vines warped and converged together, forming a circular mass of thorns in the center of the ebon sky.

Seconds later, it started to rain.

Except this was no normal downpour. Gazing up into the darkness, he saw droplets of scarlet and ivory water fall on him in perfect unison. As they landed on his skin, he found the ivory beads to be like water in every way: cold, wet and thin, dripping smoothly off his skin and onto the ground beneath him. The scarlet, however, was different altogether: warm, dry and thick, more like blood than water. Instead of slipping off his arms and landing on the ground, it stuck to his skin like glue and soon covered him entirely, coating his arms, shoulders and head with its viscous sludge.

Shaking his arms like a dog after a summer's rain, Paul flung the scarlet sludge to the ground. As it landed in sync with the ivory rain, they both sunk into the shadow and disappeared from sight. A moment later, a thousand flowers sprung out of the ground, forming a field of red and white lilies that pervaded the void, stretching out on every side farther than his eyes could see. Surprised and confused, he turned around and found himself standing before a log cabin set in the middle of the infinite field. It was small and quaint with a wrap-around deck and a purple and yellow wreath beside the front door, just like the one he and Rebecca had always dreamed of buying.

As he stared, wide eyed, at the front door, it creaked open. And there she was, his bright, shining star, standing mere feet in front of him, but even still, it felt like she was light years away. The space between them stood like an infinite chasm that he could never hope to cross.

But even if it took him an eternity to reach her, Paul was determined to let nothing stand in his way.

Ever again.

So, taking step after deliberate step, he closed the distance between them. However, as his foot hit the cabin's front step, a waft of acrid smoke blew past his right shoulder, followed by a bitter, rancid smell, like that of a thousand matches lighting simultaneously. He looked up at Rebecca, whose face was now encased in an orange glow, and suddenly, starting at her right cheek and slowly working through the rest of her face, the skin began to melt from her bones. Terrified, Paul took a step back and turned to face the field behind him, which was now set ablaze.

The entire sky burned with red and orange as Paul found himself surrounded by fire on every side. In that moment, only one thought filled his mind; he needed to save Rebecca from the flames. However, before he could take a single step toward her, a boiling liquid settled beneath his feet, a mahogany, bubbling substance like lava that puddled around his ankles and burned against his skin. Turning around once again, he found the cabin melting like a wax candle under a blow torch's flame.

And in the center of the pool stood a nearly liquified Rebecca, her beautifully crystalline eyes boring through Paul's bones and marrow, straight into his soul.

Then, she mouthed the words, "We're done."

Before he could respond, before he could fall at her feet and beg for forgiveness, the pool that once was his cabin exploded, like a can of gasoline beneath a single spark, sending bursts of blinding, white light in every direction and throwing Paul back onto the ground. Helpless, he held his hands in the air, shielding his eyes from the light, but it was useless. It broke through his defense, burning him to his core.

The next thing he knew, he was sitting up in Lena's bed in a cold sweat, nearing hyperventilation. His chest thumped up and down at hyper speed as hot and cold shivers ran throughout not only his spine but his entire body, which was now shaking in sudden stops and starts. It was as though he had lost all control himself, unable to halt the frantic groans that escaped his mouth and woke Lena from her slumber.

Shooting up next to him and placing her hands on his shoulders, she asked, "Hey, what's wrong?"

"No, n-nothing," he stuttered between faltering breaths. "G-go b-b-back to bed. I'm - I'm fine…"

"That doesn't sound like fine," she insisted, bringing her hand gently to his cheek and turning his face to hers. "Was it the dream again?"

Paul nodded. Every night since the incident, he had been unable to bring himself to sleep through the night. At precisely 3:45 every morning, the same dream awoke him in such a panic that he almost passed out. Some nights, he couldn't even bring himself to sleep, terrified that as soon as he closed his eyes, he would find himself back in the void, gazing upon Rebecca as she melted into oblivion.

Lena tried to comfort him. "Everything's okay," she promised. "Rebecca and Elle are fine. You're stressing yourself out over nothing."

"I know," Paul sighed, finally beginning to calm down. "But at this rate, it doesn't really make much a difference, does it? I'm never going to see them again."

"You don't know that," she said.

"I never pegged you as an optimist," he chuckled weakly. "Of all people, I thought you'd be the first to walk the funeral march with me, considering… you know."

"What can I say? I'm full of surprises. Besides, after the couple weeks we just had, even bittersweet news would be a welcome improvement."

"If I didn't know any better, I'd think you were actually starting to care about my happiness more than your own."

"Well, then it's a good thing you know better. Now, lay your ass down. Since it looks like neither of us will be getting any sleep tonight, we might as well make the best of it."

Shoving Paul back onto the bed, Lena lay down next to him and rested her head on his chest. Then, she wrapped her arm around his waist and placed her leg on top of his, and there they remained for the rest of the morning, talking about anything and everything other than the growing fear that had made residence in Paul's heart and soul.

It was the most at peace he had been in weeks. He wished the sun didn't have to rise that morning, but even so, it did, which meant it was time to get to work.

As the sun ascended over the top of Dragon's Wing, he stepped outside, shuffled down the steps and made his way to the top floor of the building next door, where Grace was attempting to return to what little bit of normalcy they afforded her in this life. Opening the door to her apartment, he found her sitting around the kitchen island, enjoying a bowl of cereal with her roommate, Alysha. Upon seeing Paul, Grace's eyes grew wide, and she dropped her spoon into her nearly empty bowl. Instinctively, she leapt to her feet and stood in front of him, stiff and unmoving, as though she was a soldier before her sergeant, terrified that so much as a muscle spasm could result in punishment. Meanwhile, Alysha simply looked back and forth between Grace and Paul, taking in the growing tension in the air.

"Ready to work today?" Paul asked.

"Y-yes, sir," she replied with a submissive nod.

Titling his head to the side, he motioned for her to follow, which she did without hesitation. From her apartment, they walked in silence down both sets of stairs and to his car. Without a word, he walked around the front of car and opened the passenger's side door for her. With a subtle nod of thanks, she slipped into her seat, keeping her eyes trained on the ground as to avoid eye contact. As he made his way back around to the driver's side, a satisfied smile spread across his cheeks.

She was broken, like clay in his hands that he could mold into whatever he wished.

From the house, they drove to the bus station to pick up a pre-paid bus pass to fund her coming and going from the salon. Then, they toured the main streets of Toledo, and he acquainted her with her surroundings. After all, if Grace was going to gain the trust of the locals, she had to look, talk and act like one of them. He took her past the movie theater, showed her around the mall and pointed out every teenage hangout along the way. Finally, after three hours spent playing tour guide, the sun was hanging directly overhead, meaning it was lunch time.

As Paul pulled their car to the side of a busy street, Grace asked, "What do we do now?"

"Now," he chuckled. "We eat."

After feeding the parking meter, he waltzed over to the passenger's side door and opened it with a flourish, allowing her to join him on the sidewalk. Closing the door, he rushed ahead of her, held the front door to the restaurant open and ushered her inside to their own table for two in the back corner of the main floor, per Paul's request. Then, he ordered them a large, pepperoni pizza and a pair of lemonades.

Once the waiter was out of sight, he got down to business, pulling out a custom-made, fake ID in the name of Grace Letty and sliding it across the table. It was beautiful, one of the best forgeries he had ever created, perfect in every way. He had even purchased a state-of-the-art encoder off the black market to add a magnetic strip to the back of her license, where he had loaded all of her falsified information, just in case anyone got curious. Of course, it would never fool law enforcement. However, considering Grace's newfound obedience, Paul was confident it would never need to.

Taking it in her hands and looking it over, she asked, "What's this for?"

"If we're going to make this work," he explained as he reached into his pocket and pulled out a pre-paid debit card. "We can't afford to leave anything to chance. From this point on, for all intents and purposes, you *are* Grace Letty, a seventeen-year-old, high school dropout from Lima, Ohio. Feel free to fill in whatever story you want from there. That should be everything you need to carry with you when you're out. We have all your other information, social security cards, passports, et cetera, in our files at the salon."

"What do I need the debit card for?" she wondered aloud.

"That's the best part!" he exclaimed, growing strangely excited. "Every month, for as long as this arrangement works, I'll load five-hundred dollars onto that card, which you can use for anything you want: transportation, clothing, anything, though I personally recommend saving it for nights out with any friends you make or for buying a nice purse or wallet to keep up appearances. Everyone you meet should come away with the impression that you have more money than you know what to do with. So, live it up as best you can."

"Where does the money come from?"

"As much as I wish we were bathing in money at the salon, we're not. So, as usual, we'll be tallying that amount onto your debt."

"So, another fee…"

"Oh, it's so much better than that, my dear! Like I told you before, part of the reason you're out here is to recruit. So, convince your friends that you have the best job imaginable. Feel free to take them back to the houses, show them around the salon, whatever you need to do. For every new worker you bring in, that month's spending money is taken care of. Bring in two, and we'll knock five-hundred off your overall balance. Do well enough, and who knows? Maybe you can work your way out of here."

"When do I get started?"

"All in due time. For now, you can just relax and enjoy your pizza. No sense in worrying about any of that other stuff on an empty stomach. After lunch, we'll head down to the high school and get you signed up for night classes to work toward Grace's GED. That'll be your hunting grounds. If I'm right, just about everyone in that class should be a workable target. None of the other dropouts should even have a prayer of making even half of what you do, or at least appear to, in a week. Once you're there, it should be easy. Make friends, take them to dinner and close them out. For now, you're free to do whatever you want, provided you're back home before midnight and come into work every day. However, if you're late, even just once, or we find out that you said anything that could compromise our position, you'll be back in the dark room until we can trust you again. Are we clear?"

"Yes, sir."

~

Detroit, Michigan

"Mommy, I don't understand. Why can't we live at home?" Elle asked, confused.

Looking away, Rebecca sighed. As they stood on the her aunt's porch, staring up at the front door, she wished she had a better explanation. All she wanted was to come up with an explanation that a seven-year-old would understand, something that could make leaving Elle less painful, but she couldn't. In fact, she was hardly sure she grasped the situation herself. Nevertheless, this was what she had to do, even if it broke her heart.

With a tear-stained smile, Rebecca bent down to Elle's level and tried her best to explain. "Mommy has something important she has to do," she said. "I have to convince Daddy to come back home, but in order to do that, I have to go away for a while."

"Can I come with you?" Elle asked.

"I wish you could, Muffin," Rebecca chuckled sadly, cupping Elle's face in her hands. "But part of bringing Daddy home is you being here, without Mommy. And this time, if he comes to see you, I need you to pretend you don't want to see him, okay?"

Immediately, Elle's face fell. "But maybe I can convince him to come home!" she insisted. "I can help."

"You are helping, baby. If there was another way, I'd jump on it in a heartbeat. You'll just have to trust me. As long as Daddy can see you, like when he came to your school, he won't come back, at least not for good."

"How'd you know about Daddy being at school? I didn't tell you that!"

"Honey, you try so hard to keep your little secrets," Rebecca said, pinching Elle's cheeks playfully. "But those dimples give you away every time. Now, promise me you'll be good for Aunt Marie, and I promise to be back as soon as I can. With Daddy."

With a wide smile, Elle crossed her heart and hoped not to die. Rebecca responded in suit before pulling Elle to her chest and holding on for dear life. Letting go of her was the hardest thing Rebecca ever had to do, but even that was child's play compared to the effort it took to bring her finger to the doorbell. It was as though the angels themselves were pushing against her with all their might, urging her to turn back. And normally, she would have done just that. However, for the first time in her life, not even the heavenly host could force her from her goal. Beyond all doubt, she knew her path was righteous, and she wouldn't relent until heaven blessed her.

A moment later, the door opened, and Elle rushed into the outstretched arms of a silver-haired woman, who, even though she wasn't Rebecca's mother, looked as though she could have been. Like Rebecca's, her face was soft and kind, and she bore hair that looked like it had been crafted from the rarest of silkworms. Truth be told, Aunt Marie was more of a parent to Rebecca than her own mother had been. Where her mother was distant and submissive to an abusive husband, Marie was strong, independent and the most genuine soul Rebecca had ever met. She had long since lost track of the debts she owed her aunt for their late-night talks after running away, time after time, from home, the last-minute trips to the movies when her father grabbed his fourth can of beer from the fridge or the strength she felt from what she always knew was constant and continued prayer on her behalf. And when Rebecca had called Marie to add yet another mark to the ever-growing tally, Marie hadn't hesitated.

Because sometimes, God dresses his angels in flesh.

As Marie lifted Elle into the air, holding her securely in her embrace, she glanced at Rebecca dolefully, the corners of her lips curling into a frown. In return, Rebecca smiled feebly at her, shuffling her feet and running her hands nervously through her hair.

"Sorry for the last-minute call, Auntie Em," she said, looking away.

"How could I say no to spending some time with my favorite, little ladybug?" Aunt Marie asked, pulling Elle from their embrace, cupping her face and rubbing noses with her. "Besides, I've kind of grown accustomed to only having a five-minute head start with you, Rebbie."

"Have I ever told you you're a saint?" Rebecca chuckled.

"I'm just waiting for my plaque at the Vatican," Aunt Marie joked before setting Elle back down in the ground, bending to her level and patting her on the cheek. "Hey bug face, why don't you run upstairs and check out the room I decked out for you? Make yourself at home while I talk to your mommy for a minute."

"Okay Emmie!" Elle exclaimed with an excited smile before grabbing her My Tiny Horsey suitcase and dashing around the corner and up the stairs.

As Elle disappeared out of earshot, Rebecca choked through her ever-growing anxiety, "I really should get going. Spy work waits for no woman."

"Nonsense," Marie ordered as she grabbed Rebecca by the hand and dragged her inside, shutting and locking the door behind them. "I have had long-standing, totally confidential relationships with at least a dozen, or three, spies in my years, and they always had time for tea. If I remember correctly, you're an English Breakfast girl, right?"

"Right as always, Auntie," Rebecca sighed, sitting down at the kitchen table while Aunt Marie put a teapot on the stove.

"Besides, it's not every day I get to converse with the spirits of the dead, levitical laws be damned."

"You saw the article?"

"It's kind of hard to miss your niece's face plastered all over the obituaries."

"I mean, the intent was be an attention grabber, so I guess that's kudos."

Joining Rebecca at the table while she waited for the tea to brew, Aunt Marie placed her hand on Rebecca's and smiled with tears in her eyes. "I'm so proud of the woman you've become."

"You wouldn't feel that way if you'd heard me," Rebecca sighed.

"You can't blame yourself for that," Marie insisted. "If I'd found out that Frank was involved in that sort of shady business… well, you know, before the divorce, you'd be talking to a widow."

"Paul's a good man. He just doesn't know it yet."

"You could see the good in Hitler if you only had the chance to talk to him."

"Even bad men have diamonds hidden beneath the surfaces

of their souls. Sometimes, it just takes a little pressure to reveal them."

"I hope you're right, Rebbie. I really do."

"It's times like this I could really use that old necklace you gave me," Rebecca sighed.

"You don't have it anymore?" Aunt Marie asked.

Shaking her head, Rebecca replied, "I found someone who needed it a lot more than I did."

With a beaming smile, Marie took both their hands and placed them over Rebecca's heart. "Never forget, the light's right here. As long as you remember that, it'll guide you wherever this path takes you."

"Thank you, Emmie."

"Thank me after you save the world, peanut."

Sighing, Rebecca bent over and held her head in her hands. In that moment, the weight she felt bearing down on her shoulders was excruciating. It was as though the fate of the world was weighing on her, along with the red hot rage that, if she was being honest with herself, still boiled inside her heart, mind and soul. She didn't understand how to reconcile the man she always believed Paul to be with the man she saw in Toledo. It was like pulling the mask off a cartoon villain, only for it to be the last person you expected. The only difference was that she had pulled the mask off her hero and found a villain underneath.

Even still, she couldn't fathom how the hero and villain could be anything but one and the same. Now, all she had to do was show them both the light.

Just then, the teapot whistled, drawing Aunt Marie from the table as she assured Rebecca, "All you need is a blazing hot sip of England in a cup, and you'll feel right as rain."

However, Rebecca was convinced that in order to do that, she was going to need something a hell of a lot stronger.

After tea, Rebecca left Aunt Marie's house, her heart still as heavy as a semi-truck. From there, she took the bus to the shelter, where she checked in to ensure that Georgie had everything he needed to run the place while she was gone. After that was taken care of, she hopped on the Bloodhound and rode to Toledo, clutching a paper copy of The Pulse to her chest. With every second that passed, her fingers wrapped tighter around its rolled, rounded edges, crumpling it beneath her grip. Though she knew what she had to do, it killed her to know what it would do to Paul and scared her to the grave to think that, despite her certainty, she could still fail. This was the point of no return, and she was standing with her toes touching the line in the sand, teetering over the precipice.

Once she laid the paper on the mat, there would be no turning back.

As the bus pulled up to the stop at the mall across from her destination, her heart began to beat like the gallop of a thousand horses' hooves. Walking down the sidewalk toward the house as a copper sun set over the horizon, she tapped the paper nervously against her forearm. In the distance, she saw Paul, and immediately, her heart stopped. He was walking across the street, arm in arm with Lena with an unnerving smile across his face. Rushing behind a nearby tree, Rebecca peeked her head around the side, where she saw Paul lean in and plant a soft, sweet kiss on Lena's cheek, plunging the knife deep into Rebecca's heart.

Rebecca had always known that an unspoken, chemical attraction had existed between Paul and Lena. It didn't take a detective to see. The subtle glances from across the room. How Lena always bit the bottom corner of her lip when Paul passed by. Even the way Paul looked Lena up and down when he thought Rebecca wasn't watching. And in all of her planning for this very moment, Rebecca had even imagined that, once the wheels of her plan were set in motion, he might find himself tangled between Lena's sheets in an attempt to dull the pain. However, to see them together, to know that he was sharing her bed, night after night, while he still believed Rebecca to be alive, was like heaping burning coals on her skin. It was simultaneously infuriating and heartbreaking.

In her anger, she had never realized how much their separation must have been hurting him.

Now, her only hope was that it wasn't too late for him to be saved.

As Paul and Lena entered the first floor apartment of the right-hand house, Rebecca tiptoed around the back, keeping her footsteps soft and quick. Rounding the corner, she spotted a faint light flickering from the back window and immediately dropped to the ground to avoid being seen. Approaching the back window, she took hold of the siding just beneath the window and lifted herself up so she could peer inside.

When she did, she saw Paul lying motionless on his back atop Lena's bed with the back of his head facing the window, staring at his phone, which he held, tilted up, in front of his eyes. Tears ran down his cheeks as he ran his thumb along the outline of a picture of Rebecca and Elle he had pulled up on the screen. Her eyes welled with tears to match his. For two, full minutes, neither of them moved a muscle, save for Paul's thumb, which ran laps around the picture's outline.

Suddenly, Lena's figure appeared in the doorway, dressed in nothing but a sheer, purple nightgown. She leaned against the frame, sticking her hips out to the side. Her lips moved, breaking Paul's trance. Immediately wiping the tears from his eyes, he jumped up from the bed and stuck his phone in his back pocket. Through the mirror on the other side of the room, Rebecca could see him paint a smile across his face, but it was nothing but a forgery, a falsehood. In his eyes, there was seated a deep, biting despair, the likes of which she had never seen there before.

Unable to watch for even a second longer, Rebecca dropped from the window. As she made her way back around the front of the building, she clutched the newspaper even tighter to her chest. However this time, it wasn't out of fear or apprehension, not even uncertainty. Rather, it was anticipation. She was resolved, now more than ever. Laying the newspaper on the front steps, open to her obituary, she knew that, although the news would break him, ultimately, it was the only thing that could save him.

6

FREEDOM

SPRINGFIELD, ILLINOIS

"*L*ooks like you found yourself a ripe one, Happy," a voice whispered, drawing Natasha from her dreams.

Suspicious of the voice's sinister tone, she opened her left eye slowly, being careful not to let anyone know she was awake. Instantly, she went into survival mode, scanning her surroundings for any means of escape. From what she could tell through half-opened eyes, her ride was sitting, idling, in the middle of an empty lot beside an abandoned, packing warehouse. Beyond that, there was nothing beside her but open space that stretched out for as far as she could see, only hindered by a six-foot high fence that appeared to span the length of the lot. To her left, the hunting jacket was leaning out his open window, talking quietly with what sounded like a younger man, though she couldn't tell for certain without giving herself away. So, instead of getting a closer look, she decided to listen in.

"She was a pretty good lay too. Though, a bit dry for my taste, if you know what I mean," the hunting jacket whispered. "Says she's headed to New York."

To which the younger man replied with a chuckle, "Looks like she's making a pit stop."

"We looking at the usual rate?" the hunting jacket asked.

"Depends," the other man said. "Gotta make sure she looks just as good defrocked."

Shifting in her seat so she could face the side window, Natasha groaned softly in an attempt to still appear asleep.

Suspicious, the younger man asked, "Hey, is she awake?"

Natasha gulped. Closing her eyes, she tried to calm her breathing and keep her muscles as relaxed as possible. The seat beside her squealed, and a hand rested on her shoulder, checking for any sign of life, to which she offered none, save for the rumbling of her throat in an attempt to mimic a soft snore.

Taking his hand from her shoulder, the hunting jacket turned back to his buyer and answered, "Nah, just dancing with the clouds."

Breathing a silent sigh of relief, she reopened her right eye, which was now the one closest to her seat, and took in the view, hoping to map out her escape route. However, the view to the side of the truck was nearly identical to the front: open space for miles, blocked by a high fence. The only light at the end of the tunnel was a small opening in the fence about fifty feet away, where a set of train tracks ran through it.

It was a long shot, but at this point, it was her only way out.

Without making a sound, she wrapped her hand around the door handle, preparing to run faster than she ever had in her life. However, just as she was about to open the door, something caught her eye in the reflection of the side mirror. At the back of the truck stood a heavier, bearded man in a leather jacket, who was leaning against the side of the truck with his face down, fiddling with a lighter in an attempt to light a cigarette. Despite his relative proximity, Natasha didn't consider him much of a threat, figuring that as long as she had surprise on her side, she was sure she could beat him to the tracks.

Regretfully for her, she didn't even have that, as before she could make her move, his eyes shot to the mirror, meeting hers. Immediately, they grew wide, and he took off toward her door, yelling, "The bitch is awake!"

Wasting no time, Natasha burst through the door and leapt to the ground, holding on to the frame of the door for support. As she hit the ground, her legs turned to pudding beneath her. Her knees buckled, and a painful shiver ran up all the way up to her thighs. It took every bit of strength she had left to keep from tumbling to the ground. Nevertheless, she kept herself upright and took off in a dead sprint just in time to avoid the outstretched arm of the larger man. As she passed the door, she slammed it behind her, right on top of her pursuer's hand.

Then, it was a forty-yard dash to the finish line.

However, her head start didn't last long. Almost immediately, the younger man raced after her, quickly making up ground and leaving him only a few feet behind her. He reached out to grab her, taking a hold of her hand on its backswing. Leaning forward, he tried to pull her to the ground, but, instead of giving him the upper hand, this shifted the advantage to Natasha. Reflexively, she jerked her arm forward, throwing him off balance and sending him crashing to the ground.

With only twenty feet to the fence, she found her second wind and reached the opening within five seconds. However, she knew that it would do her no good unless she found a way to keep from being followed. Luckily, her opening also came with a swinging, fence door and a padlock.

As her feet hit the tracks, she shifted to her right and stretched out her arm out, grabbing one half of the door and pulling it shut behind her. Then, turning around, she lurched forward and pulled the two sides together. But, when she reached for the padlock, it was gone. In her haste to block her exit, she had swung the door too hard, causing the lock to fall from its perch to the ground three feet from where she stood.

And there wasn't enough time to grab it.

By this point, her pursuer had recovered from his momentary stumble and was only ten feet from the fence. There was no way she would be able to open the gate, grab the padlock and lock it in time to get away. Frantically, she searched the ground around her for something, anything that could give her the upper hand. However, the only items within arms reach were a few rocks, a large stick and a metal pole. It wasn't much, but it would have to do.

After picking up the stick and the pole, she wedged both between the gaps in the chain link on either sides of the gate, effectively locking it shut. She knew it wouldn't hold long but hoped it might just give her enough time to get away from her pursuer. So, once the door was secure, she flew through the open field in front of her as fast as her legs would take her, refusing to look back to see how close she was to capture.

Two minutes later, however, she discovered just how close she was as, without warning, she was tackled to the ground. As she fell, she threw her arms in front of to break her fall. But it did her no good. The rough, frigid ground buckled her arms and broke against her skin. As she hit the ground, her whole body instantly went limp. At this point, there was no use fighting back. He was too strong, and she was too hungry, too tired and too weak to struggle. Besides, what little energy she had left would serve her better if she saved for her next escape attempt.

"Bitch," her captor muttered as he slammed his palm into her shoulder blade and dug his nails into her skin, lifting her off the ground.

But even still, she didn't fight back. She didn't scream, nor did she cry as he dragged her across the parking lot and stuffed her inside his trunk. Instead, she embraced the darkness, knowing it wouldn't hold her for long.

After all, from what she had seen, her captors had no idea what they were doing. Alexei would have never given her the chance to run.

Twenty minutes later, the car took a sharp, right turn, sending Natasha flying into the side of the trunk, before coming to a sudden stop. Bringing her ear to the deck lid, Natasha listened closely, for what happened next would determine her course of action. Two fools would be easy enough to outwit, whereas an operation would require a touch more finesse.

Thankfully, the only sounds she heard were the same ones she had heard after she was forced into the trunk except in reverse order: the slamming of two doors and two sets of footsteps approaching the back of the car. Then, the trunk opened, sending a blinding deluge of the noonday sun's glare directly into her eyes.

"Rise and shine, little pussy," the heavy man said as he bent over, smirking, and took her by the arm. "Welcome to your new home."

As they hoisted her out of the trunk, Natasha scanned the area to see what she had to contend with. To her surprise, she found herself essentially in the middle of nowhere, in the middle of a fenced-in, dirt-covered, lot behind a dingy, six apartment building in the center of Hick Town. All around her, everything was dead, including the air, which stood completely still. It was as though she was walking into a ghost town, and she was the only living thing left inside.

How are these idiots going to turn a profit in this place?

Once her feet settled beneath her, the heavy man took her by the shoulders and turned her around, looking her over and saying, "Let's get a look at you. It's gonna be nice having a bitch of our own for a change instead of handing the good ones over all the time."

Before she could finish the back end of her turn, however, the younger one swatted his hands away, ordering, "Save it for later! We gotta get her topside before old Mrs. Lampin gets back."

"Right. Sorry, Carson," the heavy man said.

"What did I tell you about using our real names?!" the younger one yelled, throwing his hands dismissively into the air.

This is going to be even easier than I thought.

From the car, the idiots led Natasha up two flights of creaky, mold-ridden stairs to the far side apartment on the third floor. After shoving her inside, the heavy man locked the door behind them while the younger one approached her, his muddy eyes littered with desire. Even still, Natasha didn't fight. As he removed her clothes, she remained limp, allowing them to fall to the floor in a heap. All the way from the kitchen to the bedroom, she let them do whatever they wanted to her, whether separately or together because that night, once they fell asleep, she would make her move.

Finally, after five, similar occurrences, which the fools seemed to think was a clever way to break her will while also popping their rocks, the moon rose over the horizon, drawing the idiots to their bed but not before a clumsy attempt at threatening her into submission.

"We own you now," the heavy man said, trying to keep a smile from creeping across his face.

"If you try to escape, we'll find you," the younger one threatened.

"And we'll hurt everyone you ever cared about," the heavy man added.

That might be intimidating if you actually knew anything about me.

Suppressing the urge to correct their folly, Natasha put on a sad face and played the part. Cowering in the corner of the room with her knees to her chest and clothes still on the floor, she quickened her breathing, allowing her chest to rise and fall almost spasmodically in an attempt to appear frightened. Then, she tightened the muscles in her arms to make her hands shake and even whimpered lightly as a few tears ran down her cheeks for good measure. Finally satisfied, the fools left her alone and locked the door behind them, convinced that they had beaten her.

"Amateurs," she muttered under her breath.

Standing up and taking the gift card out from between her knees that she had snatched off the kitchen table while they weren't looking, Natasha shook her head and chuckled to herself. As she got dressed, she almost felt embarrassed that she had allowed them to catch her in the first place. Now, all she needed to do was wait until she heard the sound of snoring echo across the hallway outside of her room.

When that finally happened, she made her move.

Sliding the gift card between the door and the doorjamb, she pressed the card down toward the handle. Silently, she jiggled it back and forth inside the gap until the latch clicked. Then, she opened the door and stepped out into the hall.

Immediately, her eyes were drawn to the kitchen table, where, glimmering under the light of the moon, she saw an unattended handgun. Tiptoeing to the table side and slipping her hand across its polished, wooden surface, Natasha wrapped her fingers around the gun's handle. Picking it up off the table, she turned it over in her hands to get used to its weight. She could feel it's bullets weigh uncomfortably on the cylinder. Then, after taking a deep, bracing breath and peering down the hallway to make sure she hadn't been heard, she tucked the gun underneath the waistband of her jeans. And as she slunk across the kitchen and unlocked the back door, she grimaced, uneasy chills cascading up her spine from the gun's cold, metallic barrel which pressed against her bare skin.

She wasn't comfortable holding a gun in her back pocket and with it, control over life and death itself. After everything she had been through, that wasn't a power she believed any person should be permitted to have over another. However, at the same time, those experiences had left her with no other choice but to wield it.

So, burying her apprehension beneath a mountain of necessity, she slipped out onto the balcony. Two flights of stairs later, her feet were on solid ground, and she was free once more.

Now, all she needed was to hitch a ride out of town before the fools realized they had been fooled.

7

MIRAGE

LAS VEGAS, NEVADA

*B*radie wrapped his fingers around the armrest as the plane plummeted toward the ground at an uncomfortable velocity, cutting through the clouds like a knife through butter. His chest grew tight, and his breathing labored. With shaking hands, he buried his head in his book and leaned into the calming sounds of jazz that played lightly through his headphones. He peered across the aisle at the other passengers who were calmly awaiting their arrival and tried to do anything but gaze out the window at his imminent destruction, but no matter how hard he tried he could't look away. Outside the window, cities sprung out of the earth like beanstalks, reaching toward the heavens like Babel. Soon, these giants towered over him, and he prayed that his demise would be swift.

As the plane bounced through a thick layer of low-hanging clouds, Stacy interlaced her fingers with his and said, "It's okay, honey. We're just coming in for landing. Everything's okay."

"There is nothing okay about dropping out of the sky like a dying bird," he replied, his voice cracking like a pre-pubescent child. "God didn't make us with wings, so why the hell do we think we're supposed to fly?"

Chuckling, Stacy shook her head and lightly scolded Anna, who was in the seat across from them, doubled over with her head against the seat in front of her and her hand over her mouth, not even trying to stifle her amusement in what was quickly becoming a Lam family tradition.

Growing up, whenever Bradie's family had taken a trip, they never traveled outside the arbitrary, three-hundred mile radius his father had drawn around Los Angeles. And they always went by car. Because of this, the idea of flying was completely foreign to Bradie. In fact, most of his life had been spent assuming that flight was a privilege relegated to movie stars and the rich. It was only when he met Stacy, a self-proclaimed, world traveler, that this belief was challenged. Since marrying her, he had flown precisely eleven times, to destinations ranging from Belize to Shanghai. However, it didn't matter how many times they flew or how rarely he heard of crashes on the news. Nothing was able to dispel the crippling fear that any moment on board a plane could prove to be his last, a fact that was somehow comical to both Stacy and Anna.

As the plane neared its landing, Bradie closed his eyes and tried to think calming thoughts. He imagined himself lounging at the edge of the ocean, watching the ebb of the tide bury his feet beneath the sand. He pictured Stacy by his side, dressed in her bathing suit, leaning her head on his shoulder as the sun's glorious rays caressed their skin. However, this paradise was soon shattered by the sudden jolt of the plane's frame as it skidded against the tarmac. Immediately, he dug his nails into the padding of his armrest and sunk his back in his seat, bracing for a crash until the plane finally came to a full and complete stop at their gate.

Still chuckling, Anna looked over at Bradie and joked,

"Don't let your guard down yet, Padre. I hear the conveyor belt is a ruthless fiend."

"Listen, just because I'm the only person here who actually values his life doesn't mean the rest of you can make a mockery of me," he replied as he unbuckled his seat belt and stood up to grab their carry-ons from the overhead compartment. "And don't forget; I can still ground you."

"Oh, you'd like that, wouldn't you?" she laughed.

"Damn it! I walked straight into that one, didn't I?" he asked.

Pursing her lips playfully at him, she reached up to grab her bag as well before following Bradie and Stacy out the front of the plane. From there, they rode down the three escalators that stood between them and their bags, and twenty minutes later, they stood outside the airport, luggage in hand, and waited for their hotel shuttle to pick them up.

As their shuttle approached in the distance, a sleek, stretch limo pulled to the curb directly in front of them. Then, the back door opened, and a smiling Nina stepped onto the sidewalk, wearing a tan chauffeur hat.

"What's this all about?" Bradie asked, perplexed. "I thought you were on the same flight we were."

"Someone had to make sure everything was in order before you got here," Nina said with a mock bow and a flourish, stretching her arm out to the side and ushering them inside. "This kind of treatment is usually reserved for celebrities and politicians, but I figured the real, good guys could use that kind of treatment for a change."

Scooting inside with Stacy and Bradie close behind, Anna's eyes grew wide. "This is incredible," she whispered to nobody in particular.

"You aren't kidding," Bradie agreed.

The inside of the limo was even more luxurious than Bradie

had imagined. Along the back and sides, black, leather seats stretched across the entire length of the vehicle. As he sat down, plush, cushioned leather wrapped around him, encasing him in a relaxing embrace. It was like sitting atop a throne made of pure cloud, but even that was nothing compared to the luxury all around them. Behind the seats sat a seemingly never-ending cascade of shelves that held at least three dozen shining, crystal glasses along with an extensive collection of aged wines, champagnes and whiskeys, which, from the look of the bottles alone, had to have cost at least a month's salary. But bar none, the best part of the whole experience was the ceiling. Across the length of the limo, it was painted as black as the night sky with tiny lights, like stars, littered across it, lighting the whole space with a dim glow.

"So, what is this big surprise that necessitated us flying down here three weeks before the show airs?" he asked.

"All in due time," Nina answered, grabbing two bottles and a handful of glasses from behind her. "For now, we relax! So, step right up and pick your poison. Wine or champagne?"

"Screw that," Stacy protested with a chuckle. "Drown me in some whiskey, baby."

"I knew I was going to like this one, Bradie. Beautiful, sassy and knows how to drink. You definitely married up," Nina said as she grabbed a bottle of whiskey, along with a pair of shot glasses, poured two to the brim and handed one to Stacy.

"Well, that's it. We're officially friends now," Stacy chuckled, clinking glasses with Nina and downing hers in a single gulp.

"And what about our favorite pair of sleuths?" Nina asked.

"I'll have a glass of Burgundy," Anna answered.

"Not on my watch, young lady," Bradie said, grabbing the neck of the wine bottle so Nina couldn't pour. "I may not have my badge anymore, but you've lost your mind if you think I'm letting you drink on my watch."

"Relax, it's not like I've never had alcohol before. You'd be surprised how many of my clients preferred a couple drinks to foreplay," she replied.

"Give the girl a break," Nina said as she wrestled the bottle from Bradie and poured Anna a glass, ignoring his protests. "Considering what she was doing the last time she was this far west, I think she could use some forget-me-juice more than the rest of us."

"Besides, Anna might not be able to drink yet, but Marina is most definitely legal," Anna added with a sly wink.

"Fine, but only one," Bradie relented.

With a mock salute, Anna took her glass from Nina and, closing her eyes with a deep sigh of relief, downed a long, lasting sip. Then, Nina handed Bradie a flute of champagne, and all the way to their hotel, they laughed, joked and forgot all about the troubles they left behind in Detroit.

After checking into their hotel and dropping their bags in their rooms, Bradie, Anna and Stacy met Nina in the hotel lobby, returned to their limo and rode along the Vegas strip as the sun set over the horizon. Staring up at the bright lights of the city, Bradie was overwhelmed by just how different it was than the movies had led him to believe. All around him, lights flashed, and life ran by at a dizzying pace, trying to force the awe and wonder out of him. But no matter how hard the buzz and extravagance tried, they couldn't.

It felt as though he was the only one who wasn't caught up in it all. Along the street side, beautiful people, dressed in their Sunday best, brimmed with hope and excitement. Businessmen and women glided along the sidewalks from casino to casino with child-like glee. Bradie even caught Stacy and Nina, though they had both, undoubtedly, seen more than most people could see in a lifetime, lose themselves in the grandeur of all. Meanwhile, he felt nothing but emptiness beneath the neon lights.

He wondered if it was the childhood stories of its depravity that he had heard from his father, who refused to come within twenty miles of Sin City. Perhaps it was the smell of money being thrown away by people who had either nothing or everything to lose. Or maybe it was the fact that he knew such extravagance always drew criminals who preyed on the unsuspecting.

But most of all, it was Anna.

Even though her face was turned away from the rest of them, trying to hide herself from the group, Bradie had known her long enough to know when she was uncomfortable. It was all in her shoulders. With every block the limo passed, they grew tenser, and the time between her bated breaths grew shorter. On top of that, she was unusually quiet. Normally, she would have been the first to revel in the craziness of the city, joke about how underdressed she felt or try to guess who was screwing who. However, nary a word had floated off her lips since they left the hotel.

Scooting beside her, Bradie placed his hand on her shoulder and asked, "What's the matter?"

"Oh — uh, nothing," she stammered, plastering a fake smile across her face. "This place just doesn't exactly hold the fondest memories for me."

"How come?" he probed further.

"It shouldn't be too hard to figure out," she replied.

"But I thought you worked out of L.A."

"Mostly, but Vegas was only a stone's throw away. So, any time there was an event going on or the police got too close, he packed us in a van and set us up with some, fleabag motel outside of town for a week or two."

"Even with prostitution legal in Nevada? Couldn't you have gone to the police?"

"Let's just say that after spending enough time in Los Angeles, we didn't have a whole lot of faith in the police."

"What do you mean?"

"Just that people aren't always what they seem."

With that, Anna turned away from him and refused to utter another word until an hour later, the limo came to an abrupt stop in front of a run-down, yellow and white, cowboy-themed bar called The Dude's Ranch. Even from a hundred yards away, it was a special kind of eyesore. It looked like it had been taken straight out of a cartoon, complete with swinging, saloon doors, a lasso and hat logo and half-dressed, cowgirl waitresses out front. It was the kind of place Bradie wouldn't step foot inside even in the wildest of nightmares. To his surprise, however, despite the campiness of it all, business was booming inside and outside the ranch. There were so many people, in fact, that Bradie could hardly make out a single face amongst the hustle and bustle.

Rolling the back windows of the limo down, Nina turned to the group and, throwing her arms dramatically out to the sides, announced, "And this, my friends, is what all the fuss is about!"

"A novelty bar?" Stacy asked.

"A brothel," Anna corrected.

"This shithole is a brothel?" Bradie asked.

"The girl's right," Nina sighed. "And one of the most popular ones in the state at that."

"How'd you know?" Bradie asked, turning to Anna.

"It's not exactly subtle," she explained. "Just look at the sign. I mean, the lasso is literally penetrating the D in 'Dude.'"

Immediately, Stacy brought her hand to her mouth to stifle her laughter, and Nina chuckled in suit, saying, "If I'm right, this place is also the number one, trafficking ring this side of Sin City."

"That was the whisper around town when I was here too," Anna added.

"Isn't prostitution legal in Nevada? At least in this county?" Stacy asked. "Shouldn't that make it easier to pick out the bad eggs? Especially with everything out in the open?"

"You'd think so," Nina sighed.

"But if anything, it just makes it harder," Anna said. "Since the pimps don't have to build covers or fronts anymore, they can focus all their energies on keeping the girls scared, secure and submissive."

"Which is why we're here," Bradie said with realization. "You're working on a story."

"And we have a winner!" Nina exclaimed. "You didn't think my friend wanted some cop from Detroit on her show for good feels, did you? We're going to take this place down on live television!"

"Which means we have some work to do," Stacy said.

"And three weeks to do it!" Nina smiled.

STANDING IN FRONT OF THE BATHROOM MIRROR IN THE BASEMENT of Matt P. Salamander's, the largest, law firm in Toledo and, since a week ago, Florian's new place of employment, he closed his eyes, took a deep, soothing breath and tried to summon the courage to survive yet another day. During his first week, he had been put through more humiliation than he had over any seven day period of his entire life. By the second day, he had already found himself on his hands and knees, scrubbing voraciously at the carpet beneath the secretary's desk in an attempt to remove a frisbee-sized pile of vomit from the floor. Then, the next day, he was forced to wade through an ankle-high sea of feces from an overflowing toilet in the fourth floor, men's bathroom. After just five days, every last one of his jumpsuits smelled like filth, no matter how thoroughly he tried to wash them.

It felt like the world was holding a jackhammer to the asphalt that was his pride, and with each day that passed, life continued to tear it down until there was nothing left. He tried to tell himself that this was what he deserved, that it was the only fitting punishment for his crimes, but even still, he couldn't help but wish for another way to atone for his sins. After all, he was supposed to be the one in the corner office. He was supposed to have the entire building at his beck and call. His name should have been engraved on the plaque outside his office door instead of stitched onto a denim jumpsuit.

As the punch of the time clock chipped another piece away at his pride, he looked himself in the eyes. "One day at a time," he whispered. "Janelle is counting on you."

That day, it took all of three seconds for his pager to buzz with his first task of the day: clearing a clog in the fifth floor, men's bathroom.

With a slight turn of his hat and a quick fix of the tie he always wore under his jumpsuit, Florian grabbed his cart and made his way up the elevator to the fifth floor. As he stepped out of the elevator, passing by offices on either side of him, he couldn't help but peer inside each and every one and imagine what it would be like to have the world at his fingertips, to be the master of his own destiny instead of indentured to the success of another. He became so enraptured that he soon found himself so lost inside his fancy that he didn't even realize he had stopped moving.

However, he was quickly put back in his place by a stern voice that bristled with arrogant authority behind him. "Are we planning on working today, Flo-Job, or are you going to decorate the hallway with your lazy ass all day?" it asked.

"Oh! I'm so sorry," Florian said, breaking from his trance.

As he moved back toward his cart, he was met by the familiar glare of Francis McEnroe, the number one lawyer in the company and, as Florian had learned over the past week, the biggest douchebag in Greater Ohio. Hardly a day passed that Francis wasn't glued to Florian's ass, ready to pounce the moment he made a mistake. Florian spent his days on edge, knowing that at any second he could find himself staring at Francis' thousand-dollar suit and looking up at his smug, condescending smile.

"Apologies don't mean shit when a man can't shit," Francis said, shooing Florian along. "Now, get your ass moving before I start thinking your face is made of porcelain."

With a plastered-on smile, Florian replied, "I hear the bathroom on the fourth floor is fully functional."

"Are you suggesting that I walk away and let you get away with slacking on the job?" Francis laughed. "Where would the honor be in that?"

"Preferably shoved up your dick," Florian muttered under his breath as he took his cart and scurried to the bathroom, hoping to get away before his fist flew into Francis' smug, little mouth.

Regretfully for him, however, Francis followed him all the way to his destination, nipping at his heels like a dog running after a mailman. Even as Florian opened the door to the bathroom, which reeked like a third-world outhouse, he was given no rest. While he bent over, plunger in hand, to unclog the overstuffed, porcelain hell-hole, Francis was right behind him, watching and waiting for an opportunity to mock him once more. Florian felt like a prison inmate, holding his cheeks together as he bent over to pick up a bar of soap out of fear that, at any moment, someone might take the opportunity to shame him beyond imagination. Finally, after what felt like an eternity spent pumping at the clog, the blockage let loose, allowing the toilet to flush.

Standing up, he held his plunger over the bowl for a moment to allow the water and sludge to slide off of it before returning it to his cart. However, before even half of the grime had a chance to run off the plunger head, Francis grabbed Florian by the shoulder and pulled him backward. In response, Florian's arm shot back and sent a glob of muck plummeting to the ground, half of it landing on his shoes and the other half on the bathroom floor.

"Aw, damnit, Flo-Job. I'm sorry," Francis said facetiously. "Looks like I've made more work for you. Oh well, them's the breaks, right?"

Is he actually trying to get me to knock his head in?

"No worries, Frannie Pack," Florian said, grabbing a mop from his cart and, with shaking hands behind his forced smile, scrubbing the floor clean. "Wouldn't want to soil that knockoff, Dulce suit of yours, would we?"

"I'll have you know I paid two thousand dollars for this suit," Francis argued, tightening his lips together in an attempt to camouflage his anger.

Then, Florian picked a loose thread off of Francis' shoulder and replied, "You should probably think about getting your money back."

Damn, it feels good to get under his skin for a change.

After that, the rest of his day was surprisingly relaxing. By the time the clock struck three that afternoon, leaving him with only two hours to quitting time, the biggest mess he had been forced to clean up was a trio of dirty dishes in the break room sink. For a split second, he even thought that he could grow to tolerate this job, providing he could avoid Francis for at least two days every week.

But, almost as soon as the thought crossed his mind, his

phone buzzed with a text from Janelle. *Come quick. Stomach pain. Doctor ASAP.*

Immediately, Florian packed his cart in the nearest janitor's closet and punched his time card. As he jumped into his car and fired the engine up, he tossed his phone in the cup holder and focused himself on getting home as quickly as possible.

As he pulled into the driveway outside his house, Janelle was sitting on the front steps, holding her stomach and breathing heavily. Jumping out of the car, he rushed to her side.

She tried to stand up to greet him, but he stopped her, insisting, "Don't move. I got you."

Wrapping his arm under her shoulder and around her back, he hoisted her up and carried her over to the car. "What's going on?" he asked.

"I don't know," she huffed. "I was having a bit of heartburn again, so I popped a couple Pepto, like I usually do. Then, all of a sudden, pain shot right through my back and stomach. It's terrible. I've never felt something like this, babe. I'm worried something happened to Iris."

"It's going to be okay," he promised as he opened the passenger's side door and helped her inside.

However, he wasn't even sure if he believed himself.

For the duration of their race to the hospital, neither of them said a word. Janelle was in far too much pain to speak. Instead, she kept her eyes closed and, leaning her head against the head rest, did little else than focus on her breathing. Meanwhile, Florian darted and weaved along the back roads with nothing on his mind but getting there as quickly as possible.

After swerving into the parking lot outside the emergency room, Florian dashed through the front doors to grab a wheelchair. Then, he wheeled her inside and checked in at the front desk. Immediately, the receptionist placed a call down to the maternity ward, and two minutes later, a pair of burly, male nurses rushed over to them and, taking the reins from Florian, led them down three hallways, up two elevator flights and through one, last corridor to a room in the maternity ward, where they hoisted Janelle onto the bed. Once she was settled in as comfortably as possible, considering the circumstances, the nurses left to find a doctor.

Turning to his wife, whose expression seemed to be stuck in a perpetual grimace, Florian asked, "How are you feeling?"

"Probably about as good as I look," she choked through the pain.

"Once the doctor gets here, he'll make everything better," he comforted her.

"Let's hope so," the voice of the doctor, who was standing behind Florian with an ultrasound machine to his back, tickled the backs of his ears. "I hear you're having some stomach and side pain, is that right?"

Unable to speak, Janelle nodded weakly.

"Why don't we take a look and see if we can't figure out what's going on?" the doctor asked as he wiggled past Florian and set the machine up next to Janelle's bed.

Over the next five minutes spent waiting for a diagnosis, Florian hardly breathed. His lungs were locked tighter than a prison cell. His head grew light, and it took everything in him to keep from shaking. In that moment, he simultaneously feared the worst and hoped for the best, though what he feared most was the ever-increasing possibility that the anticipation might cause him to pass out.

Then, they would both need a doctor.

Finally, the doctor took the monitor from Janelle's stomach and turned to face them. "The good news is that the baby is fine," he said.

"Oh, thank God," Florian said, finally breathing again for the first time.

"And the bad news?" Janelle asked.

"You have kidney stones," the doctor answered.

"That's not so bad," Florian reasoned. "You can just break those apart with the ultrasound machine, right?"

The doctor sighed in response, "Not quite. If we did that, we could wind up hurting your baby."

"Well, what can you do?" Florian probed, growing impatient for another shred of good news.

"All we can really do is give her an IV and a room for the night," the doctor replied. "Hopefully then, the stone will either break up on its own or pass through her system. Other than that, we just have to wait and hope for the best."

Then, handing Janelle a small, red pill, he continued, "It's not much, but this should dull the pain a bit. I'll have a nurse come in to get you started on your IV. If luck's on our side, we should be able to get your out of here in time for bed tonight."

However, luck was not on their side. Not even in the same hemisphere.

By the time the clock struck eleven that night, more than seven hours later, it seemed like no progress had been made whatsoever. In fact, things only seemed to be getting worse, as Janelle's pain scale skyrocketed from a seven to a nine. The doctors told them this was a good sign, indicating that her kidney stone was about to pass, but after hours spent sitting by her bedside, unable to do anything but hold her hand while she writhed and screamed in pain, their assurance did not make Florian feel any better.

Nearing the end of his strength, he began to pace around the room to keep himself awake.

"Why don't you go home for the night?" Janelle asked during a brief sabbatical from her pain. "One of us should be able to get some sleep."

Chuckling anxiously, he replied, "The kidney stone is obviously disrupting your brain waves if you think I'm leaving you here, alone, tonight."

"Then how about you pick me up something to eat?" she suggested in a mock-British accent. "I'm getting a mite peckish, and you could use the fresh air."

Sighing and nodding, he turned to leave, but she called out after him, asking, "Aren't you forgetting something?"

"Ah, of course," he said, turning around. "What do you want me to pick up?"

"Not that, silly. Get over here and give me a goodbye kiss."

He walked over to her bedside, and she took his face in his hands, pulling him toward her. Then, she pressed her lips into his. Instantly, the worry inside him evaporated.

He only wished that his lips could ease her pain like hers did for him.

As he pulled away from her kiss, her hands stayed latched to his cheeks. "And I want gummy bears and peanut butter."

"That's literally the most disgusting thing I've ever heard," Florian said, pretending to gag.

"I will have you know that I have very distinguished tastes," she joked.

With a roll of the eyes, he left the room, traveling down the same route he had been led down by the nurses on his way back to his car. Opening the door, he sat down in the driver's seat and checked his phone, which had ten, missed calls from his boss and a voicemail message.

Great, what does he want?

Taking a deep breath, he played the message. "Florian," his boss began, sounding less than jovial. "I'm sorry to hear about what happened with your wife. Please pass on my well wishes to her. However, I wish I would have heard it from you instead of having to call half the company to find out where you sped off to a full three hours before the end of your shift, which is a serious violation of company policy. Since this is only your first offense, I'm going to be lenient. I won't write you up this time, but I will need you in the building first thing tomorrow morning. We have a major leak in the pipes on the second floor and not enough manpower to get it done. Thank you for your time. See you first thing in the morning."

Are you kidding me?! Tomorrow's supposed to be my day off!

Janelle's going to have a cow.

8

BREAK

TOLEDO, OHIO

*A*s the sun set on another, long day at Dragon's Wing, Paul could barely keep his head up. For the last week, he had refused to sleep, terrified of being forced back into the void where all he saw was death. His eyes, which felt as heavy as lead, began to droop, and suddenly, everything reminded him of sleep. The high-backed, cushioned headrest of his rolling, computer chair felt like a thousand pillows against the back of his skull. The suit and tie he wore felt like soft pajamas against his skin. Even his desk and computer were like a giant, fluffy mattress that called for him to rest his head. Finally closing his eyes, he felt his head succumb to the sandman, and he fell toward slumber.

However, almost as quickly as sleep had come upon him, he jolted up, fearing the twisted visions that lay behind his eyelids and terrified of being forced to face his demons head on. Instinctively, he brought the backs of his hands to his eyes, scraped furiously at the dust that covered them and urged himself back to life. Desperate to keep himself awake, he then tried everything he could think of to keep himself from drifting off again. He organized their spreadsheets. He crunched the salon's profit margins for the fifteenth time that week, and he researched marketing ideas and strategies while blaring death metal directly into his eardrums. Finally, once he had run out of other options, he even resorted to watching cat videos on the internet, anything to keep himself glued to his computer chair and away from Lena's house, where the only thing to do was screw and sleep.

Before he realized it, the clock struck eleven, and he was stuck in the deep, dark reaches of VideoTube. Suddenly, just as he was about to hit play on yet another conspiracy theory video, the parlor doors opened. Behind them, Lena walked in slowly with her hands tucked behind her back and worry painted across her face.

Startled, Paul looked up at her and exclaimed, "Lena! You nearly scared my ass right off the back of the chair! What are you doing here?"

"I can't take this anymore," she sighed.

"What are you talking about?" he asked.

"You!" she yelled, exasperated. "I can't watch you do this to yourself! You don't sleep. You don't eat. Hell, you haven't even come home long enough to shower in a week! I thought I was protecting you by keeping this from you, and maybe I was. Maybe it'd be better if you didn't know…"

"Know what?"

With shaking hands, she brought them from behind her back, revealing a rolled up newspaper clenched underneath her right fist. "I found this on the front porch about a week ago. I thought I could keep you from finding out, but it's not right. You deserve to know."

Taking the newspaper in his hands, Paul unfolded it. Immediately, his eyes grew wide, and the breath left his lungs. In large, bold letters at the top of the obituary sections was written the headline:

Rebecca Cross, 24, A Compassionate Light Snuffed Out Too Soon.

Shaking, his hands opened, dropping the newspaper to the ground. It fell with a resounding crash, an echoing clatter that played on repeat in his ears like the clap of a cymbal or the slow-beating of his own heart. Then suddenly, the walls broke from their supports and began to close in on him, scraping along the floor as they forced themselves upon him. Soon, they were on his every side, pressing against his chest and sides with their massive weight, and he couldn't take it anymore. He burst through the doors and into the night air, leaving Lena to face the death trap alone.

As soon as his feet hit the sidewalk, he bent over, placing his hands on his knees, and breathed a sigh of relief. However, his relief was short-lived, for when he looked up, the light from the street lamps outside the building flooded his irises, turning his whole world white. He held his hands in front of his face to block the light, but it was no use. With each second that passed, everything became brighter and brighter, burning against his skin, his face, his eyes, and forcing him to his knees. In the distance, he heard a low rumble, like the fast approach of a train or the looming threat of an earthquake. However, if he listened close enough, he could have sworn it sounded like a voice.

Before he could make out the sound's source or content, the light around him subsided, giving way to a horrific blur of spiraling grey. It was like the world was made out of water-color, and the paint was running off the canvas. The ground beneath him shifted, tilting at a menacing angle.

And he found himself falling, sliding along the sidewalk at a feverish pace.

Turning onto his stomach, he reached desperately in front of him, clawing at the ground in an attempt to halt his descent. He dug his nails into every groove, every notch in the pavement, but gravity was too strong. His fingernails tore from the backs of his hands, releasing a torrent of claret and skin. As he continued to plunge into the depths for what seemed like time without end or measure, his head grew dizzy. The vicious blur of colors around him blended into a sickening whirl, turning his stomach to gelatin. Before he knew it, the paint had run off the canvas and left it empty.

He was lost in the dark, unable to keep himself from plummeting further into the abyss.

When everything finally came back to him, Paul was standing alone in a field, surrounded by nothing but olive for as far as he could see. The air swirled in every direction, covering him in a coat of ice.

And he was alone.

In that moment, a terrible loneliness settled inside his bones, a silent ache that forced him to his knees. He wished that the night would simply take him, that it would still his blood, now and forever. Everything he had done, the sacrifices and the compromises he had made, had only ever been for Rebecca, and now she was gone, along with all hope of anything but despair.

Paul sat in the emptiness for hours, staring into the darkness before him, unblinking, unmoving. Nary a thought passed through his mind, and the air itself was silent. The only sound that passed through his ears was the constant, continuous crash that still clattered in his eardrums to a beat matching the rhythm of his own heart.

Suddenly, a voice called out from behind him, its tone harsh and condescending, "What are you doing?"

Startled, Paul turned around, and behind him was Rebecca, with her arms crossed and her expression like stone. Immediately, the weight left his heart. He leapt up and rushed toward her, arms outstretched to embrace her. But, as he wrapped his arms around what he thought were her shoulders, they passed straight through. In fact, his entire body slipped through her as though she wasn't there at all.

"Oh, so close!" Rebecca cackled as Paul stumbled across the plain, trying but failing to keep himself upright. "But no Cuban."

Falling to the ground, he planted his hand on the ground and turned back toward her, but this time, she was changed. The apparition before him was almost unrecognizable. Every inch of her body was a charred husk. From her face to her hands, her skin and clothes, which were covered in a thick layer of crimson from the bone-deep gashes in her arms, festered and bubbled like molten lava. Then, as if that wasn't gruesome enough, her left arm was torn from its socket and lay on the ground behind her, drowning in a pool of blood.

Paul looked her in the eyes, trying to find his relief in their deep, crystalline seas, but even they had been ripped away, replaced by reptilian scales where they used to reside. Smiling wickedly, she walked determinedly toward him, her hips swinging from side to side.

Falling onto his back, he raised his arms in front of him, trying to halt her approach, but she paid him not attention, asking, "What's the matter, baby? Don't like the new look?"

He opened his mouth to speak, but the only sound that came out was a whimper.

Looming over top of him, Rebecca mocked, "Aw, has the clever, clever fox lost his tongue? Such a shame, I was so looking forward to ripping it from your skull."

Then, with a disappointed sigh, she said, "Well, this is getting us nowhere."

With a snap of her fingers, the horror faded from her visage, and she was back to normal again, just how Paul remembered her: radiant, beautiful, perfect. His heart feeling a smidgeon lighter, he stood up, and instinctively, his hand rose to caress her face. However, just as he was about to stroke her cheek, he remembered; she wasn't real.

So, he pulled his arm back.

"What do you want from me?" he asked, turning away in shame.

"The same thing I've always wanted," she answered. "For you to see."

"My eyes are open, aren't they?"

"And yet, you've still got those scales."

"You never even tried to understand me!" he screamed, spinning around to face her.

"What is there to understand?" she laughed. "You're a monster, only fit for torches and pitchforks."

"I gave you everything!"

"But what you gave wasn't yours to give. You didn't have the right."

"I have the right to anything I can take."

"Are those your words? Or Redd's?"

"If it wasn't me, it would've been someone else," Paul argued. "And I gave them a better life!"

"You promised them heaven when all you planned on giving them was hell," Rebecca accused.

"They were already going there!" he exclaimed. "You think those girls had some fairy tale life planned out for them? You didn't see them like I did. They were drug addicts, homeless, abandoned. I gave them a purpose!"

"But you didn't give them a choice."

"When I called, they came running."

"Because you sold them a lie and trapped them in it before they had a chance to run."

"I helped them!"

"What about Kayde?" she asked, her voice as cold as death.

"He got what he deserved," he muttered.

"And Grace?" she probed further. "Did she get what she deserved?"

She snapped her fingers again, and instantly, they were transported into the dark room, which was lit only by several, tiny rays of light that emanated from Rebecca's skin. It wasn't much, but it was enough to allow Paul to see Grace, laying atop her mattress on the floor, curled up in a ball and rocking back and forth.

Tears streamed down her face as she whispered, "Kayde... I'm so — I'm sorry. It's all — it's my fault. I-I'm sorry."

"This was the only way," he said, trying not to convince Rebecca but himself that what he said was the truth.

"There's always another way," Rebecca insisted.

"I can't — I can't just let her walk away," he stammered.

"Then who is it you're really trying to help?" she asked.

Then, in an instant, everything faded away, and Paul found himself back in the empty field with nothing but the beating of his own heart to keep him company. He turned around, back and forth, looking for Rebecca, but she was nowhere to be found. Alone again, he fell to the ground, feeling the familiar ache of loneliness settle, once again, over his chest. Closing his eyes, he tried to will himself back into the emptiness so he could see her again, even if only for a second.

But, it was no use. Rebecca was gone, and Elle was better off without him. From here on out, all he had left was himself.

However, the problem was; he wasn't sure exactly who that was anymore.

9

RETURN

TOLEDO, OHIO

*C*rouched behind a pair of bushes across the street from Dragon's Wing as darkness fell, Rebecca held her binoculars in front of her eyes and hoped that her fifth night of surveillance would prove more illuminating than the first four had. At this point, everything was just as it had been before she had left her obituary on Paul and Lena's porch, aside from the newspaper itself, which had promptly disappeared after the first night. Other than that, the only noticeable difference was the fact that Paul had begun to work late nights in the office. However, considering his past penchant for not getting home until midnight when they were in Detroit, that wasn't exactly out of the ordinary.

By all estimations, her plan had failed. Either Lena had snatched the paper before Paul could see it, or he had seen the headline and didn't care in the least. But either way, she had to know for sure so she could figure out her next move.

That night, five hours after sunset, a single light flooded out of the door to Lena's apartment. Repositioning herself in view of the houses, Rebecca peered down her binoculars' sights at

Lena, who stood at the edge of her porch with the rolled up newspaper in her hands and stared across the street, grief stricken, as though she was watching her child waste away before her eyes. Tapping the newspaper against her open palm, she stood there, motionless, for several minutes before taking a deep breath and, with eyes locked shut, crossed the street to meet Paul in the massage parlor.

As the doors to the parlor closed, Rebecca darted out of the bushes and flew behind a nearby tree, raising her binoculars just in time to see Lena hand Paul the newspaper. He opened it, and in an instant, his eyes grew wide. Even from that distance, Rebecca could see his heart shatter inside his chest. In turn, hers grew heavy. It killed her to see him in so much pain, but she knew this was the only way.

Seconds later, Paul burst through the doors of the parlor in a panic. Bending over and placing his hands on his knees, he tried to calm the beating inside his chest, and for a moment, relief washed over him. He looked up and breathed a thin puff of smoke into the night sky. Then, something inside him broke.

As he lowered his gaze, his eyes glossed over, as though pure cocaine now coursed through his veins. His knees buckled, and he fell to the sidewalk, his chest heaving so rapidly that Rebecca could hardly even see it move. Then, without so much as a break in his motion, he planted his right hand on the ground and broke into a drunken sprint down the sidewalk, zigging and zagging to every side and nearly slamming into both the buildings on his right and the parked cars on his left. Before Rebecca even had a chance to react, Paul was halfway down the street, rounding the corner onto a side street. She took off after him, determined to find out where he was going. But, when she turned the corner he had taken, he was nowhere to be found.

It was as though he had vanished into thin air.

She scoured the street for a sign of where he had gone, checking each and every side alley to see if he had collapsed nearby with her ears peeled for the sound of shuffled footsteps or a thud, anything to give her a clue as to where he had gone. However, there was nothing. The air around her was dead, and not even the wind howled through the night sky.

All she heard was the sound of her own panic.

Confused and worried, she hurried down the street, continuing her frantic search until something in the distance caught her attention. She heard what sounded like voices, arguing around a nearby corner. So, keeping her footsteps light and quick, she scurried to the corner and pressed herself against the edge. But when she finally got eyes on the situation, she found only Paul, standing in the middle of a neighborhood playground in the middle of a vicious argument with a swing set.

"I helped them!" he screamed into the empty air.

Then, his head dropped and he turned away, muttering, "He got what he deserved,"

Suddenly, it was as though the world underneath Paul shifted. He stumbled backwards, straight into the empty swing behind him. For a moment, it moved with him, rising up into the air. But a moment later, it stopped at his knees, sending him tumbling over top of it and face first into the ground below.

As he hit the dirt, he curled his knees to his chest and rocked back and forth, whispering in a soft voice that sounded nothing like his own, "Kayde... I'm so — I'm sorry. It's all — it's my fault. I-I'm sorry."

"This was the only way," he responded to himself in his own voice after a moment's pause before breaking into a stammer. "I can't — I can't just let her walk away..."

Rebecca continued to watch for another moment as Paul lay in the dirt, motionless, his eyes still layered in a glossy film. Tears fell from his eyes, forming two, tiny puddles of mud beneath him. In that moment, all she wanted to do was to rush to his side, cradle his head in her lap and whisper in his ear that she was okay, that this was nothing more than a bad dream. She yearned to wake him up from this nightmare and bring him back home, where they could reclaim the life she always dreamed they would have, without need of money or deception. All she wanted was for them to be together, as a family, to be the people she knew they could be.

But, only through brokenness would he be able to see the truth.

So, as Paul finally stood up and, sanity once again behind his eyes, made his way back toward Lena's apartment, Rebecca hid herself in the shadows of a nearby alleyway, allowing him to pass by, unaware. Then, returning to the hotel she was staying in just outside of town, she racked her brain for what to do next. Paul was broken, that much was obvious, but still, she had so many questions.

And none of those questions had answers she would be able to divine while hidden in the bushes across the street from Dragon's Wing.

They were answers that could only be found up close, straight from the source, and there was only one way she was going to be able to do that.

She had to find a way inside.

{}~{}~{}~{}~{}~{}~{}~{}~{}~{}

The next day, Rebecca lowered herself back into the bushes across from the massage parlor and studied the scene before her, scanning for anything she could use to her advantage. Regretfully, that was easier said than done. During the days, everything at Dragon's Wing ran like a well-oiled machine. Someone was always manning the counter at both shops, whether it was Paul, Lena or Izzy, making a frontal assault impossible, especially since she had already used up the only disguise she owned when she first infiltrated Dragon's Wing. A rear assault was just as risky, considering clients and workers were constantly walking by the back door as the day went on.

The only chance she had for any kind of reconnaissance was after night fell, when Paul would be, once again, alone in his office, drowning himself with sorrow.

But once I get inside, what am I looking for? I need to know who Paul thought he was talking to and what he was muttering about, but it's not like he's going to keep that written on some post-it note in a back office. I have to get eyes and ears on him, but knowing him, he'd spot a bug or camera a mile away. I'm going to have to find a way to get him to talk… to someone, but who?

Wait a minute…

Where's Florian?

Over the course of six days of surveillance, she hadn't seen hide nor hair of Florian, not even a whiff of his cologne at the end of a single day. Admittedly, it wasn't too out of the ordinary for an employee to take a week off, especially with a child on the way. However, in the time Rebecca had known him, he hadn't taken so much as a day off, much less six. It was a shot in the dark, but she had to find out where he was and what had drawn him away.

So, that night, after the sun had set and everyone except for Paul had returned to the houses, Rebecca slunk around the back of the shop. Quietly, she wrapped her fingers around the handle and turned, but it wouldn't budge. It was locked, which meant her only way inside the parlor was through the front door, where Paul was bound to see her.

She had to think fast.

As she backtracked to the front edge of the building, firmly in the shadows with her back pressed against the brick, she racked her brain for a distraction, something that would allow her to get her hands on Paul's phone for no more than thirty seconds. However, in order to do that, she needed to find a way to draw Paul away from his desk, but nothing she thought of would work.

Except for one thing. It was a long shot, but it was the only one she had.

After tussling her hair, she ran her hands along the ground, gathered as much dirt as she could muster and rubbed it across her face. Then, she crouched down and crawled across the ground, just beneath the windowsill, until she was ten feet from the building's edge. Closing her eyes, she took a deep breath and prepared to put on what she hoped would be the performance of a lifetime.

Turning toward the building, Rebecca rose up in a single, fluid motion, staring Paul down with the most twisted, furious expression she could dredge up. For ten, full minutes, she stood, unmoving, as Paul gazed into his computer screen without so much as a glance in her direction.

Desperate and feeling her resolve waver, she raised two, open hands above her shoulders and slammed them into the glass so forcefully that the resulting thud was startling, even to her. It took everything in her to keep from jumping, but she remained stoic with her eyes trained furiously on Paul. Startled, he jumped back, and his eyes fell on her. Instantly, he froze. For what felt like an eternity, not even a single muscle in his body twitched, nor did his nostrils so much as flare with breath. Then suddenly, he leapt from his seat and rushed to the door, trying to catch up with her before she disappeared.

However, she didn't give him the chance.

With a calm turn to her left, she walked out of the window frame, ducked around the corner and crouched behind an empty, garbage can just inside the alleyway. As she peered back toward the street, Paul stumbled past in the same, drunken manner he had the night before, crashing into both building and car on his way down the street. As soon as he was out of sight, Rebecca hurried out of the alleyway and through the front doors of Dragon's Wing, praying that Paul had left his phone on his desk.

Unfortunately, when she sat at his desk, his phone was nowhere to be found. She checked top of the desk, the divot in the back of the chair and even the floor underneath the desk, but she found nothing. It was gone.

Dang it! It must still be in his pocket.

Pulling the keyboard drawer out from underneath the desk, she tapped nervously at the keys and prayed that Paul still used the same password for his computer that he did at home. Without Florian's phone number, address or a clue to where he had been over the past, six days, she had little hope of seeing her plan to fruition, and every sacrifice she had made to this point would be in vein.

With a nervous crack of her knuckles, she closed her eyes and typed: *RnP4ever*

Immediately, Paul's home screen popped up. She was in. First, she pulled up that month's work schedule to see when Florian was next scheduled. To her surprise, his name didn't appear on the calendar for a single day that month, the next or any month for the next year. It was almost as though he had never worked there at all.

There must have been a falling out. Maybe I can use that to my advantage.

Next, she pulled up the start menu and rifled through the documents tab. Knowing Paul, even if Florian had burned the shop to the ground, Paul wouldn't have been so brash as to delete his personnel files. If he was half as organized as she knew him to be, they would be there. And lo and behold, as soon as she opened up the personnel folder, there it was, right at the top. In full, complete detail, Paul had the record of Florian's entire life packed into a single, clean page, complete with his mother's maiden name, his high school GPA and, most importantly, his current address.

7826 Gallop Road. Silica, OH.

After taking a glance out the window to make sure Paul wasn't on his way back, Rebecca pulled out her phone and snapped a quick picture. Then, determined to leave no sign she was ever there, she closed out each and every application, logged out of the computer and scurried out the back doors, taking the first cab to Florian's house.

It may have been the middle of the night, but there was no better time than the present to set a plan in motion.

Silica, OH

Meanwhile, Florian was in his kitchen, brewing himself a fresh cup of chamomile as he did every night before bed. As he waited, he leaned against the counter, sleep weighing heavily on his body. He raised his arms in the air, wrapping his fingers around the back of his head, and stretched both elbows as far as they would go, trying to keep himself awake long enough to hear the whistle of his teacup. However, only a few seconds later, his eyes were closed, and he was drifting off into standing sleep.

Suddenly two, loud knocks at his door jolted him back to the waking world as though a fallen power line had just sent electricity surging through his veins. Involuntarily, he leapt back to his feet and slammed head first into the cabinet door he had forgotten to close. The metal handle jammed into the bridge of his nose and sent a surge of adrenaline through his veins, finally accomplishing the thing he had been unable to do, wake himself up. Holding his hand to his forehead, he staggered over to the front door.

"Who the hell is making house calls an hour before midnight?" he muttered to himself.

As he opened the door, his jaw dropped to the floor. Before him stood a ghost, an apparition. It looked like Rebecca, but it couldn't be. She was supposed to be dead. At least, that was what every newspaper in Detroit had been reporting for the past week.

"I'm dreaming," he assured himself. "This is just a dream. A very. Painful. Dream…"

Chuckling, the ghost reached across the threshold and dug her nails lightly, but forcefully, into his flesh.

And to Florian's surprise, it hurt.

"Okay, not a dream," he said to himself, turning back toward the kitchen and grimacing. "I'm just dead."

"You're not dead, Florian," Rebecca laughed, following him inside the house and closing the door behind her. "Though, judging by the state of your house and what I know of your usual standards, you're obviously in hell."

Leaning back against the kitchen counter, he sighed, "Yeah, can't say I'm exactly living the high life."

"I never thought I'd see the day when Florian Romani settled for suburban life."

"Surprisingly, it wasn't on my bucket list."

"I don't think I'll ever get used to seeing a ring on that finger."

"Does your ring ever itch? I swear, one of these days it's going to get so bad that I actually chop this damn thing off."

"You get used to it eventually," she replied, leaning against the counter next to Florian and nudging him playfully with her shoulder. "Which reminds me, I don't remember getting a wedding invitation in the mail."

Turning away and scratching his head nervously, Florian stammered, "Well, you know — I — we — it was a small wedding, and it all just happened so fast, that-"

"I'm messing with you. Trust me, I know what a pregnant wedding looks like."

"And a marriage full of secrets."

"I take it you heard about what happened."

"Oh, trust me," Florian chuckled as the teapot whistled, drawing him over to the stove. "I would've had to have been deaf and blind to not hear *that* showdown. Care for some tea?"

"What kind?" she asked.

"Chamomile," he answered.

"Bedtime blend? Better pour me a double shot," she said.

"That bad, huh?" he chuckled, pouring two mugs full of tea. "I imagine death must make it awfully tough to get any sleep."

"You have no idea. How'd you get your hands on that article?"

"You can take the man out of Detroit, but his heart never leaves. I still get The Pulse's newsletter in my inbox every week, and it's kind of hard to miss it when someone you know ends up in the obituaries. But considering that you're standing right in front of me, I assume the story's just a way to get Paul's attention."

"Am I *that* transparent?"

"Only to those of us that understand what it's like to live that life."

"You think it'll work?" Rebecca asked.

"If there's one thing I know about Paul," Florian answered. "It's that nothing is more important to him than you and Ellie. If you're looking for a way to break him, that'd be it."

"But it won't save him," she sighed.

"It takes more than a nudge to push people like us off that ledge."

"What did it for you?"

"Seeing my daughter."

"And that should be enough for anyone."

"Paul's in far deeper than I ever was. I don't think he knows who he is anymore apart from the life."

"Then we have to show him."

Florian shook his head. "I can't go back there," he insisted. "He'd kill me."

"Paul wouldn't do that," Rebecca assured him.

"After what happened to the kid," he said, his hands shaking beneath him. "I'm no so sure."

"What kid?"

"I was long gone before any of that shit went down. But, the cops have been showing around the picture of a shooting victim who looks suspiciously like one of our parlor boys."

"Oh my God… Kayde?"

"I'm sorry Rebecca; the old Paul is dead. He died the moment we left Detroit, and what we got in his place was a madman. I wish I could help. I really do, but I can't go back there. Not with a wife to worry about and a little girl on the way. They need me too much."

Florian turned to leave, but Rebecca latched onto his arm and refused to let go. Her grip on his arm was tight, as though every ounce of her desperation was being funneled through her fingertips.

Her eyes pleaded for him to reconsider, but with trepidation, he pulled away, saying, "I can't risk it."

"I understand. It's okay," Rebecca sighed with tears in her eyes as she grabbed a napkin from the counter and a pen from her pocket and scribbled a phone number across its front. "If you change your mind, give me a call."

Swallowing down her tears, she slid the napkin toward Florian and smiled weakly before shuffling toward the front door, her head bowed and shoulders slumped. As the door closed behind her, a heaviness pressed on his ribcage. He tried to walk back up the stairs to bed, but he couldn't bring himself to so much as set foot on the first step. Something felt wrong about letting her leave, about waking up the next morning and returning to a pointless, thankless job when there was work to be done. He left the business because of Janelle, because of Iris. But, maybe he had to return to it for the same reasons.

If he helped Rebecca, he could make the world a little safer. *For* Iris and Janelle.

So, without a second's more hesitation, Florian rushed out the front doors and chased after Rebecca, who was already halfway down the street, heading toward the bus stop.

He called out after her, "Rebecca, wait!"

Startled, she turned around, her tears glistening under the light of the street lamps and the corners of her mouth curling into a grateful smile. "I forgot to finish my tea, didn't I?" she chuckled as she wiped the tears from her cheeks.

"That you did," he laughed in suit. "And I figured you could finish it while you finished telling me what you need me to do."

{}~{}~{}~{}~{}~{}~{}~{}~{}~{}

The next morning, Florian pulled up outside Dragon's Wing, fifteen minutes before the start of another work day. Before the parking brake even had the chance to engage, the front door to Lena's apartment opened. Behind it stood Paul, his expression like granite. Instantly, Florian's heart began to race, and his palms grew sweaty. He closed his eyes and breathed deep, trying to camouflage the fear that flooded like a raging river through his veins. But to his surprise, as he stepped foot onto the sidewalk and looked up toward the porch, Paul was no longer there. Instead, he was marching toward Florian with determined steps, his arms pinned to his sides and both hands balled into fists.

As Paul reached him, Florian braced for impact, expecting a firm, right hook to the jaw. However, a second later, he was thrown forward and pulled into a tight, bracing hug. Caught completely off guard, he let out an involuntary cough as soon as his chest hit Paul's.

His brow furrowed and his face still contorted in confusion, Florian patted Paul on the shoulder. "Wow, things here must be worse than I thought," he said.

"You have no idea," Paul replied, breaking from the hug with a relieved sigh. "It's good to see you, buddy."

"Which is a surprise, considering you were about to rip my throat out the last time we saw each other," Florian chuckled nervously.

"I'm sure the feeling was perfectly mutual. Come on, let's head inside. We have a lot to talk about."

When Paul and Florian first locked eyes, Florian knew something seemed different. But, he couldn't quite put his finger on what it was until they entered Lena's apartment. Inside, nothing was the way Florian remembered. It looked as though someone had taken a leaf blower to a pile of trash and spread it across the whole of creation. All across the room, papers, used coffee mugs and an assortment of pens were strewn seemingly at random, with the coffee table being the epicenter of the destruction.

As Paul sat down on the couch, clearing a pile of wrappers off the spot across from him for Florian to sit down, it became clear that things were far worse than Florian had thought. Paul's eyes had turned almost entirely to scarlet. His skin was peppered with imperfection, and there were bags the size of the state of Colorado underneath his eyes. Even his hands shook uncontrollably as he brought what looked like his fifth cup of coffee that morning to his mouth to take a sip.

Sitting down, Florian placed his hand on Paul's shoulder and asked, "Is everything all right?"

"Oh yeah, never better!" Paul exclaimed. "So, what brings you back? Unemployed life not agree with the wife?"

"Well, yeah. That, and I heard what happened to Rebecca," Florian sighed, watching closely for Paul's reaction.

Immediately, Paul's left eye twitched, and the right corner of his mouth followed suit. Then, his eyes grew wide as they moved to the door. Florian turned around to see what he was looking at, but there was nothing, just a ruffle in the window curtain.

"Yeah, it's a shame…" Paul trailed off, his eyes still focused on staring the curtain into submission.

"Do you want to talk about it?"

"Not much to say, really."

"Come on, I know you better than that. Nothing happens to Rebecca without you feeling it."

"I was already going to never see her again. So, not really much of a difference, I guess."

"Well, if you change your mind about talking," Florian offered. "I'm here."

"I'm fine!" Paul snapped, turning viciously on Florian before cowering away. "Sorry, back to business. I take it you want your old job back."

"Minus the breaking of my marriage vows," Florian clarified.

"Right. Well, in your absence, we changed things around a bit to work without you. But, we could still use an extra hand around the office. You know, to help keep things in order."

"Sounds perfect. When do I start?"

"Not so fast. Now, my memory hasn't been the best lately, but I do seem to recall you *stealing* some product when you quit. And I'm willing to take you back, but I'm going to need some assurances that you're really on board."

"What do you want me to do, boss?"

"Replace what you took. Bring me another to take Natalee's place."

10

SUMMIT

PAHRUMP, NEVADA

*B*radie sat alone on a bench fifty feet from The Dude's Ranch with a newspaper in hand, reading the same Devin and Hops comic he had been staring at for the past hour. At this point, he could have re-drawn this particular comic strip in his sleep. Impatient, his legs began to bounce up and down anxiously, and he leaned his head back, sending a thin puff of vapor floating up to the stars. Slowly lowering his newspaper back to just beneath his eye level, he canvassed the area again in the hopes that he could spot something out of the ordinary in the brothel's parking lot, but just as there had been the twenty previous times he had done so, there was nothing.

No commotion, no suspicious behavior. Just blatant, albeit legal, prostitution.

"This isn't working," he muttered to himself as he covered his face with the newspaper and started, once again, at the beginning of his comic.

"It's surveillance," Nina's voice buzzed in his eardrums. "It's not supposed to be a page-turner."

"I've got a cowboy hat and spurs on the west side," Anna said.

"That makes the score ten to seven, with the east side still in the lead," Stacy replied.

"Come on, Mom," Anna pleaded. "I let you take the side facing the parking lot. The least you could do is spot me a handicap."

"Should've thought about that before you chose the losing side," Stacy teased.

"There's got to be more to the plan than this," Bradie said, trying to get everyone back on track. "We've been at it for a week now, and these two are resorting to road trip games."

"Patience, my grinchy apprentice," Nina replied with a chuckle. "By now, I'm sure you've spent a few millennia locked in a surveillance van with nothing but deviled ham to keep you company. At least this time you've got the funnies."

"It's chicken salad, and I'll have you know that he has, on countless occasions, informed me it's his favorite part of the van," Stacy insisted.

"That's not really saying much," Bradie sighed.

"You don't like my sandwiches?!" she gasped.

"All I'm saying is there has to be a better way to figure out what's really going on behind those doors," he deflected.

"And there is," Nina replied. "We walk through them."

"What do you mean?" Bradie asked.

"Oh, you're not getting out of this conversation that easily," Stacy interrupted.

"Mom, Dad. No fighting in front of the kids," Anna teased.

"Meet me back at the car," Nina chuckled. "And all shall be revealed."

Tucking his newspaper under his shoulder, Bradie hurried down the street in an attempt to grab the front seat before Stacy could catch up with him. However, he didn't make it far before she casually strode alongside him, grabbed him lovingly, but forcefully, by the arm and proceeded to interrogate him about every dish she had ever cooked for him. Of course, being no wide-eyed fool when it comes to marriage, he swore up, down and sideways that the issue was with chicken salad sandwiches in general, not just hers, and prayed that would be the end of it. Thankfully, Anna came to his rescue a few minutes later and distracted Stacy with a conversation about her favorite topic, that week's celebrity gossip.

After an hour ride back to the city, a trip up the elevator and down the hallway, they finally reached their room. And as soon as the door closed behind them, Nina got down to business. Grabbing a manila folder from her closet, she laid it open on the bed in front of them. Inside, she had the makings of a nearly fool-proof, fake identity: a passport, driver's license, birth certificate and pages upon pages of backstory.

"This," Nina began. "Is Sarah Eaton, the girl who helped me break my first, big story back in the Big Apple. We took down a homeless shelter that was giving out expired goods so they could pad their pockets with their donors' money. Since then, Sarah's been off the grid, bouncing from strip clubs to the streets and keeping herself mostly out of trouble. Except for that one time in Chicago. Those thirty days in the clink weren't her best."

"So, you're going undercover?" Bradie asked.

"Were you really arrested?" Stacy probed. "Or was that part just for your cover?"

"Yes, and that's classified," Nina answered, pointing to each of them in order.

"This is the dumbest idea I've ever heard," Anna muttered.

"You think the cops or the press are going to care how many men walk into a brothel dressed like John Wayne?" Nina asked.

"We have to give them something that'll make their skin crawl."

"It's not that different from when we went after Henry Maxwell," Bradie explained.

"Except that nothing's the same," Anna argued. "We're not talking about a hour-long con where all she has to do is bluff her way in. They're not going to get her with the hard sell right away. It's going to take time and digging, which means she's going to have to get her hands dirty. You think she's prepared to do that?"

"I was born in the mud, sister," Nina answered for him.

Anna rolled her eyes. "But this dirt isn't the kind that goes away with soap and water. It lingers, festers, boils until it burns. Besides, do you really think you can talk your way into this kind of operation? They don't just take every bimbo with a nice rack that bats her eyes their way."

"I thought you might feel that way," Nina said with a wry smile as waltzed back over to the closet, pulled out an identical folder and plopped it open on the bed. "Which is why you're coming with me."

"You've got to be kidding!" Stacy explained.

"Absolutely not," Bradie agreed. "Anna is not stepping one foot inside that shithole."

Taking a quick look through the folder, Anna shook her head. "This isn't going to work."

"Exactly," he sighed in relief. "We'll just have to find another way."

"Because I already have the perfect cover," she said as she tossed the folder to the side. "I worked this exact spot around this time last year. Something tells me they won't have forgotten me so easily."

"Why didn't you say that before?"

"It wasn't relevant at the time. Besides, you wouldn't have let me within earshot of that place I you'd known."

"You're damn right, I wouldn't have! And there's no way I'm letting you in there now."

"You really want to send Nina in there without any real knowledge of what she's getting into?" Anna asked. "She'll be made before she even walks through the doors."

Placing her hand on Bradie's shoulder, Stacy sighed, "I hate to say it, but she's right, babe."

"You too?!" Bradie exclaimed.

"Besides, if I don't go with her, she'll just sneak out the moment we go to sleep," Anna said.

"You know me too well," Nina chuckled. "If there was another way to take these bastards down, I'd take it in a heartbeat. But you can't seize a castle from the outside. You have to do it from within."

"But if you've worked here before, does that mean *he* might be here?" Bradie asked Anna.

"Not until New Years," she answered, shaking her head. "Life with him may have been hell, but it was pretty damn predictable."

"Fine," he sighed, circling back around the bed and joining the group. "So, what's the plan?"

{}~{}~{}~{}~{}~{}~{}~{}~{}~{}

The next night, Bradie and Stacy sat in the back of a black, rental minivan as Nina and Anna made their way toward The Dude's Ranch, each dressed in little more than black heels, a pair of jean shorts that were ripped just beneath their cheeks and a plaid, shirt that was tied in a neat bow at the bottom of their breastplates. He watched reluctantly, shifting in his seat and rubbing his hands against the legs of his jeans as they disappeared amongst the crowd, leaving the faint echo of their breathing in his earbuds as the only sign that they were still alive.

"I don't like this," he sighed.

"You wouldn't be much of a father if you did," Stacy said, reaching underneath her seat, pulling out a brown, paper bag and handing it to him.

Taking it, he opened it and peered inside nervously. Then, his face fell. "Chicken salad?"

"It's a surveillance van tradition," she laughed. "Besides, you love my cooking, remember?"

"Well, I'll give you one thing; you're the best cook in this van."

"Which is why I also picked you up something a smidgeon less mayo-filled. Check under the sandwich."

Pulling the chicken salad sandwich, he set it to the side and looked back inside the bag.

Immediately, he breathed a sigh of relief. "You got Farmer Ron's," he said.

"I married a simple man," she laughed as she leaned in to plant a kiss on his lips.

"Save it for the hotel room," Anna's voiced buzzed in their ears. "Or at least when I can't hear the two of you flirt."

"We're approaching the front doors," Nina added. "Check your video feed."

Pulling out his laptop, yet another present from Nina, he turned it on. Immediately, the screen lit up with various shades of black, white and grey. They watched the view from Nina's button camera while she and Anna approached the front doors, where a muscular, bearded man stood with his arms crossed. As their feet hit the steps, his gaze turned to them.

And from the top of the screen, Bradie could see him smile.

"Well, if it isn't Magic Marina," the man's voice rang above the static that blared from the computer's speakers. "Looking pretty damn hot for a corpse. With how long it's been since your last visit, I figured Angel had sent you sky-sailing by now."

With a nonchalant roll of the eyes, Anna replied, "Because you guys are the only game this side of Mile High, right Hershey?"

"The only game that matters," he laughed, taking her by the shoulders, turning her around and giving her a once-over. "Still a few weeks before the ball drop. How come you're here so early?"

"Do I really have to answer that? After what happened last year?" she asked.

"Damn, you let one, drunk knucklehead with a lighter in, and he holds it over your head for eternity."

"Yeah, 'cause he lost a nine-hundred dollar dress, and the fire nearly took me out of the game for two weeks. You're lucky it was only first degree, or it would've been hospital bills too."

"But I don't seem to remember him seeming too torched about it come Cinco de Mayo."

"Well, he wasn't the one who got burned."

"What do you say you mosey on over to my room later, and I'll make it up to you?" he flirted as he turned his attention to Nina.

Then, striding over to her, he gave her the same treatment he gave Anna, questioning, "Who's the new bitch?"

"Fresh product," Anna answered, her tone even, though Bradie could sense her nerves break through her stony exterior. "Just off the shelves."

"Hmmm…" he muttered. "Looks like this one's past her expiration date."

Slapping his hand away, Nina countered, "I wouldn't put money on it."

Immediately, his face twisted with rage. He stepped back, crossing his arms in full view of the camera. For a moment, he looked as though he was about to put a dent in the side of her head for daring to touch him. Then, his icy gaze broke, giving way to fits of laughter.

"Damn!" he laughed. "Your boss didn't tell me he had so much spice in his storeroom. I'm impressed. So, are either of you carrying?"

"You telling me you don't remember?" Anna scoffed. "I'm banging cymbals, and this one comes bearing gifts."

"All right. They're coming in to test everyone tomorrow. So, you know the drill," he sighed.

"Ghost till they're gone," she finished for him.

"You got it. Now, get in there, find a bed and get your asses in the game."

As Anna and Nina brushed past Hershey and entered the brothel, Stacy looked over at Bradie, confused.

"I think they're talking about STD's," Bradie informed her.

"That testing's mandatory, right?" she asked. "And we've got them on camera, telling their girls to skip out."

"It won't be enough," Nina's hushed voice joined the conversation. "All that'll buy them is a hefty fine, but not enough for it to seriously hurt business. We need to bury them, which means we need to find a hell of a lot more."

New York, New York

THE SETTING SUN GLIMMERED THROUGH THE SMALL, STAINED-GLASS window in the corner of Violet's room, casting an array of red, green and blue light over her covers and directly onto the backs of her eyelids. Lifting the blanket over her head to block the light, she turned over to her side and hoped that she would be able to go back to sleep and forget the world for the next twenty or thirty years, but the damage had already been done. She was awake, doomed to face the ruins her life had become.

In the two weeks since she came to Saint Mark's, she had made no progress in fulfilling her promise to Kayde. In fact, she had hardly pulled herself out of bed for any reason other than to avoid soiling her sheets. There wasn't any other reason compelling enough for her to do so. Her bones were too weak, her muscles too stiff, and her head felt like it had a thousand pounds lying atop its crown at all hours of the day. After a while, she could no longer tell whether her progressive atrophy was caused by her depression of the lack of food in her stomach, though it wasn't for a lack of Father Christopher's trying.

Without fail, he brought her three meals a day, which he laid on the inside of her door morning, noon and night. But, no matter how delicious and tempting each, successive meal looked, she couldn't eat a bite of any of it. Every time she brought a bite of it to her mouth, every time its scent hit her nostrils, her stomach turned itself inside out, and her throat closed up and covered itself in a thick layer of saliva that made it nearly impossible to swallow or even breathe. It was as though even her body had lost the will to live.

Sitting up in bed so the light no longer burned against her eyelids, Violet stared, unblinking, at the wall in front of her. Despite all of the color that danced around her as cars sped along the street outside her window, there was something relaxing inside the pale, grey emptiness of cement. It reminded her of days she longed for but could never get back.

At least when she was at The Eclipse, there was hope of life beyond her prison bars. Back then, she had an escape; she had Kayde. Now, though she was free, she was trapped within her despair, and there was little hope of relief.

Or of life past her pain.

"You want to talk about it today?" Father Christopher, who was standing in her doorway with a tray full of her breakfast in his hands, asked.

"Not today, Father," she replied in monotone.

"You can't just keep sleeping through the days," he said. "One way or another, you're going to have to face it. Might as well do it when you have someone offering to take your hand and lead you through it."

Violet opened her mouth to refuse him, to once again forsake company and continue to allow the pain to fester inside her soul. However, as she looked him in the eyes, which were filled with pure compassion, she was no longer sure she wanted to. She had been alone for so long, and she could feel the loneliness weigh on her shoulders and drag her to the ground. If she didn't share the weight with someone, anyone, she feared she might just collapse.

So, gulping as she shrugged in an attempt to play it off, she replied, "Couldn't hurt any worse than it already does, right?"

"That's one way to look at it," he replied, setting the tray of food on top of the dresser by the door and sitting on the bed next to her.

"Except... I'm not exactly sure where to start," she sighed.

"Why don't I start, then? When I first came to New York, I was a lot like you: lost, angry, depressed. Like a lot of the people I went to seminary with, I thought the collar meant I'd made it, that I was officially holy and had punched my ticket to Heaven. But that was far from the truth. I made a lot of mistakes, hurt a lot of good people because I thought I was better than them. Almost lost everything because of it."

"That doesn't sound like you at all."

Sighing, he shook his head. "That's because you don't know me very well. See, I grew up in a pretty rough home. When I was five, my mom left. She went to work one day and never came back. After that, my father spiraled downhill. His world shattered around him, and he was angry at everything, especially me. He made my life, excuse my language, hell. As soon as I was old enough, I got out, determined to not make the same mistakes he did. Thinking it to be a one-way ticket to righteousness, I enrolled in seminary and committed my life to a greater purpose, but I never got rid of the anger. So, I took it out on every disappointed mother and angry father that walked into my parish."

"What changed?"

"I forgave them, my parents. For everything. It was the hardest thing I ever had to do, but once I did, everything changed, including me."

"And you think that's what I need to do."

"Is that what you think you need?"

"I don't know if I can," she sighed, her nostrils flaring and her entire body shaking at the mere thought. She tried to close her eyes and breathe deep, but that did nothing to relieve the tension that was rapidly growing inside her bones. "After what they've done, there's not a universe in existence where they deserve to be forgiven."

Placing his hand on her shoulder, he replied, "But you deserve to be free. No one can change the past, but the longer you hold onto that anger, the more power you give them to hurt you over and over again."

"But she won't stop. She'll never stop, and more people will suffer," she muttered, her hands still trembling.

"You don't have to be one of them," he insisted.

"You're right. I'm done playing the victim."

"That's the spirit! It doesn't have to all happen at once, though. Why don't we start with a good meal and some fresh air? You know, baby steps."

Violet nodded as Father Christopher patted her on the shoulder with a smile and stood up to leave. Before exiting the room, he grabbed the tray of food from on top of the dresser and laid it on the bed in front of her. Then, he exited the room, leaving her alone.

Hesitantly, she reached for her food. It wasn't much, little more than a peanut butter and jelly sandwich, a few crackers and a juice box, but she wasn't about to complain. She only hoped that her stomach was feeling nostalgic for her childhood staple. Taking a deep breath, she tentatively bit down on her meal. As its taste first hit her tongue, her stomach growled like an angry lion in the savanna. Before she knew what had come over her, she started to rip ravenously into the sandwich's bready flesh, tearing whole chunks out of its carcass without even taking a second to swallow her last bite before moving onto the next. In less than a minute, she had devoured her entire meal, and all she could think about was getting more.

She was a wolf on the prowl, and it was hunting season.

The sunlight and cold, December air burned on her skin as she took her first steps outside the church in weeks. But she wasn't about to be deterred. Though the buildings all around her towered over top of her like giants and the throngs of people on every side were like a fast-approaching army, ready to tear her apart at a second's notice, she pressed on, determined to fulfill her promise before anxiety overtook her.

From the church, she crossed the mile and a half that stood between her and Theresa's brothel in less than twenty minutes. With her arms tightly pressed to her sides, she marched down the New York streets like a soldier on her way to battle. Nothing was about to stand in her way, not people, not cars, not anything. The whole of the city could have stood in front of her, pressing against her chest with all their might, but she wouldn't have been deterred. Soon, she was standing across the street from a familiar site. As the sun set over the horizon, a dozen girls flooded onto the street wearing a black and white variation of the same outfit she had worn every night at The Eclipse. Closing her eyes, Violet took a deep breath, trying to ignore the pain it laid upon her soul.

It didn't take long for her to spot the girl Kayde had described. She was unmistakable, from her knotted, raven hair to the glossy, drug-dependent film that covered her eyes and the constant scratching of her arms, where she had been forced to shoot up. If she was going to get Theresa out of there, unscathed, Violet had only one option, to grab her and take shelter in the church before her pimp realized she was gone, which, if they were lucky, would be about fifteen minutes.

After making sure Theresa's pimp wasn't watching, Violet made her approach, looking Theresa in the eyes and feigning desire with a subtle bite of her bottom lip. Within seconds, Theresa caught her gaze and lifted herself off the dirty, brick wall and swung her hips from side to side as she approached her.

Reaching her, Theresa traced a finger along Violet's collarbone, smiled seductively, though it never quite reached her eyes, and said, "Hey there, beautiful. Looking for a good time?"

"Depends," Violet answered, sweeping her hand around Theresa's side and grabbing a thick piece of her backside. "Any chance I could get a piece of this ass somewhere a little more private?"

"That can be arranged," Theresa replied with a wink, taking Violet by the hand and leading her into the alleyway around the back of the building.

Once they rounded the back of the building, Theresa placed her finger on Violet's chest, pushing her against the brick wall. Then, she cupped Violet's cheek in her hands and leaned in, her lips readied for a sensual embrace.

But before their lips could meet, Violet raised her finger to Theresa's mouth, saying, "We're alone, right?"

"What's the matter, baby?" Theresa asked as she pressed her hips into Violet's. "Are you feeling shy?"

"No, it's not that."

"It's okay if you are. No one will see us back here."

"Not even your pimp?"

"Especially not him."

"Good," Violet said, grabbing Theresa by the arm and pulling her down the alleyway toward the street. "Then he won't see us leave."

But instead of following, Theresa pulled away, asking, "What are you doing?"

"I'm breaking you out," Violet assured her. "I have a place we can stay and a car to take us far away from here. All we have to do is make it one night, and we'll be out the city by sunrise tomorrow."

"How do I know I can trust you?"

"Because I promised Kayde I would get you out."

"I should've known," Theresa muttered, turning away.

"And once we're out of town, we can go get Blair," Violet said as she took a step toward Theresa.

"I already told him; he can get her himself, alone."

"He can't. Not anymore."

"Why not? Did he finally run out of pawns to sacrifice for his precious queen?"

"It's not that. He-"

"Or did he finally realize what a worthless piece of shit he is?" Theresa scoffed. "Why can't he just man up for once in his life and-"

"Because he's gone, Theresa!" Violet screamed, unable to control herself anymore. "He's dead. Are you happy now?"

Violet's words hit Theresa like a shot to the stomach. She fell

to her knees and broke down in loud, gasping sobs. "N-no…
He can't — when I said — I didn't mean… I'm so sorry."

"It's not your fault."

"But if I hadn't-"

"You couldn't have known."

"But if I hadn't!"

"What's done is done. All we can do is finish what he
started."

"Okay." Theresa nodded, extending her hand to Violet.
"Then, let's go."

Violet reached out to take Theresa's hand, but before their
fingers could touch, the alley door flew open, giving way to a
large, muscle-bound man with a face that even a mother would
shudder at the sight of. He planted his feet in front of Theresa,
who was still in tears on the ground, and stared daggers at
Violet.

"Get out," he barked in a thick, Russian accent.

"Nothing happened," Violet said, raising her hands in front
of her and backing away slowly.

"Alexei, wait," Theresa whispered.

"I hear shouts from alleyway so I come to see what is problem. When I open door, I see my girl on ground and you with
hand raised toward her. What do you expect me to think?" he
asked, taking a threatening step toward Violet.

"She tripped. I was just helping her up," Violet explained.

"She's telling the truth," Theresa confirmed.

"No," Alexei said as he continued toward Violet. "I will give
you three seconds to get out of my sight. If, after time is up, I
see your face on my street again, I will not hesitate to rip it from
your head. Understood?"

"Y-yes sir," Violet gulped, looking past him apologetically at
Theresa.

"One," he whispered.

She didn't even give him a chance to get to two before she dashed down the alleyway and onto the street, her hands shaking uncontrollably and tears pouring down her face.

She was quickly running out of options. The risk involved with stepping foot back onto that street was tremendous, and there was no way she could stand toe to toe with that brute and come away with anything less than empty hands and a punctured lung. Nearing hyperventilation, she stumbled into a side alleyway and collapsed to the ground, leaning against the brick wall behind her. As she sat there, her mind continued to race.

One thing! He asked me to do one thing, and I still managed to screw it up!

Why am I so worthless?

Kayde would have known what to do. He always knew what to do.

Why couldn't I have been the one on the other side of that bullet instead of him?

That night, as she walked the death march back to the church, her heels dragging across the concrete with every step she took, she looped around the same questions over and over in her mind. With each passing moment, her heart grew more and more weary, like the sun had set inside her heart, leaving its shadow resting across her soul. She thought she could find healing by fulfilling her promise to Kayde, but she had failed. Now, the world around her had crumbled, and no matter what path she took from there, no path gave her the one thing she wanted above all else: the ability to bring Kayde back.

11

REGRET

COLUMBUS, OHIO

*N*atasha stood on the side of the highway in a pelting rain with a soaked, cardboard sign in hand and a backpack she had given as a parting gift from the sweet family of three she had spent the last, five hours with on her back. Overhead, the moon was safely hidden behind the clouds, casting darkness all around her. The only light that lit her way came from the headlights that whizzed by her at breakneck speed. For thirty minutes, not a single car so much as slowed down to read her sign.

At this point, she looked like a stranded, wet dog and didn't smell a whole lot better. Her hair was wet and knotted, her clothes had long since soaked through to her bones, and she was becoming desperate. She could feel the cold set in, reverberating through her bones like electricity through a conductor. Soon, she feared that hypothermia would follow, and she wouldn't survive till sunrise.

So, stretching her sign out in front of her, she took a tentative step toward the road. Seconds later, she caught the headlights of an oncoming car, and immediately, she began to wave the sign up and down, hoping that she would scare them into at slowing down, even if only for a second which she hoped would be enough time for them to find it in their heart to help her.

However, it was no use.

With a blaring horn blast and little regard for her safety, the car zoomed by at top speed, splashing a cold stream of water directly toward Natasha's face as she leapt back. Landing back on the asphalt, she tried to keep her footing, but the raging torrent hit her like a runaway train and knocked her flat on her back. To make matters worse, as she hit the concrete, her sign flew from her hands and into oncoming traffic. As Natasha looked on helplessly, it soared across the highway, slamming into windshield after windshield. Then, the current latched onto its corrugated edges and lifted it into the night sky and completely out of view.

Wet, cold and signless, Natasha tucked her knees to her chest and stuck her head between them, hoping to find some reprieve from the monsoon that raged all around her. Regretfully, it was no use, and soon, a despair even heavier than her rain-soaked backpack nested atop her shoulders. She was alone and cold with no hope of rescue. In that moment, she wondered if she would have rather died in the warehouse than survive and hold onto hope, only to die with it still within arm's reach.

Suddenly, she felt something she didn't expect settle across her back: warmth. As she looked up, she found herself bathed in two, foggy streams of light that broke through the rain and darkness. In front of her, a tan station wagon slowed to a stop and flashed its high beams at her, signaling for her to approach. So, with her makeshift, jacket umbrella held high above her head, she tottered over to the driver's side window and peeked her head in.

"Any chance I could hitch a ride to New York City?" she

asked, shuffling her feet beneath her in a feeble attempt to stay warm.

The driver, who was a stocky, middle-aged man with a biker jacket and handlebar mustache replied with an unsettling smile, "What a coincidence! That's exactly where I'm heading. Hop on in."

With an involuntary chuckle and a nervous nod, Natasha hurried around the front of the car and opened the door. "You might want to set down a towel or something," she said, placing her hand on top of the car and leaning inside. "I think I have the entire Amazon River soaked into my hair."

"Don't worry about it," he laughed, waving her off. "My seats were in need of a good wash anyway."

Pushing aside the pair of half-full, potato chip bags that were sitting on the seat, she sat down and shot the mustache a thankful smile. Then, leaning forward, she ran her hands through her hair, clumping it together, and shifted it over her shoulder so the water would run down her front instead of the back of the seat. By the time she had ensconced herself in her side of the car, a tension had fallen across the car so thick that it turned her blood to molasses. It was a strain she had quickly become familiar with over the course of her brief, hitchhiking career whenever she was alone in a car with another man. Whenever she did, she immediately grew nervous and for good reason. At this point, her record was two and two, making it a fifty-fifty chance that she would wind up in chains.

In an attempt to calm her nerves and spark a conversation, she asked, "So, what takes you to the Big Apple?"

"Eh, nothing too earth-shattering. Just a bit of business," the mustache answered with a wry grin.

Rubbing her hands nervously against her still soaked jeans, Natasha gulped but tried to cover it up with feigned laughter. "Wow, so specific! What kind of business are you in?"

Out of the corner of her eye, she saw his mouth curl thoughtfully and his fingers tap against the steering wheel.

Then, he replied, "The product delivery business. I've got a package in back that I think my employer will be very interested in."

That's what I get for asking.

For the next three-hundred miles, Natasha didn't say a word, instead opting to spend those five hours being tortured by the tone deaf, country tunes the mustache blared over the radio. With every second that passed, the scene became increasingly and unbearably familiar. She tried to breathe deep and calm the anxiety that was brewing inside her soul, but it wouldn't shake. No matter how many times she told herself that not everyone was out to get her, despite every thought of Lucas, Deanna, Lynn and the missionary that she let run through her head, she couldn't bury the thought that something was wrong.

Suddenly, the mustache turned to her and asked, "So, what was a pretty girl like you doing all by herself on the side of the road?"

Why did he have to ask that question?

"Oh, you know," she chuckled nervously, the left side of her mouth twitching almost imperceptibly. "Trying to see how long it would take to drown in the rain."

"Sorry to ruin your experiment," he laughed.

Shifting in her seat, she instinctively slid her hand behind her back, double-checking to make sure her gun was still secure in her waistband, which it was. "Next time I'll just have to pick a less public place," she sighed.

"So, what's in New York?"

"I've got some business there too. The unfinished kind."

"Why didn't your boyfriend take you?"

Shit. He's fishing.

"My mail-order hasn't come in yet," she answered.

As long as he doesn't…

"What about family?" he probed.

…ask that question next.

Before he could utter another word, she drew her gun and pointed it at his head, demanding, "Why do you want to know about my family?"

"Holy shit!" the mustache exclaimed, nearly jumping out of his skin and swerving into traffic at the sight of the muzzle in his face. "God, I'm sorry. It was a question, a simple question. I just thought we could get to know each other."

"What kind of product are you delivering?" she interrogated.

"I don't," he stammered. "I don't understand what that has to do with anything."

"Answer the question!"

"Really, it's nothing."

"Pull the car over."

"Why don't you put the gun away and we can-"

"Pull over!" she ordered.

"Okay, okay," he said, breathing heavily as he turned on his blinker and pulled to a stop along the shoulder.

As he threw the car into the park, she thrust the gun in his face, insisting, "Put it in park and step out of the car."

The mustache quickly obliged, and Natasha followed out her own door, keeping the gun trained on him at all times. All around them, the rain, which had now turned to sleet, fell at a steady pace, pelting the top of her head like the pricking of a thousand needles, but she refused to pay them no attention. With the muzzle of the gun, she motioned urgently for him to approach the trunk, which he did, holding his hands in front of him the whole time. Meanwhile, Natasha stayed at a safe distance, the gun shaking in her hands.

"Open it," she demanded.

"You got it, ma'am," he replied, stopping and looking around him anxiously. "Only problem is my keys are still in the ignition."

"Then get them!" she insisted with another quick motion of the gun toward the front seat.

With calm, steady steps, the mustache slunk back across the side of the car and reached through the driver's side window to grab his keys. As he did, Natasha followed him with her gun, bending over as he reached inside the car as to not let him out of her sight. Taking the keys from the ignition, he tiptoed back around his car and unlocked the trunk.

Then, lifting the lid, he looked at her and said in a calm, even tone, "Now, don't get jumpy. There's nothing back here you need to worry about."

I'll believe it when I see it.

As the mustache reached inside the trunk to grab the product, a semi-truck barreled down the highways, its high beams breaking through the fog and covering the car in blinding light. That was when she saw it. Just over the edge of the trunk, there was a glimmer, the reflection of light off metal. It was the same glimmer that radiated off her own gun underneath the headlights. Instinctively, she pulled the trigger.

Bang!

Before she could even process what had just happened, the mustache was on the ground, clutching his shoulder, which, though it wasn't where she was aiming, was an effective landing spot. Frozen, she simply stood in place, staring at the smoke that billowed out of the muzzle of her gun and wafted into the night sky.

"Ah!" the mustache screamed, grimacing in pain. "What the hell was that?"

"You know what that was! I saw it!" she exclaimed,

wheeling around the back of the car with her gun still aimed directly at his head. "In the headlights. You had a gun. You were going to shoot me."

Shaking his head, he replied, "Look."

Without moving the gun, she turned to look inside the trunk. To her surprise, it was mostly empty, save for an open box of metallic, silver trophies sitting in the center.

"My son," he explained, choking through the pain. "Formed a little, touch football league with a few of his friends back home in the city. And he — well, since it's not an official league or anything, they don't have any trophies. But I've got a friend who makes them. He said he'd give 'em to me for free if I just picked 'em up."

"Your son?" Natasha asked, shaking with realization. "Why did you call him your employer?"

The man chuckled, "It was supposed to be a joke. You know how kids are. They always think you work for them."

Natasha staggered back as her hands shook, dropping the gun to the ground. With both hands, she latched onto the sides of her head and pulled at her scalp, trying to rip her hair out from the roots. The fog around her grew thick and heavy, making it impossible to breath, and her vision began to blur.

She tried to speak, but all that came out was, "But I-I didn't — this wasn't supposed to — I thought…"

Bracing himself with his hand, the mustache stood up and approached Natasha. He raised the one, good arm he had left and reached out to her, saying, "It's okay. Why don't we get back in the car?"

But she turned away, muttering, "No, no. You need to go to the hospital. I-I shot you. I didn't even mean to."

"And I should be glad you aren't any better with that thing," he laughed. "You only grazed me."

"But you fell, and you were clutching your-"

"It was instinct. Why don't you see for yourself?"

Taking her by the hand, the mustache raised her shaking hand to his shoulder. As he placed it on top, Natasha felt all around, searching for the wound. All she found, however, was a single rip in his jacket's leather, where the bullet had flown by. Immediately, she breathed a sigh of relief.

"My jacket probably won't forgive you for a while," he laughed. "But as for me, I can't seem to remember why it is we're letting ourselves get soaked when my wagon still has a perfectly, intact roof. What do you say we pound out the last leg of our trip and talk about what it is that had you so freaked out?"

With an insistent nod, Natasha followed the mustache back into the car, and they drove off, leaving the gun where it belonged, alone on the side of the road, where it would hopefully never to be found again. As she fastened her seat belt and let herself finally sink back into the mustache's leather seats, she felt as though a weight had been lifted from her shoulders.

And she hoped to God she would never so much as see another gun in her life.

12

SCREWED

TOLEDO, OHIO

*A*fter ushering Florian out the front door, Paul stumbled back across the living room, rubbing the base of his right palm against his temple, and collapsed on the couch, exhausted. With each day that passed, the lack of sleep wore on him like the pounding of a raging sea. For a while, it was bearable. All it took was a little concentration to keep his head above water, but now, he didn't even have enough strength left to tread water in the shallow end, much less in the midst of an ocean squall.

As his backside hit the couch cushions, his head sunk to his right shoulder. Along with it, his eyelids fell, and he descended into the depths. However, as soon as his eyes closed, the space behind his eyelids burst with flame. In an instant, he was back in the void, watching Rebecca and their cabin burst into flames over and over again. Immediately, he jumped to his feet, his eyes shooting wide open and his hands shaking wildly. Then, he dashed into the kitchen to forage for yet another cup of coffee.

However, finding relief would be more difficult than he imagined.

First, he checked the bottom, left hand drawer underneath the sink, where Lena's main stash was usually kept, but there was nothing. Next, he searched behind the blue cup in the top, right cabinet, where he kept his backup cache. Still, nothing. Finally, in a last-ditch effort to locate his caffeine fix, he frantically flung open every cabinet and drawer and looked in, behind and around every plate, bowl and cup for even a single coffee bean, yet still found nothing.

As he was just about to turn on the garbage disposal and throw himself down the sink in frustration, Lena appeared in the kitchen doorway and chuckled, "Looks like we need to start planting coffee plants at the rate you're going."

"I don't understand!" Paul exclaimed, slamming his fists on the island counter. "I just bought a whole bag less than a week ago."

"What did you do, just shove the raw grounds into your mouth?" she teased.

"No," he replied. "I mean… at least, I don't think I did. The last week's been a bit of a blur."

"That's because you haven't stopped moving long enough to actually have anything other than one, long day."

"You don't understand, Lena. I can't."

"Then, what do you say we multitask? Let's run down to the cafe, buy a truck load of coffee and maybe grab a couple cups for ourselves. I could use a sit down."

"What about the shop?"

"It'll be fine," she replied, taking Paul gently by the arm and dragging him out the front doors. "I'm more worried about how many employees we'll have left by day's end if we don't get you out for a bit. Besides, I think, after everything that's happened, we deserve a coffee date."

"Date?" he asked.

"Don't make me say it again," she said as she locked the front door behind them.

Hopping in the car, they sped off toward the outskirts of town to Rao's, Paul's favorite, little hole in that wall. It was the type of place that most who passed through wouldn't give a second thought. Located down the street from an abandoned church and directly behind a notorious, biker bar, it wasn't much to look at. Its gutters were half-torn off the roof on both sides. The front door was covered in taped-up cardboard where glass used to be, and the sign was missing two of its four letters. Inside, the atmosphere wasn't much more appealing. The floors were perennially dirty, and it wasn't uncommon to see a mouse or five running in and out of the space they had carved out of the front door.

But damn, if they didn't make a fine cup of coffee.

After ordering a dozen bags of coffee and two, triple shot, caramel macchiatos from the front counter, Lena and Paul took a seat at one of the two, functioning booths in the shop. As he sat down, Paul leaned his elbows on the table and placed his head in his hands. He tried to breathe deep and calm his growing anxiety, but at this point, it was oozing from his pores. His hands were shaking, and his nails were involuntarily digging into his scalp.

Leaning across the table and placing her hand on top of his, Lena assured him, "Everything's going to be okay."

"How do you do it?" Paul asked, releasing the grip he held on the front of his hairline. "Even with everything that's been going on, you've stayed so calm. I couldn't sleep for days after what happened with Kayde, much less now, but it's like it hasn't bothered you at all."

"I'm not sure that's an ability you should envy," she sighed.

"At this point, I'd prefer anything to this," he admitted.

"When you've been in the game as long as I have, not much gets to you. As long as you're still breathing at the end of the day, you don't break a sweat over what happens to *other* people."

"Even still, it sounds nice."

"But at what point do you stop being human?"

"Probably the same time you stop taking me out for coffee just to make sure I'm doing okay."

Smiling, she asked, "Well, are you?"

"No," he sighed. "But keep this up, and maybe one day I will be. We should probably get back to the shop, though, before Izzy screws the pooch. Possibly literally. At this point, nothing would surprise me."

With that, Paul grabbed his coffee and stood up to leave, but Lena grabbed his hand, stopping him. "You're not supposed to be okay right now," she assured him. "What happened is... worse than you deserve. But, you'll never be right if you don't face it. Stand up to that pain, stare it in the eyes and demand that it be the one that moves."

"Careful," he laughed as he slid his hand from hers and continued toward the front door. "Someone who didn't know you might think you actually care."

As they walked out the cafe doors, a sudden crash and shriek came from the alley beside the bar. Seconds later, what sounded like a scuffle followed. Then came the shouting.

A deep, gruff voice echoed across the otherwise empty parking lot, yelling, "You're gonna pay for that, bitch."

"No... no, please!" a girl's voice followed, her shaking fear evidenced by her tone. "All I wanted was a little to eat. Please, I haven't had a decent meal in weeks."

Suddenly, a third voice growled, "Doesn't matter. No one steals from Carmine."

Immediately, Paul took off in a dead sprint, rumbling determinedly toward the alley with Lena following closely behind, needing no instruction to know what Paul was planning. After all, she had been playing this game far longer than he had. At this point, there wasn't a play in the book that she hadn't read.

If there was one thing he had learned over the years, it was that the best recruitment opportunities often came at unexpected times. When those chances arose, the best course of action was always to leap first and look later, knocking down the pins before fear could take hold. So, as always, the plan was to gain the target's trust.

And what better way to do that than to save a defenseless, homeless girl from a pair of thieves?

As soon as Paul rounded the corner, however, Rebecca materialized out of thin air directly in front of him, stopping him dead in his tracks. She looked just as she had in the field, twisted and broken with blood pouring down her face and blouse. This time, though, there was something different in the way she looked at him. Gone was the hatred, the inferno that had raged behind her eyes. In its place was something vaguely resembling disappointment, like the tears of the angels themselves falling from a sunless sky.

She pleaded with him, "You don't have to do this. You have plenty of girls."

But he paid her no attention. Instead, he broke into an even faster sprint than before, passing right through her like the apparition she was. Then, as he ran, he studied the scene before him. Halfway down the alleyway, two men hovered over a teenage girl, who was on the ground, backed up against the concrete wall behind her. Across from her, the man on her right side, closest to Paul, was, by far, the easier of the two to subdue. He was short, stocky, and, though he tried to dress tough, with a spiked, dog collar around his throat, a leather jacket draped across his shoulders and skull bandana wrapped around his forehead, he looked more like the kind of guy who couldn't win a wrestling match against a third-grade, kung fu class, much less a full-grown adult.

The other thug, however, appeared much tougher to take down. He was gargantuan, standing a full foot higher than Paul with physique that would have put Redd's to shame. It looked like a flick of his wrist could send any one of them flying into the next zip code. On top of that, judging by the slight bulge in his skin-right, biker jacket, he was packing heat.

If Paul was going to take this guy on, he would have to be crafty.

Keeping his footsteps as light and quick as possible, Paul lowered his shoulder and crashed into the smaller man before either of the bikers noticed him. He wrapped his arms around the smaller man's shoulders and threw him into the larger man, knocking them both off balance. Then, as quickly as he could, Paul sidestepped the falling dwarf and reached desperately for the brute's gun, but he wasn't quick enough. Before Paul could grab the gun, the giant regained his balance and latched onto Paul's wrist. He then whirled around and threw Paul to the side.

Shuffling his feet as he landed in an attempt to keep from crashing to the ground, Paul spun around to face his foe. When he did, he saw Lena already on top of the dwarf, her heel slamming into the back of his knee, and Rebecca standing behind the giant, staring directly at Paul.

"Better get your slingshot ready," she laughed.

Shaking her off, Paul squared off against Goliath, his clenched fists raised up in front of him, ready for a battle. For a moment, they simply stood there, sizing each other up. Then, without warning, Goliath charged, his right fist flying toward Paul. Instinctively, Paul weaved to the left, narrowly avoiding the hit. But a second later, just as his feet settled underneath him, he saw something move out of the corner of his eye. It was Goliath's other fist, flying at him with cheetah-like speed. This time, Paul didn't have enough time to react. Goliath's punch proved true, striking Paul in the collarbone and sending him plummeting to the ground.

As he hit the ground, Rebecca mocked him, "Is that all you've got, darling? I didn't know I married such a pussy."

Her words hit him like a knife to the chest, causing his heart to stop and his fists to clench with rage. He lowered his head to the ground and rested his forehead on the dirt as Goliath towered over him, his shadow completely encompassing Paul's body.

"Valiant effort," Goliath laughed, his voice sending chills up Paul's spine. "But you've got to be a bit bigger to have a chance against me."

Even from the ground, Paul could feel Goliath rear back and prepare to strike him down, leaving his face defenseless. Suddenly, Paul spun around, hurling the fistful of dirt he had grabbed while on the ground directly into Goliath's eyes. It hit with a crash, and the giant staggered backward.

"Ah!" he yelled as he doubled over and held his hands to his eyes.

Then, while Goliath was indisposed, Paul made his move. He leapt off the ground and in one, fluid motion, snatched the gun from Goliath's waistband and pointed it right between his eyes.

"Go! Before I decide I'd rather repaint the bar with your blood," Paul threatened, motioning toward the road with the gun.

"My hero" Rebecca mocked, holding the back of her hand to her head and fake-swooning as the thugs circled around Paul and dashed out of the alleyway. "Now, while their backs are turned, shoot them quickly, since we both know how good you are at taking people's lives from them."

Trying to ignore her, he turned to the girl, who was still cowering on the ground, and held his hand toward her, saying, "It's okay. You're safe now. They won't hurt you again."

"Thank you," the girl said as she took his hand and stood up. "I don't know what they would have done to me if you hadn't come."

Suddenly, Rebeca disappeared from over Paul's shoulder and reappeared next to the girl. "Whatever it was, it's probably better than what he's got planned," she sighed.

"It was the least we could do," Lena replied.

"I just wish we'd gotten here before they ruined your meal," Paul said, motioning to the half-eaten sandwich that was lying on the ground behind them.

"You heartless bastard," Rebecca muttered.

"It's okay," the girl said. "There'll always be another meal."

Feigning concern, Paul replied, "Still, I feel bad. Why don't we swing you by a fast food joint and grab you a bite? It's the least we can do."

"Oh, I couldn't possibly impose," she insisted.

"You're not!" he exclaimed as Rebecca mockingly mouthed his words in perfect sync. "I insist. Breakfast is on us."

"Hefty price tag on that meal," Rebecca sighed.

"But what about after, honey?" Lena asked, leaning in and placing her hand on the girl's shoulder. "Do you have a place to stay?"

To which the girl shook her head in response. "Not for a while now."

"Are you really going to do this?" Rebecca asked, inching closer to Paul. "After what happened to Kayde? To Grace? To me?!"

Paul gulped. "Well... we've — I mean, if you want — we've got an extra room."

"What Paul is trying to say," Lena corrected, elbowing him in the side and raising her eyebrows at him. "Is that, if you don't have anywhere else to go, we'd be happy to have you stay with us. There's plenty of room. Isn't that right, Paul?"

"What's the matter, Paul? Dead wife got your tongue?" Rebecca mocked.

"No!" Paul screamed.

"No?" the girl asked, her shoulders tensing as she backed away from him. "You don't have to do anything for me, really. Not if it's too much trouble."

"It's not," he pleaded, shaking off Rebecca's taunt. "I'm sorry. I just got a little distracted."

"Are you sure it's okay?" the girl asked.

"Or maybe you just don't have it anymore," Rebecca corrected him.

Finally, Paul had enough. Pointing his finger straight at Rebecca, who was standing directly in front of the girl, he backed her against the wall, yelling, "I've had just about enough of you! You think you know everything, but you don't. You never knew me. Why don't you just leave me the hell alone?!"

Suddenly, with a flash of light, Rebecca disappeared, and Paul found himself standing only a foot from the girl's face, his finger resting almost directly on top of the bridge of her nose.

Squeezing past his finger, she apologized as she backed toward the road, "I'm sorry. I'll leave. I didn't mean to bother you, sir. Thank you for helping me out. Have a great day! "

Then, she was gone. She darted down the alley and turned the corner before Paul even had a chance to reach out after her.

"Are you okay?" Lena asked, reaching out to console him.

But as her hand touched his shoulder, her brushed her off,

walking past her toward their car and muttering, "Yeah, I'm fine."

The truth, however, was precisely the opposite. He was stranded in the middle of the ocean without a life vest and no energy left to tread water. If he wasn't careful, he would soon drown.

13

LIFE

TOLEDO, OHIO

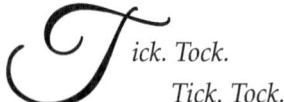ick. Tock.
Tick. Tock.

Blair stared at the clock as the final, forty seconds of her GED class flew by. Each click of the second hand felt like the rapid beat of a bass drum played at a dance club tempo. Soon, her shoulders were swaying to its rhythm, and even her wrists were twitching in suit. She closed her eyes, trying to drown out the thumping that now inhabited her soul. The last thing she wanted to hear was the hellish chiming of the school bell, which marked the end of her reprieve from the scorching flames that awaited her inside the dragon's lair. With only five seconds to go, a familiar countdown began.

Five. Four. Three. Two.

One.

She closed her eyes and braced for impact, but it didn't come. In its place, there was only a faint buzzing, like the sound of bees pollinating a nearby field. Curious, Blair opened her eyes, hoping that meant class hadn't ended. However, when she did, every student in the class was already out of their seat, packing up their backpacks and slinging them over her shoulders.

Even their teacher, Mr. Fredrick, was doing the same. "Looks like the bells are picking out their cemetery plots," he said. "Enjoy your Friday evening, everyone. I'll see you crazies next week."

Fifteen seconds later, Blair was alone at her desk, staring at the empty chalkboard at the front of the room. She knew that, eventually, she would have to bite the bullet and rip herself from her seat, but with three days until her next pardon, she would have to be dragged out of that room at gunpoint.

At this point, she couldn't bear to be back at Dragon's Wing any longer. Every moment there was excruciating, a painful reminder of everything she had lost and of how she was responsible for her demise. Every time she was alone, every time she closed her eyes, she was back in that alley. Whenever silence rang hollow through the night air, she heard the blast again and again. She even saw Kayde in her dreams. Lifeless. Bleeding. Dead. And all she could think about was how different things should have been.

If only I had gone with him the first time.

If I just hadn't been so self-righteous, thinking he needed to be taught some sort of damn lesson, he would still be here.

Since that night, the only place where those questions didn't flood through her synapses was at her school desk. There, for an hour and a half every night, she was back in a simpler time, before the bus stop, before New York, before she had simultaneously gained and lost everything in the world that was precious to her. In that room, she was a student again, and all she wanted to do was soak in every bit of knowledge she could and pretend that the world held a future for her that didn't only consist of pain.

Eventually, Blair knew that even this place would become

tainted. Lena would force her to see every second in the outside world as a chance to drag someone else to hell with her. But for now, she was determined to hold onto her freedom as tightly as she gripped the sides of her desk in that moment.

Just then, a thick-haired Latina sat in the desk next to her and tapped her on the shoulder, teasing, "You've really got a penchant for punishment, don't you?"

"What do you mean?" Blair asked.

As Blair turned toward the girl, she was immediately struck by the glow that covered every inch of her butterscotch skin. It was a wonder that Blair hadn't noticed her in class before. In no way was this girl average or the kind that could be missed even from a city away, much less a few desks away. She looked like the type of girl who was destined for Hollywood, with her wide, encompassing smile, hips as wide as a country road and hourglass figure to match. It was a wonder she had survived this long without being scooped up by the vultures in the entertainment industry.

And if Blair wasn't careful, she would have to be the one to do it.

"This place is, like, government sanctioned, water torture," the Latina laughed. "Drip after drip of knowledge, but none of it's worth shit. This place is a frickin' ghost town thirty seconds after that bell rings, but it's been at least twice that. And you're still here. Why?"

Blair shrugged. "I don't know. I guess this is the only place where I feel like anyone sees any real potential in me. Gotta hold onto that as long as I can."

"You're an odd duck, Ivory, you know that? Do all rivers run half full to you or just the ones that are laced in shit?"

"Nah, that cup always runneth over. So, now I've got something to ask you. I've been coming here for two weeks now, and

I can't remember seeing you. Now, I can't believe I would have missed a stunner like you. So, what are you doing here?"

"Well, aren't you the gorgeous, little charmer! I'm not here for much, just shooting some hoops in the gym. After all, it sure as hell beats being home. I was walking by and saw you sitting here, frozen, like you were posing for a painting. Figured I'd come see if the artist was doing you any justice."

"And the verdict?"

"Jury's still out." The Latina smiled. "So, does our model have a name? Or do I just keep calling you Ivory?"

Blair chuckled, "I've got to admit; Ivory does have a nice ring to it. But you can call me Blair."

"I'm Ciara, but you can call me Cici," the Latina said, reaching out to shake Blair's hand. "So Blair, what kind of stuff do you do when you're not staring at chalkboards? Like, for fun?"

"Well, I do eat on occasion."

"With that figure, you could've fooled me. What do you say we skip detention and head over to Suzie's? I hear they've got a four for four deal going on right now."

"If we're going to go out, might as well treat ourselves, right? What do you say I bring you some place nice? I've been dying to try Salvatore's at the end of the block. I hear even the appetizers are served with caviar."

"Damn, Ivory. You really are full of surprises. Lead the way. But, let me warn you; I will be running that tab up as far as you let me. After all, it ain't much fun if I don't see how deep that fancy pocketbook of yours goes, right?"

"I'll let you know when it starts begging for mercy."

If they're giving me five-hundred a month, I might as well find an excuse to use it, right?

From the school, Cici and Blair walked side by side down a lamplit street as the world around them drifted into slumber.

All around them, the street was empty. Not a car drove by on either side of the street. Outside of the two of them, it was as though not a person existed in the entire world. As they sat across from each other at Salvatore's, a relaxing silence fell between them, the likes of which Blair hadn't experienced since leaving New York. It was familiar and welcome but at the same time heartbreaking.

A few minutes later, the waiter came and took their orders, which, as promised, were exorbitant. Both of them endeavored to pick out the most expensive meals they could find, and a hundred and fifty dollars later, they were not disappointed. Their cocktails were magnificent, their cranberry and walnut salads divine. The Wagyu Filet Blair ordered was possibly the most succulent thing she had ever put in her mouth, and Cici said the same about her Steak and Shrimp Fettuccine Alfredo. Thoroughly stuffed, Blair sank into the back cushion of her seat, but Ciara leaned forward, her elbows on the table, and looked at Blair with a curious expression painted across her face.

"What?" Blair asked, chuckling.

"You've got to answer me something, Ivory," Cici said. "How is it that a girl like you is taking a GED class one minute and shelling out a buck fifty for dinner the next?"

Shit, please don't make me do this, Cici.

"That's the beauty of credit. You don't have to actually have the money to spend it," Blair answered.

But Ciara shook her head. "I'm not buying it. That's pipsqueak logic. You've gotta at least be raking in some kind of money to even get your hands on a credit card. And, judging by your clothes and that handbag, you've got yourself a damn high limit. So, what gives, B-loves?"

"Well, I didn't exactly buy the dress. Or the purse."

"Got yourself a sugar daddy, then! Damn girl, can you point

me in the direction of one of them? Oldies ain't exactly my type, but no way I'm gonna say no to a little purse padding."

"Not quite. Let's just say my job has its perks."

"With perks like that, why go for your GED?"

Blair sighed, "I kind of just stumbled onto this job. It's got perks, sure, but it's not exactly the dream."

"Well, I don't know whose dream you're talking about," Cici said. "'Cause that sounds pretty close to the cloud nine to me."

"Different strokes, I guess."

"Think they might let me in for an interview?"

"Well, you're certainly their type..."

"That a yes?"

"You in the mood for dessert? That brownie platter is downright calling my name."

"Don't think I don't see you changing the subject on me. What's the matter? Do you not want to work with me?"

She's not going to let this go, is she? I've got to think of something quick. Something to make her drop it.

"No, it's not that," Blair said. "I really like you. It's just that after what happened, they've been cutting down on new hires. I don't even know if they're accepting applications."

"What happened?" Cici asked.

"There was an... accident. Really big deal. Somebody was caught doing something they weren't supposed to. It was a huge scene, and my boss ended up having to pay for it out of pocket. Not a lot of money left over for new hires."

"Well, if anything opens up, you'll let me know, right?"

"Yeah, sure thing."

Let's both hope that day never comes...

14

LIBERTY

PAHRUMP, NEVADA

*A*fter three days inside the belly of the beast, Nina and Anna were no closer to breaking a story than when they first got to Las Vegas. In fact, the only progress Anna and Nina had managed to make was in giving Bradie an ulcer, and it got worse with each day that passed. Every time they pulled up to the curb outside The Dude's Ranch, his stomach tied itself up in knots, and the only thing worse than watching Anna walk out of that car was watching and listening to her every move, powerless to do anything. He had to trust her, but that was getting tougher by the second. The only solace he had was knowing that, since the thugs at the ranch thought she was still under her keeper's thumb, she was still allowed to go back to their hotel every night.

But as each day passed with no time to snoop and no end in sight, it was starting to feel more like visiting a loved one in prison than bringing them home.

As Anna and Nina continued to push through the never-ending gauntlet of client after client, Stacy leaned across the car's center console, resting her head on Brodie's shoulder, and said, "I don't understand. If these guys are traffickers, shouldn't we have seen signs of it by now? Now, I'm in no way complaining about this, but they haven't so much as threatened either of the girls since we got here."

"And they won't," Anna whispered through the earpiece. "These guys are pros. They don't beat the ones they don't own."

"Then how are we supposed to find proof?" Stacy asked.

"We have to get into their office. Next mark I nab, I'll run a switch with one of the other girls. That should buy me enough time to at least tell us where the evidence isn't," Anna explained.

"Shit," Nina sighed. "Who'd have thought getting your rocks off would be so damn tiring? I'm beat!"

"I did not want to know that, Brown," Bradie replied with an amused chuckle.

"Way too much information," Stacy agreed. "This is exactly the reason we shut off the video feed in the first place."

"Wait, you're actually screwing your johns?" Anna asked.

"Well, yeah," Nina said. "What else an I supposed to do?"

"For the most part, Anna just makes them cry," Bradie answered.

Up to this point in the investigation, whenever Anna brought a mark up to her room, she began their rendezvous with a subtle, yet pointed, interrogation in the hopes of uncovering anything she could about her client: their home life, their childhood and any trauma that might have been associated with either of those two. Usually, she managed to pinpoint their weakness in a matter of minutes, and the rest of her time was spent playing therapist. Any time that didn't work, she would perform an elaborate striptease, which included a disturbing and uncomfortable amount of sexual banter but always forced her johns to finish before she even got started.

It was an intricate scheme, which for the most part was

wildly successful. Occasionally, however, it did result in unhappy clients, typically alpha males who resented anything or anyone that tries make them feel less than kingly. They would inevitably grow to abhor Anna's incessant prodding and teasing, and most of the time, they grew violent. But, just like the clients with excessive, childhood trauma, the alpha males were also easy enough for Anna to deal with. As soon as their open palm fell across her face, she beelined out of her room and straight toward one of her handlers, who, after several rounds of threats from Anna, insisting that her keeper would not stand for such violence, promptly threw her attackers out of the building and demanded that they never come back.

Frankly, Bradie found her technique to be a sight to behold, but even still, he couldn't help but feel an ache in his heart. He couldn't imagine the nightmares this place would form in her. Back in Detroit, she couldn't sleep for weeks after only a week of investigating. Now, she was back in her own, personal hell, feeling its fires scorch her skin again and again. Bradie only hoped that they can find what they were looking for him before either she or Nina got burned.

"Oh well," Nina sighed. "I might as well get off while I still can. Once I'm back in the real world, it'll probably be another three years before I see any action, with my luck."

"We've really got to find you a boyfriend," Stacy giggled.

"You and my mom both. At this point, I have a feeling my next boyfriend's going to be made of silicone," Nina replied.

Just then, Bradie's phone rang. Taking his earpiece from his ear and setting it in the center console, he leaned forward and reached around his back to take the phone from his back pocket. The screen flashed with his old partner's name, Loman Darvey.

Holding the phone to his ear, Bradie answered. "Buddy! Long time, no talk. What's the occasion?"

"Is that Loman?" Stacy asked, taking her own earpiece out and setting it next to Bradie's. "Put him on speaker so I can hear too."

As he did, Loman replied, his voice barely audible over the whistle of the wind all around him, "Well, for starters, I just saw the promo piece they're showing for that spot on the Nickie Ocean show you've got in a couple weeks, and of course, I couldn't let that kind of info slide without giving credit where credit is due. Looks like the detective's life is suiting you well. I knew it would."

"Thank you," Bradie said, though the taste of Loman's congratulations was bittersweet going down his throat.

"Hi Loman!" Stacy added.

"Is that Stacy I hear?" Loman asked with a chuckle that sounded more like sadness than joy. "Hey Stace! Before I forget, let me tell you the good news. We've got a lead on the asshole who hurt your girl."

"Really?" Bradie asked. "How'd you manage that after all this time?"

"Ye is little faith! Honestly, I'm offended that you sound surprised. Since you left, I haven't stopped looking for him. I've been scouring the city, showing your girl's picture around to every hooker and parlor girl I could find, off the clock of course, since Chief doesn't think there's anything there."

"Of course."

"So finally, I found someone who said she knew Anna. In fact, she says they worked together under the same pimp. I'm on my way to close it out now."

"Thank you so much, partner. It means a lot to me that you kept digging into this. I know there wasn't a lot to go off of."

"No need to thank me. That's what partners do."

"Any chance I could get a few minutes with the bastard after you cuff him? I'm not too far outside the city, and I want to see his face when he finds out we beat him."

"Oh, I'm sure something can be arranged. Listen, I'd love to catch up, but I'm pulling up right now. Shoot me a ring when you're in town. Gotta run."

With a sudden click, the line went dead. Then, before Bradie even had the chance to put his phone away, there was a frantic knocking at the passenger's side door, which caused both him and Stacy to nearly jump out of the closed sunroof in shock. Turning to the right, he saw Nina, dressed in a half-shirt and jean shorts, shivering in the cold and emphatically motioning for him to roll down the window. Curious, he obliged.

"Where the hell have you two been?!" she yelled as the window slowly descended.

"I had to take a call," Bradie answered. "Why? Shouldn't you still be inside?"

Nina rolled her eyes. "If you'd been paying attention, you'd already know why," she scolded. "I've been yelling for you for the last, three minutes. Anna's gone. Somebody took her."

Those words struck like crashing cymbals in his ears, spiking his heart rate and immediately sending him into a panic. As Nina hopped into the back seat, Stacy pulled up the video feed on the computer. Meanwhile, Bradie shoved his earpiece halfway toward his eardrum so he could listen. But all he could hear was static. Even as the picture came into focus on the screen, they didn't fare much better. All they could see were ropes tied directly over the camera, blocking their entire line of vision, save for a tiny sliver of light on the right-hand side of the screen, which illuminated what, when he leaned in close to the screen and squinted, looked faintly like a highway.

Wheeling around the face Nina in the backseat, Bradie began his interrogation, asking, "What the hell happened back there?!"

"Damn Bradie, no need to turn this car into Guantanamo. I was getting there," Nina answered.

"Then go faster," he demanded. "This is my daughter we're talking about."

"Well, I was taking another mark back to my room when I heard scuffling in my earbud. So, of course, I excused myself to the bathroom and took it out for a second, assuming it was just a malfunction or something. And when I put it back in, I heard yelling, not in my earpiece but in the hallway, right outside the bathroom. So, I swung open the door just in time to see two men dragging Anna down the hall as she kicked and screamed the whole way."

"And you didn't help her?!"

"Yeah, because I'm secretly a kung fu master. What do expect me to do, take out two guys who are twice my size?"

"You could've at least tried."

"Then we would be making a trip to the hospital instead of actually being able to do something about it. Besides, you didn't let me tell you the most important part. As they were heading down the stairs, I heard one of the bastards talk about bringing her home."

"Which means *he* found her," Stacy gasped. "But how? Didn't Loman say he was on his way to pick him up?"

"He would've had to have sent those guys at least five hours ago, long before Loman called us," Bradie explained.

"Wait, your old partner called?" Nina asked. "Just as Anna was taken?"

"He had an update on her case," Bradie explained.

"And you don't think that was a little convenient?"

"Loman and I were partner's for five years. I'd know if he was involved in something like that."

"And you'd think I would've known my last husband was screwing my cameraman, but them's the breaks, kid. Proximity doesn't equal knowledge. People can hide anything from you if they're trying hard enough."

"But he wouldn't-"

"Shouldn't we at least check it out?" Stacy asked, placing her hand on Bradie's shoulder. "Just to make sure."

"Fine," Bradie growled as he turned the ignition and sped down the street toward the highway. "We're going to the same place either way so I guess we might as well pay him a visit. All right, buckle your seatbelt, love. We're headed back home."

~

New York, New York

I walk along a familiar street
As despair covers my weary feet.
A darkened sun hangs overhead,
And every step fills me with dread.
But another feeling takes me instead.
Suddenly, that old fear falls to the ground,
Replaced by a hope for the lost that I've found.
Final rest feels far, but I'm still so close
To finding those I care for most.
But for now, I must face this ghost
Of the life I once lived.

As soon as Natasha's feet hit the New York City streets, her heart rose into her throat. She couldn't swallow. She could hardly find the strength to breathe. All around her, the city buzzed in a familiar frenzy, but even still, she felt like the only person left in the entire world. Time froze as she passed her old street corner. Her hands started to shake. It was simultaneously the most terrifying and exciting moment in her entire life.

Creeping along the far side of the street and hiding herself in the nearest alley, she waited for night to fall. Only then would she be able to make her move. As she sat in the darkness, staring at the crimson door that stood between her and Blair, she played out her plan over and over again. She would only get one attempt at this, so she had to make sure she got it right.

After the girls made their way onto the street, Natasha planned to simply watch and wait. Nothing could prove more fatal than rushing into a rescue mission without first ensuring that everything was in order. Months had passed since she had been inside the warehouse, and in that time, she had gone through more changes than she could count. It was only logical to assume Alexei had done the same, especially since her own escape had gone off without a hitch.

Once she got a lay of the land, she would need to find an inside man. While Blair and the other girls were busy hitting their quotas, Natasha planned to score a mark of her own. Thankfully for her, she had kept her old outfit from the warehouse for just this occasion. Then, after giving him whatever pleasure fit his fancy, she would put her plan into action. She would ask him to do a simple favor for her; he would go into the brothel, ask for Katrianna and insist that she service him in his car. After that, it was simply a matter of running as fast as they could and leaving New York City in the dust.

On paper, it was a good plan. But as night fell over the Big Apple, that paper went up in flames.

Right on time, Alexei sauntered down the street, cheeseburger in hand, headphones in his ears, and ketchup smeared across his lips. For a moment, Natasha was taken aback by this sight. From where she stood, he almost seemed… normal. He walked with a dancing, energetic strut and a smile across his face instead of the signature scowl she had seen every night at the warehouse. If she hadn't known the devil underneath his skin, she might have even thought that he looked kind. However, when he reached the door, everything changed. He took a deep breath, taking his headphones out of his ears and wiping the ketchup from his mouth, and his shoulders slumped. As he carefully unlocked the door, every muscle in his body tensed. Then, with a wolf-like howl into the empty sky, he kicked open the front door.

Nine minutes later, the street flooded with girls, most of whom Natasha recognized and others she did not. The last to emerge from the warehouse was Theresa. Even from across the street, Natasha could see that she was struggling. Stumbling across the sidewalk, Theresa clumsily leaned against the brick wall, bringing her hands to her face to hastily wipe the underside of her crimson-stained nose. As Natasha watched Theresa's bloodshot eyes scan the street for her next client, her heart grew heavy. She wished she could do something for Theresa as well, but regretfully, there was only time for one rescue this night. And she didn't know if she would ever get this chance again.

The only problem was; Blair was nowhere to be found.

Natasha double, triple and quadruple checked every inch of the street corner, praying she had made a mistake but found the same thing, time after time. Terrified, her heart began to race, and her mind filled with the worst thoughts imaginable. She feared that her escape had finally caused Alexei to snap. She worried that Blair's punishment had been too severe for her to continue working, or, worse yet, it had been deadly permanent, making it impossible for them to ever see each other again, for her to hold Blair in her arms and melt inside her embrace ever again. But either way, only one thing was for certain; she had to find out for sure.

Just then, a familiar voice rang out of the darkness behind her, saying, "She's not here anymore."

Whipping around, Natasha found herself face to face with her old dealer, the hoodie, standing behind her and glaring over her shoulder at the scarlet door to the warehouse. At first, he looked exactly as she remembered, wholly unremarkable outside of his black sweatshirt, which perennially cloaked him in shadow. However, as she looked closer, she saw how fundamentally he had changed. The hood had been torn from his sweatshirt, and a deep, jagged scar ran across the length of his dark face. Even the look in his eyes was different. Before, he always looked happy, despite the glint of darkness behind his irises. Now, that joy was gone, replaced by a deep-seated rage. When he gazed upon the warehouse door, it was as though thermite burst out of his very sockets, turning the entire warehouse to ash.

Something had changed in him, but truthfully, Natasha didn't care. In that moment, he had information she needed, and that was all that mattered.

"What happened to her?" she demanded, grabbing him by the collar and bringing his eyes to hers.

She expected that he would flinch, but he didn't. Instead, he stared her straight in the eyes and answered, "They wheeled that bitch out not long after you booked it. Ain't seen or heard nothin' from her since."

"Where did they take her?" she questioned.

"Don't know. Don't care," he said. "If you ask me, it's good, frickin' riddance."

"You talk about Blair like that again, and I'll end you. Understood?"

"Fine, then do it. That whore already took everything from me. Might as well bring it full circle, am I right?"

"What are you talking about?"

"I was already on the outs with the Russian bear after he knocked my teeth in. But, right after she came by, it all went to shit."

"She came to see you?"

"No shit," the hoodie scoffed. "She came by, looking to score three hypes of H, which I thought was a bit crackass, but I ain't gonna turn down no free head, ya know? Well, I mean, 'course *you* know, but it was whatever. So, we browntowned it. No big deal. Well, at least it wasn't 'till that effing Cossack tracked her to me. Apparently, she only needed those hypes to replace the ones you nicked outta his pack. He came over here, all stank faced, and said some kind of angry shit. Honestly, I didn't catch most of it, but the next night, alley's empty. Not a single buyer all night. It's been that way ever since. Bastard tanked my whole business."

"You ever think about just finding another alley?" Natasha asked.

But he waved her off, exclaiming, "See, you don't get it either! Don't know why I even bother breaking it down for ya. This is *my* alley. Not his. Not yours. Mine! I built this spot from the ground up, and I ain't gon' let no Russian bitch-shit take it from me."

"Looks like you're doing a bang-up job so far," she replied.

"I'm just waitin' for an opening."

"For six months? What are you, a punk-ass, little bitch? The only chance you get is the one you take. Sit on your ass all you want, but all that's gonna get you is a dust collection. Move or get moved, shithead."

"Yeah? And what are you suggesting?"

"He cut into your business? Burn his to the ground."

"And how do I do that?"

"Take him off the market," Natasha replied.

The hoodie laughed, "By doing what? You asking me to lay

a hit? Damn, you's a crazier bitch than I thought. Dude's frickin' KGB. I lay a finger on his body, Imma lose it before I can say, 'Uncle.'"

"Just keep him distracted long enough for me to get his girls out."

"Actually... that might not be as ass backwards as it sounds."

"See? I told you it would work. Now, the first thing we have to do is-"

"Nah, it's still batshit crazy if you think we're doing this solo. But, I think I got an idea. See, I been scouting out this place for a while now."

"You going to tell me something I don't know?" she groaned.

He rolled his eyes. "Ha. Ha. Yeah, you're a regular Chappelle. I feel ya, whatever. So, everything's been pretty vanilla for a few months. But, then some bitch comes by like day before last, looking for the crank whore, the black haired chick."

"Theresa?" she asked.

"Shit," he sighed. "You want me to know names now? Damn, you ask for a lot. So, your friend, Theresa, the crank whore, doesn't seem to know the new bitch, but it's pretty damn crystal that the new bitch knows your crank whore. And the new bitch thinks she's clever by bringing her 'round back for a screw. 'Cept, even from here I know she's just planning to bust her out. I didn't exactly see what happened after that, but I got a pretty good guess. I mean, the crank whore's still out there working the street, ain't she?"

"Yeah..."

"So, the Russian must have found out and sent her packing. But the new bitch seems like the determined type so I'd put money down that she's still in town, waiting for another chance for a jailbreak."

"I guess, but how are we even supposed to find her?"

"Well, you must be one, lucky girl 'cause you just stumbled upon a regular Einstein. So, this new bitch was sportin' a pretty sweet wristband when she came by the other day. And I recognized it right away. They only give those out at one spot in the city: Saint Mark's Cathedral."

{}~{}~{}~{}~{}~{}~{}~{}~{}~{}

Walking up to the church building, Natasha couldn't help but feel a bit of irony in her situation. For as long as she could remember, God had been nothing to her but a nuisance, an imaginary friend that offered her nothing but judgment and false promises. She had blamed Him, ridiculed Him and eventually grown to hate Him. But now, with what felt like her entire world hanging in the balance, the only hope she had lay inside His house.

As the front doors swung open, the veins surrounding her heart tied themselves in knots, slowing her blood. Her mouth grew dry, and her palms began to sweat. She didn't understand why, but everything in her screamed for her to run before God once again pulled the rug out from under her. At this point, however, it was her only chance.

After closing the doors, the hoodie stepped into the middle of the room, cupped his hands over his mouth and called out, "Papa Chris! The prodigal son has returned home!"

Seconds later, the sanctuary doors burst open, and a young priest stepped into the main lobby, a wide smile across his face and his hands outstretched. He rushed over to the hoodie and wrapped him in a bracing, bear hug.

Then, the priest put his hands on the hoodie's shoulders and laughed, "Luther, my friend. It has been far too long."

"It has, hasn't it?" the hoodie said, stepping back and rubbing his palm anxiously against the back of his neck.

"But it's still good to see you. I just wish it didn't take an emergency for you to come to my door."

"You know me too well, Papa."

"That's why they let me wear the collar," the priest said, walking over to Natasha and extending his hand toward her. "And this is an extra special treat. It's not every day I get to meet one of Luther's friends."

Taking his hand, Natasha replied, "Well, you might have to wait a little longer. My name's Natasha."

"It's nice to meet you," the priest said. "So, how did you and Luther meet?"

She laughed, "Now, that's definitely not a story anyone wants to hear. Especially not here. I, for one, am much more interested in how the two of you met."

"Well, that *is* quite the story," the priest said.

"He caught me walking off with the collection plate," the hoodie said.

"Well, you weren't that hard to catch," the priest chuckled. "You just stuck it under your shirt."

"I could've been pregnant. You don't know."

"So, I catch him walking out the doors with a stomach the size of San Francisco. I call after him, trying to get him to give it back, and the dummy takes off running. But, he was a little too concerned with making sure I wasn't close enough to catch him that he forgot to check for oncoming traffic."

"Next thing I know, I'm in the hospital, and Papa Chris is at my side with rosary in hand, praying for me. He paid for my hospital bills and everything, even took me in, treated me like I was his own kid. Didn't stop me from totally failing him, but Papa's good people. Always helps, even when you don't deserve it."

"And I'm not ready to call you a failure yet, Luther. Takes a lifetime to earn that title, and even then, you can never be so sure. So, what do you need me for today, my friend?"

"You have anyone new come in here over the past, few days?" Natasha asked.

"Yeah," Father Christopher answered. "I have a young girl named Violet staying in one of the basement rooms. Why?"

"We need her help," the hoodie said.

"It's a matter of life or death," Natasha added.

"Right this way," Father Christopher replied, leading them through down a hallway, through a set of doors and down the stairs into the basement.

Then, stopping in front of the first room on the left, he leaned against the door, placing his left ear and forearm against its frame, and knocked three times, announcing, "Violet. I have some people who would like to meet you."

"Just a second, Father," a voice answered from behind the door, followed by a bed's squeal and shuffling, plodding footsteps. A moment later, a frazzled-looking girl with tangled, knotted hair and bags under her eyes opened the door nonchalantly, letting it swing into the room, unaided, and sauntered back onto her bed, pulling the corner of her pillow to the edge of her bed as she lay down.

"What does the odd couple want?" she asked with a sigh.

"Just to talk," Natasha answered as she took a step inside the dumpster fire that apparently constituted a room, passing by two, full trays of rotting food on her way in. "You went to see a girl named Theresa yesterday, right?"

"Maybe I did. Maybe I didn't." Violet shrugged.

"I saw you take her behind that warehouse downtown," the hoodie said.

"Then maybe I did," she replied. "What's it to you?"

Pulling a chair up across from Violet, Natasha said, "I think we both want the same thing."

"And what's that?"

"To help her get out, to get them all out. And I know just how we can do it."

"Alright, I'm listening," Violet said, leaning forward on the edge of the bed until her eyes were even with Natasha's.

"And so am I," Father Christopher added. "Whatever you need, I can guarantee you'll have every priest in this parish right behind you."

So, with a smile, she leaned back in her chair and said, "That gives me the perfect idea."

15

PURSUIT

TOLEDO, OHIO

*R*ebecca sat on the edge of her hotel bed with her elbows on her knees and her head in her hands. Tilting her head to the right, she reached over and checked her phone, which was sitting on the night stand next to the bed, for the fifth time in as many minutes, and just like the other, four times, there was nothing. Not a call, a text or even an email. The anticipation was excruciating. It had been three days since Florian had agreed to help her, and she hadn't heard a word from him. At this point, her plan was in motion, but she was blind and deaf to its progress. For all she knew, Lena had put a bullet in his skull, and her chances of getting through to her husband were as dead as Florian was.

Involuntarily, her legs began to shake. Soon, the tremors reverberated throughout her whole body, causing even her head to quake. Unable to take the waiting any longer, she began to pace around the room, walking the same, three-foot path over and over again until it felt like a divot was forming along the floor beneath her. If Florian didn't call soon, she worried that her hotel bill would also include the cost of a brand new carpet.

Finally, after ten minutes spent pacing, the sweet, beautiful sounds of jazz-fusion burst from her phone, echoing harmoniously all around her. She rushed to the phone and checked the called ID. It was Florian.

Immediately putting the phone on speaker and plopping down on the bed, she breathed a sigh of relief. "It's about time you called," she said.

"Yeah," Florian sighed on the other end. "Sorry about that. I just… I had to think about it a little more."

Sitting up quickly, she said, "I thought you said you were in."

"And I am," he replied. "But, it's not going to be easy. For either of us."

"I never said it would be."

"But you still don't know the half of it. Paul said that if I want my job back, I have to replace the 'product I stole.'"

"Shit! I'm sorry. I didn't — I mean… shit."

"Damn, I never thought I'd live to see the day Rebecca Cross swore."

"It was the only word that fit. Just don't tell Elle."

"Your secret's safe with me."

"We'll have to figure out something, I guess," she sighed.

"What are we going to do?" he asked. "I don't know if I can handle bringing another, innocent girl into that hellhole."

"Let me worry about that," she answered. "For now, let's focus on the big picture. When you spoke with Paul, how did he seem?"

"Like he'd completely lost it. There was no reason he should've let me within ten feet of that place, much less inside Lena's apartment. But the strangest part was that, when I got there, he hugged me. Really tight, like he was relieved that I was there."

"You guys were friends. It's not *that* weird."

"You didn't see him when I quit. He was ready to tear my heart from my chest. You don't go from that to bear hugs in just a couple weeks, but it got even stranger from there. When he let me inside Lena's apartment, it was a mess, like someone had taken a truckload of coffee and dumped it all over the living room. Honestly, I don't think he's slept since he read the article."

"Did you ask him about it?"

"That's when things got weird," Florian explained. "As soon as I said your name, it was as though I wasn't even there. He looked right past me, over at the window, and his eyes grew as wide as the moon."

Just like at Dragon's Wing.

He continued, "It was like he saw a ghost."

"Quite literally, if I'm right," Rebecca said.

"You still think your plan's going to work?" he asked.

"It will," she answered. "We just need to bring in the right girl."

"What do you have in mind?"

"Nothing you have to worry about. For now, just sit tight. I'll call you when I need you."

With that, Rebecca hung up the phone, grabbed her keys and rushed out the door. Then, hopping in her car, she sped off, barreling down the streets toward the one place that held the key to her plan: Aunt Marie's house.

This wasn't a door she wanted to open, but at this point, she had no other choice.

As she pulled into her aunt's driveway, it felt as though a thousand miles of desert stood between her and the front door.

Stepping foot on the grass, her legs turned to stone. Each step she took was immensely difficult, but even still, she pressed on, knowing that her ends would justify the sacrifice it took to get there, no matter how large. In the end, though, it wasn't herself she had to convince; it was Aunt Marie.

Trudging up the front steps and bringing her finger to the doorbell, Rebecca closed her eyes. She couldn't bear to even look at the door, out of fear that she would see the hopeful smile on her aunt's face and lose her nerve. A few seconds later, she heard the door open and felt two, soft arms wrap around her neck.

Then, she heard Aunt Marie's voice whisper in her ear, "It's so good to see you, Rebbie. But I have to say, I'm surprised to see you back so early."

"Im only here for a visit," she sighed, releasing from Marie's embrace and faking a smile, though she still refused to look Marie in the eyes. "We should talk… inside. I have something important to ask you."

"Does the fate of the world hang in the balance?" Marie asked with a chuckle.

"You could say that," Rebecca answered.

Taking Rebecca by the hand, Aunt Marie led her into the kitchen and sat her at the table before heading toward the kitchen to brew her another batch of English Breakfast.

However, before she had the chance, Rebecca took her by the wrist and said, finally looking her in the eyes, "Thank you, but I think it'll be better if we just talk."

"If you say so," Marie replied, concern spreading across her face as she sat down across from Rebecca. "What's the matter, angel? You look like you got run over by a herd of elephants."

Rebecca sighed, "Something like that. Like I said, I have something to ask you, and it's kind of a big deal."

"What do you need?"

"How's Macy?"

Immediately, Aunt Marie's face fell, and Rebecca's heart grew heavy in turn.

Macy was Aunt Marie's daughter and had always been a mainstay in the Thompson household when Rebecca was a teenager. Back then, Macy was barely high enough for the top of her head to reach the kitchen counter and still wore her hair in a pair of messy pigtails. Though they weren't necessarily close at that time, she and Rebecca spent many a night during those years playing everything from house to doctor to tea party.

But everything changed after the divorce.

It happened two years earlier, right before Macy was set to enter high school, and it hit her harder than anyone. Despite the physical resemblance she shared with her mother, which Rebecca and Elle also shared, she had always felt more connected to Frank. He made Macy feel special and, in terms of punishment, was far more lenient than her mother. So, when the courts decided to grant custody to Aunt Marie, Macy sank into seclusion. For months, she refused to speak to her mother and oftentimes wouldn't come home after school, instead electing to hang out with her friends until long past midnight. She was struggling, but no matter how hard Marie tried, Macy wouldn't open up.

After a year of rebellion and distance, Marie was at her wits end, and it only got worse after she discovered a plastic bag full of weed in the bottom of Macy's dresser.

That was when World War Three began.

Aunt Marie put her foot down, but Macy wouldn't have it. After only a week of her three month, grounding sentence, Macy ran to her father's house, convinced that he would understand. Instead of letting her stay there, however, as she expected, Frank sent her back. Another week later, she ran away for good.

"You know," Aunt Marie sighed. "A whole lot of the same."

"She still won't talk to you?" Rebecca asked.

"If she so much as sees me walking down the street, she books it in the other direction. I haven't seen her in months," Marie answered.

"Do you know where she is?"

"What kind of mother do you take me for? I've had a friend of mine keep tabs on her."

"Why don't you just call the police? I'm sure they'd bring her back home."

"All that would do is drive her further away. My daughter's a strong-willed girl, just like her hard-headed cousin," Marie said with a sad wink. "If I push too much, she'll shove back even harder. She'll figure out that I only ever wanted what was best for her, eventually. It's just a realization she has to come to on her own."

"So, where is she?" Rebecca probed.

"Why do you ask?" Aunt Marie asked in turn, a small smile pursing across her lips.

Rebecca stammered as a lump formed in her throat, "I mean, no reason, really — I just thought that-"

"The answer is yes."

"The answer to what?"

"You want to know if it's okay for you to ask Macy to come with you to Toledo. You think that, if you bring her to Paul, it might send him over the edge."

"Everyone always did say how much she and Elle look alike."

"It's a good plan," Marie said, swallowing hard. "And my

daughter's decided she's old enough to make her own decisions. It's only right to let her make this one too."

"Nothing bad will happen to her. I promise," Rebecca insisted.

"I hope you're right," Marie sighed. "But even if it does, maybe it'll be just what she needs. Last I heard, she was still hanging out under Ambassador Bridge with a group of her new friends."

Standing up from the table, Rebecca wrapped her arms around her aunt's neck and said, "Thank you, Auntie. You have no idea how much this means to me."

"I think I do," Marie choked, tears welling up in her eyes. "Elle deserves better than Macy got from Frank and I. If I had known there was a way for us to make things work before things got so out of hand, I hope someone would've been willing to do something like this for me. Just… when this is over, bring her back to me."

"I will."

{}~{}~{}~{}~{}~{}~{}~{}~{}

That afternoon, the sun hung high in the middle of a cloudless sky as Rebecca parked her car across from the Ambassador Bridge. It took only a few seconds for her to spot Macy, who was leaning against the bridge footing with three of her friends, having a smoke. Rebecca's heart leapt to her throat the second she saw her. The last time she saw Macy, she was beautiful, with long, blonde curls that fell well past the shoulder straps of the flowery sundress she always wore. She had the kind of smile that created little craters on either side of her mouth and was always joyous and full of life. She looked like a girl who had a bright future in front of her.

Now, however, she looked as though she had spent the

night sleeping in a gutter. Her hair was short, unwashed and matted, and she was dressed in a pair of dirty, ripped jeans and a pale, green jacket that looked like it hadn't been taken off in at least a month. As she blew a puff of smoke high into the sky, Rebecca stepped out onto the asphalt. Immediately, Macy's eyes shot up, wide, as though she had just heard her greatest enemy call her name, and they fell directly onto Rebecca. Then, without so much as taking a second to breathe, Macy hightailed it in the other direction, motioning frantically for her friends to follow.

Not to be denied, Rebecca ran after her but soon found herself doubled over, huffing and puffing about twenty feet behind Macy.

I knew I shouldn't have cancelled that gym membership.

Finally, in desperation, she called out, "I just want to talk!"

"You can tell my mother that I'm fine," Macy replied, whirling around to face Rebecca as her friends did the same.

"I'm not here for your mother," Rebecca insisted.

"Then we *really* have nothing to talk about," Macy said before turning around and continuing on her way.

"But what if I told you I had a place you could stay?"

Suddenly, Macy froze in her tracks, but she didn't turn around.

Instead, the camo-clad boy to Macy's right did it for her, walking up to Rebecca until her was only inches from her face and saying, "Macy's fine where she is, bitch. So why don't you just-"

"Wait," Macy ordered, placing her hand on the boy's shoulder and stepping between him and Rebecca. "What kind of place are we talking about?"

Rebecca gulped. "My... husband runs it," she said. "In Toledo. You'll have everything you need: clothes, food, a place to stay. All for nothing."

"What's the catch?" Macy asked, raising her eyebrows in suspicion.

"You just have to do a little work," Rebecca replied. "He owns a massage parlor and a salon across the street. Just give him your nine to five, and the rest of your time is yours."

"Sounds too good to be true."

"Well, you know what they say when something sounds too good to be true."

"It probably is?"

"Some say that. But, you know what I say? Even if the truth is half as good as the lie, you'd still be crazy not to at least check it out."

"You drive a hard bargain, Rebbie," Macy laughed, holding out her hand toward Rebecca. "You've got yourself a deal. But, this had better not just be a ploy to get me back to my mother's."

"Oh, trust me," Rebecca said, shaking Macy's hand. "It isn't. But, you have to promise me one thing, honey. This is my only request. If I bring you to my husband, you can't tell him you saw me. Can you do that for me?"

Macy nodded.

"Good," Rebecca continued. "Then, let's get you going."

Sometimes, the only way to cure a demon is to sell one's soul.

STARING OUT THE WINDOW WITH HIS FOREARMS RESTED ON THE kitchen counter, Florian waited for Rebecca to arrive with the fresh weight that was to be placed atop his heart. Ever since he had gotten her call, not a moment had passed when he wasn't trying to convince himself that what he was about to do was right. It went against everything in him. He could't bear to so much as think about throwing another girl into the fire, of sacrificing her on the dragon's altar. No matter how pure his intentions may have been, it just felt wrong, like daring to utter "Macbeth" before the curtain's rise.

But this is Rebecca. She wouldn't go through with this if she didn't know beyond a shadow of a doubt that this was right.

Would she?

The minutes passed like grains of sand falling to the bottom of the hourglass in zero gravity. In fact, he stood there for so long, gazing at the uncertain future held by the outside world, that the colors all blurred together, turning what once was perfect reality into what looked more like an abstract painting. Cupping his hands over his face, he pressed down on his cheeks and rubbed his wrists against his jawbone. Every molecule in his body begged for him to turn away, to dash to the front door and lock it tight. The urge pulled so hard against his bones that he almost gave in. However, just as he was about to, Janelle joined him at the counter and laid her head softly on his shoulder.

"Are you sure this is what you want?" she asked.

"No," he sighed. "But I think I might just have to."

"It's not too late to walk away."

"And I just let them continue to hurt people?"

"You're not responsible for the choices of others."

"Still, if I see a man bleeding on the side of the road and turn to walk on the other side of the street, was that not my choice? Is that man still dying because I refused to act?"

Smiling, Janelle took him by the shoulders and turned him so he could face her. "Did I ever tell you about the moment I fell in love with you?" she asked, wrapping her arms around his neck and gazing into his eyes with a twinkle that made him feel as though he was the only person in the world. "Like, when I *really* fell in love with you, not just when I told you at the motel."

"I don't think so," he answered, sliding his arms around her waist and swaying with her to the love song that played silently in both their ears.

Leaning forward and laying her head on his chest, she said, "We were standing by the alleyway, right after that adorable speech you gave when that man screamed. Any other man would have looked the other way, called the cops and left them to do the dirty work. But not you. You didn't hesitate. You didn't think about all the things that could go wrong. All you cared about was making sure he was okay. It doesn't matter that he tried to rob us. All I know is that it was at that moment I realized that my man was a hero. And seeing you now makes me so proud. You're still the man I fell in love with, running head first into danger, not thinking about yourself, concerned above all else with making sure everyone is safe."

"But what if it isn't that simple?"

"What do you mean, baby?"

"What if that's not who I am? What if I only did those things to impress you?"

"Then color me impressed."

Breaking from their slow dance, Florian turned away and ran his hands anxiously through his hair. He couldn't stand lying to her anymore, letting her believe that the love story he had scripted for them was the true story of how they had come together. He wanted to tell her that she was the true hero of their tale, not him. *She* was the knight in shining armor who had slain the dragon and set *him* free from the tallest tower. He wished she could know of the difference she had brought to his life, but he also knew that knowledge would change everything. And he couldn't stand the thought of watching the love and adoration that shone from her eyes whenever she looked at him fade into oblivion. Without that one light in his life, he would surely die.

So, he turned around, faked a smile and said, "If I'm going to do this, I'm going to have to do some things I'm not comfortable with. I need to convince them that I'm back for good. Do you think the hero in your story would do that?"

"I think he would do whatever it took to save the day," she answered, placing her hand on her cheek and leaning in for a decadent kiss on the lips.

As the taste of her lips faded from his tongue, Florian's gaze drifted back to the window, where he saw Rebecca's silver, rental car pull into the driveway. His chest grew tight, and he closed his eyes, sighing heavily. Then, after saying his goodbyes to Janelle in the form of one, last, lingering kiss to the lips, he walked out the front door and toward the dragon's lair.

As he turned the back corner of Rebecca's car, he peered into the back seat to get a look at the poor soul Rebecca had roped into acting as their sacrifice. At a quick glance, the girl looked like a near-perfect replica of what he imagined Elle would look like in about ten years. The resemblance was striking, but what was even more disturbing was that she was even dressed like Elle. She wore a short, pink skirt and white, striped blouse that was unbuttoned down to sternum. Her hair was braided in two, thick strands that fell over either shoulder, and she wore a pair of prop glasses that topped off the ensemble. The only difference between her and Elle was that, while Elle perpetually bore a dimple-inducing smile, her clone appeared frozen, uncertainty, anticipation and fear simultaneously painted across her countenance.

But, if it was a psychotic break Rebecca was going for, this girl would give Paul that in spades.

Tapping on the driver's side glass, Florian leaned into the

window to talk to Rebecca, who looked about as conflicted as he felt. "I can certainly see the family resemblance," he said.

"Well, that is, more or less, the point," she sighed.

"What do you want me to do once I drop her off?" he asked.

"We need a way to get inside his head. Seeing Macy will drive him to the edge. Knowing Paul, though, he's still going to need a little extra. I have an idea, but in order for it to work, I need to know everything."

"What do you have in mind?"

"Take this," she said, handing him a flash drive. "Install this program onto the computer in the parlor, and I'll be able to stream his camera feed onto my phone. After a few days, I should have enough to push him in whatever direction I want."

"How are you going to do that?"

"Leave that to me. Just text me when the program's up and running. I'll take care of the rest."

After that, Florian wheeled back around the car to collect Macy from the back seat and transfer her into his own car. From there, it took only thirty minutes for him to navigate the highways and byways on the way to Dragon's Wing. Though in reality, it felt much longer, considering it was done in absolute silence. Neither he nor Macy made a sound for the duration of the trip. It was as though they both felt the same tension in the air, like they were breathing in the same, polluted smoke. Soon, his lungs felt as heavy as steel, filled to the brim with a sickly brand of tar.

Pulling up to the curbside across the street from the parlor, he turned off the ignition, but he didn't get out of the car. Not yet. Once he opened those doors, he would be crossing the point of no return. And truthfully, he didn't know if he was ready. Before, he had always made his home in the grey, but now, everything in front of him looked inescapably black. He only hoped that this dark was the one that came before the dawn.

As he wrapped his fingers around the door handle, Macy spoke in a weak, shaking voice, "Is this place really as nice as Rebecca says?"

"Even better," Florian choked, swallowing the bitter taste that was in his mouth. "But it's the kind of good you have to see to believe. Trying to describe it leaves it so hollow."

"I hope you're right. After the month I've had, I could use something good for a change," she said.

"Me too," he agreed before finally opening the door and stepping out onto that familiar, nightmarish curb.

Taking Macy from the back seat, he walked her up the front steps like an executioner leading an innocent victim to the gallows. He held onto the back of her forearm with a vice-like grip, which was more due to his own trepidation than any sort of animosity. As he reached the front door, he tentatively rang the door bell before stepping back and waiting for the blade to fall.

A few seconds later, Lena opened the door. As soon as she saw Florian, her already terrifying frown turned into a deadly scowl. If looks could kill, he was convinced he would have already been dead. However, as her eyes drifted over to Macy, Lena's expression softened.

She looked Macy up and down before opening the door even wider and stepping aside to let them enter. "Good to see you, Florian," she said. "Now, don't just stand there. Come on in. Let me get a good look at our new pet."

Leaning over as Macy's shoulder as they stepped in the living room, he whispered in her ear, "Lena can be a bit of a character, but don't worry. She's just trying to be funny."

"Good work," Lena said, circling around them like a shark to its prey. "With a little training, this one looks like she could make one hell of a worker. We've got an extra bed in 3B, just upstairs. Why don't you take her up and get her ready for her first day?"

Nodding with an air of reverent submission, Florian took Macy by the arm and led her toward front door. However, as he turned her around, he nearly ran them both head first into Paul, who, upon seeing Macy, froze in his tracks with his eyes wide.

"Wh-what's she — I mean, who's this? H-how did she get here?" Paul stammered, blinking rapidly in an attempt to ensure he wasn't dreaming.

"Meet our newest recruit," Lena answered. "Florian was just about to start her training."

"Why don't you let me take care of that?" he asked as his face vacillated rapidly between concern, worry and feigned excitement.

Before Lena even had the chance to respond, Paul took Macy by the arm and dragged her anxiously across the street and straight through the doors of the salon.

Florian looked to Lena for instruction, but she just rolled her eyes and waved him off, saying, "Or you can just get to work, I guess."

With a subtle nod, Florian stepped out of Lena's apartment and onto the porch. As the door shut with a crash behind him, he hurried across the street toward the parlor with his right hand stuck inside his pants' pocket, nervously fiddling with Rebecca's flash drive. Opening the salon doors, he shot the same wink and mock salute at Monica, who was busy soliciting a rich-looking man in a fur coat, that he did every morning as he started his day. Then, he sat down at the computer and got to work. Taking the flash drive from his pocket, he stuck it in its slot and checked last week's profit spreadsheet while the program installed in the background. Before he even made it halfway through the document, the speakers dinged.

After checking around to make sure no one was watching him, he pulled out his phone and typed up a quick message to Rebecca. *Should be all set. Is it working?*

A second later, he got her reply. *Like clockwork. Good work, Florian. Thank you. I know it's hard, but you're doing the right thing.*

Now, all he had left to do was hope that he hadn't just made the biggest mistake of his life.

16

WAKING

TOLEDO, OHIO

From Lena's apartment, Paul hauled Macy across the street, through the front doors of the salon and into the back room, where, letting her go, he began to pace around the room. Furious and confused, he ran his hands through his hair and dug his nails into his scalp. He titled his head back and tried to take a deep breath, but nothing could calm the cyclone that raged inside his soul. Unable to look at her, he turned around and bent over in frustration, placing his elbows on the cold, metal filing cabinet in front of him and clasping his hands behind his neck.

"Is something wrong, Uncle Paul?" Macy asked.

You mean other than everything?!

As his grip tightened around his own neck, he felt a presence loom over his shoulder. Warm breath fell on his neck. Immediately, his spine grew cold, and his hair stood on end.

Closing his eyes, he muttered to himself, "This is a dream. Just a horrible, twisted… nightmare."

"Oh, but honey," Rebecca whispered in his ear. "This nightmare is real."

Closing his eyes and rocking back and forth, he repeated, "This is a dream."

"Then, wake up."

Enraged, Paul slammed his foot into the filing cabinet and spun around to face the phantom, but she was gone. Not a sign of her remained except for the faint echo of her voice that still resonated behind his ears. As he shook off the icicles that had formed on either side of his spine, a terrified Macy raised her hands defensively in front of her and backed away from him. He took a step forward to calm her. However, as she stepped back underneath the dark lights of the back room, he was struck by just how much she looked like Elle. He had always thought they shared a slight resemblance, but in that moment, he could have sworn he was watching his little girl's eyes fill with fear at the sight of the monster he had become. Overcome with emotion, he gulped, and his eyes welled up with tears.

"I-I'm sorry," she stammered. "I shouldn't have come. I-I'll just — I'll get going. It was good — I mean, nice to see you again."

"No, it's okay," he said, regaining his composure, closing the distance between them and placing a comforting hand on her shoulder. "It's good to see you too. I'm sorry if I scared you. I was just… surprised to see you. That's all."

"Are you sure? I don't want to stay somewhere I'm not wanted," she said. "I had enough of that back home."

As if I have a choice at this point.

With a forced smile, he reassured her, "Don't be ridiculous! You are more than welcome here, Macy, as long as you'll have us."

"Is everything I heard about this place true?"

"Depends on what Florian told you. Because, despite appearances, I'm pretty sure Lena isn't actually a fire-breathing lizard. However, I wouldn't test that hypothesis if I were you.

People have been known to get a little charred when they're around her."

"He said that, if I gave you my nine to five, I could have a place to stay, food to eat and all the new clothes I wanted."

"Then you heard right."

"What kind of work would I be doing?" she asked.

Paul choked. "You're looking at it," he replied. "I've been meaning to reorganize these files for quite some time now. It's just that, you know, with a business to run, I haven't had the time, which is why I need you. Then, once you're done with that, you can start getting all this data input into the computers so we have it all backed up. Does that sound like something you can do?"

"You want me to do math?"

"It's not so much math as it is data entry. Everything's in the files. I just need you to get it all to make sense. Do that for me, and you can have everything Florian told you about. No strings attached. So, what do you say?"

After thinking it over for a second, Macy's face lit up as she answered, "When do I start?"

"About five minutes ago," Paul said as he forced a chuckle through his closing throat. "Listen, I have a few things to take care of up front so you'll be on your own for today. So, don't worry about getting too much done over the next, few hours. Just get yourself acquainted with the room, take a look through some files and settle in. We'll get to the real work over the next few days. Think you can handle that?"

"You got it, boss," she said as she grabbed a chair from the far end of the room, sat in front of a file cabinet and started rifling through a drawer.

As Paul strode out of the back room, he couldn't hide his fury anymore. At this point, he didn't care if it was an honest mistake or a blatant attack, someone was going to pay. Darting past employees, clients and cubicle, he burst out the front door, turned the corner and blew through the parlor doors. Then, he marched up to the front desk, which he promptly leaned across, and grabbed Florian by the collar.

"You're coming with me," Paul ordered. "Now."

With little effort, he lifted Florian from the chair and dragged him out the front door with one hand. He hauled him around the corner and halfway down the alleyway to the side of the building before throwing him against the wall.

"What the hell were you thinking, bringing her here?" Paul asked, flame building up behind his eyes.

"You told me to bring a girl," Florian replied. "So I brought you one. What's the problem?"

"You did this on purpose," Paul accused.

"I don't even know what's going on!" Florian exclaimed, waving Paul off in frustration.

"Did you not see the resemblance, or did you conveniently choose not to notice?"

"Shit, she's family?"

"Where did you find her?"

"Not far outside Detroit. She was hanging with some homeless kids under a bridge. I had no idea she was related to you. How could I have?"

Wheeling on him, Paul got in Florian's face and backed him against the wall, asking accusatorially, "Why were you in Detroit?"

"I didn't have time to scout out new territory," Florian said, squeezing out from between Paul and the wall and backing away. "You gave me pretty short notice, after all. Why don't you let me take her back? I'll see if I can find another girl."

"No," Paul sighed. "It's too late. Lena's seen her, and she sure as hell won't give a shit about family ties. For now, I'm keeping her busy in the back room, reorganizing a few files.

That should keep her busy for a couple weeks until I figure something out. In the meantime, we need to make sure she doesn't leave that room except to use the bathroom or cross the street. I won't be back till the end of the day, so for today, that job falls to you. Are we clear?"

"As a bell," Florian answered as he returned to work.

At this point, Paul couldn't take it anymore. In all his distraction, his despair and pride, he had avoided going back to Detroit at all costs. Just the thought of seeing his little girl alone, mourning her mother and feeling her father's callous abandonment was more than he could stand. But now, after seeing Macy, the thought of spending another minute apart from Elle was even worse. So, marching back across the street, he hopped in his car and stuck his keys in the ignition.

But, instead of starting the engine and speeding off right away, he sat there with his hand still held tightly around his keys, unable to bring himself to move. Leaning forward, he placed his head on the steering wheel and tapped his forehead over and over again to its leather. With each moment that passed, his heart grew heavier until he felt as though he was about to collapse. So, there he stood before the point of no return, his toes hovering over the edge, staring down at the thousand-foot fall before him.

As long as he stayed in Toledo, Rebecca's death was only a story. There was still a chance at reconciliation, and Elle wasn't alone in the world. However, as soon as he took that step and breathed Detroit air again, it would all become real. Once he saw her, reality would break through the walls of fiction he had built around himself.

And he would have to deal with it, for better or for worse.

He was just about to step back out of the car and reenter his fantasy when Rebecca's voice once again echoed in his ears.

Wake up.

Those words, the same ones that had before cause shivers to run up his spine, struck an ominous chord in his soul, freezing him in place with his fingers wrapped around the door handle. Real or not, his tormentor was right; he was living in a dream. He was ignoring the truth while Elle dealt with the real pain of losing her mother. And by doing nothing, he was forcing her to do it alone. At this point, he didn't know if Rebecca had told her everything. For all he knew, Elle didn't even want to see him. Chances were high that, as soon as he stepped foot outside of Rebecca's aunt's house, he would be forced to leave, never to return.

But he had to at least try. Until he did, he would never know.

{}~{}~{}~{}~{}~{}~{}~{}~{}~{}

Detroit, Michigan

Paul pulled up to the curb about a hundred yards from Aunt Marie's house in the middle of the afternoon with the sun still hanging high above the tree line. Taking out his binoculars, he peered through the kitchen window as she and Elle were enjoying what used to be one of Paul's favorite, Saturday traditions: breakfast for lunch. Aunt Marie stood in front of the stove, whipping up a pair of western omelets while Elle sat patiently at the kitchen table, her head hung low and her mouth curved into a frown.

It broke his heart to see his precious girl so heartbroken. All he wanted to do was run up to her, wrap her up in his arms and take all her hurt away, but in order to do that, it wasn't only his pride he had to overcome; he also had to make it past Aunt Marie.

"She'll never let you in," Rebecca's voice rang condescendingly in his ears.

Dropping his binoculars, he spun around in his seat to face Rebecca's ghost, who was leaning across the space between the front seats, peering past him at the house with a wicked smile on her face.

"You know how close she and I were," she continued. "Do you really think I didn't tell her about just how much of a piece of shit you are?"

"I have to try," he said.

She laughed, "You're still determined to do this, aren't you? Damn, you really are a sadist. Good thing I'm three hundred percent down for watching you get crushed. Come on, this'll be fun! Let's get this show on the road."

Rolling his eyes, he swung the door open and stepped out onto the asphalt. As he made his way toward Aunt Marie's house, Rebecca followed closely behind, now carrying a full bucket of popcorn and munching away with every step he took.

"Hey honey, can you do me a favor?" she asked a few seconds later as she chomped on another mouthful of popcorn. "When Marie's done ripping out your heart, do you think I could have a go at it? I want to see how easily it crushes in my hands."

"Sure thing," he sighed as he reached the front steps. "And *when* she lets me in, how about you just leave me the hell alone?"

"You've got yourself a deal," she said.

As Rebecca threw a kernel into the air and caught it in her mouth, Paul pressed his finger to the doorbell and rang. A few seconds later, Aunt Marie opened the door. As soon as her eyes fell on Paul, they narrowed, fury billowing out of them like waterfalls. Checking back around her to make sure Elle wasn't close behind, she stepped out onto the porch and shut the door behind her.

Then, she asked, "What are you doing here, Paul?"

"I want to see my daughter," he answered.

"Told you she wouldn't be happy to see you," Rebecca mocked.

"And what makes you think that's something I'm about to let you do?" Marie asked, crossing her arms in front of her.

"Because a girl deserves to have her father in her life," he said. "I thought you would've understood that by now, considering that mistake is what brought Macy to my door this morning."

"That may be so," she said. "But that doesn't mean her father deserves to have her in his life. What makes you think she even wants to see you, after all you've done?"

"You told her?"

"She deserves to know the kind of monster her father truly is."

Behind him, Rebecca snorted so suddenly and so viciously that she almost choked on her popcorn.

Once she cleared her throat, she laughed, "Is that her hand going through your ribcage, or are you just that crushed?"

"Please," Paul said, reaching out and taking Marie by the arm. "I've already lost Rebecca. You can't take Elle away from me too."

But Marie just shook her head as she reached back to open the door and stepped inside the house. "I'm not," she replied with a sigh. "You did that on your own."

With that, the door closed, and Paul was left alone on the porch with his heart in pieces on the threshold and his blood seeping through the slats of the porch.

"Aw damn," Rebecca said, setting her popcorn on the

railing and picking the fragments of his heart off the ground. "Looks like she already got it pretty good."

"Why don't you just leave me the hell alone?" Paul asked as he stormed back to his car, trying to shove her aside but once again finding his arm passing right through her.

And in that moment, the truth became abundantly clear; he had lost everything. He had awoken from his nightmare only to find that the world he opened his eyes to was worse than the one that lay behind his eyelids.

17

PRESSURE

LOS ANGELES, CALIFORNIA

*W*ith unbound ferocity, Bradie pounded at the door to Loman's downtown apartment as the sun painted the sky with its morning glory. This was not the reunion he had been hoping to have with his old friend. It should have been a happy occasion with high fives and hugs all around as well as an exorbitant dinner that neither of them could afford. Even under the circumstances, Bradie had wanted to wait until lunch hour before storming through Loman's doors like a wolf in pursuit of its prey. That way, Loman could have at least enjoyed a few hours of what Bradie knew was his only day off before feeling the weight of the Spanish Inquisition fall on his head. However, that morning had found Bradie pacing back and forth across his hotel room floor hours before sunrise, and he couldn't wait any longer. This was no time for decorum. Anna was missing, and nothing mattered other than finding her.

He would rain down the wrath of God on Loman's head if necessary.

After two minutes spent trying to knock the door from its

hinges and ignoring the shouts and complaints from angry neighbors, the door finally opened. Behind it, Loman stood, dressed in a bathrobe and rubbing his eyes.

"Where is he?" Bradie asked, blowing past Loman and into his living room.

"And a good morning to you too," Loman yawned as he stumbled back into his wall, nearly toppling over from the hurricane force winds formed by Bradie's passing.

Patting Loman on the shoulder, Nina squeezed through the doorway as she whispered, "At least he didn't drag you out of bed by both feet while it was still dark out."

"I'm loving the bathrobe, Loman. It's very Playboy mansion," Stacy laughed, following closely behind Nina.

"Well, it was either this or the full monty," Loman said as he closed the door behind them. "But I figured I'd spare you the horror show."

Quickly losing patience, Bradie turned on Loman, backing him against the wall. "Where is he?!" he demanded.

"Your dad just left," Loman answered, placing his hands gingerly on Bradie's shoulders and moving him out of the way. "But he wanted me to let you know that he really enjoyed my company."

As Loman took his hands from Bradie's shoulder, Bradie latched angrily onto his wrist and said, "You know who I'm talking about, partner. Anna's pimp, where is he?"

"What's this all about?"

"Anna's gone."

"Shit, are you serious?"

"Two of his men grabbed her, not even a minute after you called me."

Suddenly, Loman's face twisted into an expression that bordered between horrified and as though he had just been stabbed in the back by his closest friend. "And you think I had something to do with it," he said.

"Not at first," Bradie replied. "But Nina said some things that really got me thinking."

"In my defense, I'm a journalist. It's my job to assume that everybody sucks," Nina said.

Ignoring her, Bradie continued, "It's been seven months since I left town, seven months. You've had that long to find him. And for every one of those two-hundred plus days, you've given me nothing. You didn't answer my calls and ignored every email I sent. Hell, you didn't even find the time to shoot me a text, just to give me an update. But now, now that I'm back in town with Anna by my side, you find him, which would be awesome if your call hadn't been immediately followed by *my daughter* getting kidnapped. Forgive me if I'm out of line, but if it stinks like a pile of shit, it probably is one."

"What about you?" Loman asked, turning to Stacy. "Do you think I was involved in this?"

To which she replied, "I don't know what to think right now."

"Personally, I'm only about seventy-five, twenty-five that you're a kidnapping asshole," Nina said. "Though, I'm sure my opinion doesn't hold that much weight right now."

Sighing, Loman shuffled over to the couch, sat down and said, "Five years together. We spent five years in that squad car, side by side, and you still think I would do that to you?"

"If these last seven months have shown me anything, it's that you can't give anyone the benefit of the doubt, especially those you think don't have it in them," Bradie answered.

"Prove us wrong," Stacy said as she sat beside Loman and placed her hand on his shoulder.

"I'm sorry I didn't call sooner," Loman said. "There were just so many dead ends for so long that I didn't want to get your hopes up before I knew for sure. The truth is, I had all but given up on her case. The files were sealed up in a box on my desk, ready to be stored with the rest of the cold cases when I got a call."

"From who?" Bradie asked.

Loman sighed, "I wish I knew. The line went dead before I could get a name. She said she got my number off a business card I left with a friend of hers. After that, all she gave me was an address and assured that *he* would be there."

"Which was when you called."

"It was my first, legitimate lead since you left, and I heard about all the shit that went down in Detroit. I figured you could use a win, but honest, I had no idea they were going after Anna."

"They played me."

"They played us both, partner."

"The men at The Ranch must have given her pimp a call right after we showed up," Nina explained.

"And he knew just how to throw us off our game," Stacy said.

"Did you find anything at the address she gave you?" Bradie asked.

"Nothing useful," Loman answered. "Just a matchbook, a used condom and a shattered mirror. Other than that, it was bare, wiped down and totally useless. I couldn't even find a fingerprint."

"Shit!" Bradie screamed, slamming his fist into the couch cushions. "You've got to be kidding me!"

"I'm sorry, buddy. I wish I had more for you," Loman said.

"What kind of matchbook was it?" Nina asked.

"It was from Man of L.A. Mancha," Loman answered. "A bar down on the west side of the city. I went in and asked around, but I got nothing. Just another dead end."

"All right then, let's check it out," Bradie said, taking Stacy by the hand and leading her toward the door.

As they got to the doorway, Loman jumped from the couch and ran after them. "And I'm coming too," he announced.

"You don't have to do that," Bradie replied.

"An old friend comes to town after his adopted daughter's been kidnapped, and you expect me to sit on the sidelines?" Loman asked. "You must not know me at all."

"For all I know, you could just be leading us on a wild goose chase. How can I trust you?"

"At this point, I guess you can't. But I'm coming either way."

"And I'm not going to be able to stop you, am I?"

"I'd like to see you try."

"Fine. You can tag along, but I'm running point," Bradie said.

"Wouldn't have it any other way," Loman replied. "So, how do you propose we get them to talk? Everyone was pretty tight-lipped when I was there last."

"We don't," Bradie answered.

"I do," Nina said, breezing past both of them and striding down the hallway with a confident strut as her hips swung from side to side with a familiar, practiced flair.

Fortunately, when Nina first told Bradie about the talk show, Anna had a feeling that there might be some undercover work involved and had packed both of their outfits from when they had gone to see Henry Maxwell. Adding to their fortune was the fact that Anna and Nina were roughly the same size, give or take a few inches. So, after stopping by the local Grittles and Bits for a quick bite of breakfast, Nina and Bradie hopped into the bathroom to slip into their disguises while Loman and Stacy waited in the car. Then, they headed off to Man of L.A. Mancha.

As they stepped out of the car and onto the curb outside the bar, which was, unsurprisingly, only a few blocks down from the First National Bank, where he and Anna had first met, Bradie couldn't help but feel a sense of ominous familiarity in the air. Like Illuminate, Man of L.A. Mancha stood out from every building around it, although the way they differentiated themselves made them the inverse of each other. While Illuminate was a star in the night, the only modern-looking building in a rundown sea, L.A. Mancha was surrounded on every side by bright, sleek buildings. But even still, it stood out, as though it was a remnant from a time long lost.

It was small in stature, standing a full, three stories shorter than every other building on the street, and was made of aged oak, as though it had been built from the ashes of a California brushfire. Even its sign was covered in only a slightly lighter shade of brown with a large, running windmill on the roof being the only part of the building which truly felt like it belonged this close to Hollywood.

And the inside was built to match.

Centered around a burnt mahogany stage in the middle of the room, the tavern earned every iota of its namesake, with its chili pepper carpets and cowboy hats and bull horns that covered the length of the walls. On the left side sat the bar, which was stocked full of every kind of liquor imaginable, and on the right, there was a life-size, mechanical bull surrounded by plastic, gym mats, a padded wall and a slew of tables and chairs, which took up every last inch of the remaining space.

Well, doesn't this look awfully familiar.

That morning, as Nina and Bradie breezed through the front, saloon-style doors, the bar was mostly empty, apart from a large, tattooed man behind the bar and a few, grey-haired patrons sitting at the bar stools.

"The bartender's name is Samuel Burns, but everyone calls him 'Smokey,'" Loman said through their earpieces.

Reaching the bar, Bradie sat down at one of the stools and rested his cane against the bar's lip while Nina stood to the side, munching demonstrably on the stick of gum she had stuck in her mouth seconds before they entered the building. Smokey, who to this point had been turned away from the front door, mixing a trio of drinks, turned to serve his customers, and his eyes immediately fell on Bradie. Upon seeing Bradie's bright purple ensemble, Smokey burst out laughing, nearly dropping his drinks on the floor.

A few seconds later, after delivering his drinks off to their destinations, Smokey shuffled over to Bradie, obviously trying to contain his amusement. "What's your poison, Petunia?" he asked.

"Thanks for the offer, Smokey," Bradie replied in the gruffest Southern accent he could muster. "But I'm here for business, not pleasure."

"You hoping to have your girl perform?" Smokey asked, glancing over at Nina, who smiled and shot him a flirtatious wink.

"That's one way of putting it," Bradie answered.

"Uh… yeah, sure thing, Eggplant."

"He's not biting," Loman said. "You're going to have to drop a name. Tell him Aster sent you."

"Aster said that you were the man who could hook me up," Bradie said.

Suddenly, Smokey's face grew dark, and his eyes lit with fire. Placing his hands on top of the bar, he leaned over until he was face to face with Bradie and growled, "I told that bastard I didn't want to have anything to do with his business. So, you tell him Smokey said that if I see another one his goons inside my bar, he'll be scraping their blood off my bull's horns himself. You've got five seconds to get out of my sight. Five. Four. Three…"

Bradie didn't give him the chance to get to two. Standing up and taking Nina by the hand, he led them out of the bar and marched straight toward their car, which was parked a half block down the road. When they reached the driver's side door, he swung it open and threw himself into the front seat.

Then, he whirled violently upon Loman, who was sitting in the back, and asked, "What the hell was that?!"

"I took a chance," Loman replied. "There was whisper on the street about a man named Aster running the trafficking underworld."

"And you thought that was the time to test your theory?"

"Well, it worked, didn't it? Now, we know two things; first, Anna's not at L.A. Mancha, and second and more importantly, whoever has her is somehow connected to this bar. All we have to do is figure out how."

∿

New York, New York

NATASHA LEANED UP AGAINST THE WALL ON THE BACK SIDE OF THE church, watching the clouds dance the tango across the morning sky. Hand in hand, they spun and swayed together to the rhythm of the wind as they filled their heavenly dance floor with tantalizing motions. As she continued to watch, breathless, she felt the story they told move through her bones. It was a story of love, of joy and above all, freedom, one that she hoped she would soon be living.

As she stood there, enraptured by the celestial scene, Father McCreedy, one of the more seasoned priests, sidled next to her, dressed in a bright, Hawaiian shirt and khaki shorts. Natasha couldn't help but chuckle at the sight of the man, who, over the week she had spent at the church, she had come to know as the most serious man she had ever met, dressed like a tourist whose deck was several cards short of full. She looked over at him, and immediately, every muscle in his five-foot frame tensed up.

For three minutes, they stood in silence, neither of them saying a word, though it wasn't for a lack of trying on Father McCreedy's part. Over that time, he looked over at Natasha a total of seven times, by her count, and opened his mouth in the attempt to say something, but every time he tried, his vocal cords remained locked tighter than Fort Knox.

Unable to stand the awkwardness anymore, Natasha broke the silence. "Hey there," she said in a breathy tone as she turned to him, sticking her hips out to the side. "What can I do for you, stud?"

"I — uh…" he stuttered, turning an uncomfortable shade of red. "I was — well, if you wanted — I though that maybe we could, you know, go somewhere… quieter?"

She chuckled flirtatiously, "And once we got there, what kinds of things would you like to do?"

Immediately, his eyes grew wide as he gulped, "Things."

"What kinds of things?"

"Bedroom… things?"

With a sudden burst, Natasha bent toward until she was mere inches from Father McCreedy. Grabbing him by the collar, she pulled him closer, bringing his ear to her lips.

Then, she whispered seductively, allowing as much of her breath as possible to tickle the grey hairs on the side of his lobe, "You won't believe the *things* I'm going to do to you."

At the touch of her breath, his cheeks flushed, and his skin turned hot. He tried to take a deep breath, but the frog in his throat caught hold of each atom of hot air, forbidding that he manage to take a single breath for what seemed like an eternity.

"I think I'm going to need a cold shower," he replied before finally breaking character. "Did you like that?"

"Why don't you ask them?" Natasha replied, turning to Violet, the hoodie and the rest of the priests, all of whom were holding their hands in front of their mouths in an attempt to keep from laughing.

"Did I — did I do okay?" Father McCreedy asked.

Suddenly, the entire group erupted with a chorus of raucous laughter. Violet doubled over, clutching her stomach. The priests turned to each other and placed their hands on each other's shoulders, trying to keep themselves from falling over. Father Christopher shook his head with an amused chuckle, and even the hoodie couldn't bring himself to keep a straight face. Throwing his head back, he cackled into the open air. Then, his knees buckled, and he tumbled to the ground, flailing his arms as legs as he literally rolled on the floor, laughing.

Turning to her pupil, Natasha assured him, "That was your best attempt yet. At least you didn't offer to pray for me this time."

"I'm never going to get this right," Father McCreedy sighed, hanging his head in shame.

"You were so close," she said, smiling at him before addressing the group. "Remember, it doesn't have to be perfect. I'm not expecting any of you to give the performance of a life-time tonight. You don't have to be the perfect, pardon my French, asshole. All you need to do is make it inside your girl's room. If you have to, let her do all the talking. None of them are going to care as long as they think they're getting one mark closer to their quota. If you're nervous, that's okay. Use it to your advantage. In my day, I saw a lot of first-timers. Believe me, it was not uncommon for them to turn a little red. And you can refer to sex as a lot of things. Just… not 'bedroom things.' That might raise an eyebrow or two. So, is everyone ready for round two? We're four hours from show time. Let's split off into groups. Left side, go with Violet. Everyone else, stay with me. We're going to get this right."

"And no cold showers until it's mission accomplished," Father Christopher teased as the group split off.

{}~{}~{}~{}~{}~{}~{}~{}~{}~{}

That night, Natasha stood with Violet and the hoodie in the alley across from the warehouse, cloaked by the shadows, and waited for the last of their pieces to fall into place. So far, eleven of the twelve priests had made it inside the warehouse, leaving only Father McCreedy to go. Natasha's lungs tightened as she watched him approach Jasmine, the only girl, apart from Theresa, who had yet to be solicited. Though she knew Jasmine would be, by far, the easiest mark of the night, she couldn't help but feel nervous now that McCreedy was with a real pro.

As Father McCreedy tapped Jasmine on the shoulder, Violet and the hoodie crowded over Natasha's shoulders to watch. Jasmine turned to him, biting her lip seductively, and ran her finger down the side of his arm. His eyes grew wide as she grabbed his hand, leaned in and whispered in his ear. After that, he didn't blink. He didn't speak. All he could do was nod, which wasn't much, but it was enough. Jasmine smiled, laced her fingers with his and led him into the warehouse.

The stage was set, and all that was left to do was wait.

Once the priests were inside the warehouse, that was when the plan really began. Earlier that afternoon, Natasha gave them specific, detailed instructions for what they were to do. As soon as they made it inside their assigned girl's room, they were to drop their charade immediately and tell them that Natasha had sent them, in case any of the girls got spooked. Then, they were to detail every aspect of the plan their girl before asking them to distract Alexei for exactly fifteen seconds while they high-tailed it into an empty storage room toward the middle of the room, where they would wait for their cue. That way, once the final play was set in motion, every girl in the warehouse would have a priest who could take them to safety.

All of the girls, that is, except for Theresa. Violet and Natasha wanted to personally see to it that she was taken care of once the hoodie's part was done.

Ten minutes later, Natasha turned to the hoodie, placed both hands on his shoulders and asked, "Are you ready for this?"

"I was ready the moment you stepped your whore ass out of the state," he replied as he brushed her off and stepped out of the alleyway.

He didn't make it very far, however, before Natasha darted after him, seizing him by the wrist. "Remember," she implored. "All I need to do is give us enough time to get the girls out. We don't need any complications."

"Don't worry. I'll get you your time."

With that, he shook her off and marched across the street, his eyes set on the warehouse. And in that moment, though she couldn't explain why, Natasha couldn't help but feel that, some-how, bringing him along would prove to be their undoing.

But, a card laid was a card played. She had no choice but to let the hand play out the way she dealt it.

Violet and Natasha followed quickly, yet slowly, behind the hoodie as he burst through the crimson, iron curtain and into the warehouse. Stepping onto the sidewalk only seconds behind him, they scurried to the door, placing themselves on either side of it, and waited for the hoodie to divert Alexei's attention. Meanwhile, a clamor rose up on every side of them. On both sides, most of the girls, who to this point had been outside the building, searching for their marks and waiting for the moment of truth, started to whisper amongst themselves.

Soon, the entire side of the street was brimming with both excitement and terror. Even Natasha couldn't keep her heart from racing with anticipation.

Crouching quietly beside the door, Natasha and Violet slid it open without a sound. Then, they peered inside. As they did, they saw Alexei and the hoodie halfway down the hallway in the middle of a shoving match. However, to Natasha's surprise, it was the hoodie who did most of the shoving as he bobbed and weaved around, beneath and over Alexei's flailing arms. Whenever one of Alexei's swings missed, the hoodie slammed his shoulder into Alexei's stomach, pushing him back. This pattern continued for a few moments until finally, the hoodie landed a right hook to Alexei's jaw and sent him crashing to the ground

Without delay, Natasha and Violet made their move.

They dashed through the door, weaving around confused clients who were simply standing in the hall, eagerly watching the gladiator match. Then, the two of them zipped through a space in the curtain and into Theresa's room. Flinging the curtains open, they found Theresa lying naked on the bed in the middle of servicing a thin, disrobed man, who lay over top of her, slamming his hips into her over and over again. Without so much as giving him a chance to land another thrust, Violet ripped him off of Theresa while Natasha gently lifted Theresa to her feet.

Immediately, the thin man shook Violet off and exclaimed, "What the hell, bitch?! I paid good money for her!"

"Why don't you find a picture of some skank to jack off to, pervert?" Violet said, grabbing the man's clothes from the floor and shoving them into his arms.

As the man stumbled angrily out of the room, clutching his clothes to his chest, Theresa struggled to maintain her balance, muttering, "What's going on? Natasha?"

"No time to explain," Natasha said as she snatched the sheets from Theresa's bed and wrapped them around her. "We're getting you out of here."

Just then, they heard the hoodie's voice echo over the crests of the curtains, yelling, "You'll pay for crossing me!"

That was the signal. With both of their arms wrapped around Theresa's shoulders, Natasha and Violet rushed her out of her curtain and into the hallway, where what seemed like a horde of half-dressed girls, priests and angry customers flooded through every inch in a furious procession that was headed toward the front door. Quickly, Violet and Theresa joined the fray. But, as they reached the front door, Natasha turned back to check on the hoodie, who was standing over Alexei on the far end of the building with what looked like a gun trained to Alexei's forehead.

Immediately, Natasha took off after the hoodie, hoping to talk him off the ledge, but Violet grabbed onto her arm and urged, "We have to go."

"Get Theresa out of here," Natasha responded. "I'll meet you at the church. Just go."

As Violet rushed Theresa out the door, Natasha darted down the hallway toward the hoodie, yelling, "It's done! Just knock him out, and let's get going."

However, he paid her no attention, choosing instead to press the gun further into Alexei's temple, tilt it to the side and lean in close. "Have any last words, commie bitch?" he whispered.

"What are you doing?" Natasha asked, grabbing the hoodie by the shoulder and trying to pull him back.

But he didn't budge. Though she tugged at him with all her might, he didn't waver.

He simply stared Alexei in the eyes and said, "What I should have done the first time I met this asshole."

"This wasn't part of the plan," she insisted.

"Maybe not yours," he replied. "But this was *always* my plan."

"It figures," Alexei choked as he spit a giant wad of blood and spit at the hoodie's feet. "You don't have enough balls to come up with plan on your own. Poor, little man, always following lead of cowardly bitches."

"Don't listen to him. He's just trying to get inside your head," Natasha warned the hoodie.

Alexei laughed, "Let weak man dig his own grave, Natasha."

"No," she replied. "I won't let him throw his life away."

"You will do as told, whore!"

"I'm done taking orders from you, Alexei. You don't own me anymore."

"You think that, but you will always be mine."

"No!" she screamed, her hands shaking.

Surprised by her outburst, the hoodie turned to Natasha, loosened his grip around the pistol and asked in a strangely calming tone, as though he was seeing her for the first time, "He really hurt you, didn't he? I've only been thinking of myself when, really, it should be you doing the honors. Here, do it. Right between the eyes, like this bitch deserves."

Hesitantly, Natasha took the gun in her hands, planning to simply take it and leave the second the hoodie let go. However, as she stood there, with the gun resting against Alexei's temple and the balance of his life hanging between her fingertips, something strange and powerful began to course through her veins. She rested her finger on the trigger and took a deep breath. With everything she had, she fought against the darkness that raged inside her soul, urging her to fire. Finally, a moment later, she lowered the gun and determined to let Alexei wallow in the fact that, though he was alive, she had still beaten him.

But just then, Alexei looked up, and his eyes met Natasha's. They were black and empty, just like Thirteen's. Ebon smoke spilled out of his sockets, completely enveloping the air around his head.

Instinctively, Natasha twitched, and he smiled. "I should've known you didn't have it you," he said. "Whore, I should have killed you when-"

Bang!

Quickly and, this time, without hesitation, she raised the gun and pulled the trigger. The shot rang out across the warehouse, echoing throughout the space as Alexei's body slumped to the floor. Horrified, Natasha dropped the gun and covered her ears in an attempt to quell the vicious ringing that pounded at her eardrums like a thousand hammers against a single nail. Hands shaking, she backed away. She couldn't believe what she had just done but, at the same time, felt incredibly invigorated by the finality of it all.

And that was the part that scared her the most.

As she made her way out the warehouse doors, Violet tapped Natasha urgently on the shoulders, asking, "What took you so long? Come on, let's go!"

"He's dead," Natasha muttered, barely registering anything around her except for Alexei's lifeless body that she could still see through the open, warehouse door.

"Shit," Violet said. "Are you serious?"

"It all happened so fast."

"Well, good riddance. The bastard deserved it."

"Yeah, I suppose he did."

And as Natasha walked away from the warehouse that night, she looked down at her hands, which were now as black as tar. Dark, watery tendrils pulsed and flowed around them, seeping in and out of her skin as it encased her arms in darkness. She could feel it flow, simultaneously scorching and cold, through her veins, her marrow, her very being.

When she left Minnesota, she thought she had escaped the darkness, but instead, it had infected her, seeped into her soul. Now, the darkness wasn't simply around her.

She *was* the darkness.

> *I thought I was free,*
> *Didn't think of the cost.*
> *In my complacency,*
> *All light I have lost.*
> *With no will but my own,*
> *I took up arms to fight.*
> *But now the sun's left me alone,*
> *For I have become the night.*

SHE DID IT. SHE ACTUALLY DID IT.

As Natasha shuffled away from the warehouse, her head down and her shoulders slumped, Violet stayed behind, shocked that the cautious, timid girl she had come to know over the past week actually had the gall to take the life of the man who had stolen hers. A pang of jealousy washed across Violet's chest, along with the heavy weight of sorrow. Theresa was free. Luther got his revenge, and even Natasha had managed to take control of her life back. Everyone around her was getting everything they had ever wanted, and, as much as she wanted to be happy for them, Violet couldn't help but feel that she had been cheated of the one thing that could give her even the slightest bit of release: revenge.

If only I could get my hands on Natasha's gun.

Breathing a sigh of defeat, Violet started after the group, her eyes instinctively drifting to Natasha's waistband in search of the gun. However, it was nowhere to be found, not in her hands, not around her waist, not even under the lip of her boots. And it was in that moment that Violet came to a realization.

The gun was still in the warehouse.

As the group rounded the corner, Violet took a step back and waited for a minute to ensure she wouldn't be followed. Then, once she was convinced she was alone, she turned around and tiptoed through the door to the warehouse, excitement and anticipation coursing like lightning through her veins. Reaching the midpoint of the warehouse, she saw it. Lying in a sea of a maniac's blood, her salvation glimmered beneath the fluorescent lights and shone like a beacon in the night, drawing her to itself.

She reached out hesitantly, grabbing hold of the gun and holding it in front of her. Turning it over in her hands, she gazed upon its dark, metallic surface, and in an instant, a monstrous, desperate hunger settled inside her stomach, growling like a beast about to pounce. Suddenly, the gleaming plastic she held in her hand became as much a part of her as her own skin. The truth was, as much as she tried to deny it, she needed that gun. She needed revenge.

She needed to find that bitch and make her pay for what she did to Kayde.

18

HAPPINESS
TOLEDO, OHIO

"*Y*ou're kidding me!" Blair snorted, laughing, as she sat across from Cici at Milk King, their newfound favorite dessert stop, and took another bite out of her leaning tower of caramel covered brownies.

"I shit you not," Ciara replied, digging into her own, triple-scoop of rocky road. "Somehow, Frankie managed to literally strap himself to the ceiling fan and was spinning around the room like a frickin' whirlybird! By the time I woke up, he had been up there for fifteen minutes, and the whole room was covered in half-chewed waffles and puke."

"Your parents must have been furious," Blair said.

"Well, they would have been... if they ever found out," Cici said.

"How did you hide that from them?"

"Let's just say it involved a shitload of paper towels and so much bleach that I smelled it for days."

"Damn, Frankie must have been grateful to have a sister like you around to clean up his messes."

"And yet, I still found five, dead frogs inside my pillowcase the next morning."

"That ungrateful bastard!"

"That's just brothers. What, you're telling me you don't have a shithead brother of your own?"

"Yeah," Blair sighed. "But he wasn't really the prankster, risk-taker type…"

Setting her empty bowl to the side, Cici leaned across the table and squinted at Blair. "Okay, what gives?" she asked. "We've been hanging out for two weeks now, and I've now counted three things you downright refuse to talk about: your job, what brought you to Toledo and your family. You gotta level with me, B-loves, are you a secret agent or something? Am I gonna find a dossier or some shit with just your name and a shit ton of black scrawled across it?"

Ashamed, Blair looked away, tears welling up in her eyes. The truth of the matter was that Cici was right. Over the two weeks they had spent together, which, truthfully, had been two of the best of Blair's life, they had talked about everything, from politics to movies to sex and bathroom habits. But every time their talks grew personal, Blair found herself doing anything she could to keep the spotlight off of herself. All she wanted to do was forget, even if it was only for a few hours every night. At the salon, she couldn't get away from it. There, the shame and despair covered her like sludge. Desperately, she wanted to tell her everything, to spill her guts all over the floor of the ice cream shop, but she also knew that Cici wouldn't understand, not in the way she needed. It was moments like these that she missed Natasha more than she could bear.

Blair opened her mouth to, once again, deflect the attention off of herself, but before she could, Cici reached across the table, placing her hand on top of Blair's, and said, "You know you can talk to me about anything, right? I'm in your corner, Blair. You ain't got nothin' to be ashamed of with me."

"It's..." Blair gulped, trying to smile, albeit weakly, at Ciara. "It's just that my brother... Kayde. He — it's all my fault! He's gone because of me, and now he's never coming back!"

Unable to hold the tears back any longer, Blair fell forward and buried her face into the table, hoping to hide her sorrow behind her outstretched arms. But the hysterical sobs that escaped her throat, like a herd of frogs in an empty swamp, betrayed her. Soon, a murky river of snot and tears flowed like a flood down the edge of the table, dripping steadily onto her shoes, which sat directly underneath her.

Immediately, Cici rushed to her side, kneeling beside her, picking her off the table and taking all of Blair's weight upon herself. Though Blair continued to fight to keep herself together, it was no use. She was a shattered puzzle with all of her pieces strewn across the floor, and Cici had no hope of ever picking up all the pieces.

"I'm so sorry," Cici whispered, her voice cracking beneath her own, trickling tears. "I can't even imagine how hard that must be for you, but I'm here. I'm always here, and I'll do whatever it takes to help you. Hell, I'll carry you if that's what you need. You got that, B-loves? All the way to Mordor and back. Now, how about we get you some fresh air? I think everyone thinks I just proposed."

Snorting back yet another bubble of snot and chuckling through her sorrow, Blair lifted her head from Cici's shoulder and nodded. Planting her hands on the table, she lifted herself up as Cici slid underneath her shoulder to help. Then, they grabbed what remained of Blair's brownie platter and walked out the front doors to a mixed reaction of silent claps from most of the crowd, except for one, suspender-wearing, old man in the corner, who stared at them as they left with a deadly portion of side eye.

As the parlor door closed behind them, Blair wiped her eyes, a small smile spreading across her face. "Did you see the look on that guy's face?" she giggled.

"He's just jealous because we make such a damn sexy couple," Ciara said, nudging Blair playfully with her hips before taking on a more serious expression. "So, you want to talk about it?"

"I don't know," Blair sighed.

"Hey," Cici said, jumping out in front of Blair and placing both hands on her shoulders. "I meant what I said in there. You can talk to me about anything. I don't care about whatever baggage you come with. I care about you, okay?"

"I know you do. It's just... bad stuff tends to happen to people I care about. I don't want that to happen to you too."

"Isn't that my decision to make, Care Bear? I'm a big girl. I can take it."

"You wouldn't say that if you knew."

"Why don't you give me the chance?"

"All right fine," Blair said, shaking her head. "I got involved with... the wrong crowd a couple years ago. They convinced me to run away from home, and not long after that, I wound up in New York, all alone and convinced that everyone had given up on me. Except my brother never did. He crossed the country to find me and bring me back home, but in the process, he got on the wrong side of those same people. It happened a few weeks ago. We ran, and they — they shot him. Now, he's dead, and it's all my fault."

"Damn, that's heavy, Blair. That's a heavy weight to carry on your shoulders, but you can't blame yourself for that. It wasn't your finger pulling the trigger," Cici said.

"It might as well have been. He only got mixed up in that shit because of me."

"It's a bad rub. There's no skirting around that, but cause and effect ain't linear like that. There's still a lot of bad shit that had to go down to bring him to that place, right? Are you gonna go around laying blame on every person he came into contact with between you leaving and how it all ended?"

"I guess not."

"Exactly! In the end, what happened to him is the fault of one person and one person alone: the ass-trunk at the other end of that bullet."

"You make it sound so simple," Blair chuckled uncomfortably.

"That's 'cause it is, Boo," Cici replied with a comforting smile, linking arms with Blair as they continued to stroll together down the sidewalk. "So, is that why you came to Toledo? To get away from the bad shit you got involved with?"

"Yeah," Blair sighed.

"You don't sound to happy about that."

"It's complicated."

"You left someone behind back there, didn't you? Someone you cared about."

"Am I really that open of a book to you?"

"You just gotta know how to read the signs."

"I didn't so much as leave her behind as she left me," Blair explained. "Not that I blame her for it. I basically forced her out so she could make a break for it while she still could."

"But you're afraid that, now that you've left, she won't be able to find you if she comes looking," Cici said.

"Pretty much," Blair replied, staring off into the night sky.

Placing a hand on Blair's cheek, Cici stopped her and looked her in the eyes. "If she cares about you as much as you do for her, she'll won't give up until she finds you," she said. "I know I wouldn't."

{}~{}~{}~{}~{}~{}~{}~{}~{}~{}

That night, Blair hopped off the bus across the street from Dragon's Wing, feeling a hundred pounds lighter. Though talking to Cici may not have changed anything, she had forgotten how good it felt to not hold onto that burden by herself any longer, to no longer be the only person standing inside of the storm. It was a weightlessness she hadn't felt since Natasha left New York. For the first time in ages, she had hope, and she felt free.

It was a freedom, however, that didn't last long.

As she took her first step up the stairs that led to her apartment, a firm hand grasped her wrist and pulled her back. Turning around, Blair found Lena standing behind her with her arms crossed and the heels of her boots tapping against the porch at an anxiety-inducing rhythm.

"How goes it in the outside world?" Lena asked, her expression cold and her tone icy.

"Oh, it's — uh — actually, fantastic," Blair stuttered. "I haven't enjoyed myself like this in quite a long time. Thank you for allowing me the opportunity."

"Don't thank me yet. There's still the matter of repayment," Lena said.

"Repayment?" Blair asked. "But Paul said-"

"Yes, I know what Paul said. As long as you work hard every day and make it back every night for a month, this arrangement could continue with some provisions. However, I am spending a lot of money to give you this privilege, and I expect something in return for my kindness."

"Lena, please. I haven't had the time."

"You have had three weeks. Are you telling me you haven't made a single friend in twenty-one days?"

"Well, I mean, I have, but-"

"Then you shouldn't have a problem finding me a new play thing by the end of next week."

"A week? But I was told I had the first month just to see how it worked," Blair said. "I should have ten days still."

"And now I'm changing the rules. Do you have a problem with that?" Lena asked as she backed Blair slowly against the side of the house.

"No, ma'am," Blair replied as she looked down, more out of fear than reverence.

"Good," Lena whispered. "Because, if I don't see you back here with a new girl by the end of the week, I'll have to reconsider all of the privileges you've been afforded. Are we understood?"

"Yes, ma'am." Blair nodded as Lena marched back down the porch steps, leaving her to return to her room, alone.

And that night, she fell asleep, feeling that old ball and chain wrapped around both her hands and her feet once again.

19

POWER

TOLEDO, OHIO

A choral cacophony of shouts, screams and the distant beating of drums filled the otherwise empty air. Startled, Paul opened his eyes and immediately found himself lying face down on a cold, metal platform. On every side, iron, prison bars trapped him inside a deadly cage, every inch of which was enveloped by flowing streams of black and white lightning that crackled across its surface, dancing to the rhythm of the drums, which grew louder and more chaotic by the moment. Even the floor beneath his feet warped and swayed to the beat, and beyond his cell, everything was black.

As he raised his arms in front of him, he saw that the skin on his arms was raw and cracked, covered in scales like vines that ran across every inch of his exposed skin. Backing away in horror, he felt his back run against the prison bars behind him. As soon as he grazed against their surface, a brilliant surge of electricity raged down his spine and through his feet into the ground beneath him. It was simultaneously excruciating and exhilarating, scorching and soothing. In that moment, immense power surged through his bones and resonated throughout his entire body, evidenced by the arcs of lightning that leapt between the scales on his arms, shedding shards of his skin in their wake.

Meanwhile, an equally powerful sensation, like fire mixed with liquid nitrogen, fought with the lightning for control over his body. In equivalent arcs, bands of darkness flowed directly behind the lightning, rebuilding every set of scales that the lightning had shed. As the power coursed through his veins, his body grew as cold as the arctic before catching fire again. Looking down at his hands, which now pulsed with the same black and white lightning as his prison bars, Paul felt himself become one with his cage. He walked to the edge of it and brought his hands to the bars, and to his surprise, there was no shock, no pain, not even a buzz. This time, instead of punishing him, the light and darkness used him as a conduit, flowing through his arms, down his chest, into the ground and back again as freely as they pleased.

With his hands still latched onto the bars, Paul gazed into the void before him, where, in the distance, he saw a faint light hovering within the black skies, like a firefly in the midst of a field at night, small and unassuming. However, soon it began to move toward him, pulsating and growing until it was right in front of him, life-sized and fully illuminated. Within the light, there sat a room, no larger than the suites at Dragon's Wing. Against the far wall, a single bed stood beside an old, oak dresser, surrounded by pale yellow walls that were completely empty, aside from a single painting that hung, uneven, above the headboard.

Suddenly, the door to the room creaked open, and a greasy, overweight man led a young, pigtailed girl into the room. As they entered, they walked with their backs toward Paul, the outlines of their faces covered in shadow. The greasy man led her to the bed, wrapping his arms around the little girl and thus tying Paul's stomach up in knots. But even that was nothing compared to the nausea that overtook him when the shadows fell from their faces, allowing Paul to see them for the first time.

In front of the bed stood Elle, and before her was Izzy, biting his lower lip as he looked down at her.

While Izzy brought his hand to her cheek and cupped her head in his hands, Paul's grip tightened around the bars of his cage. He tried to yell after them, to scream for this nightmare to end, but it was no use. It was as though he was stuck inside the emptiness of space, and no matter how hard he tried, even if he screamed until his lungs burst inside his chest, no one would ever hear him scream.

Taking Elle by the waist, Izzy hoisted her onto the edge of the bed, where she sat as stiff as a board with her eyes squeezed shut. He ran his hands down the length of her body, and her face twisted with horror. Immediately, Paul lost control. He rammed his body into the edge of his cage and shook the bars with all his might, trying to break the prison walls down. With every strike of shoulder against metal, the darkness and lightning flashed and grew, shooting out in every direction like the blast of a shotgun. Just as Izzy was lowering the shoulder straps of Elle's dress, a bolt of lightning struck him in the shoulder, causing him to turn around.

Upon looking into Paul's glaring eyes, the corners of Izzy's mouth twisted into a wicked smile, and he whispered, the ominous hiss of his voice echoing throughout the void, "Open your eyes, Paul. You've got to wake up."

Suddenly, the ground beneath Paul's feet began to shake. Trying to keep his balance, Paul gripped the bars in front of him until he felt as though he might just rip the door from its hinges. However, his effort was in vain. Seconds later, hurricane force winds ripped off the top of his cage and took him with it. Helpless, he flew up into the darkness as the scales on his body evaporated in an instant. The wind pushed, pulled and ripped violently at him, leaving him spinning, uncontrollably, within the vacuum of space. Desperately, he reached out toward the ever-shrinking room below him where Elle was left powerless to defend herself from the beast of Paul's own machination.

Then, the world around him flashed with blinding light, and he found himself sprawled across Lena's couch, covered in coffee grounds, wrappers and papers with his hands wrapped around Lena's throat and her hands clasped onto his shoulders.

"Listen," she coughed, hardly able to speak through her crushed windpipe. "I'm all for being choked, but maybe not first thing in the morning."

Embarrassed, he released the vice grip he held on her neck and collapsed back onto the couch. "Sorry, Lena," he said. "I was having a nightmare."

"Was it the house again?" she asked as she sat down next to him and placed her hand on his knee.

"N-no," he sighed. "I—I almost wish it had been. This was so much worse."

"What happened?"

"It was — it was Elle. She—she was... with someone. In a room. A man. He—he had her and — oh God, all I could do was watch, helplessly as he — as he..."

"Say no more. It sounds terrible."

"It was."

"And it also sounds like you've been thinking a lot about her lately."

"I have. It's so hard not being able to see her, especially after everything that's happened."

"Why can't you?" Lena asked.

"Rebecca's aunt won't let me within twenty yards of her," Paul replied.

"She can't do that!" she exclaimed. "A girl deserves to be able to see her father."

"Even if I could, doesn't she deserve better than just a few hours at a time?"

"Hey, that gives me an idea! What if you brought her here? To stay. She could live here with us. I know I can't replace Rebecca. No one could ever hope to do that, but I like to think I'm not the evil queen everyone makes me out to be. We could spruce this place up a bit, make it nice for her. She'd never have to know what we do for a living or ever want for a thing. And who knows? It might even make you happier, at least a little. I can't bear seeing you like this."

"I can't bring her here."

"Why not?"

"You can't expect me to raise my daughter in the same place I killed her mother."

"You did no such thing," Lena insisted. "Here or anywhere. Rebecca died in a car accident. What happened to her is not your fault."

"But I drove her to it!" Paul exclaimed. "She would have never been driving that fast, never been on that highway, never died if she hadn't found this place, if I hadn't been such a fool to think I could hide it from her in the first place."

"All you ever did was do the best you could for the people you care about," she replied.

"And still, it wasn't enough," he sighed.

"Listen, I know I can never hope to be half the woman she was, but I want you to know that I care about you. I just hope that, even after everything, you can say the same about me."

"Of course I care about you, Lena. Nothing could change that."

"You may want to hold off on making any promises until you hear what I'm about to say."

"What's on your mind?"

"It's about Macy."

"What about her?"

"She's been here for a week now," she sighed. "And all you've had her doing is reorganizing our papers, which, in case you've forgotten, is something you already did like a month ago during your sleepless phase."

"Then she can just do the massages," he said.

"That's not how this works," she replied.

"What are you saying?" he asked, his skin turning cold and his eyes dark.

In an instant, he felt it again: the power. Just like in his dream, it surged through his spine and ran along the length of his arms, causing his hair to stand on end. He could feel electricity crackle in the air like lightning before I crashes. His fists clenched, and his heart began to race. Taking a deep breath, he tried to quell the rage that now boiled inside of him, but he couldn't help but feel as though it was only a matter of time before he struck.

Sensing his anger, Lena took a step toward him and raised her shoulders authoritatively before answering, "We have a simple arrangement here; our girls do the work, and we give them everything they need. That's how we stay in the black. It's a good plan, *your* plan. Now, I understand that she's family, but I can't make exceptions. Not now, not ever. So, what I'm saying is that-"

"No."

"Macy either needs to-"

"No!"

"Do the work, just like everyone else, or-"

"You won't touch her!" Paul screamed as he reached out and took Lena by the arm, squeezing until his nails broke her skin. "I won't allow you!"

"You won't allow me?" she scoffed, taking him by the wrist, pinching his pressure point and twisting until he let go. "Just because I allow you in my bed doesn't mean you have power over me. I *own* you, and you do as I say."

"I said you can't have her!"

Before he knew what was happening, his clenched fist flew into her jaw and sent her crashing into the wall behind her. As she landed, her head whipped back and slammed into the door frame, leaving a massive dent in its surface. Leaning forward, she grimaced and brought her hand to the back of her head. When she brought it back around to look at it, it was stained red. Immediately, her eyes shot up at Paul, turning an unsettling shade of crimson.

"Listen, I'm sorry," he sighed. "I shouldn't have done that, but if you would just listen to me…"

Bending over, he placed his hand under her shoulder to help her up, but she slapped it away, choosing instead to pick herself up. "Get out," she growled. "I've put up with a lot of shit from you over the past few weeks. I've sat with you during your sleepless nights, ignored your outbursts, even cleaned up the piles of coffee grounds you constantly leave on my floor, but I will not permit you to lay a hand on me. That is the last straw. I want you out of my sight. Now. I don't care what you do. Hop a plane, take a vacation, jump off a bridge, I don't care, but I don't want you within a mile of this place until you've dealt with whatever the hell is wrong with you. Are we clear?"

"Can't we at least talk about this?"

"I'm done talking. Now, get out before I force you out."

"Do I at least have time to get things settled across the street?"

"Fine. But if I so much as see your face when I cross the street in fifteen minutes, I'll consider that your resignation."

Without another word, Paul stormed out of Lena's apartment and marched across the street, fuming. Bursting through the parlor doors in a huff, he stomped over to his desk and rifled through the drawers, searching for his keys, but he couldn't find them. It was as though they had vanished into thin air. For the next, five minutes, he searched relentlessly, even ripping every file, every folder, every staple and pen out of his desk. But still, he couldn't find them. Unable to take it any longer, he screamed in frustration and slammed his fists down on the only empty spot left on the desk, immediately silencing the room and drawing every eye inside it to him.

"What are you looking at?!" he yelled. "Get back to work."

"Looking for these?" Florian, who had just exited of the back room with a stack of files in his hands, said from behind him, his voice immediately followed by the jingling of keys. "Sorry, I borrowed them for a second because my old keys don't work for the back door anymore. But, if I'd known it'd cause an international incident, I would've asked first."

"It's fine," Paul huffed as he whirled around and snatched the keys from Florian's hand.

"What do you need them for?" Florian asked.

"I'm taking a leave of absence, Lena's orders," Paul explained.

"When are you coming back?"

"I don't know."

"Where are you going?"

"Anywhere but here, apparently."

"You know what?" Florian asked, patting Paul gently on the back. "I think this will be good for you. No one can expect to come back from something like what you went through without taking some time away. Who knows? Maybe it'll give you the time you need to grieve."

"Yeah, maybe. If she'd just leave me the hell alone for once," Paul muttered.

"If who would leave you alone?" Florian asked.

Paul opened his mouth to answer, but just as he did, Rebecca appeared in the doorway, dressed in tattered clothes and covered in blood. A second later, their eyes met, and she winked at him.

Instinctively, he shuddered, sighing, "Too late. She's already here."

Florian followed Paul's gaze to the door, confused. "Are you okay, boss?" he asked.

Ignoring him, Paul grabbed a picture of Rebecca and Elle from his desk and marched out the front doors, leaving Florian to clean up the desk by himself. As he stormed through the doors, passing straight through Rebecca, she turned with him and followed him across the street toward his car.

Smiling, she asked, "Where are we going?"

To which he replied, "Somewhere even you won't be able to bother me."

"Oh, I've always loved a challenge!"

CURIOUS, FLORIAN WATCHED PAUL AS HE WALKED ACROSS THE street toward his car. From where Florian stood, though Paul was the only person on the street, it looked as though he was talking to someone. Passing the back corner of his car, Paul turned his head to the right and shouted something over the top of the car. Then, as he sped off, barreling backwards out of the driveway with reckless abandon, Florian could have sworn that he saw Paul push against the empty air across the center console from him.

Interesting.

So, pulling out his phone and hiding it under the table as he began to pick through the paper ruins atop Paul's desk, he shot a quick text to Rebecca. *Did you see that?*

Three stacks of replaced files later, his phone buzzed with her reply. *Every second.*

FLORIAN: *Who was the 'she' he was talking about?*

REBECCA: *Our only hope.*

FLORIAN: *What do you need me to do?*

REBECCA: *Keep an eye on Macy. With Paul gone, there's no telling what Lena will make her do. Make sure she doesn't have the chance.*

Before Florian could put his phone away, Lena kicked the front door open as thought it had just insulted her family, nearly sending it through the window on the other side of its hinge. She stormed past him in a huff, straight toward the back room, where Macy had just started on the parlor's paperwork. Immediately leaping out of his chair without even taking the time to put his phone away, he followed quickly after Lena. As he did, he felt something slip from his hands, crashing to the floor behind him, but there was no time to see what had fallen. He had to get to Macy before Lena was through with her.

As he paged the curtain to the back room, an exasperated Macy asked, "Can I finish with this drawer first?"

"No," Lena answered. "You've wasted enough of my time."

Taking two, quiet steps into the room, Florian kept himself against the back corner of the wall, waiting for the perfect opportunity to intervene. Immediately, Macy, who Lena had backed up against a large filing cabinet on the opposite side of the floor, spotted him, and her eyes grew wide, pleading for him to do something, anything to help her before the tigress pounced on top of her and ripped the flesh from her bone.

Instead, however, he raised his hands in front of him and urged her to take a deep breath, which she did before replying, "But Paul said-"

"Paul isn't here anymore," Lena growled. "And I have a whole week of training to make up for."

"Why don't you let me take care of that?" Florian asked, taking three more, confident steps into the center of the room.

Suddenly, Lena turned on him, getting in his face in an attempt to intimidate him. "Speaking of Paul's mistakes," she said. "Just because I haven't set your head on a pike doesn't mean I haven't thought about what you did. And right now isn't the time to test my resolve."

But Florian stood his ground.

Staring straight into Lena's eyes, he replied in a calm, smooth tone even though his heart was quivering inside his chest, "We're a man down, which means everyone needs to pull their weight. And you can't do that while you're dragging five tons of rage in your wake. If Macy's going to get trained, she needs to be trained by someone who's going to do it right. Do you honestly think you can do that right now?"

"I do," she answered, her face contorting with rage before softening as she sighed. "Not."

"Then let me do my job."

"But you'd better do it right. As far as I'm concerned, you're still on thin ice. One misstep just might leave you drowning."

With an agitated grunt, Lena stormed back out of the room, throwing the edge of the curtain dramatically as she left. Relieved, Macy breathed a sigh of relief and, turning around, began to tap her head in frustration on the edge of the filing cabinet.

Laying a hand on her shoulder, Florian said, "I told you she's a bit of a character."

"I'm not sure I quite get her humor," she sighed.

"She's had a hell of a morning."

"What did she mean about you being on thin ice?"

"That's a story for another time. Right now, we have some training to do."

Suddenly, Monica barreled into the back room.

"Florian," she said, breathing heavily. "It's your wife. Your phone — it was — so I — she says her water broke."

"What?" he asked. "No, she can't be. We've still got eight weeks."

"She was pretty insistent," she replied.

"Shit! It'll be twenty minutes before I can even get home, much less get her to the hospital. She'll-"

"Be fine. She called a Ryde. So, all you have to do is meet her at the hospital. Now, go. Don't worry about telling Lena. I already took care of it."

Turning back toward Macy, Florian looked at her apologetically, but she shrugged, smiling weakly. "Maybe she'll grow on me. Get out of here, go. I'll be fine."

If only that was true…

Wasting no time, Florian dashed out of the salon and barely got the door to his car closed before he hit the freeway. With every minute that passed along the crowded highways and byways, his grip on the steering wheel tightened, and his mind raced with every conceivable worry. And as much as he tried to tell himself that everything was going to be okay, he couldn't help but fear the worst. In the end, there were only so many reasons Janelle's water could have broken this early that weren't a cause for concern. After a while, he couldn't even bring himself to think of one that didn't feel like a scimitar to the heart.

And it didn't get any better once he got the hospital.

Rushing through the sliding doors of the maternity ward, he bolted up to the front desk, pushing past several, expectant couples and forcing himself to the front of the line. At the front desk sat a thin woman with horn-rimmed glasses and pink scrubs.

As soon as she saw Florian, she rolled her eyes and sighed in monotone, "You'll have to wait your turn. One at a time, please."

Ignoring her, he planted his hands defiantly on the desk and demanded, "I need to see my wife! Where is she?"

"Back of the line, sir," she repeated.

"I don't give a shit about your line," he said. "I need to see my wife."

With yet another sigh, the woman pressed a button on her computer, leaned forward and spoke into a microphone, "Jerry, we've got another one."

A second later, a strong, bulky hand latched onto Florian's shoulder and dragged him into the center of the lobby, where he was spun around. When he finally regained his footing, he found himself standing in front of a gargantuan security guard whose hands alone looked like they could wrap around Florian's waist. Though he wore what Florian could only assume was the largest security uniform the hospital had to offer, the guard's muscles still managed to keep him from being able to so much as tuck in his shirt. Furious, he flared his nostrils at Florian, daring him to so much as think about crossing him.

But in that moment, not even a gun to his face would have deterred Florian. This was about Janelle, and he would not be denied.

So, he puffed out his chest, pressed his chin to the guard's chromium pecs and said, "I need. To see. My wife."

"Then, you'll have to wait. With everyone else," the guard replied.

"She's thirty-two weeks pregnant with my little girl," Florian said. "She's already had kidney stones and placenta previa. Her water broke, and I don't know what's going on with her. All these people standing at the counter have their partner by their side to get them through, but right now, my wife has no one. *I* have no one to let me know whether or not my daughter is okay. So, you can put me at the back of this line if you want. I have no doubt you're strong enough. But you'll have to rip my head from my shoulders first because I'm not going without a fight."

For a moment, the guard didn't move. He simply looked down at Florian with intense eyes, trying to stare him into submission.

Then, his face softened, and he said, "Any man willing to stand up to me like that is all right in my book. What's your wife's name?"

"Janelle Romani," Florian answered.

"I'll find her," the guard replied with a nod before marching off in the direction of answers.

The next, three minutes, as Florian waited for the guard to return, felt like hours spent with his arms and legs strapped to a medieval, torture device. With every second that passed, the crank turned over notch after notch, stretching the limits of what he thought he could endure. As his limbs continued to be stretched in every direction, he paced across the lobby. Then, he sat in the waiting room with his head in his hands, hoping to take his mind off his anxiety, even if only for a second. He even tried to step outside and get some fresh air, but nothing could calm the storm that raged inside his soul. Finally reaching the limits of his patience, he opted to stand in the center of the hallway and stare, unblinking, down the same path the guard had taken just moments before.

That was when he saw them. About thirty feet down the hallway were the only two people in the world with any hope of keeping him from becoming unhinged: the guard and, more importantly, a doctor.

Immediately, he rushed down the hall to meet them. "Where's Janelle?" he asked.

Taking a deep breath, the doctor placed his hand on the small of Florian's back and led him off to the side. Florian looked to the guard for reassurance, but all he received was a sympathetic half-smile. Once they were sufficiently out of sight, the guard nodded at the doctor and returned to his station at the front door.

"Where's Janelle?" Florian repeated. "I need to see her."

"I'm afraid that's not possible," the doctor replied.

"What do you mean?" Florian asked.

"We were hoping she would be able to deliver naturally, but she's lost a lot of blood."

"Is she okay?"

"For now. We had to rush her in for an emergency C-section. We're doing everything we can, and we're hopeful. But, situations like this are touch and go with even the strongest of women. And your wife's so young."

"When can I see her?"

"I don't know. Hospital policy is that, whenever we have to give a patient anesthesia for a C-section, no one is allowed in her room outside of hospital staff. I'll do what I can, but for now, you'll just have to wait."

With those words, a crushing weight was laid atop of Florian's shoulders, a burden so heavy that he could hardly stand. As the doctor returned down the same hall he had come down, Florian braced himself against the wall, trying to hold himself up. However, six seconds later, his knees buckled, and he threw himself against the wall and slid to the floor, where he remained until the world around him faded into the never-ending void that was his despair. For the next, three hours, he didn't move. He didn't speak, nor did he even look up from the six inches of carpet in front of him until he felt a warm body sidle up next to him and saw a dark, delicate hand hold his phone in front of his eyes. Looking up, he saw Lena on the ground next to him, her expression unreadable, stuck somewhere between compassion and rage.

"You left this at the parlor," she said. "I figured you wouldn't be back for some time tonight so I thought I'd deliver it myself. Though, I'm sorry to hear about Janelle."

Stuffing his phone in his back pocket, he replied, "Thanks. The doctor says they're doing everything they can, but I can't help but worry that something awful has happened."

"Well, worrying about it isn't going to help her. It'll just make you more useless when she does actually need you," she said.

"Did you come here to make me feel better, or are you actually trying to make me feel worse?" he scoffed. "Because with you, it's sometimes tough to tell the difference."

"Neither. My reasons are my own."

"What's that supposed to mean?"

"I figured you'd want an update on how Macy's training went today."

"I thought I told you I'd take care of it."

"That you did," Lena said. "And I was going to let you, but then, your ice broke."

"What are you talking about?" Florian asked, his throat closing tight as he scooted away from her.

"Imagine my surprise when I got off the phone with your wife," she said. "And found an unread text message from Rebecca Cross, which is obviously impossible because, if I remember correctly, she's dead."

"Listen, I can explain…"

"I don't care about your explanation, Florian. Truth be told, I'm quite impressed with the both of you. Pulling one over on Paul, much less myself, is not so easy a task. So, kudos to you, but now that I know your secret, why don't you tell me all about Bec's little plan?"

"I don't really know much. I'm just-"

"You had better choose your next words carefully," she ordered. "Because you aren't the only one your actions affect. By my count, there are two, other lives that hang in the balance."

"What do you want from me?" he asked.

"Nothing much. When the doctor comes back, I want you to visit your wife and see your sweet, precious child for the first time. Then, I want you to say your goodbyes because, as of this moment, you're getting a promotion. The pay isn't any better, but it does come with a few perks, such as you and everyone you ever loved being allowed to continue to breathe. Your job is to find that treacherous whore, Rebecca, and bring her to me. And if you so much as breathe a word of this to anyone, I will destroy everything you ever dreamed of caring about."

"You wouldn't dare."

"Do you really want to test me right now?"

Just then, Florian heard a door open to his left. Instinctively, his eyes shot down the hall, where he saw the doctor making his way down the hallway toward him. Leaving Lena behind, Florian leapt to his feet and rushed to must him.

From ten feet away, Florian asked, "Is she all right?"

The doctor smiled. "Thankfully, I come bearing good news. It was touch and go for a while, but your daughter's stable. And Janelle is sleeping soundly. She'll be awake in a couple hours. You're free to see her if you'd like. Just follow me."

Nodding, Florian took a step to follow the doctor but was immediately stopped by the outstretched arm of Lena, who had latched onto his wrist as she whispered in his ear, "Remember what I said."

From the ground floor, it took three dings of the elevator,

four hallways and six doors for Florian and the doctor to reach Janelle's room. As they stopped outside the door, the doctor patted Florian on the shoulder with a reassuring smile and left him to enter the room alone. Slowly opening the door, Florian crept inside, where both Janelle and Iris were sleeping soundly.

The first thing he did was stand over the top of Iris' plastic crib and look down at the little bundle of joy that lay inside. Immediately, he was filled with an overwhelming pride that brought tears to his eyes. She was the tiniest, most perfect being he had ever laid eyes on. It was as though God, in all his power, had channeled every ounce of his majesty into a single, five-pound frame. She was so delicate, so beautiful, and in that moment, he knew that he would do anything to protect her.

Even leave her forever.

So, picking up a pen and notepad from the table beside Janelle's bed, he wrote with shaking hands:

Janelle, my life, my love,

My love for you is as boundless as the sea. There is nothing that can contain it, nothing that can destroy it and no one who can deter it. I want you to know that first because, after reading what I have to say next, that truth may become easy to forget.

Over the course of our relationship, I have never lied to you about my feelings for you. You have always been my muse, my inspiration, and you have given birth to the most beautiful, most precious gift imaginable. I am in awe of the pure strength of your heart. I only regret that I was unable to be with you to carry you through what I imagine were the scariest moments of your life.

And I wish that I was able to stand with you through what is to come next.

Regretfully, there is a part of my past that I have not told you about, and it is threatening to tear apart everything we have worked so hard to build. Because of that, I can never see you or Iris again. I will always provide for you what I can, even from a distance. And I truly hope that you and Iris have the most spectacular life possible.

I love you to the heavens and back,
Florian.

As he walked out the door, he took one, last look back at the life he was leaving behind. His first step into the loneliness before him was simultaneously the hardest and easiest decision of his life. It hurt to leave them, but at the same time, he couldn't live with himself if either of them got hurt because of him.

So step by step, he left them in the distance, only looking back to wipe the tears from his eyes.

20

DELIVERANCE

LOS ANGELES, CALIFORNIA

"*I* don't understand!" Bradie exclaimed as he threw himself against the wall beside the door of the Man of L.A. Mancha after another, unsuccessful day of searching. "A girl can't literally disappear."

"We'll find her," Stacy assured him, leaning next to him and laying her hand on his shoulder.

He sighed, "It's been a week. We've combed every inch of this street, and she's not under, in or around anything within a mile of this place. She's just… gone."

"You know, Bradie could be right." Nina backed against the wall next to Stacy and laid her head on her shoulder. "What if this guy's really a wizard, and he just up and took her to Hogwarts? Unless one of you has some super convenient, magical powers you haven't told me about, that could be, like, the perfect plan. We'd never find her."

Shaking her head, Stacy laughed, "Barring an escape to a secretive, magical realm, there's only so far she could have gone."

"Are we sure she was even here?" Nina asked.

Bradie replied, "Loman said-"

"Yeah, he did," Nina scoffed.

"What are you insinuating?"

"That there's a reason he never got promoted to detective. He's what, a hundred years old, and still a beat cop? If the dumbass was going to move up, don't you think he would've done it by now?"

"They offered a few years back, but he turned it down, said he'd rather keep making a difference on the streets."

"Yeah, and I don't have a boyfriend because I *really* enjoy masturbating every night."

"You've got to admit," Stacy said. "He doesn't have the best track record with this case. He spends seven months tracking Anna's keeper and finds nothing. Then, when he actually finds a lead, it turns out to be a dead end."

"Meanwhile, you took down a whole ring of traffickers and unmasked a dirty judge in that same time," Nina added.

"What do you suggest we do?" Bradie asked.

Smiling, Stacy planted a kiss on his cheek. "You? I don't want you to move a muscle. *I'm* going to see if I can get some answers out of Smokey."

"He wasn't exactly what I would call cooperative the last time we tried to talk to him."

"Oh, but honey. You know no one can say no to this ass."

Pulling her neckline down and hiking up her skirt until she showed just enough skin, Stacy sauntered into the bar with a skip in her step and a swing in her hips. As she opened the door, Bradie's gaze lowered to her backside. He bit his lip.

I sure as hell wouldn't.

"I sure as hell wouldn't," Nina said, biting her lip as she followed Bradie's gaze to Stacy's rear end.

"Will you let it go?" he chuckled. "It's not going to happen."

"I'll believe that when I hear it from her beautiful lips," she replied.

"She's not going to go for it."

"Want to make a bet?"

"Twenty bucks says she says no, and you never bring it up again."

"You've got a deal. But, if she says yes, I get her to myself for a whole night."

Rolling his eyes, Bradie reached out to shake Nina's hand, saying, "Easiest Jackson I've ever made."

"I wouldn't be so sure," Nina replied, shaking his hand.

As they were mid-shake, Stacy came bounding out of the bar doors with a wide smile on her face. Immediately, both Nina and Bradie let go of each other's hands and backed away into opposite corners, ashamed. Turning away, Bradie rubbed the back of his neck uncomfortably as Nina did the same, turning a bright shade of pink.

Confused, Stacy looked back and forth between them with an eyebrow raised and asked, "Did I come out at a bad time?"

"No," Bradie replied a little too quickly, clearing his throat. "No, of course not. We were just making a bet…"

Wrapping her arm around Stacy, Nina led her down the street away from the bar as Bradie fell in line beside them. "About whether or not you'd be able to get anything useful out of Smokey Bones," Nina said with a wink toward Bradie. "For the record, I bet on you."

"Wow," Stacy said, looking at Bradie with her mouth agape. "Ye of little faith."

"I have all the faith in the world in you. I'm just not sure Smokey actually knows anything," he replied as he peered around Stacy's back to give Nina the stink eye.

After sticking her tongue out at Bradie, Nina linked arms with Stacy and asked. "So, did I win the bet?"

"It looks like it," Stacy answered. "Because, according to Smokey, Aster isn't a trafficker at all. He sells fake booze, and in Smokey's words, he 'doesn't stand for that shit.'"

"So we're back to square one," Bradie sighed.

"Not exactly," Stacy said with a playful hip bump to his side. "I asked him where I could find the best pimp in town, and he told me to go to the corner of San Pedro and Ninth."

"Right down the street from where Loman found the match-book. Good work, honey."

And just a skip and a jump away from First National Bank.

"Was there ever any doubt?"

"I, for one, always believed in you," Nina answered, biting the bottom corner of her lip. "You're damn sexy when you're playing private eye."

"Why, thank you," Stacy said. "You're not so bad yourself."

"If you weren't a married woman, I'd jump your bones right here and now," Nina said.

"Why should you let that stop you? Bradie will be out late investigating tonight so my bed'll be empty."

"Not for long, it won't."

"So, I'll see you tonight?"

"Wouldn't miss it for the world," Nina answered, reaching behind Stacy's back taking a twenty dollar bill from Bradie before leading Stacy ahead of him down the street.

As they continued down the street, hand in hand, Stacy looked back at Bradie with a wink.

Confused, he chased after them, asking, "Wait, you're just messing with me, right?"

To which Nina replied, "If you want to find out, you'll just have to join us. But fair warning, when the clothes come off, this girl plays rough."

{}~{}~{}~{}~{}~{}~{}~{}~{}~{}

That night, after convincing himself that Stacy and Nina were just toying with him, he left them in their hotel room and made his way into the center of the city, planting himself on the corner of San Pedro and Ninth. Across the horizon, the sun painted the sky with a wash of red, orange and purple as traffic came to a screeching halt along the street. For what seemed like forever and a day, the line of cars in front of him didn't so much as move. Meanwhile, the sidewalks filled with tourists and pedestrians, all of whom were taking in the sights and sounds of the Garment District and doing their best to make it impossible for Bradie to spot a single face in the crowd, much less Anna's.

After fifteen minutes spent scanning every face he could pick out in the crowd and still finding no trace of her, the only option he had was to blend in with the horde and hope the zombies didn't bite. So, as he entered the crosswalk, he kept his head down and peered out of the corners of his eyes. Over the next hour, he walked every inch of not only that corner but every side street, alley and main path within five blocks, but there was still no sign of Anna.

In fact, to his surprise, he hadn't seen a single prostitute during the entire course of his search. It was beginning to feel as though he was chasing a wild goose, holding a needle while sifting through a pile of haystacks, and all he could find were red herrings.

Exhausted and exasperated, he collapsed to the ground in the exact spot he had started, on the Northwest corner of South San Pedro Street, and stared up into the night sky, wondering what he was supposed to do. As always, he was so close to salvation but still stood in the middle of the second circle of hell.

Where he was doomed to be punished for all of eternity.

Just then, a dainty finger tapped lightly on his shoulder.

Turning his head to the side, he was met by the deadpan glare of a curvy, caramel-skinned girl in a faux, fur jacket, a purple half-shirt and full-length, fishnet stockings. She tried to smile seductively at him as she pressed her exposed breasts closer to his face. But it was hollow, empty. No matter how hard she tried, her eyes were devoid of sparkle and covered with storm clouds.

"You look like you could use a pick-me-up," she said in a practiced, breathy tone.

Finally!

Standing up, Bradie smiled and ran his hand along her side until it rested on her thigh. "And it looks like you could be just the thing I need," he said.

"For seventy, you can have any part of me you want," she replied.

"How much would it be to double the fun?" he asked.

"Double the fun, double the price. Any type of girl you have in mind?"

"Actually, I do. I'm already bringing the chocolate. You've got the caramel. How about we add a little vanilla to our sundae? Maybe one with a few golden flakes on top. You got any girls like that?"

"I think I've got just the one."

Taking Bradie by the hand, she led him around the corner, down a back alleyway and into a brick building on the right. Then, she took him up three flights of stairs and through a mold-ridden, wooden door on the left.

As she stepped into the living room of what looked like a small apartment but was so poorly furnished that Bradie couldn't imagine anyone actually living inside, she called out, "Harmony, I've got a double dipper coming through! Get your sexy ass out here!"

Seconds later, a girl's voice rang out over the moaning,

pounding ruckus that was coming from the other room, saying, "Keep him warmed up for me, Jazz. I'll be out in a second."

Taking Bradie's hands in her own, Jazz smiled seductively and began to backpedal toward the open room on the left, saying, "Looks like I get you all to myself."

"I was hoping you'd say that," Bradie gulped.

Once inside her room, Jazz closed the door behind her and backed up against it, arching her back and running her hand down her every curve. Then, she lifted herself from the doorway and puckered her lips as she drew closer to Bradie's.

But before her kiss graced his lips, Bradie raised his finger to Jazz's lips and said, "I think I'd rather watch to start."

"That can be arranged." A smile crept across her face as she placed a single finger on his shoulder and pushed him onto the bed. "Now, why don't you be a good boy and sit down. Let Jazzy take good care of you."

As Jazz raised her arms above her head and began to sway to a slow rhythm, her hips swinging in wide passes to each side, her jacket fall to the floor. Then, she brought her hands behind her head and turned around slowly. Backing up, she rubbed her backside against Bradie's chest, and every muscle in his body tensed. While she lifted her shirt above her head, he crossed his fingers, praying that they would be interrupted soon.

And he hoped to God that Jazz had brought him to Anna, or he didn't know how he was going to get out of this one.

Thankfully, after another thirty seconds of dancing and the removal of two more pieces of clothing, the door opened, and to Bradie's relief, Anna was standing on the other side. Immediately upon entering the room, her eyes fell on Bradie, and they grew wide, followed by waves of joyous relief.

Without another second's hesitation, Bradie pushed Jazz off

of him, ran over to Anna and wrapped her in his arms. "Thank God you're here," he said.

"Same goes for you," she replied. "I always knew you'd find me. Though, it sure as hell took you long enough."

"Sorry about that. We hit a few bumps in the road," he explained.

"Excuse me!" Jazz, who was still standing over by the bed, completely undressed, exclaimed as she raised her hands in frustration. "What the hell is going on?"

"How do you feel about getting out of here?" Anna asked. "This is the man I told you about, the one who talked me off the roof of First National. He's here to take me home, but there's always room for one more."

Anna reached out to take Jazz's hand, but she pulled away, saying, "Are you kidding me? If we run, he'll find us. You should know that better than anyone."

"But it'll be different this time. We'll be halfway across the country. He can't find us there."

"Yeah? And how'd that work out for you last time?"

"That was different too."

"No, it's always the same. Every. Single. Time. Why can't you get that through your head?"

"Because I found someone who proved that to me," Anna said. "Come with me, Jazzy. With Bradie, we can make it. I promise."

With a hesitant nod, Jazz put her clothes back on and followed them toward the front door. But, as they stepped into the stairwell, Jazz latched onto Anna's hand. "I'm sorry, sissy, but I can't get punished again," she said before cupping her free hand over her mouth and yelling down the stairwell. "Harmony's making a break for it!"

Immediately, three doors below them swung open in unison, and large, tattooed men streamed onto the stairs and dashed up after them. Turning to Anna, Bradie's expression grew serious as he gave her a determined nod as if to say that if they were going to go down, they would go down swinging. She nodded in reply, and, clinging tightly to her hand, he started to pull her down the stairs.

But she stopped him, saying, "While I appreciate your willingness to die, I know a better way. Come on."

Dragging him back into the apartment, Anna rushed into her room and over to her window, which she kicked open with ease. Then, together, they climbed out of the opening and onto the five-inch windowsill that stood between them and certain death.

"Quite the view," Bradie said, looking down at the three-story drop to the concrete. "But I'm not sure it helps us all that much."

"Then you're looking in the wrong direction," Anna replied as she leapt up and grabbed hold of the rooftop above, using the top of the window shutters to hoist herself up. Then, she turned and leaned over the edge of the roof, offering Bradie her hand. "You been keeping yourself in shape?"

"Not if you ask Stacy," he chuckled as he reached up, grabbed a hold of her hand and tried to get a footing on the shutters.

But, as his toes grazed the top of the window, his foot slipped, almost sending him plummeting to the ground below. Thankfully, Anna's grip held true, giving him just enough time to swing his feet back onto the windowsill. Bending over, he peered quickly through the window to see how much time they had. When he did, he saw two of the three men storm into the room with their arms outstretched to grab a hold of him.

He looked up at Anna and sighed, "It's now or never."

With a primitive grunt, he jumped as high as he could off the ledge, stretching his arms as far as they could go. The fingertips of his free hand wrapped around the ledge as Anna tugged against his other hand with all her might, allowing Bradie to get his elbow on the ledge. He swung his right leg onto the roof and started to push himself up, but before he could, a strong hand seized his left foot and pulled him back down toward the ground.

Desperately, he fought as hard as he could to avoid capture. He jerked his knee back and forth and kicked wildly at his pursuer's wrist. However, it was no use. Seconds later, a second hand took hold and pulled him down, leaving him helpless to do anything but fall. As his forearms slipped from the roof's edge, he knew he had only one way out. So, rotating his foot, he loosened his shoe's grip around his ankle. Then, with his wrists planted on the roof's edge, he pushed with all his might and jerked his foot to the side, wrenching free from their grasp. Suddenly, he flew forward, straight into Anna, and his shoe went in the other direction. Helpless, it plummeted thirty feet to the ground below, crashing into the windshield a parked car on the street level and setting off a slew of car alarms along the street side.

Pushing Bradie off of her and panting heavily, Anna said, "Damn, Stacy wasn't kidding. We've got to get you a gym membership, a running buddy, something. I can't keep lifting you like that. My arms will fall off."

"Ha ha," Bradie replied, rolling his eyes. "You're hysterical. Come on, let's get moving before they catch up."

From there, it was a foot race across the rooftop to the other side, where they slipped down the fire escape to the ground below. Then, after checking around to make sure their pursuers were gone, Bradie took Anna by the hand and pulled her toward the street for their getaway.

But before they could so much as take a single step onto the road, Anna was ripped from Bradie's arms. He spun around, ready for a fight but froze just as quickly when he saw whose face he would have to cave in to get her back.

"Loman?" Bradie asked, his heart skipping a beat as he laid eyes on his old partner with one arm around Anna's neck and the other holding a gun, which he pressed against her temple. "It was you the whole time?"

"Now you're catching on," Loman cackled. "Though, I must say; I'm surprised you found her this quickly. I thought the detour to L.A. Mancha would at least give me another week before I had to move. What gave me away?"

"Smokey," Bradie answered. "All Stacy needed to do was ask him the right questions."

Sighing, Loman shook his head. "I should have known that clever, little bitch would throw a wrench in my operation."

"How long have you been on *his* payroll?"

"His payroll? You better check yourself, partner. I'm not working for him. I *am* him. At least the only one you need to care about. Anna's always been working for me, even if it was originally for one of my lieutenants."

"So, that day at the bank?"

"I was trying to retrieve my product."

"Why do you think I wrote you that message in the interrogation room?" Anna asked.

"Not here," Bradie muttered to himself. "Why didn't you say anything?"

"I didn't want to hurt you," she answered. "I could see how much he meant to you as your partner, and we were far enough away that I didn't think it mattered anymore."

Loman smiled. "I've got to admit; you've impressed me. I never thought you'd follow through with that impulsive promise you made her. I figured I could get her back the second you hopped the plane to Detroit without her. But, to take this little whore across country with you and make her a part of your family, you really are a Hallmark kind of hero. It brings tears to these dry, old eyes."

"Then why didn't you just leave us alone?" Bradie questioned.

"When I heard you were going to be in town, I couldn't resist. Besides, her escape not withstanding, Harmony here was my best girl. I can't just let talent like that be wasted."

"You can't have her."

"Oh, but she was only ever on loan to you. She's always been mine. I don't know if you noticed, but I'm the one with the gun, the badge and the forethought to have a credible alibi. What exactly do you have, partner? Grit? Determination? None of those will do you any good when you're spending the night picking her brains off the concrete. Sorry to say, buddy, but you lost this one, pure and simple."

"Oops, spoke to soon," a voice called out from behind Bradie.

Startled, Bradie spun around to find Stacy and Nina standing behind him with wry smiles on their faces and a tape recorder in Nina's hand.

Pressing the stop, rewind and play buttons in sequence, Nina let the recording play back. "When I heard you and Stacy were going to be in town, I couldn't resist," Loman's voice echoed through the alleyway.

Loman growled, "You two are getting to be a real pain in my ass. Let me guess; you want to trade."

"Oh no, you figured us out. What will we ever do?" Nina said with a dramatic roll of the eyes. "You got it, dumbass. My tape recorder for Anna."

"And what's stopping me from shooting you as soon as I get that recorder in my hands?" Loman asked.

"Because then you'll have four murders to clean up after,"

Stacy answered. "And we both know how much you don't like to sweat."

"Fine," Loman sighed, releasing his grip around Anna's neck and pushing her toward Bradie, who immediately wrapped her in his arms and led her behind Nina. Then, Loman raised his gun toward Nina. "Now, the tape. Don't think that because I let her go first doesn't mean I won't put this bullet in your skull if you don't fulfill your end of the bargain."

Carefully, Nina laid the recorder on the ground and kicked it toward Loman, who, as it landed at his feet, bent over, took it in his hand and stuffed in into his jacket pocket. Then, with his gun still raised, he disappeared into the shadows, leaving nothing in his wake but a thick layer of tension in the air.

Anna looked up at Stacy and Nina, tears welling up in her eyes, and said, "Thank you both. I don't know how I can ever repay you, but how did you know how to find us?"

"You think I don't keep a GPS lock on my husband at all times?" Stacy laughed. "It's the only way I survive being a policeman's wife."

"But I thought you two were back at the hotel," Bradie said.

"We were," Nina replied with a wink. "But I've only got so much stamina, you know. My tongue can only keep running for so long, and you were sure taking your sweet-ass time."

"Wait, what's going on?" Anna asked, her eyes growing wide with confusion.

"We thought we might need the element of surprise," Stacy chuckled. "And what good is surprise if everyone's in on it? Trust me, nothing went on except a job well done."

"Could've fooled me," Nina said with a wink.

Shaking his head, Bradie said, "Well, thank you, Nina. I don't know what I would have done if you hadn't shown up. It's just too bad we lost the tape. I really wish we could take that bastard down."

"Who's to say we can't?" Stacy asked, reaching into her jacket pocket and pulling out a duplicate recorder.

"Loman wasn't kidding," Bradie laughed. "You really are a clever, little bitch."

"It's why you married me," she replied.

Wrapping his arms around Anna and Stacy, who, in turn, wrapped hers around Nina, Bradie looked up into the night sky and sighed. It was a bittersweet walk to freedom. On one hand, he had lost his old partner, his brother, to the darkness, but at the same time, he finally had everyone he could ever need standing right beside him. His family was finally complete.

And that made all the difference.

FORGIVENESS

NEW YORK, NEW YORK

*N*atasha took a deep breath. As she looked up at the behemoth before her with its ornate, sloping arms threatening to take her by the throat and choke the life out of her, its shining mahogany called out to her in mockery. After all of her grandstanding, all her false shouting about her hatred of religion, there she stood, with a confessional as the only thing left that could take her pain, her guilt, away.

To this point, she had tried everything to shake the darkness from her soul. She threw herself into helping Theresa deal with her withdrawal, hoping that keeping her focus on another would lead her to forget her pain. Whenever she wasn't doing that, she was holed up in the room the priests had given her at the end of the basement, trying to drown her sorrow in an ocean of dreams. She had even tried to rip the darkness from her wrists with the edge of a knife's blade. But after four days, Theresa's symptoms were worse than ever, and Natasha was teetering on the edge of sanity.

The truth of the matter was, though she still didn't believe in God, He was the only thing left that she hadn't yet tried. So, with bated breath, she wrapped her blackened fingers around the door handle and took a tentative step inside the ligneous prison.

Inside, everything around her turned to a darkness that rivaled the one which now inhabited her soul. She held her hand in front of her face, but it was dim, lit only by the streams of fluorescent light that trickled through the checkered slats that separated her from the minister of her false relief, Father Christopher.

Sitting down on the hard, cold bench on the far side of the cubicle, she repeated an old, yet hauntingly familiar, refrain. "Forgive me, Father," she said. "For I have sinned. It has been — I don't know — five years… or so, since my last confession."

"That's a long time to live without relief from the weight of sin," he replied.

"I hope it's not too long," she said.

"There's no statute of limitations on forgiveness," he assured her. "That's just a long time to carry that burden on your shoulders, alone."

"But you see, I never thought I needed forgiveness. Until now."

"We all need forgiveness, daughter."

"I suppose. But up until this point, my sins weren't really my own. I was just a cipher, without enough free will to elicit guilt. This time, though, the choice was no one's but my own."

"What happened?"

"We don't have to play games," she sighed. "I know you priests get quite good at recognizing voices after a while so I'm sure you know the story by now."

"But I'd rather hear it from you, Natasha," he replied.

"Of course you would… It all happened so damn fast — I'm sorry, I mean — now I'm just adding to the list of grievances I need to ask forgiveness for."

"There's no need to apologize. All God cares about is your heart. Besides, I've heard far worse within these walls. Go on."

"I was just so angry. He hurt me so bad, and there he was, completely at my mercy. His life was in my hands, and it was so... invigorating. I felt powerful, strong, like the tables had finally turned, and I was no longer his bitch. Instead, he was mine. So, when he mocked me, when he pushed me, I lost it. And in that second, it felt good, right."

"And now?"

"I feel dirty, disgusting. There's a darkness inside me, and it wants to break free. Before, the black was always on the outside, and I was under siege. But now, it's like I am that darkness, and everyone else is feeling its wrath."

"There's darkness inside all of us, Natasha," Father Christopher said.

Natasha shook her head. "Not like this."

"I wouldn't be so sure," he replied. "Most people aren't aware of how fallen they are. That means you're ahead of the curve, but you can't let the darkness win. No matter how hard you have to fight, you can't let it take control."

"You can't let the darkness win," she whispered, chuckling.

"What is it?"

"Nothing. I've just — someone said that to me once before, and it looks like I failed her after all."

"Is it really forgiveness you're seeking today, or did you come here looking for something else?"

"Honestly? I don't know anymore."

"Do you want to be forgiven?" he asked. "Are you sorry for what you've done and ready to turn away from the bad things you've done?"

Swallowing hard, she answered, "Yes. I mean, I came all the way up from the basement for this so I might as well try something."

"Then God forgives you," he said.

"Wait, that's it?"

"Were you expecting a hundred Hail Mary's and a thousand Our Fathers?"

"To be honest, yes. Something like that."

"And you can do that if it makes you feel better. That's really all those are for, to help us feel like we've done something to earn His forgiveness. All He really wants us to do is talk to Him."

"Then how come I don't feel forgiven?" she asked.

"Because maybe you still need to forgive yourself," he answered. "Now go, my daughter, and may you find the peace you're looking for."

But as Natasha stepped out of the confessional and felt the daylight once again wash across her skin, she didn't feel peaceful. Nor did she feel forgiven. Instead, she felt even more guilty than she did before, and the darkness still covered her hands and arms like tar.

You say I'm forgiven,
But I'm not sure I agree.
Why should this villain
Receive any clemency?
Forgive me, Father,
For I have sinned.
But why should he bother
When I'm still lost in the wind?

That night, Natasha tried to go to sleep, but she couldn't. Nothing but darkness lay behind her eyelids, and every time she closed her eyes, she could feel it closing in on her again, threatening to drag her with it into the depths of hell. So, as the hours, which seemed like days, passed, she simply stared, unblinking, at the ceiling above, fighting like hell to keep her eyes from closing.

Suddenly, after a passage of time Natasha couldn't even hope to estimate, there was a rustling outside her door. Curious, she jumped out of bed and crept toward the sound. She pressed her ear to the doorframe and cracked the door open a few inches so she could peer through the slat and out into the hallway. However, when she opened the door, she saw nothing, just an empty hallway. Confused, she swung the door open and stuck her head into the hallway, but still, there was nothing.

Not a light. Not a sound. Nothing but a dark, empty hallway.

Rubbing her eyes and shaking her head, Natasha turned back into her room and wrapped her fingers around the door's edge to slam it back shut, convinced that her exhaustion was causing her to hallucinate. But, just as she was about to close the door, she heard it again: the faint rustle. This time, it was coming from the stairwell. Turning her head to the side, she calmed her breath and listened closely. Seconds later, she heard the church's front door fling open and slam shut again within a matter of milliseconds.

Growing increasingly curious, Natasha bounded up the steps and out the front door. As soon as she stepped out into the freezing, winter air, she spotted her. It was Theresa, scurrying along the lamplit streets with her arms curled across her chest to keep her bare arms from catching frostbite. As soon as she heard the door open, Theresa spun around. Her eyes grew wide, and she took off in a dead sprint. Natasha followed after her, running as fast as her legs would carry and quickly making up ground as Theresa tripped and stumbled across the pavement, barely able to keep up her pace due to the buckling of her knees. Seizing the opportunity, Natasha sped up and caught up only a few seconds later.

Reaching out, she wrapped both her arms around Theresa and pulled her back. "Where are you going?" Natasha asked.

"You can't keep me there!" Theresa cried as she bucked and kicked like a raging bronco, trying to knock Natasha off her shoulders.

But Natasha wouldn't budge. With all her might, she clung to Theresa as she assured her, "It's what's best for you."

With a sudden burst of strength, Theresa's arm lurched forward before swinging back into Natasha's stomach, nearly knocking her over. Instinctively, Natasha's hands moved to her stomach, trying to absorb the shockwave that rippled through her core, and she let go of Theresa. This time with determined speed, Theresa took off again. However, before she could make it more than a few steps, Natasha lunged forward, grabbing hold of Theresa's arm, and pulled her into a tight embrace. She wrapped her arms around Theresa's elbows, locking her arms in place. Though Theresa fought against her with everything she had, it wasn't enough. She couldn't break free from Natasha's clutches.

Finally, she gave up, slumping helplessly into Natasha's arms. "I can't do it, Natasha," she cried, shaking uncontrollably.

"Yes, you can," Natasha said.

But Theresa shook her head. "I thought I could handle it, but I can't sleep. Can't eat. Every time I even think about food, I want to vomit. Hell, I can barely stand up without falling over. Nat, I need it. The heroin. My body needs it. I thought the warehouse was the worst thing that could ever happen to me. But I was s-s-s-so — so wrong. I-I hope your r-r-ready to catch me 'cause I th-th-think I'm gonna pass…"

Suddenly, Theresa's body grew limp, and her legs gave out from under her. Natasha tried to brace herself, but it was no use. As Theresa's body came toppling to the ground, it took

Natasha with it. And soon, they were both lying on the cold concrete, the breath knocked out of their lungs. With the last bit of her strength, Natasha slid out from underneath Theresa. Then, standing up and bending over, she draped her arms underneath Theresa's shoulders and tried to drag her back toward the church. However, as she reached the church steps, her arms turned to gelatin. Unable to hold on any longer, she set Theresa on the ground and collapsed onto the front steps.

I can't do it. Not alone. I don't have the strength.

Just then, as if summoned by her thoughts, Violet rushed out the front door, followed by Father Christopher, sprinting down the sidewalk from the rectory next door.

Kneeling beside Natasha, Father Christopher asked, "What happened?"

"I couldn't — I couldn't sleep," Natasha stammered, out of breath. "And I heard a noise outside my room. She — she was trying to — she said she couldn't take the withdrawal anymore. I tried to — I stopped her, but then she just passed out. I tried to get her up the steps, but I wasn't strong enough. I'm sorry."

"Don't be," Violet said as she and Father Christopher took Theresa by the feet and shoulders, respectively, and carried her back to her room. "You did a good thing, but you don't have to go it alone. You've got us. We're here for you."

And for a reason Natasha couldn't quite explain, those words struck a deep chord inside her soul.

As Father Christopher and Violet disappeared into the church behind her, Natasha leaned her head back and stared up into the empty night sky, feeling a tsunami of despair wash over her.

A thousand miles' journey was finally about to lead her to the devil's doorstep, where Blair sat, imprisoned, and she didn't know if she had any strength left in her bones to pull her from perdition.

But thankfully for her, she wouldn't be doing it alone.

Greenville, Michigan

As the morning sun broke through the windows of the old, fleabag Motel Eight on the edge of town, Rebecca rolled over in bed, trying to catch just a few seconds of shut-eye before the day began. Over the past week, she had left no stone unturned in her search for Paul, though she had still had no luck. When he sped out of Toledo, he had made sure that no one would be able to follow him. He shut off his phone, dumped his car in a Detroit parking garage and had even taken out a thousand dollars in cash so his credit cards couldn't be tracked. Even Shepard, with the entire breadth of the police department database at his disposal, couldn't find him. Paul had gone entirely off the grid, but Rebecca didn't give up hope.

After all, she knew him better than anyone, meaning it was only a matter of time before she found him.

Initially, she theorized that Paul had run to try to get as far away from Lena as possible. However, since all of the logical and defensible hideaways had been dead ends, that left only one thing he could be trying to escape: his pain. It was that realization that brought her to their hometown. Once midday came, she would go to the only spot in town that held any sentimental value to either of them, where she was sure that she would find him.

But in order for her plan to work, she needed to prepare. So, rolling onto her back, she opened her eyes. But, when she did, she saw something she didn't expect. Florian was looming over top of her with a pained expression on his face.

"Florian!" she exclaimed, jumping up and scurrying to the

back of the bed, startled. "What are you doing here? Don't scare me like that!"

Sighing, he looked to the back of the room, where a dark figure sat in the shadows. "She's all yours," he said.

Slowly and ominously, the figure rose from the darkness and stepped into the light. As it did, the light wrapped around the stranger's dark, heeled boots that clacked viciously across the motel's cold, cement floor. Rebecca didn't need to see its face to know who had found her. It was Lena, and immediately, Rebecca knew that she had been sold out.

"I thought we were in this together, Florian. Why'd you bring her into this?" she asked.

"I'm sorry. I had no choice," he sighed as he stood up, rubbing the back of his neck, and retreated into the darkness.

Sitting at the edge of the bed, Lena smiled, though from the look in her eyes, it was clear that it wasn't happiness she was trying to convey. "It's good to see you too, Rebecca," she said. "Let's talk."

"I have nothing to say to you," Rebecca said.

"Oh, but I think you do," Lena replied as she planted her hand on the mattress and leaned closer until she was only a foot from Rebecca's face. "Why don't you start with telling me where he is?"

"Where who is?" Rebecca asked, feigning confusion.

Lena chuckled, "You always were the only person who could truly make me laugh. And it's for that reason and that reason alone that you're sitting here right now instead of in the ground, where you're supposed to be. So, I'll ask you again. And I'd answer honestly if I were you before all that good will runs out. Where is Paul?"

"I don't know."

"Don't lie to me!"

"I'm not lying. I've been looking for him, the same as you."

"So, it's just supposed to be a coincidence that you're renting rooms under a fake name in your hometown?"

"I had a theory," Rebecca answered. "But there was only one place in this town that he would have gone, and he wasn't there. So, I guess it's back to square one."

"I think she's telling the truth, boss," Florian chimed in from the back of the room.

"Did I ask for your opinion, traitor?!" Lena exclaimed, whirling around to stare daggers at Florian before calmly turning back to Rebecca. "Give me one reason I should trust you."

"Well, my plan doesn't exactly work too well if I'm actually dead, now does it?" Rebecca replied.

"And what is your plan, exactly?" Lena asked.

"To turn him against you."

"I thought you were smarter than that, Rebecca. What makes you think he would choose you over me? He made that decision a long time ago."

"Is that why he's in the wind instead of in your bed?"

"I never pinned your as a Peeping Jane, but I certainly hope you enjoyed watching your husband enjoy a real woman."

Rebecca smirked. "If only your tits weren't made of plastic," she said.

"Enough of these games!" Lena exploded, slamming her clenched fist onto the bed next to Rebecca's leg. "Where would he have gone?!"

"The Milk King on Washington Street. It's where he proposed."

"If you're lying to me, you know what I'll do to you."

"He wouldn't go anywhere else. It was the only good memory either of us had in this place."

"Fine," Lena scoffed, latching onto Rebecca's arm and

forcing her onto her feet. "But you're coming with us. That way, I can put your ass in the ground if you're lying."

After stepping into the bathroom to get herself dressed, Rebecca followed Lena and Florian to their car. As she slipped into the backseat, she sat herself against the driver's side door, directly behind Lena. The whole way to Milk King, she closed her eyes and drew up a map of the town in her head. Once they got to the restaurant, it was only a matter of time before Lena discovered she was lying, which meant she needed an escape route and fast.

Thankfully, this wasn't a neutral field. They were playing on her home turf.

Five minutes later, they pulled up to the curb on Washington Street, about twenty feet from Milk King. Lena stepped out onto the curb first, followed by Florian. Meanwhile, Rebecca simply waited and watched. Squinting through the glare off the nearby windshields, Lena took a step forward and tried to look through the windows in search of Paul while she motioned for Florian to circle around the car and open Rebecca's door, which he did.

Opening the door and bending down to her level, Florian took Rebecca by the arm and whispered, "She threatened Janelle. I have to do what she says. Don't be too upset with me."

"I understand," she replied, bracing herself on his shoulders as he helped her to his feet. "Which is why I hope you'll understand that it's nothing personal when I do this."

With a sudden burst, she shot her knee into his groin, doubling him over in pain. Turning him to the side, she positioned him in between herself and Lena, who still hadn't noticed the commotion, and with both hands, threw him into the back of Lena's knees. After that, she didn't linger to see how much of a head start she had earned

herself. She darted around the back of the car like a grey-
hound after a hare. Then, as her feet hit the sidewalk, she
zipped right before whipping left, heading down the alley
next to Smith's Hardware, a store owned by the father of
her seventh grade boyfriend, and knocking a trio of trash-
cans over to block Lena and Florian's as she passed. Immediately, a pungent odor filled the air around her, like
spoiled milk a second after opening the carton, nearly
knocking her flat on her back. But, she shook it off and kept
running.

As she rounded the corner toward the other side of Smith's
she looked back just in time to see Lena and Florian arrive at
the alley's entrance and abruptly stop in front of it, surprised
and nauseated by the smell. Sweat began to drip from Rebecca's brow as her lungs started to ache. Regretfully, she had
always been more of a Saturday morning cartoon girl than a
track and field girl.

*I won't be able to keep this up much longer. There's got to be a way
to lose them.*

While Lena and Florian tiptoed around the trash pile, being
careful not to take a header into a pile of wood scraps or week-
old shepherd's pie, Rebecca dashed to the other end of the alley
and back onto the street. Then, she wheeled back around to the
front of the building and shot through the front doors of the
store with a desperate crash.

As she stepped into Smith's Hardware, the familiar smell of
sawdust and soil filled the air, transporting her back into a
simpler time, when she wasn't running for her life from a
traitor and a psychopath. During her two-year romance with
Freddy Smith, the most popular boy in the seventh grade, she
had spent countless hours in the back room of this exact store,
checking out his horror movie collection and testing the waters
of her newfound sexuality. Above all of that, however, the thing

she remembered most of all was the solid, sliding door that separated the store's main floor from the back room.

That afternoon, the store was empty part from Mr. Smith, who was manning the front counter, and Freddy, who was restocking hammers and screwdrivers along the back wall. So, ducking under the tops of the shelves as to hide herself from anyone who might come looking for her, Rebecca shuffled around to the back of the store. Then, taking Freddy by the hand, she pulled him toward the back room.

Initially, he stumbled along with her, but upon seeing her, he stopped in his tracks, dumbfounded. "Rebecca?" he asked. "Aren't you-"

"No, I'm not dead, and yes, I'm still married," she answered as quickly as she could. "I can explain later. For now, I need you to take me into the back room. And don't say a word."

Nodding politely, he checked over both shoulders and slid open the door to the back room, which was only a few feet to his left. As he did, she wheeled around to his back, using his body to shield her. Then, they backed into the room, and Freddy locked the door behind them.

After being ushered into the farthest corner of the room, Freddy turned to Rebecca and chuckled, "You always were the dramatic one, weren't you? If you wanted another make-out session, all you had to do was ask. You didn't have to fake your death and skip town just for me."

"Very funny." She rolled her eyes and pushed him playfully. "My life's been... a little complicated lately. You probably wouldn't believe me if I told you."

"I'm offended," he said, gasping facetiously and holding his hand over his heart. "After everything we went through, you still don't trust me."

"Well, you did leave me for Heather Sanders three days into high school."

"A mistake that has haunted me ever since."

"Either way, thank you for taking me back here."

"Anything for little Becca Badass."

"Have I ever told you how glad I am that nickname never stuck?"

"I, for one, think it's a shame," Freddy replied with a chuckle. "So, now that we're both here, in the back room of my dad's shop, all alone, is there anything else I can do for you?"

"Now that you mention it, I may need a small favor," Rebecca answered.

"Just say the word."

"Are you still as obsessed with horror movies as you were when we were kids?"

"Even more so, if you ask my exes."

"And do you still have that horror makeup collection you used for every Halloween?"

"Of course," he replied. "Right underneath my bathroom sink. Why do you ask?"

She laughed, "Because I figured, since everyone already thinks I'm dead, I might as well lean into it."

22

CLOSE

GREENVILLE, MICHIGAN

*S*itting alone under the shade of an oak tree as a frigid, December wind blustered on every side, Paul stared across the horizon at his ghost of his own Christmas past. Bending over, he straightened out the creases on the edge of the picnic blanket and wrapped his fingers around the fourth, full flute of champagne he had drunk that afternoon. As it bubbled and fizzed, flowing smoothly down his throat, he peered at the empty spot across the blanket from him, at the second, untouched glass he had set there, and, for the first time in the week he had spent atop that hill, wished he didn't have to drink alone. Originally, he climbed that hill to escape Rebecca's ghost, but now, he felt empty without her beside him.

Because even if all she did was antagonize him, at least she was there. At least he got to see her beautiful face and gaze into her shining, crystal eyes. In the end, the guilt didn't burn as hot as the loneliness. By leaving him alone, she was inflicting a punishment far worse than he could have imagined.

As morning passed into the afternoon, the cold seeped

through the five layers that separated his skin from the air and sizzled against his skin. Soon, numbness crept through his bones, starting in the back of his neck but quickly making its way through his arms, his legs and all the way down to his toes. After six hours, he lost all feeling in his body, but even still, he wasn't about to leave. He was determined to stay there until he saw Rebecca again. It didn't matter if she came that by hallucination or death. He was done living without her in his life.

Even if he passed to the other side that day, at least he would see her again. Though, deep down, he feared that, even in death, an infinite chasm of flame would still stand between him and his love.

As the sun set across the horizon, painting the skyline a brilliant shade of red, yellow and blue, the blanket rustled beside him. Immediately, pure relief washed over him, which only escalated as he saw his Rebecca sitting across from him, just as beautiful as he remembered her. Despite the blood, the scars, the skin that hung, haphazardly, from her hands, face and hair, she still bore a radiance that drove away the darkness inside his soul. In that moment, they were back in high school with a whole world of possibility in front of them, and it was perfection.

Paul smiled. "I was hoping you might show up," he said. "I've missed you."

"I thought you were getting sick of me," Rebecca replied wryly.

"Though a thousand lifetimes pass between us, I could never feel anything but love for you," he said.

Looking down at the champagne flute on her side of the blanket, she raised her eyebrows at him and chuckled, "You know I can't actually drink this, right?"

"I know. But I wanted it to feel as much like that afternoon as possible."

"It's even December."

"Almost eight years to the day since the best day of my life."

"But we didn't get married until February."

"You know," he sighed. "I used to think I could find no greater happiness than I did while I was standing beside you in that courthouse, but now, after everything that's happened, no. This was it. I had everything I could ever need on top of this hill. I was just too young and dumb to see it."

"Why did we ever need anything more?" she asked.

"Because it was always about me! Hell, maybe that's all it still is for me. I was afraid, afraid of failing you, of not being able to provide enough for you or give you all the things you dreamed about."

"But I never wanted any of that. I never wanted money or the biggest house or even the shelter. All I wanted was you."

"But what if I wasn't enough?"

"Then *we* would have been."

"How can you know that?" he asked.

"Because deep down, you do too," she answered. "After all, aren't I just a projection of your guilt? Could I say it if it wasn't already what you believed?"

"It was the only thing I could think to do!" he exclaimed, raising both arms toward the sky.

"Kidnapping women? Forcing them into your harem? Damn, Paul. Are you really that uncreative?"

"I didn't mean for it to — I wasn't trying — it didn't start out that way. Just... one thing led to another and another and another. Soon, I was in over my head."

"Then why didn't you swim back to shore?"

"I was in a riptide, Bec! The ocean was swirling around me

so fast that I didn't know which way was up, down or side-ways. So, I reached. I grabbed onto the first boat that came my way. They gave me a job, and I was damn good at it. Shit, I was great at it. How is that even a skill that someone has? I mean, it wasn't all bad, was it? I gave them a place, a job, a life."

"And a nice pair of chains for their hands and feet," Rebecca scoffed.

"Do you really think it was better for them out there?" Paul asked.

"At least they had a choice."

"Come on, hun. You saw those same girls every day at the shelter. You gave them their meals. What were they supposed to do? What was really in the cards for them when they went into the real world? You can offer them all the classes, the food, all the good conversation you want, but it doesn't change the fact that this world is a shit-hole. The second they leave your shelter, they're back in hell, and they have nothing. I tried to give them something better!"

"And what about Kayde?"

Suddenly, Paul stopped pacing and turned away from her, ashamed. "It wasn't my finger on the trigger," he said.

"But you still think he deserved it," she said.

"He betrayed me!" he screamed as his fist flew into the trunk of the tree, splintering its bark beneath his knuckles.

"Can you blame him?" she asked. "Wouldn't you do the same for me? For Elle?"

Just then, the shadow of the setting sun fell across Paul's face, and immediately, everything went dark. Across the horizon, there was nothing except the glimmer of his own skin and a faint light in the distance, like a firefly in the night or a long-distant train. And with every second that passed, it grew larger and closer, but it wasn't the light that was approaching; it was him. Beneath his feet, the ground beneath flew at a blistering speed, so fast that he could hardly keep his feet. He stumbled and swayed against the wind that blew at his back, but he refused to lose his balance. Spreading his legs and chopping his feet to counter the shifting ground underneath him.

But it was what he saw when the light came into full view that sent him tumbling to the ground.

Suddenly, he was back inside the hotel room from his dream. Elle was sitting atop the bed, and Izzy stood before her, lowering the shoulder straps of her dress. As they slipped from her arms, Izzy turned and looked Paul directly in the eyes.

With a wicked smile and a spine-tingling wink, Izzy said, "Don't worry, Paulie. I'll take good care of her."

Leaping to his feet, Paul made a break for Izzy, his arms outstretched to tear him in half. However, before Paul could reach him, the ground split in half. Then, it shifted violently, sending Paul sprawling onto his back. He tried to reach out for her, but it was too late. As quickly at it appeared, the hotel room faded into oblivion, and he was helpless to stop it. Before he even knew what was happening, he was back in Tower Park with his blanket on the ground and Rebecca's ghost by his side.

Desperate, he reached out toward the sun, which had now disappeared behind the city skyline, screaming, "I'll tear you in two, you disgusting motherfu-"

"You know what you have to do," Rebecca said.

"I-I can't..." he sighed.

"Why not?" she asked.

"First, I lost you. Then, I lost Elle. If I lose this, there will be nothing left. I won't — I'm not sure I'll know who I am anymore."

"Not the same man. That's for damn sure."

"I'll have nothing."

"Not for long."

"How can you be so sure?" he asked.

"Because, all that other stuff be damned, you're still Paul Cross, the man who stood by me when the rest of the world left me in the ditch. You're the man who, despite the fact that he never even graduated high school, became the best father, the best husband I've ever seen. If there's one thing you've proven, it's that it's not what you've done that defines you. It's what you do next."

"Why are you being so nice to me?" he asked.

"What do you mean?" she asked.

"Ever since you showed up, you've done nothing but insult, ridicule or downright torture me. But now, here, you seem... different. If I didn't know any better, I'd say you seem more like the Rebecca I remember. What changed?"

"I think you did. All I've ever told you is what you needed to hear. I guess what you needed today was just a little dash of hope."

"But what am I supposed to do with that?"

"That's up for you to decide."

With that, she was gone. The wind gusted, blowing through the tree's empty branches and drawing his attention toward the setting sun. When he turned around, he was alone again with only his two flutes of champagne and his thoughts to keep him company. For the next, two hours, he stood there, at the apex of the hill, gazing upon a clear, infinitely starry sky. And it was in that moment, as he was dwarfed by the vastness of the universe that he realized for the first time how truly small, insignificant and alone he truly was. Up until that point, he had always been responsible for someone else's well-being, whether it be Rebecca's, Elle's or Lena's. But now, the only person he was responsible for was himself.

At the end of the day, the only thing he wanted was to see his little girl again, to be the father that Rebecca always believed him to be, one who Elle might, one day, come to forgive and want back in her life.

So, sitting back down by his side of the picnic blanket, he pulled out his phone and dialed the only person left in the universe who could redeem him.

∼

Las Vegas, Nevada

"OKAY, IT'S SHOW TIME!" THE NINETEEN-YEAR-OLD, OVER-enthusiastic production assistant who had been hounding Bradie all morning, from make-up to interview prep, whispered as she put a hand on each shoulder and directed him toward the stage. "You'll do great out there."

However, Bradie didn't budge, not even an inch. Instead, his legs froze to the floor beneath him as he stared out onto the stage at the seat that had been saved specifically for him. The deafening roar of applause echoed on every side, encasing him in a audial prison of fear. His mouth grew dry. His throat closed up. He looked around him for a means of escape but found none. Behind him were Stacy and Nina, each of whom bore a hopeful smile on their face and shot him a nervous thumbs up. Beside him stood the production assistant, who was now attempting to literally push him onto the stage, her back pressed against his and her legs churning like they were attached to bicycle pedals.

And next to him was Anna, who looked over at him with a smile and planted a warm kiss on his cheek.

Then, she whispered in his ear, "I'll be right next to you."

Somehow, that gave him the courage he needed to take that first step toward his own sort of lethifold.

However, it didn't allot him enough to grant speech to his vocal cords.

As Anna and Bradie took their seats in front of the live, studio audience, their host, Nickie Ocean, the salacious, silken-voiced siren of Sin City greeted them with her usual high-energy flair, looking directly into the camera that stood right in front of the audience and saying, "Good morning, Oceaneers! I hope you are all having a great day as we sail on into the holiday season. This morning, I have the privilege of spending time with a pair of bonafide saints, Bradie and Anna Lam. When I first heard about these two, I was so blown away by their story that I had to bring them on the show. Why don't we give them a Oceaneer's hello?"

As Nickie lifted both of her hands toward the audience, a chorus of cheers and applause once again echoed off the walls of the soundstage, assaulting his ears from all directions. In that moment, watching the audience rise and fall in delayed unison, like the coming of the tides or a sea of avid, sports fans, Bradie felt like a gladiator in the arena, terrified that one wrong move could turn the crowd against him and cause the day to end with all of Vegas calling for his head on a platter.

Once the commotion died down, Nickie continued, "These two have the kind of story you have to hear from the horse's mouth in order to believe. So, I'm going to let them tell it. Why don't we start with how you met? You weren't originally father and daughter, were you, Bradie?"

Suddenly, every eye in the building turned on Bradie, and just as quickly, his heart started to beat at a marching drum rhythm. He opened his mouth to speak, but all that came out was a squeal. After that, all Bradie heard was silence.

Looking directly into the camera with both eyebrows raised,

Nickie laughed, "Looks like our hard-boiled detective is a little camera shy."

"He can stare the criminal underworld in the face, unblinking," Anna chuckled. "But put a camera in front of his face, and he forgets his own name."

A ripple of laughter made its way through the audience as Nickie said, "You should've seen me the first time I saw this motley crew. Let's just say my assistant had a hell of the time cleaning the barf off her shoes. While our fearless sleuth gets his wits about him, Anna, why don't you tell us about First National Bank?"

"Well, in order to tell you that, I think I have to start further back with how I met *him*."

As Anna detailed her story, starting with her introduction to the trafficking industry and quickly moving to that fateful morning atop First National Bank and beyond, the audience scooted to the edge of their seats and leaned forward to listen with bated breath to every detail. With every story Anna told and every follow-up question Nickie asked, Bradie's heart slowed to a ballad beat. As he breathed in, every ounce of anxiety flowed out of his body and into the couch cushions beneath him. The lights around him dimmed, and the audience and cameras faded into the background.

It's just like having a cup of coffee with a friend. No pressure. Just tell the story.

"I didn't know what to expect when we walked into that club," Anna explained. "It was the first time I had been inside that world since Los Angeles. But honestly, I wasn't as afraid as I expected I would be. None of the stuff from my past really mattered anymore. It was about rescuing those girls. There's no way I could have found that strength on my own. Really, I owe it all to Bradie. He taught me how to be strong."

"I really appreciate the compliment, sweetheart," Bradie

said, finally feeling the last of the weight on his shoulders dissipate as he spoke. "But I think you give me far too much credit. That strength you found in me wasn't my own. I got it all from you."

"Are you viewers at home eating up the father-daughter love as much as I am?" Nickie asked the camera before turning back to them. "So, how did it feel to finally get your man?"

"It felt good at first," Anna chuckled.

"Yeah, really good," Bradie sighed. "Until the court let him off with just a slap on the wrist."

Nickie shook her head. "I read about that in the papers," she replied. "But you were still a huge part of getting Rodney Marshall finally put away for good. How did that come about?"

"With blood, sweat and a lot of illegal activity," Bradie replied. "After doing some digging, we found out that Allan Mathis, the judge assigned to Rodney's trial, was another flunky on Rodney's payroll. So, since the justice system wasn't doing us a whole lot of good, I took the story to Nina Brown from The Pulse. Her article got Judge Mathis fired and gave Rodney a re-trial and a life sentence to boot."

"A smart move, one that, from what I hear, also cost you your badge. I imagine that must have hurt," Nickie said.

"Honestly, it wasn't as bad as I thought it would be. In the end, justice is far more important than a position. The only thing I miss about having a badge is being able to make a real difference out there every day."

"Word on the street is that you haven't let that stop you from doing it."

"Once your eyes are opened to that world, it's impossible to look away."

Turning back to the camera, Nickie said, "We've got a special treat for you today, Oceaneers: exclusive, undercover video from *inside* a trafficking den *in our own backyard*. You're not going to want to miss it or the *surprise ending* that will knock your socks off. Stay tuned!"

As the cameras turned off, signaling the crew to set up for the next segment, Nicky stood from her seat and walked over to Bradie.

Then, sitting on the edge of the coffee table, she placed her hand on his and Anna's knees and said, "You both are such an inspiration to me. You have such determination, such inscrutable integrity. These stories are just further proof to me that the two of you are just the type of people that I need working with me on my team."

"What are you talking about?" Anna asked, tilting her head in confusion.

"My producers have been buzzing for *weeks* about this episode, since before we even booked you," Nickie explained. "This is a hot button topic right now. Forget politics, forget football. Women's rights are today's water cooler talk. I mean, just look at social media. It's everywhere, and I want to jump on the bandwagon with both feet. Picture this, a monthly segment where we take down trafficking rings, expose dirty cops and bring justice to judges. It'll be a hit, and you two will be the stars. I can't think of anyone better for this job."

"Wow," Bradie said. "That's really quite the offer. I don't know what to say."

"All I want to hear is that you'll think about it," she said.

Just then, his phone rang. Reaching down, he pulled it from his pocket and checked the caller ID.

The number was blocked. Instinctively, Bradie went to put his phone away. Usually, if he didn't know a number, he wouldn't answer it. But that evening, for a reason he couldn't quite explain, he felt compelled to answer it.

"I-I'm sorry," Bradie stammered. "I think I-I need to take this."

So, standing from his seat, Bradie scurried off stage, past the production assistants and cameramen who were crowded around the snack table, stuffing their mouths full of finger foods, and through the back doors.

Once he was outside, he brought the phone to his ear and answered, "Hello?"

"Yes, Bradie?" the voice on the other line asked. "It's Paul Cross. There's something I need to talk to you about."

Paul? How the hell did he get my number?

"Yes… uh, of course. What — well, what's going on? I can't say yours was the voice I was expecting to be on the other line," Bradie chuckled anxiously.

"And I'm sure you won't be surprised to hear that you were the last person I thought I'd ever be calling," Paul sighed.

"After all this time, why call me now?"

"Because I need your help."

"You're going to have to be a lot more specific if you want me to stay on this line."

"I made a mistake. A long time ago."

"What kind of mistake?" Bradie asked.

"The kind that changes a man into something he never thought he'd be," Paul answered. "The kind that has… permanent consequences."

"Yeah, I heard about Rebecca. I'm sorry that happened. No one deserves to go through that kind of pain."

"Except for me, that is."

His voice. He sounds almost sincere. Rebecca must have really done a number on him.

"Why do you think that?"

Gulping, Paul answered, "Because I've done horrible things. Unforgivable things. And I know how it's going to sound when I say this, but I need you to trust what I'm about to say."

"You know I can't promise that," Bradie replied.

"Then I just need you to listen. Since closing Illuminate, Lena and I have been in Toledo, Ohio, running a massage parlor and nail salon called Dragon's Wing. But of course, you know what's really going on behind those doors. One week from tonight, as night falls, I will be at my desk in the parlor with a stack of files in my hand that will be more than enough to prove your suspicions to a court. And I want you to be there to arrest me."

"But I don't have a badge."

"If you're half the man I believe you to be, that won't matter."

"How do I know you'll be there?" Bradie asked. "How do I know I won't be walking into a ghost town, just like the last time?"

"I guess you don't," Paul answered. "One way or another, I'll be there. We may only have one shot to do this. So, I really hope you'll be there."

With that, the line went dead, leaving Bradie floored. Even though he knew what Rebecca's plan had been, he never believed it would actually pan out.

And if he was being honest with himself, he still wasn't sure it would.

So, as he walked back through the studio doors, past the food table and up to the stage, a thousand doubts ran through his mind, saddled atop another million questions. For his whole life, he had believed that people never truly changed; they only appeared to change when it suited them, when convincing others of their goodness was a matter of survival. But in Paul's case, there was no gun to his head, not even the threat of being found out. In fact, if Paul actually showed up at that parlor and turn himself in, he was guaranteed prison. No district attorney in their right mind would pardon him of the charges he was sure to face.

So why would he turn himself in?

As Bradie approached the stage, Anna rushed over to him, saying, "Hey, good timing. We're just about to get started again. Who was the call from?"

"It was Paul Cross," Bradie answered. "He said he wants to turn himself in."

23

GREY

TOLEDO, OHIO

*B*lair's chest tightened as the echo of the clock's incessant ticking resonated in the back of her ears, raising the hairs on the back of her neck. With every second that passed, she grew more and more anxious. Soon, the bell would toll, signaling the end of her reprieve, and she would have no choice but to decide between freedom and friendship.

For six days, Lena's threat had played on repeat in the back of Blair's mind. When she was in the salon, when she was at school, when she was out to eat, she was subject to her torment. There was hardly a second that she didn't feel the ball and chain dragging behind her feet, tethering her to her cage. As the clock struck eight, the school bell rang, marking the end of the seventh day.

And just like that, her time was up.

The hour of reckoning had come, and Blair's mind was made up. Now, she had to act before she changed her mind.

So, quickly stuffing her books into her backpack, she slung it over her shoulder and bolted out the doors, hoping she could make it out the front doors of the school before Cici caught up with her. She couldn't stand the thought of having to say good-bye. After all, Ciara was the first, real friend Blair had made since leaving New York. And as much as it hurt to leave her behind without an explanation, it would sting even worse to see the disappointment that was bound to be etched across her face upon learning that they would never see each other again. It was easier this way. She only hoped Cici would come to realize that some day.

However, just as Blair stepped out the front doors and into the night air, Cici's hand latched onto hers, pulling her back.

Desperate, Blair fought against her, trying to wrench herself from Cici's grip. "I'm sorry. I have to — I've got to get back. Lots of homework."

But Cici refused to let go. Reaching around Blair's side, she grabbed her and held on tight, insisting, "No, you're not getting off that easy. You've been 'busy' for a week now. What gives, B-loves? I've missed you. Did I do something wrong?"

"Of course not," Blair answered, feeling a heavy weight press against her chest. "There's just been a lot of my plate."

Ciara shook her head. "Bullshit," she said. "We've been friends for almost a month now. I know that's not a lifetime or anything, but you get to know someone pretty damn well when you see them literally every day. What do you expect me to think when you suddenly drop off the face of the earth?"

"Please, I've really got to get going."

"Not until you tell me what the hell's going on with you. You can always talk to me, hun. You know that."

"Don't make me do this."

"Don't make you do what?"

"Say goodbye!" Blair exclaimed, finally prying herself from Ciara, tears now streaming like rivers from her sockets. "I didn't want this to be my last memory of you. I wanted us both to remember the friendship, not the farewell."

"So, you were just going to let me sit here and wonder what I did to drive you away?" Ciara asked, the hurt seeping from her own eyes.

"No! I mean… Cici, it's not that. You didn't do anything."

"Then why?! Why would you leave someone who cares about you more than anything without even giving her the courtesy of a goodbye? I'm trying to wrap it around this crumb-sized brain of mine, but I can't, love. I don't understand."

"I'm sorry."

"Fine, whatever. You do you, B-loves. Shit, I thought you were different, but I guess I was wrong. Eventually, everyone leaves. Even you."

"Goodbye, Ciara," Blair said as she turned and walked away, refusing to look back out of fear that she might change her mind.

After leaving the school, Blair didn't go home. At least, not at first. For two hours, she walked aimlessly down every city street and parkway within two miles of the salon until every inch of her body was numb. After a while, even her tear ducts froze, forming what felt like tiny icicles at the base of her eyelids. As she walked, she tried to take in as much of the city as she could. That way, she would never forget what it felt like to be free, what it meant to be human. She stared at the light from the street lamps as it reflected off the snow-covered ground, encasing the air above it in a shroud of white. She watched the cars whip past her, flying down the city streets, and listened to their wheels skid against the wet pavement, and she gazed upon the night sky, watching the stars dance a celestial tango and taking in every detail she could, no matter how small.

That way, when she lay in bed at night, unable to sleep due to the cinema of death and pain that cycled without reprieve through her mind's eye, she would have somewhere to go back to, free from that pain and filled with nothing but peace.

Stopping at the gate outside the houses, Blair turned and leaned up against it, taking one last look at the horizon before returning to her dungeon. She closed her eyes and breathed a final, lasting breath into the emptiness. And as she walked the death march back to her apartment, the chains wrapped around her wrists and ankles once more.

Her door creaked open like the slow cranking of the guillotine, and behind it stood her executioner.

Upon seeing that Blair had returned alone, Lena sighed angrily, "I can't say I'm surprised. You should never send a bitch to do her master's job."

"I'm sorry, ma'am," Blair said, hanging her head in a show of submission. "I couldn't get anyone to come with me."

Lena rolled her eyes. "I don't want excuses," she said as she took a step forward, dug her nails into Blair's arm and pulled her toward the door. "Right now, all I want is for you to squirm."

"Where are we going?"

"To the dark room. And you'd better get yourself comfortable because you won't be leaving it anytime soon."

"But I don't understand. You said I just wouldn't be able to go out anymore."

"I changed my mind. And, you'd better shut your damn mouth while I'm still feeling generous or I'll make you join your brother."

Blair's hands shook as Lena dragged her toward the door. As they passed the threshold, Blair looked around for anything she could use as a means of escape. Deep down, she knew she could never actually get away from Lena, but she couldn't go to the dark room, not again. She would rather die first, and an attempted escape was the best way to ensure that this night would be her last.

But, just as she was about to hoist herself over the handrails and make a break for the outside, she heard the sound of footsteps ascending the stairwell. Peering over the edge, a familiar, brown streak turned the first corner toward the second floor.

"Cici?" she whispered as her heart fell into her stomach.

"Maybe you aren't so useless after all," Lena whispered as she hauled her back inside the room. "Now, reel her in. And just in case your own safety isn't enough to motivate you; ether you persuade her to stay, or I will."

Closing her eyes, Blair swallowed through the thousand frogs that were sitting inside her throat, trying to force down the bitter taste of fear that now lingered on her tongue. As Cici's feet hit the top of the stairs, Blair opened her eyes and pasted on a smile. Then, she met Cici at the door, wrapping her arm around Cici's shoulders and leading her inside the room.

And with that, her performance began.

"Ciara, my love!" Blair exclaimed. "I'm so glad you're here! I was just about to give you a call."

Immediately, the muscles in Cici's shoulders tensed, and she looked quizzically at Blair. "You okay, B-loves?" she asked. "You're kind of giving me a Tyler Durden vibe right now."

"Don't be ridiculous," Blair chuckled, pulling Cici closer and kissing her on the forehead. "I'm sorry for being so silly earlier. Turns out, I was freaking out over nothing. See, my boss was planning to transfer me out of state tomorrow. I was devastated when she told me because it meant I wouldn't be able to see you anymore. But, she and I just had a little talk, and she says I can stay."

"Providing she helps me find a replacement for the girl I'm sending in her place," Lena said with an ominous wink.

"Isn't that great?" Blair asked through gritted teeth.

"Wait, replacement?" Cici asked. "Does that mean…?"

Pointing to the room beside Blair's, which to this point had been perpetually empty, Lena answered, "As of tonight, that room is officially open. For the right candidate."

Immediately, Cici left Blair's side and marched over to Lena, taking her by the hands and begging, "Oh, you've got to pick me! I'd be perfect for this job."

"What has Blair told you about what we do?" Lena asked.

"I mean, not much, really, but like, what is there to know? All I do is a little grunt work, and I get everything I could ever need? Sign me up."

"You won't be able to live at home anymore."

"Dude, is supposed to be a downside? I've been looking for a way to get away from my asshole family since I turned thirteen."

"I don't know. I mean, we've got interviews lined up, some really good candidates too."

"There ain't nobody on your list who'll do a better job than me," Cici said.

"And why's that?" Lena asked.

"Because I need it more than those other bitches. Ain't one of them gonna beat my drive."

"You make a compelling argument, but I'm not sure I'm convinced. The other applicants all have references and a work history. I can't just hire you without someone to vouch for your character."

"Why don't you ask Blair? She can tell you how it is."

"That's a fantastic idea," Lena said with a wicked smile. "So, what do you say, *Blair*? *S*hould I hire your friend?"

"Absolutely," Blair gulped, nearly choking on her own lies. "I can't think of anyone better suited for this life."

"Then it's settled!" Lena exclaimed, clapping her hands together as a wide, mischievous smile enveloped her face.

"From now on, this is your home. Don't even worry about going back to pack because as of tomorrow, everything you need will be right here."

Then, taking Blair by the arm, she led her toward the door, turning back to Cici and saying, "Sit down, kick your feet up and make yourself at home. If you don't mind, I'm going to borrow Blair for a day or two. She and I have business to take care of."

Confused, Blair looked to Lena as the door closed behind them and asked, "What business?"

"You, my dear, have a date with the dark room," Lena answered.

Immediately, Blair's eyes grew wide, and the breath left her lungs. "I don't understand," she choked. "I did what you asked; I brought her in."

"Don't think I don't recognize a happy accident when I see one," Lena replied. "You weren't expecting her to be here, which means you still failed me. And I don't accept failure."

And with that, as Lena hauled Blair across the street and threw her into the dark room, the last piece of Blair's soul was devoured by the darkness. For, when push came to shove, she had sold it to the devil for mere trifles.

24

REVENGE

NEW YORK, NEW YORK

"Okay, we know *where* she is," Natasha said, leaning across the bed and tapping her fingers on the sheets. "But how do we get in?"

Across the mattress, Theresa shook her head and looked away, biting her lower lip in frustration. Meanwhile, Violet paced around Natasha's room in the church basement, holding her thumbs to her temples in an attempt to force her neurons to fire and trying to avoid giving the answer they all were thinking.

Which was that none of them had a clue how they were going to rescue Blair.

To this point, the only part of the plan they could agree on was where to park the car. Once that was settled, they quickly sunk in the quicksand. Regretfully, the only information they had was the little Violet had been able to gleam from her boyfriend, and even more unfortunately, that wasn't a whole lot. All they knew was that they were dealing with a massage parlor and nail salon turned trafficking den called Dragon's Wing. But besides its name, purpose and general location, they had nothing, and without first-hand knowledge of its inner workings, they were stuck throwing stones at the stars, hoping to make one fall.

"I still say we burn those bastards," Violet muttered.

"I hate to admit it," Theresa sighed. "But I think I agree with Violet."

"This isn't about getting revenge. We're going there to get Blair, and that's it," Natasha said.

"That's great and all, but how are you planning to actually do that?" Violet asked.

"We'll figure it out," Natasha answered.

"You keep saying that. But we've been at this for days, and we're still no closer to a plan," Violet said.

"It would save us a lot of trouble if we just took them out," Theresa said.

"And make us just as bad as they are," Natasha replied. "Okay, let's go back to square one. Violet, you said you saw Blair and your brother come out of a house?"

"I didn't have the best view from down the street, but yeah, that's what it looked like," Violet answered as she ran her hands roughly through her hair.

"So Blair must be in one of those rooms," Natasha said.

"But good luck getting to her," Violet scoffed. "If Dragon's Wing is anything like The Eclipse, they'll have their people living on the first floor. They'll spot us a mile away."

"Could we sneak in while the girls go back home at the end of the day?" Theresa asked. "I still have my clothes from the warehouse."

"So do I," Natasha said.

But Violet shook her head. "I mean, I have my hooker threads too, but it's not going to matter," she said. "There's no way they're letting their workers walk all that way unguarded. Besides, when I saw Kayde, he was in some sort of flamingo-pink uniform. Somehow I doubt our old clothes will do us any good."

"And you're sure there's no way we can sneak in?" Natasha asked.

"Not without getting ourselves killed," Violet replied.

"What if we created a diversion?" Theresa asked.

"It'd have to be big enough to pull everyone they've got across the street," Violet said. "But if we did it right, it could work."

"What are you thinking?" Natasha asked as both she and Violet crowded around Theresa, eagerly awaiting her answer.

"I-I don't know," Theresa stammered, her eyes fluttering nervously around the room. "Maybe something like… a fire?"

"Oh my god, that's perfect," Violet muttered to herself before grabbing Theresa by the shoulders and kissing her excitedly on the forehead. "Terry, you're a genius!"

"And if they're anything like Alexei, they'll deal only in cash. Which means, as soon as they see the fire, they'll barrel straight out of the houses to make sure their money doesn't burn," Natasha said.

"We'll need a lot of gasoline," Violet said.

"And something to light it with," Theresa added.

"Then let's get going!" Natasha said, unable to keep the excitement from oozing out of her pores. "Violet and I will grab some gas cans and fill them up. Theresa, talk to Father Christopher and see if we can nab a few packs of those matches they keep for the Advent candles. Once we get that, we'll have everything we need to make this dragon breathe fire."

With a thankful pat on Theresa's shoulder, Natasha stood up and started to follow Violet out the door.

But before she made it to the doorway, Theresa stopped Natasha, grabbing her by the hand and saying, "Hey, before we go, there's something I've been meaning to give you." Then, reaching into her back pocket, she pulled out a gleaming, silver necklace and held it out toward Natasha. "After you left the warehouse, Blair snuck into your room and took this before Alexei could find it. When they sent her away, she gave it to me. I think, deep down, she knew you'd come back for her. And now that we're going back for her, I think it's only right that you wear it."

Reaching out, Natasha took the necklace in her hands, holding the cross pendant in one hand and letting the chain fall into her other. Its loops cascaded down the space between her hands like a glorious, familiar waterfall and swirled like a whirlpool in her palm. Under the morning light that flooded through the stained glass, basement window, its faded silver almost looked brand new as it reflected an array of colors as extensive as a rainbow off its surface. As she held it up, unclasping it, and looped it around her neck, her body filled with the most reassuring kind of warmth. It was as though she was returning home after a lifetime away. She looked down at her hands, which, since putting a bullet in Alexei's skull, had been encased in darkness every moment of every day, and in that moment, the darkness didn't appear so dark. In fact, if she didn't know any better, she could have sworn it was starting to look grey.

"Thank you," Natasha said as she wrapped her arms around Theresa and held her to her heart. "This means more to me than you could imagine."

"We 'warehouse girls' have to stick together, right?" Theresa replied.

"For life," Natasha said before following after Violet out the front doors of the church.

As she rounded the front corner of the church, she felt as though nothing in the world could squash the joy that pumped through her veins. The sun was shining on her back, massaging her shoulders with a pulsating warmth. She looked up into the clear blue sky and watched the birds pass overhead, fluttering effortlessly in the light breeze that moved across the sky. There was hope in the air, and she was bathing in it. Soon, all the puzzle pieces would be back where they belonged. Finally, after all these years, she would be complete.

As she approached Violet, who was sitting in the passenger's seat of her car, fiddling with something in the glove compartment, Natasha called out, "Are you ready to get this party started?"

At the sound of Natasha's voice, Violet jumped back, startled, and hurriedly stuffed something black and metallic into the glove compartment, closing it tight before Natasha could reach her. "Born ready," she replied. "I was just making sure we were going to have enough gas to make it to Ohio."

Drawing her keys from her pocket, Violet dangled them from her fingers, offering them to Natasha, but instead of taking them, Natasha leaned across the front seat and reached for the glove compartment. "In the glove compartment?" she asked. "What do you have in there? A calculator?"

But before she could wrap her fingers around the handle, Violet grabbed her by the wrist. "I was just checking the manual for the gas mileage."

"If that's the case, then why are you so determined to not let me see it?"

"I'm not. I'd just like to get this all taken care of as soon as possible. We're wasting time."

"And you're squandering more by being so suspicious."

"Fine," Violet said, releasing Natasha's wrist and squeezing past her into the parking lot. "See for yourself."

As Natasha opened the door to the glove compartment, she immediately saw what Violet had been hiding. Inside the drawer was a fully loaded, black revolver with its handle facing toward the inside of the car to make for easy access. She recognized it immediately; it was the same gun the hoodie had brought into the warehouse, the same one she had used to kill Alexei. Immediately, Natasha's mind flashed with images of her own finger on the trigger, of Alexei's lifeless body lying on the floor of the warehouse, of blood and darkness seeping into her skin. She could feel them burn as they entered her over and over again, infecting her with their stench. Her heart began to race, her brow began to sweat, and her hands started to shake.

Turning on Violet, she asked, her voice trembling like a ship lost at sea, "What the hell are you doing with that?"

"I thought we could use a little insurance," Violet answered, stepping out of the car to face Natasha. "Just in case things get out of hand."

"If that's all this is about, how come you didn't bother to mention that fact when we were trying to plan?" Natasha asked as she planted her feet firmly on the pavement, fire raging behind her eyes, and took two, deliberate steps toward Violet, forcing her to back up against the car. "Why were you trying to hide it?"

"Because, crazy me, I thought you might freak out," Violet said.

"No one's getting hurt on my watch."

"Yet you're totally fine with burning a store to the ground."

"It's the only way to get to Blair."

"What if someone gets hurt?" Violet asked, rolling her eyes condescendingly. "How will you ever live with yourself?"

"They won't," Natasha answered. "Their sprinkler system will put out the fire long before it gets out of control. And even if it doesn't, the fire department won't be far behind. I'll call them myself to make sure."

"Why are you trying to protect them?" Violet accused.

"I'm not. I'm protecting *you* from doing something you're going to regret!"

"And you were *so* concerned about everyone's safety when you shot your old pimp. Or is killing only okay when you do it?"

"I made a mistake! And I don't want you to do the same."

"But see, this is different," Violet said. "You were brash, scared. You pounced on him like a cornered animal. I've been planning this for weeks. You couldn't possibly understand."

"I understand better than you ever could," Natasha replied.

"Oh really? Did you have to watch your boyfriend *die* in front of you? Did you see their hands pull the trigger? No? Then get off your high horse and come back to me when you have a damn clue."

"We're not killing anyone."

"I'll kill anyone the hell I want!"

"Not on my watch, you won't."

"Who died and made you queen of the whores?"

"At what point do we become no better than they are?" Natasha asked.

"The moment we allow them to keep hurting others the same way they hurt us, how they hurt Kayde," Violet answered.

"This is not a discussion," Natasha ordered, reaching into the glove compartment, taking the gun in her hands and shoving it into Violet's chest. "This stays here, or so do you. Now, while you're taking care of that, I'm going to get us ready to go. Are we understood?"

"Yes, ma'am," Violet said, taking the gun from Natasha and shooting her a mock salute before sighing angrily and marching back inside the church.

STORMING THROUGH THE FRONT DOORS OF THE CHURCH AND slamming them behind her, Violet tilted her head back and screamed at the ceiling. At this point, she was fuming. The boiling blood that flowed through her veins could have scorched lava. Closing her eyes, she tried to breathe deep and calm herself down, but all that served to do was to remind her of her pain. In the darkness behind her eyelids, she saw Kayde, dying in her arms, blood pouring from his chest and turning her skin crimson. Shaking, her fingers tightened around the gun's handle, and she held it to her temple, ready to fire.

If Natasha won't let me have justice for Kayde, then there's nothing left for me here.

However, as she was about to pull the trigger, a soft, familiar hand wrapped around her wrist, pulling it back to her side.

Clenching her jaw, she said, "Father Christopher. You would do better to just let me end it already."

"I don't believe that," he replied, pinning her arms to her side gently yet with no small modicum of force. "If God still allows blood to flow through your veins, it means He still has a plan for you. It's not our job to choose who still has worth."

"But what about the ones who leave us?" she asked, choking back the tears. "Were they worth nothing to Him anymore? Is there not more they could have done?"

He sighed, "I wish I had all the answers. Regretfully, we may never know why God allows some to continue living while others die. At least not on this side of Heaven. Now, I'm more than happy to try to continue talking like this. But, why don't you let me have the gun, and we can continue this conversation in the sanctuary?"

Hesitantly, Violet released her grip on the revolver, allowing it to fall into Father Christopher's hands. Then, he placed his hand on her shoulder and led her through a set of large, mahogany doors and into the sanctuary. As she stepped foot inside, she was encased within a wash of light which emanated from the stained glass windows on either side of the sanctuary as colorful and extensive as the entire breadth of the visible spectrum. At the front of the room, past the rows upon rows of oaken pews, stood a stage, at the back of which was an ornate, marble statue of what looked like a poor man, kneeling down to the ground with his hand outstretched toward a beaten, broken man who had fallen on the road before him, and in front of that statue sat a large, wooden pulpit.

Taking a seat in a pew toward the front of the auditorium, Violet bent over and held her head in her hands. She breathed in deep, trying to end the war the waged inside her soul between rage and despair. However, all she felt were arrows piercing her chest on each side. As Father Christopher sat beside her, he placed his hand on her shoulder and simply stayed with her in silence. For the next, ten minutes, neither of them spoke. Neither of them breathed until her armies decided to retreat, at least for the night.

Finally, she broke the silence, whispering, "It's not fair…"

Even still, Father Christopher remained silent, as if he knew that all she needed was a trickle to make its way through her dam before a flood would burst forth.

Unsurprisingly, he was right.

A moment later, Violet let loose, drowning him in a sea of emotion. "Who does she think she is?!" she exclaimed. "She doesn't understand. How could she? She has someone to go back to. What do I have?"

"Yourself," he answered.

"Sometimes, I wish I didn't," she sighed.

"Well, I, for one, am glad you're here," he replied. "If you weren't, who else would I get to teach the priests to not be such wooden stiffs all the time?"

"Natasha did most of the work."

"If I remember correctly, you trained half the priests for that rescue. Without you, they would have never made it through the doors of that brothel. I know I wouldn't have."

"You would have done just fine."

"I was shaking in my cossack at just the thought of walking up to one of those girls. You gave me confidence. You gave all of us the courage we needed to make that plan work. That is no small feat."

"Why do you care so much about what happens to me?" she asked.

"Because I care about what happens to all of God's children," he answered. "But beyond that, I know special when I see it. It would be a shame to see you leave this earth before you saw it in yourself too."

"You wouldn't say that if you knew what I was going to do."

"It's only natural to want revenge."

"Oh... you heard us?"

"It was hard not to."

"What gives her the right to tell me what I can and can't do?!" Violet exclaimed, standing up, throwing her hands in the air and pacing back and forth across the center aisle.

Following her, Father Christopher took her by the shoulders and held her in front of him. He tried to look her in the eyes, but, ashamed, she refused to meet them, moving her head to the side every time he craned his neck to her level. Then, refusing to give up, he placed his hands on either side of her jaw and held her face in front of his. But even still, she looked away, only to return his gaze a moment later.

"No one can tell you what to do," he said. "This is a decision that only you can make. However, I hope you don't choose revenge, for your own sake. It may taste refreshing when it first hits your stomach, but it soon turns sour. It won't be long before you wish you had never tasted it at all. But regardless of what you choose, you are always welcome here. I will keep your room open for you always. That way, whenever you come back, whether tomorrow or in two years, you'll have a home."

"Thank you," she said, breaking free from his grip and walking out of the sanctuary. "But one way or another, I have a feeling this is going to be a one way trip."

Storming down the stairs and slamming the door to her room behind her, Violet prepared herself for the night that was to come. She strapped on her favorite pair of fishnet stockings, her old, black and white top and shorts combo from The Eclipse and the pair of knee-high, leather boots Kayde had bought for her during the week after their escape. Then, after sticking a photo strip of her and Kayde inside the backs of her right boot, she sat on the edge of her bed and waited for Natasha to return.

And with every second that passed, the war within her, between rage and release, continued to escalate, though neither side was able to gain the upper hand.

Finally, after almost an hour of stewing inside her emotions, Violet heard footsteps rush down the steps and march past her door. A second later, Natasha burst through Violet's door with Theresa over her left shoulder. Without a word, she strode over to Violet, stood her up and raised both of her arms to the side before patting her down.

"Is this really necessary?" Violet scoffed, rolling her eyes as Natasha ran the backs of her hands along her sides.

"After the stunt you were about to pull," Natasha answered. "I'm not taking any chances."

"We just don't want anyone to get hurt," Theresa said.

"While you're checking out my tits, you think you could take a second to rub my nipples too?" Violet asked, taking

Natasha's hands and bringing them to her chest. "It's been a while since they've had a good fondle."

Shaking her off, Natasha grabbed Violet forcefully by the waist and turned her around before checking the pockets on both sides of her shorts. "I could always strip down naked and make this a hell of a lot easier," Violet sighed. "Though, I'm sure you'd like that, wouldn't you?"

"Anything in your boots?" Natasha asked as she turned Violet back around to face her.

Lifting her right boot onto her mattress and pulling the photo strip out from inside it, Violet answered, "Just a picture of my boyfriend and I to keep me company during the ride. You want to check the other one too?"

"Come on, Nat," Theresa said. "She doesn't have anything on her. Let's just get going. We want to make sure we make good time."

"No," Natasha replied, shoving Violet's right foot off the bed and forcing her left boot to take its place. "I need to know for sure."

After checking both sides of Violet's boots once, twice, three times, Natasha came up empty-handed. Finally, after a fourth search, though the look in her eyes still screamed suspicion, she relented, whipping around without a word and storming out the door with Theresa at her side. And as they walked toward Violet's car, no one said a word. Not even the sound of one's breath could be heard all the way from the church door to the car door.

Throughout the entirety of the eight hour ride to Toledo, the hush lingered, hanging in the air between them like sickness. At first, it settled in Violet's gut like a quiet churning, but soon, she felt it through her entire body. Her head grew light. Her bones began to ache, like they were battling to break through all three layers of her skin, and soon, even the blood that raged like rapids through her veins burned against her arterial walls. Watching the mall across from Dragon's Wing break across the horizon, she could feel the tide turn within her.

As she stepped onto the asphalt outside the mall, she could almost see Kayde standing outside that same alleyway with his hands raised and that woman's gun to his chest. She slammed her door, and the pistol fired, burying a bullet deep into his sternum and sending him falling, lifeless, to the ground.

And with that, rage drove the final spear into the heart of release, and now, the only thought she allowed to flutter across her synapses was that of revenge.

Taking the matches and canisters of gasoline from Violet's trunk, the girls made their way around the back of the salon, where it was Violet's time to shine. Kneeling in front of the back door, she took her lock picking tools from her pocket and brought her ear to the door handle as she guided her torsion wrench and hook pick through the keyhole.

After a moment spent scrubbing at the back of the keyhole, she passed the first pin.

Click.

Then, she moved on to the next pin, raking and scrubbing in circular motion until…

Click.

After that, it took all of seven seconds to pass the final, three pins and pry the door open. Immediately, Natasha and Theresa rushed inside with their gas canisters at their sides while Violet doubled back to grab hers. Then, she joined the fray.

Starting from the back corner and working their way to the front, the three of them poured, splashed and sprayed all ten gallons of gasoline across the front rooms of both the salon and the massage parlor until every computer, every massage table, every divider was soaked in fluid. After only a minute, the overwhelming stench of diesel flooded the air around them, almost knocking Natasha and Theresa flat on their backs. The odor was so strong that their coughing became so vigorous that they had to open the front, two windows just to be able to breathe. Violet, however, simply breathed it in, allowing its sweet scent to work its way through her lungs and into her blood. In that moment, the lightness that coursed through her veins was euphoric, poetic, hungry.

She felt like a lion on the prowl, who wouldn't be satisfied until she devoured everything in sight.

Once all the gasoline had been poured, Natasha trickled a small stream all the way back to the doors, where she turned to Theresa, tossing her canister into the center of the room, and asked, "Would you like to do the honors?"

"Did you even have to ask?" Theresa smiled as she took a matchbook from her back pocket, struck a match and tossed the flaming stick into the center of the room.

Immediately, the room exploded with flame and heat, quickly casting the room in an ominous orange and reddish glow. Within seconds, the row of cubicles in front of them was engulfed in masses of five-foot-high flame. Then, it began to spread through the room, devouring everything it touched in a single bite.

As the storefront burned behind them, Natasha, Theresa and Violet hid in the darkness of the side alley, waiting for the commotion to catch someone's attention across the street. And it didn't take long. Not even a minute later, three figures came rushing out of the houses across the street, barreling toward Dragon's Wing like gazelles on the run from a predator.

Except, instead of running away from the danger, they were heading right into Violet's trap.

Under the light of the street lamps, she saw them: a greasy, overweight man, a slick-haired Romeo-type and the object of her rage, the olive-skinned woman who had stolen everything from her. Upon seeing her, every muscle in Violet's body tensed, and the air inside her lungs grew heavy. As the gazelles ran into the blazing building, Natasha and Theresa took off toward the houses. But, Violet didn't follow them. Instead, she wheeled around the front of the building and stood before the doors.

Then, reaching underneath her shirt, she pulled out the pistol she had been hiding beneath her bra.

As the doors opened, the fire's heat washed across Violet's skin, turning her rage to ecstasy. The smell of burning wood and fabric filled the air around her, like the glorious scent of a bonfire on a cool, summer night. Smoke billowed from the tips of the flames, painting the ceiling with a thick layer of fog and activating the sprinkler system, which poured like a monsoon on Violet's head as she walked calmly, unwaveringly, through the gaps in the flames toward the back room, where her targets were frantically trying to salvage what they could of their files.

With her gun raised, Violet stood in the doorway to the back room and said, "Surprise."

Immediately, all three gazelles stood and turned to face her, only to recoil at the sight of Violet's gun trained on them. All except for the woman.

With determined strides, she marched toward Violet with a wicked smirk across her face, saying, "I was wondering how long it would be until I saw you again. How's Kayde? I sure hope he's made a full recovery."

"He's dead, you bitch!" Violet exclaimed, taking an instinctive step backward and pointing her shaking gun toward the woman.

However, the woman paid her no attention, instead taking step after step toward her. "I'm sorry to hear that," she said with no subtle hint of mockery. "But that's what happens when you're a backstabbing cunt."

"Don't talk about him like that!"

"And what are you going to do about it, little girl? You're not going to shoot me. You're too much of a coward to take me down."

"You want to bet?" Violet asked, whipping her gun to the right and firing a bullet just past the woman right ear.

The bullet flew smoothly through the flame-painted air like a rocket, plunging deep into the greasy man's forehead and sending him to the ground in a pool of blood.

Instinctively, the woman turned around, and upon seeing her man, dead, on the ground, a twinge of fear washed across her eyes, only to be replaced a second later by a blank, icy stare.

She took another step. "If your plan was to shoot me," the woman said. "Why let me know you were coming? Why not just shoot me in the back and get it over with?"

"Because," Violet said with a smirk as she twisted her gun to the left and sent another bullet sailing into the Romeo's chest. "I wanted to look you in the eyes so you could know what Kayde felt the moment you pulled the trigger, bitch!"

Then, without hesitation, Violet fired a bullet directly into the center of the woman's skull, sending her plummeting to the ground with a sickening crash. Taking two steps forward, Violet stood over her, watching the blood ooze from the back of her head and cover the ground in a pool of scarlet. Then, channeling every ounce of rage left into her body into two pulls of the trigger, she lodged a bullet into each side of the woman's chest.

But, in the reflection of the diminishing flame that reflected off the sea of red that now covered the ground, Violet saw something that sent shivers down her spine: her face, staring down at the lifeless body of the woman she had waited so long to enact revenge upon. A twisted smile was spread across her face, and a monstrous gleam sat just behind her irises. As she looked closer at the sick joy that enraptured her countenance, she found herself back outside the alley, watching the woman that now lay, dead, beneath her take Kayde's life, with that same, smug expression across her own face.

It was then that Violet realized; in her quest to avenge her one, true love, she had become the monster that had killed him.

So, with shaking hands and her breath locked tightly inside her lungs, she dropped the gun where she stood and sprinted out the front doors and down the street, leaving everything behind her. She threw herself into the driver's seat of her car and fired the ignition with tears raining from her eyes. For hours, she simply drove, never looking back and fearing that somehow, on the other side of death's curtain, Kayde was looking down on her, no longer seeing the girl he loved but a disgusting, hollow shell.

And no matter how far she ran, she feared she could never find forgiveness or healing. There was no garment or cloak for her to reach out for this night. She was irredeemably broken, lost and alone.

25

REDEEMED

TOLEDO, OHIO

*A*fter setting Dragon's Wing ablaze and watching its proprietors rush inside to salvage what they could, Natasha and Theresa raced across the street like the judgement of God Himself was about to obliterate everything that lay behind them, refusing to look back, lest they be turned to salt. While their distraction would buy them some time, there was no telling how long it would keep Blair's keepers occupied. And with what looked like eight rooms to search through in order to rescue Blair, there was no time to waste.

So, as they passed by the front gate outside the houses, Natasha veered to the left while looking over at Theresa, pointing to the house to the right and saying, "Check every room, every floor. Let everyone you find know that we're breaking them out. And if you see Blair, don't let her out of your sight."

Theresa nodded, and they took off in opposite directions, hitting the front steps of the houses and bursting through the doors in sync. After leaping over the first, three steps, Natasha bounded up the first staircase and up to the first door on her right. Unbolting the three sets of locks that sat on its outside face, she flung the door open, letting it slam into the drywall with a crash on its backswing.

Then, planting herself in the center of the doorway, she slammed her hands on the wooden doorframe and yelled, "Cavalry's here! Everyone out on the front lawn, now! Get your asses moving!"

Refusing to wait a second longer than was necessary, she zipped across the hallway and repeated this process in the room across the hall. As she unbolted the doors to the second room, she checked back in with the first room's inhabitants, who were streaming into the hall and down the stairs. She studied each of their faces, hoping to find Blair. However, after clearing every room in building, Natasha hadn't seen a sign of Blair anywhere.

Theresa must have found her. Dear Lord, I hope she found her.

Dashing down the final set of steps and onto the front lawn, Natasha combed the crowd in search of Blair, but still, she was nowhere to be found. Immediately, Natasha began to panic, and her anxiety went into overdrive, leaving her heart racing faster than the speed of sound as her ribcage closed in on itself. Her head grew light. Her hearing dulled as though she was listening to the world through a thick pair of earmuffs, and her line of vision shrunk to the size of a pin head. No matter how hard she tried to assure herself that everything was okay, that there was a reasonable explanation for Blair's absence, she couldn't help but fear the worst.

In equal parts rage and fear, Natasha marched over to Theresa, grabbed her firmly by the collar and lifted her until their eyes were level, exclaiming, "Tell me you saw her!"

"I'm sorry, Natasha," Theresa sighed, shaking her head sullenly.

"Blair?!" Natasha screamed, her voice nearly cracking beneath the tears that were now flooding from her eyes. "Blair!"

Just as she was about to collapse to the grass in agony, a tentative finger tapped her on the shoulder. Immediately loosening her grip around Theresa's collar and letting her drop to the ground, Natasha spun around to find a worried Latina standing behind her, looking as though her heart was racing as fast as Natasha's.

"Excuse me," the Latina said. "Did you say you were looking for Blair?"

"Yes, do you know where she is?" Natasha asked as she latched onto the Latina's wrist, her eyes pleading for good news.

The Latina's eyes grew wide with realization as she pointed across the street, toward the burning salon, and answered, "In one of the rooms on the second floor. But I don't know which one."

Bang!

Suddenly, a shot rang through the silent, night sky, drawing every eye to the salon, where a flash of pure, white light, infinitely brighter than the flames that still raged inside the building, flashed through the open windows.

Bang!

As the echo of a second blare settled to a dull hum, Natasha came to a realization; not only was Blair nowhere to be found, but neither was Violet, which could only mean it was her gun behind the fireworks show. Natasha took off in a dead sprint toward Dragon's Wing, praying that she could make it through the doors before the third blast of Violet's gun, which would complete her quest for vengeance. However, she didn't even make it halfway across the street before...

Bang! Bang! Bang!

Dropping to her knees in the middle of the road, Natasha's

heart began to burn, as though she had been the one on the receiving end of all five bullets. The breath left her lungs as she latched onto the front of her scalp, feeling the weight of her failure press down on her shoulders.

No one was supposed to get hurt.

No more than three seconds later, Violet burst through the front doors of the salon like the hounds of hell were on her tail, taking a sharp, right turn as soon as she was through the doors and racing off into the distance toward the rising moon. Quickly, Natasha leapt to her feet and raced toward the salon, squeezing through the doors before they had a chance to close. She weaved around the charred remains of desks, hopped over the piles of ashes that were once reclining chairs and zoomed past the burning embers that had once been a towering inferno of her own design, now drowned by the monsoon that still poured all around her, soaking her to the bone.

As she approached the back doorway, that was when she saw them: three bodies, one of which looked strangely familiar, lying on the floor, pools of blood and water festering on the ground around their bodies. Bending down beside the body of a woman, who was lying flat on the ground beside Violet's gun, Natasha brought her fingers to the woman's neck, hoping to find a pulse. But, there was none. She was dead, and from the looks of it, the others seemed likely to have suffered the same fate.

If only I hadn't been so single-minded.

Now, three people are dead. Because of me.

"Oh my God," a voice echoed from behind her.

That voice. I know it.

No, it can't be.

Slowly and without turning around, Natasha slid her hand along the floor, carefully wrapping her fingers around the handle of Violet's gun. As she did, she craned her head to the side in an attempt to get a look at the owner of the voice that still sent shivers down her spine. Finally, out of the corner of her eye, she saw him.

Him.

Paul...

Taking the gun in her shaking, wavering hands, she stood to her feet as she spun around, pointing the gun directly in Paul's face.

"You," she growled, the darkness around her hands buzzing and rippling like electricity.

{}~{}~{}~{}~{}~{}~{}~{}~{}~{}

Detroit, Michigan. Four years earlier.

As the sun rose over the horizon, painting the sky with a glorious array of color, Natasha walked down the busy, Detroit streets with her belongings on her back and the necklace she had received from the kind-faced lady at the homeless shelter the day before in her back pocket. Though she had been offered a room at the shelter for as long as she needed, Natasha couldn't help but feel as though she was stealing a bed from someone in more desperate of a need than she was. Homeless shelters were supposed to be for people with no place to go, with nothing else keeping them from sleeping in a cardboard box on the side of the street. That wasn't her. She still had somewhere she could go. After all, she still had friends back home in Kansas City who would offer her a room at the drop of a hat once they heard that she had run away from home.

All she had to do was get a hold of them, but regretfully, she had no change for a payphone.

As the morning wore into afternoon, the noonday sun bore down on her back like a thousand, burning coals. After three hours spent on the side of the street, trying to scrounge up enough change for a few long-distance phone calls and mapping out the route to Missouri, just in case she had to hitchhike across state borders, the skin on the back of her neck started to burn, and her brow began to drip with sweat. So, hungry and exhausted, she collapsed on the concrete footing of a nearby bridge, hoping a little shade and maybe some sleep would grant her the energy she needed to wait until her friends got home from school so she could give them a call.

However, she didn't make it through more than five minutes of shuteye before she felt two, rough hands wrap around her forehead, covering her eyes and pulling her back. At the same time, another pair of hands latched onto her feet, and she was hoisted into the air before she even had a clue as to what was happening. She kicked, flailed and screamed, trying to free herself from her attackers' grip, but it was no use. They were too big and too strong for her to overpower. With no effort at all, they carried her around the back of the bridge's supports and laid her on the grass before finally letting go.

When she opened her eyes, a tall, slick-haired man was straddling her just beneath her waist, so her legs couldn't move, and was leaning over top of her, pinning her arms to the turf. Meanwhile, his smaller, stockier weasel of a friend got to work trying to rip her shirt off her chest.

Desperate, Natasha screamed, "Someone! Please, hel-"

But before she could finish, the smaller man's hands clamped onto her mouth, and he leaned across her face, saying, "I wouldn't do that if I were you. If you try to fight, we're just going to have to get rough. And I don't think you want to know what happens when I get rough."

"Let go of her, you freaks!" a voice from behind the slick-haired man call out, drawing both his and the weasel's heads away from her.

"Yeah?" the slick-haired man scoffed as he let go of Natasha's hands, kicking her firmly in the ribs as he stood and sending her rolling over onto her stomach in pain. "And what are you going to do about it? You're outnumbered. Two against one."

"I like those odds," the other man responded.

As the crunching sounds of knuckles against bone and muffled grunts filled the air, Natasha tried to lift herself off the ground. However, when she pushed against the turf, a stinging pain shot through her side, sending her crashing back onto the grass.

"Is that all you've got?" her rescuer said as the slick-haired man flew over top of her and crashed to the ground on her left.

"You ain't seen nothing yet," the weasel said.

Her rescuer laughed, "Well, in that case…"

"Shit!" the weasel exclaimed. "Florian, he's got a gun! Let's get out of here."

Finally, as the sounds of rushed footsteps faded into the distance, the pain in Natasha's chest subsided, allowing her to finally roll onto her back. When she did, her rescuer knelt beside her and placed a comforting hand on her shoulder.

"Don't strain yourself," he said, looking down at her with a reassuring smile that lit his deep, hazel eyes with a calming radiance. "Are you okay?"

Wrapping his arm around the backs of her shoulders, he helped her sit up. "Thank you so much," she said. "I don't want to think of what would have happened if you hadn't come along."

"Neither do I," he said, lifting her onto her feet as she slung her arm around his shoulders and leaned the bulk of her weight on his strong arms, allowing him to lead her back toward the city. "What were you even doing under the bridge? Don't you know how dangerous it is out here?"

She sighed, "I thought I could get out of the sun for a minute. I'm sort of… a stranger to this area, trying to get home to Kansas City. But I don't have a ride, and frankly, I don't know the way."

"Would you color that a coincidence? I was actually on my way to Missouri to visit my family when I saw those guys going after you. Why don't I just take you where you need to go?"

"You don't have to do a thing like that. We don't even know each other."

"Then let's get to know each other. How about we start with names? My name's Paul. What's yours?"

"Grace."

"That's a beautiful name!" Paul exclaimed, opening the door to his car and allowing her to slide into the passenger's seat. "See? We're friends already."

"I guess so," she chuckled as she swung her legs into the car, grimacing from the pain that reverberated through her side.

"Does that hurt?" he asked as he leaned across her and opened his glove compartment, pulling out a bottle water and a bag of pills and handing it to her. "Here, take a couple of these. They'll help you feel better until we can get you to the doctor. Don't take too many, though. It's strong stuff. Does a hell of a number on my migraines."

After popping two of the pills in her mouth and downing a quick swig of warm water, she replied, "Thank you. I don't know how I'm ever going to repay you."

"I'm sure you'll think of something."

As Paul slammed her door shut, Natasha's body grew heavy. Her muscles became weak, and her eyelids began to close. Leaning against the seat cushion, she tried to keep her eyes open, but they refused to cooperate. A second later, her eyelids locked shut, forcing her to into a deep slumber.

And when she opened her eyes, she found herself lying atop a small, cold mattress in New York City, staring into the cold, soulless eyes of the man that would soon become her master.

That was the day Natasha was born.

Toledo, Ohio. Present day.

"...GRACE?" PAUL ASKED AS HE RAISED HIS HANDS SUBMISSIVELY in the air and backed away from the still smoking gun that stood mere inches from his face.

The acrid scent of spent gunpowder filled the air around them, mixing unceremoniously with the already putrescent odor of half-extinguished flames and burnt rubber, wood and plastic. On every side, a battle raged between the fire nations, which had spread out in camps throughout the salon, and the water tribe that rained down their power from above, holding the blaze at bay and soaking everything in its path. It felt like they were standing in the middle of the Amazon during the rainy season. Water flowed like rivers down his face and shoulders, forming ponds at Paul's feet. Meanwhile, Grace huffed and puffed under the torrent, as though she was fighting off hypothermia, but despite the shaking of her body, her aim didn't waver. Her gun remained as still as ever and pointed directly between his eyes.

"Oh, I'm flattered," she replied, her eyelids fluttering manically and her expression rapidly oscillating between amusement and anger. "After all these years, I didn't think you'd remember little 'ole me. But alas, I'm not Grace anymore. You made sure of that."

As he opened his mouth to speak, Rebecca's presence loomed over his right shoulder. Her breath fell on the backs of his ears. "How could you forget?" she whispered. "She was your virgin conquest. You don't forget a thing like that."

"How could I forget?" he chuckled anxiously.

"I trusted you," Grace said, taking a definitive step toward him and thrusting the barrel of the gun even further toward his face.

"That was your first mistake," Rebecca sighed. "And my last."

"I know. And I broke it," Paul replied.

"Along with everything else in my life!" Grace screamed as she took another, frenzied step and pressed the gun to his temple.

Closing his eyes and bracing himself for a bullet, Paul said, "I can't even imagine the pain I put you through. Back then, I thought I was doing good, but now I understand how wrong I was. I'm sorry."

"You're sorry?" Grace chuckled angrily.

"Yes," he insisted.

"No," she growled, the muscles in her neck tensing monstrously as she stressed every word that came from her mouth. "You don't get to be sorry."

"I deserve that. I-"

"Sorry doesn't give me the last four years of my life back."

"But I didn't-"

"You don't get to apologize until you've laid your dignity bare on a city street."

Gulping, Paul stammered, "B-but I'm trying — I came here so I could-"

"Until you've been spat on by every prick who thinks you like it," she continued, ignoring him.

"Listen, I'm-"

"Until you've been *fucked* by thirty guys in one night, you don't get to apologize."

"I'm trying to make things right!" Paul screamed.

Suddenly, Grace's eyes grew wide, and she took an instinctive step back, breathing heavily. "P-please, d-don't yell," she stammered. "I didn't do anything wrong. I didn't…"

"Now look what you've done," Rebecca scoffed.

Taking a step toward Grace, Paul reached out to place a comforting hand on her shoulder, saying, "I'm sorry. I didn't mean to yell at you. It's okay."

But as his hand fell on her skin, Grace turned on him, shoving the gun back in his face. "Don't move!" she yelled before, once again, backing away in horror and pacing in front of the door to the back room, muttering to herself. "Breathe in, breathe out. Please, don't… don't yell. I didn't — I didn't do anything wrong."

"Look at her," Rebecca ordered. "Take a good, long look. Do you still think that giving up the business, turning everything over to the cops is enough to atone for your sins? Do you truly believe that you deserve forgiveness after all you've done? Look at her!"

As Grace continued to pace back and forth in front of the doorway to the back room, where Lena still lay, lifeless, her body oozing blood, a familiar glimmer of light, reflecting off the dying fires around them, caught Paul's eyes. It was emanating from Grace's chest. Squinting his eyes and leaning forward, he tried to get a closer look. Like a beacon in the night, a flash from days long past, it called to him and stole the breath from his lungs. Instinctively, he felt himself drawn to it, the silver, cross necklace that hung from Grace's neck, the same one that Rebecca used to wear when they were in high school, the one she had worn at Tower Park the day his life changed forever.

"That necklace," he whispered, reaching out to run his fingers across its surface. "It's… beautiful. Where'd you get it?"

"Oh come on, Paul, you know exactly *who* she got it from," Rebecca said, rolling her eyes.

As his hands neared the necklace, Grace turned violently away, clutching her necklace with one hand and using the other to wave her gun defensively at him. "You can't have it," she said.

Suddenly, from just outside the salon, the sound of sirens filled the air, blaring through the open windows and echoing all around them. Paul's eyes grew wide as he peered through the windows, only to see the rotating, red and blue glare of police lights flood through the windows and bounce off the walls, drowning the whole salon in a purple haze.

Shit! They weren't supposed to be here for thirty minutes.

"Get on the ground!" Grace ordered, motioning to the ground with her gun only to flick it upward a second later. "No, stand up. Wait, don't move! Shit, what am I going to do?"

"Oh, that's right," Rebecca laughed. "Tonight was the night you were going to turn *everything* over to Detective Shepard. Ha! Just when you thought you couldn't give this girl more heartache. At least she'll have her prison bars to remember you by."

Slowly standing up from the ground with his hands raised in front of him, he approached her, saying, "Listen, it doesn't have to end like this."

"My prints on the canisters," she muttered. "My hands holding the gun. This is it. My life's over."

"But it doesn't have to be," he said, taking another step toward her.

Rebecca's head titled to the side. "What are you doing?" she asked.

"How else is this supposed to end?!" Grace screamed, whirling around and pointing the gun back in Paul's face.

"No one has to get hurt. You don't have to go to prison today," he answered. "If you give me the gun."

"Are you crazy?" Grace asked.

Rebecca smiled. "No. For once in his life, I think he actually might be sane."

"You'll kill me," Grace said.

"You just have to trust me," Paul replied as he checked back at the door, only to see Bradie, Shepard and an entourage of firefighters racing toward the doors. "No time to argue. Just give me the gun!"

"Fine," she sighed, loosening her grip on its handle and letting it dangle on her index finger. "Either way, I'm dead. So I guess it doesn't matter."

As Paul took the gun, the salon doors flew open. Behind them, Shepard charged into the room, gun drawn, with Bradie and a host of firemen not far behind.

"Hands in the air!" Shepard yelled as he weaved around the heaps of ash that littered the salon floor.

"Paul?" Bradie asked, stopping in his tracks upon seeing the gun in Paul's hands. "I thought you were turning yourself in. What are you doing?"

"The right thing," Rebecca said, wiping away the tears that had just fallen from her eyes. "My little boy's finally growing up."

Suddenly, Paul turned on Shepard, who at this point was only a few feet away, and fired, purposefully sending a warning shot past his ear and right between the eyes of one of the jade frogs on the wall and making sure that plenty of gunpowder residue fell on his wrists as to ensure he would take the fall.

Then, he whipped the now empty gun toward Grace, raving like a lunatic, "Don't take another step! I'll kill her! You hear that, you dirty whore? I'll kill you, just like I killed the others. You mean nothing to me. You're just another speck on the sidewalk. Another bloodstain on the wall! Just a face without a name. I hate you, you worthless-"

Before he could utter another word, Shepard was on top of him. Reaching over Paul's right shoulder, Shepard knocked the gun out of his hand and latched onto his wrist. In turn, Paul turned and delivered a vicious elbow to Shepard's gut, sending him doubling over in pain. After all, if he was going to sell the bit, he had to make sure he put up a fight. Squaring off against Shepard, Paul raised his arms in front of his face to fight. But, as soon as he did, Bradie's fist connected with his jaw, throwing him into the wall.

Then, not even a second later, Shepard pinned both of Paul's arms behind his back and latched a pair of handcuffs around his wrists, saying, "You have the right to remain silent."

"Don't think this is over!" Paul yelled, throwing his body toward Grace in a show of anger while also shooting her a wink beneath his false rage. "I'll kill you! You hear me?!"

Ignoring him as he led Paul out the doors, Shepard continued, "Anything you say can and will be used against you in a court of law."

And as Shepard lowered Paul into the back seat of his cruiser, Paul took a final look back at the salon, where Grace now stood in the doorway, staring back at him in disbelief with the ghost of Rebecca at her side. Then, he blinked, and Rebecca disappeared from view, vanishing in a puff of smoke.

But he could still hear her voice echo in his ears, saying, "I'm proud of you."

∾

STANDING OUTSIDE THE SALON IN THE FRIGID, DECEMBER AIR AS firefighters rushed past her on every side to extinguish the final embers of her making, Natasha watched the police officers take Paul away in handcuffs. In just a few moments, her entire view of the world had flipped on its head. A friend had become a murderer, and her demon had become her deliverer. For the first time in her life, everything that tied her to her former life was gone. Alexei was dead, the warehouse was no more, and now, Paul, the man with whom it all began, had just taken a place which, by all rights, should have been hers. He was gone for good, and now, Natasha was all that was left.

And so was Blair.

Wrapping an orange blanket around Natasha's shoulders, one of the firemen led her away from the burning building as hoses and firefighters flew toward the salon. "Come on, Miss," he said. "Let's get you where you'll be safe."

"But my friend!" she pleaded, trying to rip herself from his grip and rush back into the building after Blair. "She's still in there. In one of the rooms upstairs. I was trying to get to her when that madman came after me."

"Don't worry. We'll make sure she gets out," he assured her as he dropped her off with the others, who were still huddled together across the street.

As the firefighter left, grabbing an axe from the back of his truck and rushing inside the salon to get Blair, Theresa wrapped Natasha in a tight, bear hug, nearly tackling her to the grass. "Thank God you're okay!" she exclaimed. "I heard the gun go off, and I was so afraid."

Without taking her eyes off the front doors of the salon, Natasha returned Theresa's embrace and said, "So was I."

"What happened in there?" Theresa asked.

"To be honest," Natasha sighed. "I'm still not sure."

"Did you find Blair? Is she okay?" the Latina, who was now crowded anxiously over Natasha's shoulder, asked.

"I don't know. I haven't seen her yet," Natasha answered as

Theresa detached herself from Natasha's neck and stood next to her, her eyes transfixed on the salon doors.

The minutes passed like hours as Natasha waited for Blair to walk triumphantly through those doors and into her freedom. With every second that passed, she found herself inching closer and closer to the sidewalk, with Theresa and the Latina close at her sides. At this point, the anxiety that gripped her was unbearable. It felt like her heart was inside a pressure cooker, bombarded on every side by a thousand tons of steam. At any second, it could either turn into a diamond or shatter into a million pieces.

Then, in the distance, Natasha saw something beautiful. Covered in a matching, orange blanket with a fireman at her side, Blair strode through the salon doors, the glorious, golden glimmer of her hair reflecting off the street lamps and filling all of Toledo with its light. Their eyes met, and immediately, they each dropped their blankets and ran toward each other, coming together in a rapturous embrace in the center of the street.

As Natasha wrapped her arms around Blair's waist and pulled her close, she could no longer contain herself. Joyous tears broke through her dam and rushed down her cheeks like a flood, forming rivers that flowed down either side of Blair's neck.

"I never thought I'd see you again," Blair sobbed, her tears also cascading down Natasha's shoulders. "I told you not to worry about me."

"Did you actually think I could get through life without my best friend?" Natasha chuckled.

"Well, I'm glad you couldn't," Blair said.

"So am I," Natasha replied.

"It was terrible, Natasha, without you."

"I know."

"My brother... he-"

"I know. I'm so sorry."

"What about you?" Blair asked, pulling away from their embrace but still keeping her hands attached to Natasha's shoulders. "You should still be pregnant. Did the baby…?"

"Hope's fine," Natasha answered, reaching up and wiping the tears from beneath Blair's eyes. "I left her with some new friends of mine. Would you like to meet her?"

"Yes, I would. Very much so."

Suddenly, Blair's eyes shifted to the left, where she saw the Latina, who was anxiously creeping toward them.

Immediately, Blair's arms fell from Natasha's neck, and she leapt into the Latina's arms, exclaiming, "Cici! Thank God you're okay."

"Of course I am," Cici replied. "You don't think I'd let anything happen to me while you were gone, did you? And let you go through that kind of pain? No way."

"Listen… B-blair," Theresa stammered, shuffling her feet anxiously. "I'm sorry. About Kayde. It's my fault. If I had just-"

"No," Blair said as she walked over to Theresa, running a hand down her hair and cupping her cheek in her hands. "He wouldn't want us taking the blame, and neither do I. Speaking of which, where's Violet? I assume she's the only reason you were able to find me."

"She ran off before I had a chance to stop her," Natasha sighed. "I don't think she wanted to stay and have to face what she'd done."

"I hope she'll be okay," Blair said.

"She will be. If that girl's anything, she's a fighter. Wherever she ends up, she'll turn out okay."

"I hope so."

"So, I'm totally digging this reunion tour we're having," Cici said. "But what happens now? I don't know about the rest of you, but I ran away from home for a reason. I'm so not in the mood to go back."

"And I, for one, do not want us to get separated ever again," Blair replied to a definitive nod of agreement from Theresa.

To which Natasha replied with a chuckle, "I hope you all like the Vikings."

{}~{}~{}~{}~{}~{}~{}~{}~{}

Duluth, Minnesota

"Are you sure they're going be okay with *all* of us being here?" Blair asked as she, Natasha, Theresa and Cici stepped off the bus at the end of the Pierson's cul-de-sac. "I know they're nice people and all, but eight people and a baby in the same house?"

Theresa nodded. "We're talking clown car vibes."

"Trust me," Natasha said. "If anyone's going to make the room, it's them."

"…But what if they don't like some of us?" Cici asked, rubbing her hands anxiously against her thighs.

"I'm not even sure 'not liking' someone is in this family's DNA," Natasha chuckled.

"And that's great and all," Cici said. "But I'm not really, you know, one of you guys. I kind of just tagged along for the last fifteen minutes of the movie."

Wrapping her arm around Cici's shoulders, Blair pulled her in close and kissed her on the top of the head. "You'll always be one of us," she assured.

As they approached the front door, Natasha walked up the front steps first, with the rest of the group filing in nervously behind her. Then, taking a deep breath, she brought her knuckles to the door and knocked in syncopated rhythm before looking back to the group to offer them a final, reassuring smile. Seconds later, Deanna cracked the door open, her head turned away from the girls toward the living room, mid-conversation.

"Seriously, just pause the movie for, like, five seconds!" she laughed before shaking her head and looking to see who was behind the door.

Upon seeing Natasha, she flung the door open and pounced on her, wrapping her arms around her neck and exclaiming, "Oh my God, Nat! You're back!"

Suddenly, a chorus of surprised voices erupted from inside the house.

"Wait, what?!" Rylee screamed.

"Nat's here?" Jessica asked.

"You hear that, baby?" Lynn asked. "Mommy's home!"

"Out of my way," Rylee ordered. "I want to see her!"

Without warning, Jessica and Rylee bolted out the front door, wrapping their arms around Natasha in unison. "We missed you so much," Rylee said, refusing to let her go.

"It's been so sad without you," Jessica said. "It's like we were missing a piece of the group."

Behind Natasha, Blair gulped, "I hope you guys are accepting applications…"

"Well, the process is pretty lengthy," Deanna said.

"And challenging," Jessica added.

"Many of our candidates don't even make it past the second interview," Rylee said.

"Is that before or after the three-headed snake?" Jessica asked.

"But for Nat's friends," Deanna chuckled. "I suppose we could make an exception and skip to the final section, which is a simple, yes or no question. Do you like cheesy, romance movies?"

"Of course," Cici replied to nods from others.

"Then you're in!" Rylee said as she and Jessica took the girls by the arms and led them inside.

As Natasha stepped through the doorway, her gaze shifted to the kitchen, where Lucas was leaning against the wall, a wry smile painted across his face.

Running her hand behind her right ear and tucking her hair neatly behind it, Natasha took a step toward him. "So, about me running off in the middle of night," she said.

"Without so much as saying goodbye," he replied, lifting himself off the wall and taking a step to match hers.

"Sorry about that," she chuckled.

"Is that something you do often, kiss a guy and run away, only to return the second he finally stops thinking about you?" he asked.

"It's kind of my trademark move."

"How many guys have you tried it on?"

"At this point? I don't know, maybe a couple thousand? But usually, they're the ones who come running back."

"Can't say I blame them."

Meeting in the middle of the living room, Lucas threw his arms around Natasha's waist as she slung her arms around his neck and buried her head in his shoulder. In that moment, everything around them melted away, and time slowed to a stop. Closing her eyes, she felt her body fill with warmth, heating well past her melting point. But, she didn't care. The world could have been ending around them, and she would have still wanted nothing more than to simply dissolve into his arms.

Their embrace ended far too soon, considering eternity was Natasha's benchmark. As she released from him, she found Lynn standing next to her, cradling Hope in her arms.

"There's someone who would like to see you," Lynn said,

holding out her arms so Natasha could take Hope from her. "We took good care of her while you were gone, but even still, there's no replacing Momma."

Taking Hope in her hands, Natasha held her to her face and nuzzled her nose against the top of Hope's head, breathing in the familiar, intoxicating scent of her hair. As she cradled her baby to her chest, Natasha finally felt the weight of the past month wash off her shoulders. She felt like a puzzle that had been missing half of its pieces, and holding Hope was like putting them all back into place. She was home, and she was finally complete.

Walking into the center of the living room, where the girls were huddled across every inch of the couch, watching the opening scenes of *My Fifteenth, First Date,* Natasha tapped Blair on the shoulder. "Hey," she whispered. "I've got someone who's been dying to meet you."

Immediately, Blair leapt off the couch and rushed to Natasha's side. "Oh my God, she's so beautiful," she said. "Just like her mother."

"Would you like to hold her?" Natasha asked, holding Hope out toward Blair.

"Do you even have to ask?" Blair replied, taking Hope in her arms and rocking her back and forth, a wide, proud smile spreading across her cheeks. "Hi Hope, it's your Auntie Blair. I know you don't know me yet, but you're going to be seeing a lot of me over the next, eighteen years. You are the luckiest, little girl in the universe because your mommy is the strongest person I've ever met. If you inherit even half that strength, watch out world! Little Hope's coming to change it."

"So, Matthew and I have been talking," Lynn said as she entered the living room with her husband by her side, carrying a freshly baked platter of chocolate chip cookies.

"And things might get a little tight around here," the

STRAYED

missionary, who to this point had been slaving away in the kitchen, said. "But, we would love to have all of you girls stay with us for as long as you need."

"If that's okay with you, Deanna," Lynn added.

"Are you kidding?" Deanna asked. "It wasn't even a question in my mind."

"I can sleep on the couch so the girls can have my room in the basement," Lucas offered.

"That's really nice of you," Theresa said. "But I don't want to be any trouble."

"It's no trouble at all," he replied. "I actually find the couch to be rather comfortable."

"That'll still be kind of crowded, though, won't it?" Cici asked.

"Actually, it might not have to be," Rylee said. "I'd have to check with my parents first, but my twin brothers just left for college a few months ago. Honestly, the house has been kind of empty without them, and I'd love a couple, new roomies."

Looking over at Cici, Blair asked, "What do you say, Ciara? You want to move in with me?"

"I thought you'd never ask," Cici chuckled.

"I can take the couch if you'd rather, Lucas," Theresa said.

"No way I'm letting you rough it while I sleep like a king," Lucas answered.

"Really, it'd be no trouble," she insisted. "This thing's already twenty times more comfortable than the shitty bed I've been using for the last, four months."

"Or you could just stay with me," Jessica said. "My parents have a room above their garage that hasn't been rented out in a while. I'm sure it'll be no problem for you to take it over."

"I mean, as long as it won't be a problem, that sounds amazing," Theresa said.

"Yay!" Jessica shrieked, clapping her hands excitedly.

"Well, I guess that just leaves Natasha and Hope with us," Lynn said with a smile.

"I wouldn't have it any other way," Natasha replied. "Except, I've been thinking about it, and I'm not sure Natasha really fits me anymore. It was the name they gave me when I entered that life. But now that I'm leaving it all behind me, I think I'd rather go by something else."

"What were you thinking?" Lynn said.

"Evangeline."

As she spoke her new name, Evangeline looked down at her hands, which, to this point, had still been wrapped in darkness. In an instant, the ebon vines splintered apart, fading into oblivion.

Finally, she was free. Everyone she cared about was around her, and the whole world was in front of her, ripe for the picking.

And that was the best news of all.

26

STRAYED

TOLEDO, OHIO

*B*ang! Bullet piercing through flesh. Body wavering. Falling. Crashing.

Except, Florian never felt the crash. Instead, he felt his consciousness floating, like he was being pulled toward heaven. Or, as would be much more fitting for him, hell.

He watched his body fade into the distance as he passed through the ceiling, traveling through the roof and ascending into the sky above until even the earth faded into oblivion.

Until the world turned black.

Then, everything went cold. Bitter cold, like bathing in liquid nitrogen whilst inside an iceberg. Starting from the tips of his fingers, which, somehow, despite being a million miles away from his body, he could still feel, and quickly moving through every vein, every artery, his blood slowed to a crawl, decelerating like a traffic jam to a stoplight until...

It stopped. Everything stopped, and he felt nothing except for twin thoughts that ran through his mind simultaneously.

Janelle. Iris.

Suddenly, from within the darkness, dozens of lightning bolts flashed on every side of him, surging in sync with a sort of warm power that coursed through him, melting the icicles around his consciousness, before fading back into the frost. A second later, the power flooded through him again, though this time it was stronger and more profound, like he was burning from the inside out. This happened over and over again, each successive occurrence growing stronger and hotter until he felt a pair of hands, like talons, latch onto his shoulders and drag him back toward the ground. He plummeted past the stars, through the clouds and back into his body, which was lying on a gurney with an oxygen mask over its mouth, as it was being rushed into an ambulance with a paramedic on each side, one pushing the cart and the other manning a pair of defibrillator paddles.

Jerking up as he, all at once, felt every iota of pain that he hadn't felt while in the void rush through his nervous system, Florian gasped for air and fought against the restraints that were wrapped around his chest, stomach and legs. He open his mouth to speak, to yell, to cry for help, but all that came out was a faint gurgle that resonated from somewhere deep inside his chest cavity. Opening his eyes, he tried to make eye contact with one of his paramedics, hoping to communicate his distress. However, when he did, the light from the street lamps above him seared against his retinas, leaving everything around him a bright haze of white.

As he shut his eyes to quell the pain, a hand landed on his shoulder. "It's okay," a voice assured him. "You're going to be okay."

Then, he heard nothing. He felt nothing. Everything faded into the void.

Janelle. Iris.

The next thing Florian knew, he was lying on an unfamiliar, and remarkably uncomfortable, bed with his entire body, save for his arms and head, wrapped tightly beneath a soft, yet somehow grating, set of blankets. The smell of latex and disinfectant wafted through the stale air, turning his stomach sour. When he opened his eyes, the first thing he saw wasn't the tubes or wires that ran out of every inch of free space on his arms. It wasn't the fluid bags that stood on either side of him nor was it the computer monitor that beeped quietly behind him.

No, it was Janelle.

At the edge of the bed with her fingers wrapped delicately around his, she sat with her head slouched to the side and her eyes closed, sleeping peacefully. For a moment, he simply watched her, unable to do anything but smile at the sight of her. As always, she was the most beautiful sight he had ever seen, and her presence made everything bearable. Just having her beside him dulled the pain more than any amount of morphine ever could.

Sitting up slightly in an attempt to find a more comfortable position, he tried to move carefully so he wouldn't wake her. However, as soon as he moved even a centimeter away from her, she jolted awake with a gasp.

"Oh my God, you're awake!" she exclaimed with an involuntary smile before immediately growing concerned. "Are you okay? Does anything hurt? Do you need me to get a doctor?"

Reaching out and pressing the top button on his bed panel so the bed could lift into a seated position, he chuckled, though it was quickly stifled by the pain in his chest, "No, no, I'm okay. I was just trying to sit myself up a bit."

"Probably not the best idea you've ever had."

"Yeah, I've been having that problem lately."

"You know, I noticed that," she teased, rolling her eyes playfully. "What's up with that?"

"I've made such a mess of everything," he sighed.

"Well, I'm glad you're finally admitting it. You know, the first step to recovery is admitting you have a problem," she laughed.

"Lately, it's felt more like a problem after a dilemma before becoming a situation," he said.

"So you thought the best plan was just to run away from them? From us?"

"It wasn't like that."

"That was certainly what it felt like. When we got married, you promised to stick with me through the better and the worse. I wish you would have just talked to me about what you were going through instead of turning tail."

"It's not that simple."

"Isn't it?" Janelle asked.

Florian looked away. "You'd look at me differently," he said. "I'd rather die than have that happen."

"You'd rather I remember you as the man who walked out on his family?"

"Even that's better than what I am."

"And that would be…?"

Sighing, he ran his hands through his hair, rubbed them against the back of his neck and looked up at the ceiling. More than anything, he wanted to tell her everything, but at the same time, he was terrified of what telling her the truth would mean for him, for them. Almost certainly, it would be the end of their relationship as he knew it. However, if he remained silent, it was unlikely to turn out any different. So there he lay, between a sinkhole and a landmine, with no choice but to choose which one would cause the least pain, not just for him but for Janelle.

And Iris.

At least if he told Janelle, she could have the chance to teach Iris how to avoid stumbling into a similar fate.

So, despite his shaking hands and trembling heart, he looked her in the eyes and told her everything. Starting at the beginning, from when one of his mother's "cash cows," or boyfriends, taught him to run his first game at the age of sixteen, and ending with the moment the bullet pierced his ribcage, he left no detail unexplained. With every story he told, the expression of horror on Janelle's face grew and grew, as did the rivers of tears that collected behind her eyes.

As Florian concluded his story, Janelle brought both hands to her face and wiped her tears with her palms. "Wow," she said. "That was… wow."

"I guess at least you've got a story for the tabloids, right?" he chuckled.

"Wait," she said, shaking her head in disbelief. "You think I'm going to leave you?"

Taken aback, he stammered, "Uh… well, yeah — I mean, after how much pain I put you through, how much more I planned to put you through, what reason would you have to stay? I'm not the man you thought you fell in love with."

"That's where you're wrong. You are *exactly* the man I fell in love with. Sure, maybe you weren't that man then, but you certainly are now. Just the fact that you were willing to tell me the truth, even though you were so sure it would mean the end of everything, speaks volumes to who you've become."

"So, you're not hurt?"

"No, I'm hurt as hell. I forgive you, for everything, but you still betrayed me, several times by my count. It's going to a long time until I'm able to trust you fully again, but it's a start. A real one. Like I said I'm the courthouse, for better or worse, right?"

Interlacing her fingers with his, she smiled weakly at him

with both love and pain shining from her eyes. And in that moment, he finally understood.

The truest of loves don't only survive the butterflies. They last well beyond the good feelings, scale every hill, every mountain and persevere even through the greatest of storms.

And true love wears no mask.

27

HOME

DETROIT, MICHIGAN

*P*aul lay in the back corner of his holding cell on the cold, cement floor, staring up at the cracked, white ceiling above him. He was alone, and for once in his life, that was a good thing. Over the forty-eight hours he had spent in that cell, hardly a moment had passed where he wasn't being accosted by someone. Whether it was one of the four drunk and disorderlies he had roomed with over that time or another of the countless defense attorneys who wouldn't stop trying to badger him into entering a "not guilty" plea, no one wanted to let him have a moment of peace and quiet.

But at this point, quiet was all he wanted.

Because once his arraignment hearing ended with him pleading guilty, it was something he would never have again.

As he lay there, motionless, he let his mind go completely blank. For hours, not a thought passed through his synapses. Even just three days before, having enough time alone for his thoughts to linger on his pain would have been nothing short of torture. However, after everything that had happened, it was almost relaxing. His circumstances hadn't changed. Rebecca was still gone, and he would probably never see Elle again. But, he was finally at peace with himself. He had tamed the restless beast within, and as a result, a thousand pound weight had been lifted from his shoulders. So, closing his eyes, he allowed himself to rest in the darkness behind his eyelids until, for the first time in weeks, despite the concrete bed he lay upon, he fell asleep.

And surprisingly, as he slept, not a single vision of death danced through his dreams. Nor did his demons torture him with thoughts of impending doom. Instead, there was only stillness.

Only peace.

Several hours later, as he opened his eyes, a familiar voice tickled the backs of ears. "You know, they make beds for that sort of thing," it chuckled.

You've got to be shitting me. What's she doing back here?

Sitting up laboriously after twisting uncomfortably from side to side in an attempt to force the knots out of his spine, Paul turned around and, once again, laid eyes on his ghostly tormentor, who was leaning against the iron, prison bars with an amused smile on her face.

"What are you doing here?" he sighed.

"Oh, come on, Paul," Rebecca laughed. "You didn't think you could get rid of me that easily."

"You call this easy?"

"Depends on who you ask. I'm sure there are plenty of people who would like to see a lot worse than prison happen to you."

"You included, I'm sure."

"I wouldn't be so sure about that."

Chuckling, he shook his head. "And what *would* you like to see?" he asked.

"Rebirth," she answered.

"What the hell is that supposed to mean?"

"A phoenix can only rise after it first turns to ash."

"So, that's why you haven't stopped tormenting me? Because you, or I guess I, think that I can become a better person or some shit like that?"

"It worked, didn't it?" she asked.

Standing up, Paul rushed toward Rebecca, grabbing the cell bars on either side of her face and exclaimed, "Yeah, bang up job you did there, Casper! Now, I'm just the deadbeat father who left his daughter parentless. Elle will go through the rest of her life as the daughter of a devil, and she'll hate me for it. Sure, I did a 'good deed,' but you wanna know why I did it? Because I was tired, Rebecca, tired of the lying, the deception, the running from who I am and what I've done. For the longest time, I tried to convince myself that I was a good man, deep down, but I'm done lying to myself. I was never good, and one, decent action doesn't change that."

"No, it doesn't," she said, turning and placing her hand on top of his. "But it's a start."

Surprised, Paul looked down at Rebecca's hand, which was still perched atop his, her fingers sliding along his skin. Reaching through the bars to his cell, he ran his hand up her arm, feeling every hair, every curve. Then, he cupped her cheek in his hand. As he did, she leaned into his touch and kissed his wrist.

"I-I don't — I d-don't understand," he stammered between huffs of breath. "Y-you — you're supposed — supposed to be…"

"Six feet under?" she asked, smiling.

"But I read the story. How did you-"

"With a little help and no small modicum of subterfuge."

"So, at Tower Park…?"

Nodding, she chuckled, "Definitely not a hallucination."

"That was a hell of a makeup job," he said. "You looked exactly like the other one."

"I do hope Ghost-Me treated you well while I was gone."

"To be honest, she was kind of a bitch."

"Sounds like she was just what you needed," she said.

"I guess you could say that," he chuckled. "But I still don't understand. At the parlor, you said we were done, and to be honest, I wouldn't have blamed you if you had turned me in right then and there. So, after everything I did, everything I've done, why do all of this for me? Why not just turn me in?"

"Because in the end, I believed that my husband, the man I fell in love with, was a good man, deep down, and that he could still be saved."

AFTERWORD

From the bottom of my heart, I want to thank you for reading the final installment in the Ebon Sky Series. This was a story that truly touched my heart in so many ways. So many hours of blood sweat and literal tears were packed into this novel, and I hope the story and characters became as personal to you as they were to me.

Though the stories and characters I've presented in these novels are entirely fictional and are creations of my own mind, the problem is real and in our own backyards. In the shadows, often time right in front of our eyes, men and women like Paul, Izzy and Lena are selling women like Blair and Theresa for profit. They are giving them false hope and promises or a life outside the walls of their prisons and turning them on their own, other girls desperate for a second chance like Cici. Meanwhile, brave men and women like Bradie, Nina and Anna risk it all, even without a badge, to rescue those women and make their lives better. The work of the numerous non-profits that are at work today is instrumental in what I hope will eventual defeat of the human trafficking scourge. Then, there are those like Violet who have lost everything because of the life and want nothing more than to end their lives. Depression and mental illness is real in this community and takes the lives of so many.

In Branded, we were met with a dark image of the human trafficking industry. In Caged, we saw the reasons why that model, which we often assume is the only reality in which human trafficking exists. Here, in Strayed, we saw a brief picture of how trafficking typically exists. Like Paul and Lena tried with Blair, oftentimes pimps rely on having their girls out in the world to help their recruiting efforts. Some of these women go to school, others have jobs, some even have families. However, in the dark, unbeknownst to everyone around them, they are being controlled.

This is why we need to be more vigilant than ever.

You can help them, and you don't even have to go into law enforcement or write a book to do it. If you've been inspired like I have, you can go to any of the following websites and donate or find out more about the real stories.

http://www.freeinternational.org - F.R.E.E. International
http://www.ijm.com - International Justice Mission
http://www.endslaverynow.com - Project Rescue

Or get involved at the local level. There are countless organizations in our towns and cities that do amazing work to help the women in our own backyards. Do some research in your area and attend their events, get involved.

Contact your local representatives as well. The sad truth is that, as we explored throughout Bradie's story in Caged, our judicial system does not do much good for trafficking victims. As it stands right now, prostitution is a criminal act for both buyer and seller. This means that human trafficking victims like

Erica are getting arrested and fined every day for things they had no choice but to do. Though the authorities do everything they can to identify human trafficking victims, the task is daunting. As you have seen through both Branded and Caged, trafficking victims are often too afraid to come forward, even to the police. I don't know what the answer is at a governmental level, but something needs to be done.

Because of this, law enforcement has to rely on people like us to tip them off to trafficking. If you come across a prostitute, please don't write them off. Even if they chose "the life," they might still be victims. Whether they're at a strip club or the side of the road, they may still be beaten behind closed doors and cheated out of a living. Take a moment, talk to them, and most of all, look in their eyes. And as we saw in Strayed, just because prostitution is legal in your area doesn't mean that women aren't still being trafficked every day in your own backyard. If you think someone might be a victim of human trafficking, call the National Human Trafficking Hotline.

1 (888) 373-7888

This also applies to online, pornography profiles and adds online for sex. Be vigilant and speak out. It might save a life.

NOTE FROM THE AUTHOR

As is always the case with an author, my success or failure as well as the success of the message, depends almost exclusively on you, the reader.

One of the most important ways you can be of help is by leaving a review on Amazon. New readers who are searching for books to read often base their decisions whether or not to buy solely off of the reviews. If you liked this book, if it spoke to you at all, I would greatly appreciate an honest review.

Also, never underestimate the power of word of mouth. A simple recommendation to a friend can often be enough to convince them to pick it up.

Be sure to also follow me on Facebook at http://www.facebook.com/ctdanielsauthor and check out my website http://www.ct-daniels.com.

And if you've liked this series, keep an eye out for the upcoming box set, which will include an exclusive prologue and epilogue available nowhere else, which releases January, 2019!

GLOSSARY OF HUMAN TRAFFICKING TERMS

Branding: A tattoo or carving on a victim's skin that indicates ownership by a pimp/brothel owner.

Bottom or **"Bottom Bitch"**: A female appointed by the trafficker/pimp to supervise the others and report rule violations. Operating as his "right hand," the Bottom may help instruct victims, collect money, book hotel rooms, post ads, or inflict punishments on other girls.

Exit Fee: The money a pimp will demand from a victim who is thinking about trying to leave. It will be an exorbitant sum, to discourage her from leaving. Most pimps never let their victims leave freely.

Finesse Pimp/Romeo Pimp: One who prides himself on controlling others primarily through psychological manipulation. Although he may shower his victims with affection and gifts (especially during the recruitment phase), the threat of violence is always present.

Gorilla (or Guerrilla) Pimp: A pimp who controls his victims almost entirely through physical violence and force.

Madam: An older woman who manages a brothel, escort service or other prostitution establishment. She may work alone or in collaboration with other traffickers.

Quota: A set amount of money that a trafficking victim must make each night before she can come "home." Quotas are often set between $300 and $2000. If the victim returns without meeting the quota, she is typically beaten and sent back out on the street to earn the rest. Quotas vary according to geographic region, local events, etc.

Seasoning: A combination of psychological manipulation, intimidation, gang rape, sodomy, beatings, deprivation of food or sleep, isolation from friends or family and other sources of support, and threatening or holding hostage of a victim's children. Seasoning is designed to break down a victim's resistance and ensure compliance.

Stable: A group of victims who are under the control of a single pimp.

The Game/The Life: The subculture of prostitution, complete with rules, a hierarchy of authority, and language. Referring to the act of pimping as 'the game' gives the illusion that it can be a fun and easy way to make money, when the reality is much harsher. Women and girls will say they've been "in the life" if they've been involved in prostitution for a while.

Traffickers: Traffickers are people who exploit others for profit. They can be any demographic, individuals and groups, street gangs and organized crime, businesses or contractors.

Trick: Committing an act of prostitution (*verb*), or the person buying it (*noun*). A victim is said to be "turning a trick" or "with a trick."

The Wire: (1) A pimp hotline, like a phone tree pimps use to get the word around, to find out which city is on/off. (2) Wiring money from victim to pimp in different cities/states ("put it on the wire").

Glossary of terms taken from:

https://inpublicsafety.com/2014/07/know-the-language-of-human-trafficking-a-glossary-of-sex-trafficking-terms/

ABOUT THE AUTHOR

C.T. Daniels is an author, poet and playwright who has been writing for more than ten years. He studied the art of story-telling at the University of Massachusetts, Amherst under play-wrights Will Power and Marcus Gardley. Since then, he has turned his attention to giving voice to those in our society who do not have one of their own, particularly those involved in the scourge of human trafficking.

For more information…
www.ct-daniels.com
CTDanielsBranded@gmail.com